"On a day I should ha[illegible] ovel, I spent hour after hour immer[illegible] g of Tamara Leigh. Once I started reading *Stealing Adda*, I simply could not break away until I had read the last page. Laugh-out-loud humor combined with unforgettable characters and a message of hope make this book a surefire winner."

— TRACEY BATEMAN, president, ACFW;
author of *Leave It to Claire*

"A dream of a book: High drama, sheer delight. Simply divine!"

— SIRI L. MITCHELL, author of *Kissing Adrien*
and *Chateau of Echoes*

"Stealing Adda is romance as you've never seen it before: heart-stirring, rib-tickling, and spirit-lifting from start to finish. Who wouldn't love Adda?"

— LINDA WINDSOR,
author of the MOONSTRUCK romantic comedy series:
Paper Moon, Fiesta Moon, and *Blue Moon*

Stealing Adda

A Novel by
Tamara Leigh

NavPress
P.O. Box 35001
Colorado Springs, Colorado 80935

ISBN 1-57683-925-7

Cover design by Wes Youssi, The DesignWorks Group, Inc. www.thedesignworksgroup.com
Cover photo: Istock and Getty Images
Creative Team: Rachelle Gardner, Lissa Halls Johnson, Darla Hightower, Arvid Wallen, Pat Reinheimer

Published in association with the literary agency of Alive Communications, Inc., 7680 Goddard Street, Suite 200, Colorado Springs, CO 80920 (www.alivecommunications.com).

Leigh, Tamara.
Stealing Adda : a novel / by Tamara Leigh.
p. cm.
ISBN 1-57683-925-7
1. Love stories--Authorship--Fiction. 2. Women novelists--Fiction. 3. Divorced women--Fiction. 4. Writer's block--Fiction. I. Title.
PS3612.E3575S74 2005
813'.6--dc22

2005024653

Printed in the United States of America

1 2 3 4 5 6 7 8 9 10 / 10 09 08 07 06

DEDICATION

There must be one for "Dorothy doll."
Thus, I dedicate *Stealing Adda* to Dorothy Elizabeth Schmanski,
beloved mother-in-law who, despite all manner of adversity,
never let her eyes waver from Jesus,
never let her hand slip from his grip,
and never let her feet stray from his path.
I aspire to a faith so deeply rooted as to be visible to the human eye.
July 11, 2005

And to Wilson Hoffman, Jr.,
a true southern gentleman who first welcomed
and embraced the "transplants" by
lovingly sharing himself and his family.
Those who called him father, grandfather,
and friend are blessed indeed.
April 21, 2005

ACKNOWLEDGMENTS

As always, the tale I had to tell could not have found its way from imagination to manuscript without the support of my loving husband, David, and our wonderful sons, Skyler and Maxen. Thank you for believing in me.

Heartfelt thanks to my Tennessee sister, Renee Hoffman, who laughed out loud and insisted that I pursue publication of Adda's tale (wink, wink . . .)

Special thanks to my agent, Chip MacGregor, who aided in my transition from the secular market to the Christian market by opening the door, and his successor, Beth Jusino, who ushered me in.

I am deeply grateful to all those at NavPress who set in motion the leap from manuscript to publication: Rachelle Gardner for her enthusiasm and gracious insight; Lissa Halls Johnson for her patience, keen editing, and prompt, "Tell me your testimony," which enabled me to go deeper; and Darla Hightower for her attention to detail.

I also wish to acknowledge the support and friendship of

past critique partners: Mona Prevel, Jeanne Nicholson, Shannon Snow, and GayNelle Doll—I miss you all!

Above all, I thank my Heavenly Father for answering prayers in His time, and my Savior, Jesus Christ, for delivering those prayers on my behalf.

ONE

If I smoked—and I'm told I ought to start before I'm too old—I would light one up. But contrary to others of my species, smoking is not among my vices. So I sigh, fit a satisfied smile in place, and watch as the end credits of *Pride and Prejudice* begin to roll. Love this movie. Absolutely love it!

As the bubbly music fades away, I turn the face of my wristwatch toward the television's glow. And grimace at the time that glares back at me. Not that Jane Austen's romantic tale wasn't worth the entire evening, but it had never been my intention to watch it in its entirety, especially with this deadline breathing down my neck. The movie had been but an attempt to correct the tactical error made in allowing my date—AKA Gorgeous—to talk me into inviting him in for a nightcap. Far too much temptation for a single woman who hasn't been in a relationship for . . . well . . . a while.

I sigh as I conjure a vision of Jake Grainger—every angle sculpted to perfection one rarely sees off the cover of a romance novel. But then, he has graced quite a few. Over a candlelit dinner at a trendy French restaurant, he boasted he had just finished his 767th cover. And again on the way to my townhouse. And again after I let him talk his way in.

And those covers don't lie. As depicted, Gorgeous is tall, broad-shouldered, and oh-so-muscular. Then there's his face. Beneath a stylish thatch of hair, he has the most incredible cheekbones, appealing mouth, and sculpted jaw.

And don't get me started on his voice, which went straight to my toes each time he leaned near and loosed words on his warm breath. Whew! If not for one little glitch, he would be the perfect male specimen. The glitch? His eyes. Oh, they smolder, all right—big time!—and sparkle in a charmingly, boyish way; however, it turns out the phenomenon occurs only when specific criteria are met. And I'm ashamed to say, it took me a while to catch on, as I was too busy glowing at being the envy of so many women.

So what was the criteria? Plain and simple—Jake. Talk about him or respond to his attempts at seduction, and one could practically drown in his eyes.Talk about one's self, current events, even the mouth-watering food set before us, and the best one could do is wade around in those same eyes. Not that I'm complaining, as only a fool believes the perfect male exists.

Still, what woman, in her heart of hearts, doesn't want to be the one—the one worth battling dragons . . . crossing a desert . . . even dying for? More than just another conquest. Certainly more than just a sounding board.

But I fantasize, something at which I excel well enough to make a good living. At least, until recently . . .

I flinch, and once more wish I hadn't invited Gorgeous in for that nightcap—not only because of the temptation he presented, but because of the hours that could have been put to better use. I'd tried to discourage him from lingering, first by pouring him my idea of a nightcap. Remembering his disbelief when I handed him a goblet of 100 percent pure guava juice—shaken, not stirred—I smile. Unfortunately, he quickly recovered. Without warning, he swooped down and planted a kiss on my mouth. And after surfacing for air, I'd gone and kissed him back.

Memories of that kiss cause a guilty flush to warm my cheeks. It was nice. Real nice. And I would be lying if I said I hadn't wanted another one . . . or two . . . or three . . .

But I'm a good girl. Of course, my agent says I'm simply deprived.

It hadn't been easy to disengage from Gorgeous, but somehow I managed. So there we stood looking at one another, an expectant silence filling the space between us. Not good.

Knowing it was past time Gorgeous was on his way, I slyly suggested we watch a movie. To my surprise, he liked the idea— at least, until I guided him past the sofa. Almost in a daze, he settled into the chair beside mine.

I never expected him to last through the first half of *Pride and Prejudice*, but it turns out the man has staying power. With the exception of a brief snooze, complete with snoring, he'd hung on until I inserted the CD that spun out the second half of the tale. Then he suddenly remembered an early-morning photo shoot and headed for the door. Of course, by then I was hooked on the timeless romance between Elizabeth Bennett and Mr. Darcy. And it's all Gorgeous's fault.

Well . . . not all. And it's not as if I didn't enjoy being wooed, especially the kissing part.

Hmm. Perhaps I shouldn't have evaded Gorgeous when he tried to kiss me again before leaving—

Not! Prim protests, suddenly appearing on my left shoulder. *Midnight. Just the two of you. WAY too much temptation. Besides, the kid is twenty-eight-years young to your middle-aged thirty-five.*

Cruel. So Cruel.

Of course, what's Prim without Improper, who promptly plops down on my right shoulder. *Just one more kiss. Couldn't have hurt.*

Could have.

Could not.

Could have!

Could not!

I go back and forth between the two until their bickering jerks me back to the purpose of tonight's interlude: writing chapter twelve of *The Gifting.*

"Adda, Adda, Adda," my agent had purred, "you've been holed up too long. Get yourself a man, let him sweep you off your feet, and the *bleepin'* chapter will write itself." Okay, she didn't say *"bleepin',"* but it sounds better than the words that often spew from her mouth.

So I had finally accepted one of several dinner invites from Gorgeous and, overall, enjoyed his attempts to woo me. Now all that remains to be seen is if the chapter will, indeed, write itself. And what better time to test it than past midnight—especially considering my deadline.

I press "power" on the remote, promptly sending my beloved *Pride and Prejudice* into a black hole, and push out of the chair. Smoothing the skirt of the little black dress I wore for my night out, I pad through the living room on bare feet and head up the stairs. At the first landing, I consider going directly to the computer.

Nah.

First comfortable clothes, then writing.

I bound up the stairs to the next landing and enter my bedroom. In the time it takes to cross from one side to the other, the little black dress is history. As I tug the belt of my old terry robe tight, I nod. Better. Of course, I doubt Gorgeous would agree, I concede as I turn in front of the full-length mirror. In fact, I'm certain he wouldn't. Though the first half of *Pride and Prejudice* hadn't sent him running for the hills, my thick, old robe surely would have done the trick. Gone is all visible proof of the past six months' brutal work with my personal trainer, Ludwig. Lumpy, bumpy Adda Sinclaire has returned—for the time being.

Not until I cross to the doorway of my bedroom do I realize I'm still wearing my underwire bra. I pluck at the elastic, consider removing the offending bit of lingerie, but in the end, reason that the chafing will keep me from falling asleep at the keyboard. Not that I could possibly doze off with so much fresh material for Robert and Philippa's long-awaited love scene—an eye-popping kiss, a candlelit dinner, and the ever-inspiring *Pride and Prejudice*.

"Show time," I declare and start down the stairs. However, at the landing to my office, I pause. "Tea would be nice," I murmur, "and maybe a few nibbles."

You're stalling, Prim warns.

Ten . . . fifteen minutes tops, Improper scoffs.

In the end, I side with Improper. After all, when you're talking hours, what's fifteen measly minutes?

With Prim grumbling at my ear, I grasp the railing to descend the last flight of stairs. And not for the first time this evening, my brightly painted nails glare at me. Ugh. Romeo Red polish looked much better in the bottle than out of it. Maybe I should change—

Don't even think about it.

Wouldn't take but fifteen . . . twenty minutes tops.

● ● ●

Robert lowered his head, brushed his mouth across Philippa's, then stepped to her back and began loosening her laces.

Click click click.

Thud.

Click click click click.

Thud.

I just love the sound of words flying from my brain to the keyboard—almost as much as I love perfectly polished nails.

I lift my hands and spread them before my face. Admiring the ovals that tip each digit, I catch my reflection in the newly applied Heavenly Crimson polish. Unfortunately, despite reassurances otherwise, it took over thirty minutes to clean, file, and paint my nails. Worth it, though, as they look beautiful. In fact, excluding my glutes, my nails are my best feature.

Vice? Obsession? Whatever. Every woman ought to be in some sort of committed relationship. So what if mine comes in fifty-two colors with shameless names like Vabulous Vermillion, Torrid Tamale, and Goddess Gold.

With a satisfied sigh, I lower my hands to the keyboard and use the nubbies on the F and J to guide me to home row. Now where was I?

Oh, yeah. Robert is undressing his new wife—*has* been undressing her since I determined my polish was set enough to endure a nail-pounding workout.

And some workout that was. I stare at the single paragraph I managed to download from my vacationing imagination. Sheesh! What is my problem? I've done this a hundred times—and done it well and tastefully according to readers.

Readers . . . *hmmm* . . .

I look to the pile of fan mail perched on the corner of

my desk and recall a time when I dreamed of such evidence of adoration. Now they're a reality. And burdensome. Though it's true my personal assistant—ooh, that still gives me tingles!—handles the bulk of my correspondence, which typically consists of praise followed by a request for bookmarks or bookplates, she sets aside letters of special note. Such as—

I snatch my hand back.

"Oh no, you don't."

I know exactly where one little letter will lead: straight off the page of my miserable love scene.

I glare at the paragraph—if it can even be called that. It is, after all, just one long sentence.

Don't think about it, I tell myself. Just write. Get something on the page. Anything!

" . . . began to loosen her laces." I read back the last words and momentarily pity my medieval lady who will never hear the sensual strains of a zipper tracking down her back.

"Her loss," I murmur, and try to remember the last time I heard a zipper track down my back. Loooong time ago. Still, I press on.

Click. Thud. Click click click. Thud.

A few moments later, he parted her bodice to reveal the creamy flesh of her back. "Philippa," he breathed, then lowered his head and pressed his lips to the base of her neck.

She gasped and murmured his name with such longing he . . .

"He . . . " I prompt. "He . . . " What? What does he do? I close my eyes and concentrate . . . concentrate hard . . . real hard. . . .

Blasted bra! Through the material of my robe, I pluck at it. Of course, it snaps right back into place. I grind my teeth, open my eyes, and refamiliarize myself with the words on the screen. "Right. He . . . "

Come on, Adda, what does your hero do?

He . . . he . . .

"Aarrgh!"

I grab the remote control of my leather office chair and press "power."

"Okay," I murmur as the seat begins to hum and vibrate, "now we're getting somewhere." I lean back, push the "full body" button, and feel the vibratory wave move from the seat, up my back, and down again. "Oh, yeah."

My eyelids drift down.

Love this chair!

Bought it when I signed my first six-figure deal four years ago, parting with a few of those figures at the insistence of the salesman that the chair would do wonders for writer's block.

I'd smiled, smug in the knowledge I didn't suffer from writer's block, certain such an affliction was merely an excuse of the lazy.

Plunk your rear in the chair and it will come, is my motto. Discipline, discipline, discipline! With that reminder, I take a deep breath, lean toward the screen, and command my slug of a brain to produce.

. . . with such desperation he . . .

Click click click click click click.

Yes! With bated anticipation, I read the word.

. . . snored.

I flop back in the chair, drum my fingers on the chair arms, and glare at the ceiling. It glares back—no answers, no inspiration.

"Great," I grumble as I swivel around and catch sight of the tray perched expectantly on the credenza. It beckons to me, tempting me to take a well-deserved break.

"If you insist," I murmur and lift the silver pot. But it's black liquid that streams into my porcelain cup. Black, not brown.

I set the pot down, lift the cup, and peer into its depths. Once again, I forgot to remove the tea bags, turning a lovely comfort drink into bitter disappointment. And of course, no steam is in evidence.

The clock above my office door proclaims that two-and-a-half hours have passed since the closing credits of *Pride and Prejudice*. I lower the cup and eye a gold-rimmed bowl. Ben and Jerry have melted into a puddle of mauve foam. Poor guys. However, in the midst of my mourning, Lady Godiva peeks at me from behind the teapot.

I smile at the one true friend who hasn't abandoned me. A moment later, I take a bite of her and sigh as dark chocolate coats my tongue. Telling myself I'll work her off later—and to heck with Ludwig's lectures on taking care of my body so it will take care of me!—I finish off the piece. And two more.

It's a go, I tell myself as I swivel back around. Determinedly, I punch the backspace key and watch as d, e, r, o, n, and s disappear.

All righty, then, talk to me, Robert. What are you going to do next? Come on, write this scene for me. You can do it.

" . . . he . . . "

What?

" . . . he . . . he . . . "

What? What?

"Men!" I jab the monitor button. As the screen dissolves to black, the fan mail once more grabs my attention.

Maybe that *is* what I need. Some reader slobbering praise and pleading for my next book. After all, what better inspiration? I pull one letter from the middle of the pile and scan to the area highlighted by my personal assistant.

Ms. Sinclaire,

No "*Dear* Ms. Sinclaire"? It does not portend well.

I have just finished reading "Thorn of the Rose" and would love to know your research source for the plague.

There the highlighting ends, but I read on, fully aware I should run from this one.

Though I do not claim to be a historian, it is my understanding that once the disease reached the stage it did with Lady Margaret, the victim could not be saved. And yet your heroine recovered on the merit of little more than the hero's declaration of love. A bit contrived, don't you agree?

I do not! It's called fiction for a reason! And yes, the chance of recovery was nearly nil, but it happened. And I *am* in the business of happy endings.

I do hope you will personally answer my letter and address my concerns about this rather sub-standard offering.

Sub-standard!

Your devoted fan, Brandy Reynolds.

Ah. Brandy Reynolds. I snort. "You again, hmm?" As the letters of this "devoted fan" usually run a minimum of two pages, during the course of which she attacks everything from characterization to pace to point of view, it didn't occur to me that this stabbing letter might be from her. She must have been pressed for time.

I flip the letter and eye the envelope stapled to the back. It's postmarked "Phoenix, AZ." As for a return address, it's absent as usual. Of course, she isn't looking for a reply. Just wanted to get in a dig. I turn the letter over and read it again. No punctuation or grammatical mistakes—excepting artistic license exercised by beginning a sentence with "And" for impact. As for the signature, the initial letters are written with the usual flourish—big "B," bigger "R."

I grind my teeth. Though I have no concrete proof, I'd stake my fifty-two colors of nail polish on the "B" in Brandy standing for Birgitta and the "R" in Reynolds standing for Roth. As in Birgitta Roth, nemesis extraordinaire.

Hoping she left a trail, which she often does, I jump out of my chair, step to the bookshelf, and grab the most recent edition of *Women's Fiction Writers Quarterly*. In the section that details upcoming conferences for aspiring and published writers, I find it—the Phoenix Women's Fiction Writers' Conference held two weeks past.

"Aha!" "Brandy's" last letter was postmarked Houston, before that Chicago, before that Orlando, etcetera, etcetera. Always a different city where a romance writers' conference is being held and Birgitta is present, which explains how the envelopes of my "devoted fan" are always postmarked outside of New York, where Birgitta Roth resides a mere four blocks from me!

Searching for further proof, I scan the conference particulars, and sure enough, Birgitta Roth is listed as the keynote speaker. Topic: Breaking Out of Mid-list.

As if she has the slightest idea! Shaking my head, I take another look at the postmark. It corresponds with the last day of the conference.

Yep, it's Birgitta, or Stick Woman, as I call her. I'm certain of it. In fact, I wouldn't be surprised if she's responsible for all the dirty fan mail I receive. Not that I get much. After all, one does not make best-seller lists with legions of disgruntled readers in tow. Which is exactly the reason Stick Woman hates me. The closest she has come are the bottom slots of extended best-seller lists.

Wondering how anyone can sink so low, I toss the quarterly on the shelf.

"Birgitta Roth," I mutter. "That . . . that . . . that . . . "

Truly, I don't have anything against the woman. Did I get

mad when she bribed her way into the award for Best Up-and-Coming Women's Fiction Writer eight years ago? No. I got even by writing a better book the next go around, which was nominated for Best Historical Romance. Okay, I didn't take home the award, but her second book wasn't even nominated.

Did I get mad when her third book made the Book Club Selection and mine didn't? No. That's a matter of politics, after all, and my agent at the time—a mealy-mouthed woman—had no clout whatsoever. Too, as a New York news anchor, Stick Woman received plenty of free press.

Did I get mad when she was awarded five stars for her fourth book, and I was given a dismal four? No. Everyone knows it's the reader's opinion that matters. Four print runs of my book, and it's still out there racking up respectable royalties. Six months after Stick Woman's release, the covers of her surplus books were stripped and returned to her publisher for credit.

Did I get mad when my career faltered five years ago after my publisher declined my option book, and Birgitta signed another two-book deal? No. I fired my worthless agent, hired Noelle Parker, and worked up a new proposal that started a bidding war. Sweet!

Did I get mad when my ex-husband, Richard DeMarco—AKA Dick, which he *hates* to be called—had an affair with Stick Woman three years ago? No.

Well, come to think of it, I did get mad.

Dick, always rooting around for a foothold in sports broadcasting, hounded me until I finally tossed aside pride and introduced him to my arch enemy. And *that* was the beginning of the end. Stick Woman and Dick had an affair, and all I got was a lousy serving of divorce papers.

Well . . . not all.

I smile in remembrance . . .

Although I caused a scene during a writers' conference when Stick Woman showed around photos of her and Dick, the hunk of hair I wrenched from her bony head right there in the hotel lobby was worth it. Six months for it to grow back . . . six months of sporting a wig like a scarlet letter.

Oh, I could go on and on about why Birgitta Roth has no reason to detest me, and I have every reason to loathe her every blackhead-filled pore, but then I'd sound as petty as her.

Well, maybe one more thing . . .

Did I get mad at a workshop last year when I overheard her comment to a fellow writer that Adda Sinclaire ought to update her publicity photo to reflect her advanced age and thirty-pound weight gain?

Advanced age!

She's five years older than me! As for the thirty pounds, it was fifteen. And that, plus an additional ten, is now history—thanks to Ludwig, my personal trainer, and the whip he threatens to crack every time I even think about cheating on a sit-up. And I do mean whip, as in *snap . . . craaack*! The man trained lions for a traveling circus before realizing he could charge upward of two hundred dollars an hour wielding a whip over rich people with nothing better to do than throw money at him. Not that I'm rich, mind you.

Well . . . maybe just a little.

And that's another reason Stick Woman detests me. She's at five figures, and if I can just finish this last book for Farnsworth Publishing, I'm headed for seven. Or so my agent assures me.

So get to work, Prim pops up on my shoulder.

Better yet, Improper chimes in, *post dear Birgitta an e-mail. Address the poor thing's concerns.*

I blink.

That's a thought.

A good one.

Though I've never let Stick Woman know I'm onto her, perhaps it's time.

Think again, Prim urges. *Don't sink to her level.*

It would be sinking to her level. And there is a certain amount of satisfaction in being better than her.

Okay . . . okay . . .

A yawn in the works, I start to cover my mouth, then remember I'm alone and dispense with the manners. Though fatigue is starting to drag at me, I return my focus to the love scene and tell myself I can get past Robert's inability to consummate his marriage to Philippa.

Of course, after being terrorized by Birgitta, it *would* be inspirational to read a letter gushing with praise. I eye the pile and catch sight of pink parchment between sheets of white and cream.

Back to work, Prim chants, tempting me to flick her from my shoulder.

Just one, Improper purrs.

Once more siding with Prim, I shake my head and come back around my desk. As I drop to the seat, Brandy Reynolds' letter sticks its tongue out at me where it lies in the path between keyboard and monitor. I stare at it.

Don't you dare, Prim scolds.

"Hush!" I hiss.

Well, don't say you weren't warned.

I struggle a bit longer, then turn on my monitor, log onto my server, point, click, and pull up Birgitta's e-mail address.

Ms. Brandy Reynolds, Thank you for your letter regarding "Thorn of the Rose." I am so pleased you enjoyed it. As, by your own admission, you are not a historian, may I suggest "Ravages of the Plague in Fourteenth-Century Europe" by Sir C. R. Walsingham? Please understand, Ms. Reynolds, that I write romantic fiction, the culmination of which is a happy ending. If you are searching for something less romantic and, therefore, tedious—

Not to mention sub-standard!

—I highly recommend mid-list author, Birgitta Roth. I am sure you will quickly become her devoted fan. Happy reading! Sincerely, Adda Sinclaire ***NEW YORK TIMES BEST-SELLING AUTHOR***

Couldn't resist the *New York Times* parting shot. Smiling, I click "send," and off it goes. No regrets. No turning back.

Very nice, Improper murmurs.

As I slide my pointer to the "X" that will disconnect me, I notice the Barnes & Noble advertisement for free shipping. I bite my lip, tell myself I don't need any more research books, and click on the advertisement.

Some time later, bleary-eyed and yawning, I disconnect.

Nice going, Prim quips.

I stare at my paragraph and blink a couple of times to bring it to focus.

" . . . he . . . "

A fearful glance at the clock confirms it. I laid to waste nearly five hours.

Tears sting and a sob rolls up my throat as I press my forehead to the desk. I have no choice but to admit the unadmittable.

I have a problem.

A serious problem.

Hoping there's a nearby chapter of Writer's Block Anonymous, I reach for the phone.

"Why in God's name are you calling me at five in the morning?" my agent grumbles.

I take a deep breath. "I need help, Noelle. My hero can't consummate the marriage."

"Has he tried Viagra?"

"Noelle!"

She sighs, and I hear the snap of a lamp switch. "Adda, I've already advised you on this."

"And I took your advice. I got myself a date and let him

sweep me off my feet."

"Really?" There's surprised admiration in her tone. "Then what are you calling me for?"

"I—"

"You did bring him home, didn't you?" she barks, admiration giving way to suspicion.

She's not going to like it, but my conscience refuses to allow her to think I'm easy. "Yes, and we spent an enjoyable evening viewing *Pride and Prejudice*."

A long silence, and I wince in anticipation of her squeal of horror.

"Adda Sinclaire!"

Do I know her? Or do I know her?

"Are you telling me you subjected your inspiration to that sappy movie? All umpteen hours of it?"

"Hey!" I protest. "*Pride and—*"

"What happened, Adda?"

I brace myself for another squeal. "We watched the movie and he went home."

Her teeth grind across the phone line. "Then noth . . . ing hap . . . pened?" she punctuates each syllable.

Remembering Gorgeous's kiss, the urgency of which took my breath away, I almost sigh. "We . . . uh . . . " I clear my throat. "We kissed."

Once more, silence descends, the only sound that of her breathing. Finally, she says, "Okay."

Deep breath.

"Okay."

Deep breath.

"*Bleep!*" she explodes. "Did you let one of those Bible-thumpers in your front door again?"

I sink lower in my chair. Bible-thumpers—a weakness of mine. The young Southern Baptist missionaries who show up on my doorstep once or twice a year are so sincere and caring that I can't close the door in their faces. More, I have only to spend a few minutes with them to realize they have something I don't. Something I find myself wanting, though I can't say what, exactly, it is. All I know is that when they speak of God and Jesus, their eyes sparkle and their smiles grow wide. When they set their bodies to what they believe, their hands fly with such excitement a certain amount of distance is required to ensure I don't get slapped upside the head. And when they ask if I'd like to accept Jesus into my life and I decline, they're nonjudgmental. There's just this . . . peace about them.

"Adda?"

So where does that peace come from? Though I know they'd like me to believe Jesus—

"Did you let one in?" Noelle shrills.

I certainly heard that. Wincing, I say, "No," and before she can heave a sigh of relief, add, "I let in two." After all, they travel in packs. New York City is *not* Mayberry, U.S.A.

"How many times do I have to tell you—" Noelle begins her rant.

Which is why I decide against mentioning the little black book . . . er, Bible . . . or something like it . . . that I accepted from one of the nice young men I invited into my kitchen.

Rant. Rant. Rant.

If she were to know I've actually been flipping through those almost translucent pages, I might never hear the end of it. Of course, it doesn't sound like I'm about to hear the end of this. Time for a potty break . . .

I set the handset on my desk, and when I return a minute later, her miniaturized voice is still working over her absent audience.

"All that preaching about love and forgiveness and doing unto others," she says as I return the handset to my ear. "What, I ask you, is this world coming to?"

Before I can cover the mouthpiece, a snort explodes from my mouth.

"What?" Noelle demands.

I clear my throat, shake my head. "Nothing. Just . . . something caught in my throat."

"Um hmm," she grumbles, then sighs. "Listen, Adda, you've got to get serious here. Your deadline— "

"I know all about my deadline," I snap, surprising both of us as I drop the "passive" in "passive-aggressive."

"Oooo . . . kay," she intones.

Though I try to breathe through the emotions that are piling one atop the other, my throat tightens, nose tingles, and eyes water. Oh no . . .

"Adda?"

"I'm done for," I burble, voice breaking. "Finished. Dried up. Nothing left. Nada. I . . . I have . . . " Realizing I'm about to hyperventilate, I take another long, cleansing breath as Ludwig urges me to do in stressful situations.

"What is it?" Noelle prompts.

I snap my teeth. "I . . . have . . . writer's . . . block!"

A long pause follows, and I wonder if she's fainted dead away. For years we've shared the belief that no such disease exists. And now I've gone over to the other side.

How humiliating.

"What am I going to do?" I moan.

More silence, and I just know she's kicking herself for giving me her home number. But then, with her hefty 15-percent cut, she has a vested interest in this, too.

"Find yourself another date," she says.

Though tempted to slam the phone down, I grip it tighter and bark, "No!"

"Fine!" she barks back only to give an exasperated sigh. "Look, get some sleep and meet me at The Ivories at one. We'll talk over lunch."

Calm, Adda. Calm. I swallow hard, nod.

"Are you there, Adda?"

Oh, yeah, she can't see me. "I'll meet you," I say.

"Good. 'Night." She slams down the phone.

Night? Don't I wish. I look to the blinds through which

sunlight is beginning to filter. It's morning in Manhattan.

Sickened by all the wasted hours, I return the phone to its base and glance hopefully at the computer.

Oh, what's the use? With every intention of sleeping away what I dare not call depression, I trudge upstairs and flop down on the bed. But sleep eludes. Anxiety pressing in on all sides, I find myself considering the little black book and the young man who gave it to me. Josh was his name. . . .

So go get it, Prim suggests, *maybe it'll help.*

Yeah, as in putting you to sleep, Improper derides.

Sounds like a win-win situation to me. Thus, I bang around the townhouse until I finally locate the book in the kitchen. I pause at the sight of it. It's so cute, especially compared to the inches-and-inches-thick phone book beside which it lies. Very cute.

"It's the second part of the Bible," Josh said, explaining the book's rather abbreviated size. Of course, the incredibly small type and über-thin pages have a lot to do with it, too.

Settling on a bar stool at the eat-in counter, I turn the little black book right side up and frown over its condition. Not that it's beat up. It's just that, like so many books, it doesn't appear to have been treated with the respect books are due. The binding is creased in a dozen places, the cover is worn, the page edges are somewhat warped, and the gold-stamped title is fading. I focus on the latter, and with my finger trace the letters that spell out: *New Testament.*

"Jesus' life and death," Josh had said with a reverence that deepened his charming southern drawl.

The next line reads: with *Psalms and Proverbs.*

"Old Testament Poetry that teaches life principles," Josh had explained.

I lower my gaze to the *NIV* stamped at the bottom.

That he had not explained, and if I were completely ignorant of the Bible, I'd guess it to be the author's name. I shrug. Probably some kind of Bible code.

I take a deep breath. "Okay, save me or put me to sleep."

As with each time I open to the "Presented to" page, I can't help but feel guilty over how I ended up with Josh Holman's little black book, which his best friend, Dustin—the same young man who accompanied him to my home—gave him two years ago, according to the inscription.

Though I was only being kind in expressing interest in their pamphlets that talked about Jesus and what it means to be a Christian, Josh's enthusiasm had been so contagious I found myself asking questions. Next thing I knew, *he* was asking questions, foremost among them—would I like to be saved?

Saved? I'd backpedaled as fast as I could, edging him and his friend toward the door and telling them I'd have to look into it some more before making a decision like that. At the door, Josh had turned back and asked if I owned a Bible. I told him I didn't but that as soon as I found time to pick one up, I would—a lie, but anything to make the Bible-thumpers go away. Josh had stood there a long moment, chewing the corner of his lip. Then he exchanged glances with his friend, pulled the little black book from his shirt pocket, and handed it to me.

"You can have mine," he said with a smile on his lips and a light in his eyes.

It was reflex that made me accept it and astonishment that held my tongue from protest. There I stood, wide-eyed, as he told me that though it wasn't the Bible in its entirety, the life of Jesus and Psalms and Proverbs was the best place to start. Not until he had shaken my rather limp hand and stepped outside did I find my voice. Catching the sleeve of his friend as he started to follow, I asked him to return the book to Josh, but the young man just leaned near and said, "Josh is aching to lead someone to Christ. Read it, and maybe you'll be his first."

So now I'm stuck with the book, a very personalized book, it turns out—complete with highlighting, margin notes, favorite Bible sayings handwritten on the pages at the back of the book, and a list of people he has forgiven. Among them, his father . . .

Feeling like the voyeur I do each time I enter Josh's private world, I turn to the back where he listed issues he must have dealt with—anger, fear, lust, and so on. Beneath each are references to different chapters, along with numbers and colons which, I'm pleased to say, I've decoded. Thus, let's see what God has to say about dealing with writer's block.

Not surprisingly, it isn't among Josh's issues. But there must be something related to it. As googling isn't an option, I run a finger down the pages in search of a compatible issue.

"Ah," I say, "desperation." Though Josh has listed half a

dozen sayings, I choose the first—Psalm 138:7. "Though I walk in the midst of trouble," I read aloud, "you preserve my life; you stretch out your hand against the anger of my foes, with your right hand you save me."

Hmm . . . sounds like a pretty serious situation this guy is in. Not that the passage isn't comforting. It's just that a life-and-death situation hardly equates with writer's block. Or does it?

Regardless, it was obviously written for someone who already possesses faith—and I don't.

This time my finger lands on "discouragement," which is more in keeping with what's happening in my life. I return to Psalms, and the highlighted words of 77:1 immediately draw my gaze. "I cried out to God for help; I cried out to God to hear me."

Sounds like the author is advising prayer—of which I know very little.

Back to Josh's issues. "Failure?" Though I'm not at that point—yet—my curiosity over how the young man dealt with it makes me go searching for 1 Chronicles 28:20. Keeping an eye on the headings, I fan through the book, but there's no Chronicles. And the index confirms it. Guessing it must be part of the Old Testament, I wonder—not for the first time—if I should get hold of a complete Bible.

Nah.

"Suffering?" I stare at the blue-inked word. *That* I am. "Psalm 69:1-3," I repeat several times before locating the passage. "Save me, O God, for the waters have come up to my neck. I sink in the miry depths, where there is no foothold. I have come into the deep waters; the floods engulf me. I am worn out calling for help; my throat is parched. My eyes fail, looking for my God."

Well isn't that depressing—makes my own suffering seem rather petty. Still, I wonder what nugget of wisdom might be found in all that misery. So I read on, wading through enemies who seek to destroy this guy named David and force him to restore something he didn't steal. Then there's weeping, scorn, mockery, disgrace, shame, and downright groveling for help from God who doesn't seem to be answering his phone. But for all that, David continues to trust in him and praise him. And the next Psalm is more of the same stuff, and the Psalm after that . . .

Very depressing.

Temples throbbing, I drop my forehead to the open book and am surprised at how heavy my eyelids feel. Well, at least the little black book was good for something.

TWO

Still can't get used to paying twenty bucks for a sandwich. À la carte, no less! But Noelle has no qualms. In fact, she'll likely order another "to go" to avoid cooking dinner.

"So?" she says, sipping her six-dollar-a-bottle water.

"So I took your advice," I grumble.

She smiles. "Got yourself another date, hmm? And on such short notice." Her perfectly arched eyebrows bounce. "I'm impressed, Adda."

I shake my head. "Not *that* advice. I got some sleep." No need to mention that most of it was had face down in a little black book.

Noelle rolls her eyes. "You're a hopeless cause." With a pitying purse of her lips, she takes a long drink of water—about a dollar's worth. "So who's the poor sap that took you out for a nice dinner and, for all his trouble, was rewarded with—" she shudders, "—*Pride and Prejudice*."

Feeling the tips of my ears begin to warm, I tell myself to not take her dislike of my favorite movie personally. Still, I'm tempted to retaliate by holding out on her.

Petty, Prim reprimands.

So? Improper whispers.

So! Prim shrills, being the little eavesdropper she is. *Don't sink to her level.*

"Adda?" Noelle waves a hand in front of my face. "Hello, Adda. You there?"

"Jake Grainger," I blurt before I slip over to the dark side.

"Ah." Noelle's eyes brighten. "Grainger has been after you since he joined you on that publicity tour a couple years back."

Not that I could forget. Jake had modeled for each of the covers of my *Winds of Change* trilogy—once with black hair and moustache, once with blonde, flowing hair, and once with red hair. Always the same bod readers drool over. Much as I hate to admit it, I probably wouldn't have sold half as many books at those signings if he hadn't added his autograph to mine.

"Is he a good kisser?" Noelle asks with a suggestive leer.

I stare at her brightly painted mouth and realize I've never seen it any other way—not even after a three-course meal. Though I've heard of tattooed makeup, surely it's not done with the lips? Perhaps some new lipstick that actually lives up to its claim of being long-lasting and smudge-proof?

"Adda?"

"Hmm? Oh! Uh . . . yes . . . a really good kisser." I frown. "Not at all what one expects from a man who snores."

She does a double-take. "Snores?" Suspicion narrows her

lids. "You didn't say anything about snoring."

I did leave that bit out when we spoke in the wee hours of morning. However, before I can explain away any lascivious conclusions she might draw, she gives a snort of disgust. "Let me guess—he fell asleep in the middle of your movie."

Why do I suddenly feel sheepish? "Yeah."

Her eyes go rolling again.

Don't take it personally, I counsel myself. And, in an attempt to avert another argument between Prim and Improper, say, "Can you believe Jake Grainger snores?"

Noelle waves a dismissing hand. "In my experience—and it's extensive, darling—most men snore."

I frown. "Not *my* heroes." Nor my ex. Of course, he cheats, doesn't he?

"Which is why it's called women's *fiction*," Noelle reminds me.

Her remark pulls me back to last night and the e-mail I sent Birgitta. Did I really do that?

Never let them know how you feel, my mother had drilled into me from a young age. *Think what you want, but act the lady and smile, smile, smile*. And I've aspired to make her proud, but when I learned Birgitta was "entertaining" my husband, . . . well, I haven't been the same since.

"Excuse me, Ms. Sinclaire," a male voice speaks beside me.

I look up. It's Brad, our regular waiter, a plate balanced in each hand. I'll just bet he's hoping Noelle picks up the tab. Her 30 percent tip beats my 15 any day.

I sit back and fix on the plate he sets before me. Grilled veggie sandwich, Prim's favorite. And as usual, it's gussied up with sprigs of this and that—all of which are inedible and merely meant to make a girl feel she got her twenty bucks' worth.

I glance at Noelle's plate, and Improper peeks out to gaze lustfully at her triple decker that spills over with thinly sliced prime rib, avocado, cheese, and mayo.

Ludwig will be proud of you, I assure myself.

"Anything else, Ladies?" Brad asks.

"Another water, please," Noelle says, though she's barely halfway through the first.

She's *definitely* picking up the tab! "I'm fine," I say, and continue to stare at the forbidden sandwich as Brad drifts away.

"Want a bite?" Noelle asks.

I meet her knowing gaze and, throwing pride to the wind, say, "Yes!"

She chuckles and slices off a third.

"So what are you going to do about your deadline?" she asks as I sink my teeth into juicy, medium-rare prime rib. I sigh, roll the bite around in my mouth and, in the next instant, get a taste of . . . horseradish?

My eyes bulge, throat closes, and nostrils flare as the offensive muck burns my nasal passages.

"Adda?"

I stare at Noelle, wanting to spew the nasty mouthful, but

painfully conscious of the dining accommodations we share with Manhattan's finest. My napkin! I fish around my lap but, as usual, the crisp white linen has gone south.

Just swallow, I tell myself. Get it over with and wash it down with water. But I can't, and a moment later Noelle is coming around the table.

I shake my head, but she keeps coming. Then she's behind me, dragging me up, pressing a clasped fist beneath my sternum, and giving a sharp, upward thrust.

I clench my teeth, but the pressure is too great and I cough up the ugly little offender. It lands in Noelle's glass of bottled water.

"Did I get it all?" she asks, whipping me around to face her.

The room breathlessly silent, my face hot, I nod. Man! Did she break a rib?

Noelle heaves a sigh of relief. "Whew! You made my bank account flash before my eyes. Scary."

Did I hear right? Did she really say that? Of course she did—a sharp reminder that as friendly as an agent and editor may be, they are *not* your friends. It isn't your best interest they're looking out for, but theirs. You are nothing more than a dollar sign to them. The moment you take on water, they toss you the bucket and tell *you* to bail. Been there, done that, thank you!

I grab my glass and drain it. "I was not choking," I hiss.

"Oh?" Face creasing into confusion that not even her latest plastic surgery can deflect, Noelle steps back.

"Horseradish," I rasp, wincing at the ache in my lower-left

rib. "I *hate* horseradish!"

She flips her hair back. "You could have saved me the embarrassment by simply spitting into a napkin."

Now why didn't I think of that?

I glare at her as she strides back to her chair.

As I lower to mine, I glance around. Though conversations are beginning to resume, I remain the object of interest. And disdain.

I can see the headline now: BESTSELLING AUTHOR, ADDA SINCLAIRE, COUGHS UP HORSERADISH SANDWICH AT POSH MANHATTAN EATERY. HOW ROMANTIC.

Brad appears. "Are you all right, Ms. Sinclaire?" he asks as he wipes up the mess without so much as a grimace.

"Better now, thank you," I manage, wondering what shade of red I am.

"Another water is on the way, Ms. Parker," he says, "and I'll put in an order for a replacement sandwich."

I look at her plate. It seems my mess didn't confine itself to her water. *Tsk, tsk.*

"Thank you, Brad." She waves him away.

He hurries off bearing all evidence of my humiliation. Maybe he *is* worth 30 percent.

"So?" Noelle says.

I rub my ribs. Gosh, for fifty-something, the woman packs a punch! "So what?" I gripe.

"Your deadline! What about your deadline?"

I sigh, push the grilled veggie aside. "I've never asked for an extension, but that's what I'll have to do—the full three months allowed by contract."

She's quiet a long moment, then leans forward. "You know it will push everything back. Artwork, advertising, editing . . . "

And her cut of the second half of my sizable advance.

"You might even lose your June slot—prime time, you know."

Trying to calm my resentment, I take a long drink of my *free* ice water. "Look, Noelle, I'm on chapter twelve. As in barely halfway. As in *have been* on chapter twelve for *two* months. As in six weeks to deadline. Even if I could get through this . . . blasted love scene, the chance of turning in the manuscript on time is nil."

Brad appears, sets another glass of ice and six-dollar-a-bottle water in front of her, and as quickly disappears.

Noelle pours her water. "If you weren't so obsessive, you wouldn't be in this jam."

I know what's coming. We've been through it several times these past months. "I don't write like that, Noelle."

She lifts her glass. A long swallow later, she sets her water down. I stare at the rim—not the faintest smudge of lipstick. And her mouth—as perfectly painted as ever.

"Other writers do," she says. "Hit a *block*, move on, and come back later."

Just had to emphasize "block." I square my shoulders. "As your bank account can attest—you know, the one that flashed before your eyes—I am *not* other writers. For me, everything has a flow." Though vaguely aware my voice is rising and heads are once more turning, I can't stop myself. "What happens in the bedroom between my hero and heroine affects every scene thereafter."

Prim gasps, and I flick my shoulder as though to unsettle a piece of lint.

"If the heroine makes the first move, *BIG* difference, especially if it turns out my hero isn't as adventurous— "

Never have I seen Noelle's eyes so round. In fact, I would have sworn it was an impossibility considering how many times the skin alongside them has been stretched and stitched into her hairline.

Stomach clenching, I look around and find that, once more, I'm the main attraction. The expressions of other diners range from disbelief to disdain, startled to stumped—as in, why doesn't management throw her out?

Show a little remorse, for goodness' sake! Prim urges as she crawls back to my shoulder.

Give 'em both barrels! Improper cheers me on.

Too far gone after last night's failure and now this meeting with my unsympathetic, money-grubbing agent, I press my hands to the table and stand. As Noelle hisses at me to sit, I paste a smile on my face. "I'm a romance author, okay?" I address the stuffed shirts and bras. "A best-selling romance author. Who, here, has a problem with that?"

"Oh, *bleep*," Noelle moans.

Some of my fellow diners raise their eyebrows, but most

look away. Satisfied, I resume my seat, but as I look toward Noelle, a man sitting alone at one of three coveted tables against the windows catches my eye. He's staring at me, though not with disgust. Amusement? I narrow my gaze on his mouth, the corners of which are tilted. And there's a sparkle in his deeply dark eyes. He's laughing at me!

Though I have never given anyone the finger, I'm tempted to flick a Fire Brigade polished fingernail—yes, I changed the color again. Sooo tempted . . .

Turn back! Prim warns.

Full speed ahead! Improper counters.

Fortunately, good breeding prevails and I opt for sticking out my tongue.

"Oh *bleep*!" Noelle gasps.

The man raises his eyebrows and smiles, revealing brilliant white teeth and a left cleft dimple.

My heart lurches, and I blink as attraction punches me in the gut. Not that he's young and flawlessly gorgeous like Jake, but he's a breath-stopper. Probably tops six feet, broad shouldered, jet-black hair silvered at the temples, early forties.

Resisting the urge to check his left hand, I avert my gaze. It's been a long time since any man turned my insides to goo, and why this particular one does, I don't understand.

Arrogant jerk!

"Brilliant, Adda," Noelle says as she looks around, having followed my gaze. "Real brilliant."

I shrug. "It's not as if I'll see any of these people again."

Something leaps in her steely, narrowed gaze that sends flutters of uncertainty up my spine. "You're probably right about that, especially where Nick Farnsworth is concerned."

My skin prickles. Farnsworth of Farnsworth Publishing? But before that sinking feeling gets a grip on me, I recall he's no longer with my publisher. The black sheep left the family-held company years and years ago—and not on amicable terms. Okay, then, I'm all right. I think . . .

She nods in the direction of the recipient of my juvenile gesture. "As in the new president of Intrepid Books."

Not all right.

Told you so, Prim socks it to me.

"As in the publisher who has been courting you in hopes of outbidding Farnsworth Publishing on your option book," Noelle plunges the dagger deeper.

I sink into my shoulders, grip a hand over my face, and peer at her from between my fingers.

"As in the one talking seven figures, Adda dear," she delivers the final blow with a smile so saccharine it's hard not to dislike her. Sure she helped rebuild my career when practically everyone pronounced me a goner, but she can be such a meanie—which is probably the reason she's so successful. Sometimes I really hate this business.

Determined to salvage my pride, I lower my hand, sit up straight, and force a smile. "Well, can't say this is the best day of my life." I keep my voice low. "But the good news is that Nick Farnsworth probably has no idea Intrepid even has a romance line."

"Wrong." Noelle leans forward. "It's Nick Farnsworth who has acknowledged what his predecessors would not, in spite of all the industry statistics—romance is where the money's at. Thus, he's personally overseeing the overhaul of Intrepid's romance division in order to make them *the* publisher of fine romance." She pats my hand, and though the gesture might appear motherly, I feel the condescension down to my toes.

My stomach is ready to revolt, but I hold steady. "Well, at this point, my little scene has no bearing on my career, does it? I mean, if I can't finish this book, what are the chances I'll finish the option book for anyone to bid on?"

Noelle sighs, and her sarcastic demeanor slithers back into its hole. "Look, what if you just put this one aside and start fresh?"

"Start fresh? Six weeks, Noelle!"

"Eighteen if we opt for the extension."

I shake my head. "I've never written a book in under six months. You know that. I am *not* prolific."

"Not at one hundred thirty-thousand words a book, but if you pare down—"

"I can't." As she well knows, the reason for the blip in my career was a zealous, tree-hugging editor who was more concerned with the amount of paper it would take to print my book than the story I had to tell. Thus, *Whispers in the Night* had been put on a diet and forced to shed thirty-thousand words. It had been cruel and the reviews even crueler. The book squeaked by with a three-star rating.

Of course, the publisher blamed me and declined the option book. I *won't* go that route again.

"All right," Noelle says and pauses as Brad appears with her water and replacement sandwich.

Eew! How did I miss that smell? Stomach turning as horseradish wafts across the table, I sit back.

"And you, Ms. Sinclaire?" Brad asks with a glance at my untouched sandwich. "Is there anything you need?"

I hand him the plate. "'To go' box, please."

He nods and hurries away. Pretending to follow his retreat, I snatch a glimpse of Nick Farnsworth. He's still alone, head bent toward the newspaper open on the table before him. Is he waiting on someone? Yep—two menus. I just hope it's not the editor Noelle has been talking to.

Nor a wife or girlfriend . . .

I look to his hand on the newspaper and feel a thrill at the absence of a wedding band.

"So you won't leave the love scene until later," Noelle interrupts, "and you won't start over. What's left, Adda?"

"Left? Well . . . "

Therapy, perhaps?

"Maybe I'll just drag out the option book my first publisher rejected and rework it." Of course, I have no intention of doing so. What had my editor at Gentry Books written? As if I could forget!

You simply haven't grown sufficiently in your writing for us to offer a contract on this proposal. Of course, the acquisition of books is of a subjective nature, and another editor may feel different. We wish you every success in placing it elsewhere.

Wished me success . . . *not!* But who's crying now that Adda Sinclaire is a *New York Times* Best Seller?

"You might have something there," Noelle cuts through my bitterness.

"Where?"

"Pulling out the option book."

I stare at her. "I was being facetious."

"Were you? Well, I'm not."

Though her lips remain untarnished, there are bits of horseradish between her teeth. My stomach lurches again, and I look around to see if Brad is on his way with my "to go" box. He isn't.

"If I remember right," Noelle says, "*Winds of Love*—"

"*Wings of Love.*"

"Whatever. The story was set in thirteenth-century France—"

"Twelfth, and it was England."

"Close enough."

Hardly, but before I can argue, she's barreling on. "The stories share the same premise—enemy forced to marry enemy. Just swap the stories out and you'll meet the deadline."

"Maybe the same premise," I say, "but that's all. *Wings of Love* in no way resembles the proposal for *The Gifting* that Kathryn approved."

Noelle scoffs. "Do you honestly think your editor will

remember a proposal she read a year ago? And even if she did, everyone knows the finished product is often markedly different from the proposal."

What she says is true, but I simply can't imagine doing it. *Wings of Love* was a long time ago and still bears the weight of painful memories. Dick and I argued often during its writing, setting the stage for his adultery a year later—which in no way absolves Stick Woman of her duplicity. Shameless hussy! But I won't think about her now. If I never again lay eyes on that woman, it will be too soon.

"What do you say?" Noelle prompts.

Forget the sandwich. I snatch up my purse and stand. "Get me my three-month extension." I turn away.

And there's the woman I hoped to never again lay eyes upon—Birgitta Roth. And, lordy lordy, she's lowering to the chair Nick Farnsworth has pulled out for her. Might Intrepid Books be thinking of signing her? A huge step up from Heart Core Publishers with whom she's been since her first book.

Fortunately, I become aware of my gaping and snap my teeth closed.

Is there any way I can slink out without her noticing? Without her revealing to Nick Farnsworth the identity of the loud-mouthed, haughty romance author who shot a mouthful of food across the table?

There's only one thing I can think of. I pull my dark sunglasses from my purse and slam them onto my face. Shoulders back, head up, veering slightly right, though the exit is left, I hold my breath as I draw even with their table.

"Adda Sinclaire? Is that you?"

Are you really there, God?

"Well, of course it is!"

I halt. Though I feared she might point me out, *never* would I have expected public acknowledgment. After all, I am the competition, and somehow she has wrangled a lunch date with the president of a prestigious publishing house. So it's one of two things. Either she wants to rub it in my face, or she sees gain in aligning herself with a best-selling author. Of course, she can't possibly know of the low to which I sank previous to her arrival. Poor thing.

I turn. Stick Woman advances on me and, to my horror, embraces me with those bony arms of hers. It's a first. And a last, I vow as her perfume assails me. She must buy it in bulk.

"How are you?" she asks, drawing back to survey me.

Past her shoulder, Nick Farnsworth is watching. "Birgitta Roth," I say, looking up at her where she tops my five-foot-seven by several inches. "What a lovely surprise."

"Isn't it?" Though she's smiling and anyone watching would think we're old friends, the daggers in her eyes tell different—something to which I refer each time I write a villainous woman into one of my books. Believe me, my heroines have battled and beaten quite a few Birgitta Roths.

"You look . . . " She slides her gaze down me and up again. " . . . good. How long did it take to lose all those extra pounds?"

Hag.

"Not long," I say, grateful for my dark glasses. "And you look great, yourself. Finally grew out your hair, hmm?"

Her lids narrow.

"It's lovely," I continue, "though I think I prefer it short."

As in torn from your head!

Her mouth twitches, but she holds on to the smile and leans near. "You know Richard. So passionate about long hair."

Then she and my ex *are* still together. Good. They deserve each other.

"Richard?" I put confusion into my own smile. "Oh! You mean *Dick*."

I declare, the woman has a tic! I stare at her right eye, the corner of which jerks spasmodically.

Strike!

Though it's true I could have come up with a more creative nickname for my ex—say, "Two Timer"—not only is Stick Woman's dislike of the shortened form of "Richard" nearly as great as his, but the nickname is perfectly acceptable to speak aloud in public. Kind of like the use of a silencer whereby only the victim feels the shot, allowing the shooter to slip away unnoticed.

Nice.

With a forced laugh, Stick Woman turns me toward her table. "Have you met Nick Farnsworth, the new president of Intrepid Books?"

Only over my tongue.

"No?" she gloats, and pulls me forward.

Straining backward, I glance over my shoulder, but Noelle isn't about to rescue me. She lifts her blasted six-dollar-a-bottle water and shrugs.

"I . . . " I gasp. "I'm in a hurry, Birgitta."

She looks around. "Come now, Adda, it will only take a minute."

"No, really—"

The Amazon is strong-arming me! And Nick Farnsworth is rising. A moment later, I'm standing before him, Birgitta's arm looped chummily through mine.

That goo feeling is back as I stare at him through my dark lenses. I was right about him topping six feet—by at least two inches. And yes, he does appear to be in his early forties, though he's a darned good-looking middle-ager. Definitely not the pretty boy Jake is. Nick Farnsworth has too many flaws for that, and I have the sudden urge to explore each one, from the tiny lines at the outside corners of his dark eyes, to the deeper grooves in his forehead, to that left cleft dimple that appears as I stand mutely before him.

" . . . Adda Sinclaire," Birgitta's voice squeezes into my consciousness, and I realize she has finished introductions.

"Best-selling romance author," Nick Farnsworth reminds me of my earlier outburst, which causes Birgitta to startle.

Blushing hotly, I look to the large, long-fingered hand he extends. Nice nails . . . clean . . . clipped . . . trimmed cuticles . . .

"A pleasure to meet you, Ms. Sinclaire."

If it's possible for a voice to have muscles, his does. I slide my hand into his and feel the goo invade my knees as he presses my palm. I'm holding my breath, I realize, and wonder if any man has ever made me do that.

"A p-pleasure, Mr. Farnsworth," I stammer.

For certain, *no* man has ever reduced me to a speech impediment.

He gives my hand a parting squeeze before releasing it.

Disappointment curdling my insides, I tell myself to get a grip.

Stick Woman, still clutching my arm, pats my hand. "Adda and I go back a looong way, Nick."

Nick. That familiar, hmm? Telling myself I'm not jealous—how could I be?—I wonder what Dick would think of Birgitta's lunch date.

Nick Farnsworth shrugs up his jacket and shoves his hands in his pockets. "A long way. Is that right?"

Stick Woman laughs huskily. "Our first books were released within months of one other." As if suddenly remembering something, she gasps. "Oh! Remember the awards ceremony the following year, Adda?"

It's coming, and just like vomit, there's no holding it back.

"We were both nominated for Best First Historical, Nick. Imagine that!" She giggles, and I can't help but be embarrassed for her. She *has* just hit the big four-O.

Nick Farnsworth is smiling, but he's looking at me—

studying me, making me feel like a specimen under glass. And despite my impenetrable dark glasses, it feels as if he's looking right through them.

Stick Woman sighs. "It was a close one, and to this day I still can't believe *I* took home the award."

Neither can I. Though I've walked away with more prestigious awards since, that one still smarts.

Nick Farnsworth steps aside. "I realize you were on your way out, Ms. Sinclaire, but perhaps you can spare a few minutes to join us for a drink?"

Stick Woman tightens my arm against her side, squeezing it against her bony ribs—honestly, I can feel the ridges! Though tempted to tick her off by accepting the offer, and knowing how much Noelle would want me to accept, I say, "I'd love to— " Stick Woman's arm tightens further, cutting off the blood supply to my lower arm, "—but I have another obligation."

"Oh." Stick Woman thrusts her bottom lip forward, eases up on my arm. "Pity. I was looking forward to doing some catch-up."

The story of her life.

"Maybe another time," I say, and meet Nick Farnsworth's x-ray vision. "Thank you for the offer."

He inclines his head, and that left cleft deepens.

Steady, girl. Steady.

At last, Stick Woman releases my arm. "Lovely meeting up with you," she says.

And I am dismissed. As I turn away, I see her step toward Nick

Farnsworth and lay a hand to his arm. Her claws—artificial nails that obscenely extend past the tips of her fingers a full inch—sink into his sleeve with a familiarity that suggests their meeting might be other than business.

And I see green.

I swing back around, startling Stick Woman into dropping her hand from Nick Farnsworth. "Forgive me, Birgitta," I say with an apologetic smile. "I forgot to ask after Dick. How *is* he doing?"

Her lashes flutter, and she appears to squirm inside her tacky pastel pink two-piece. "Oh. Didn't he tell you?"

Beneath the cover of my shades, I steal a look at Nick Farnsworth, and his mouth curves into a smile. He *does* have x-ray vision!

"He took a job in Houston," Stick Woman says and taps a considering finger to her lips. "What? Six months past?"

I jerk my gaze back to her. Richard's gone? Six months gone? I talk to my mother at least once a month, and she *never* mentioned it. As she's best friends with my ex's mother, she *must* know. Or is Stick Woman lying?

"Sports anchor for a local television station," she says. "Just too good to pass up."

Then Dick's hooking up with Stick Woman and her broadcasting connections paid off? He finally attained that which so long eluded him?

If not that the position was ill-gotten gain—paid for with our marriage—and that he'd been such a jerk, I'd be happy for him.

"I'm happy for him," I say. "Next time the two of you speak, give him my regards."

"I'll do that," Stick Woman says.

If she talks to him again. After all, it sounds as if he dumped her. In the middle of my smug revelry, I'm accosted by a memory of my beloved Shar-Pei's sad eyes. "I assume Dick took Beijing with him?"

Stick Woman lifts a hand to examine her claws. "Actually, no. The dog would have been too much of a hassle with the new job . . . the move . . . "

My heart leaps. "Then he left Beijing behind?"

"Yes," she purrs, "the little darling is staying with me." She lowers her hand. "But once Richard settles in, he plans on sending for him."

And when might that be? Already Beijing has endured six months of solitary confinement with *this* woman. Trampling my pride, I say, "Well, if it becomes too tiresome—"

"Oh, it won't. Beijing and I have become . . . " She heaves a sigh of contentment. " . . . inseparable."

Biting off a smile, I say, "I'm pleased to hear it." Resisting another glance at Nick Farnsworth, I incline my head. "Bye, then." I turn and am barely three steps removed when Stick Woman calls me back.

"Oh, Adda."

Feeling like a yo-yo on a dangerously frayed string, I look over my shoulder.

"You inadvertently posted me an e-mail intended for one of your fans."

Don't know how I could have forgotten that. With a supremely innocent smile, I ask, "Did I?"

"You did. I just wanted to thank you for recommending my books to the woman. I will, of course, reciprocate."

Told you so, Prim says, all smug and superior.

"You're quite welcome," I manage, though what I really want is to tear out another hunk of bottle-dyed blonde hair. But not in front of Nick Farnsworth. So I nod and, ignoring the stares pelting me, thread among the tables. At last, I step out into a muggy Manhattan day.

I'm certain there will be an urgent message from Noelle when I get home. Certain there will be an urgent message from Noelle when I get home—doubtless, she watched the whole Stick Woman scene—I decide against hailing a taxi. A nice, long walk is what I need. Of course, a new shade of nail polish wouldn't hurt either . . .

Putting my chin up, staring straight ahead as I pass the window behind which Nick Farnsworth and that little tramp sit, I head for Saks Fifth Avenue.

Two hours later, an elegant shopping bag in the crook of one arm, I let myself into my townhouse. And halt as Nick Farnsworth's voice—rippling with muscles—calls to me from the kitchen.

THREE

s. Sinclaire, Nick Farnsworth. 212-555-2540. I would appreciate a return call."

Rewind . . . play.

I listen again—for the umpteenth time since he left the message two days ago. And still I haven't returned his call, though Noelle swears that if I don't do it today, she'll call him herself. Maybe I should let her, but he called *me*, not *her*, meaning—

"Nothing," I mutter. He's just bypassing the middle man. Still . . .

"Wrong," I speak to the kitchen that stares back at me from stainless steel canisters, stainless steel spice racks, stainless steel fruit baskets. And even if he were calling about something other than business, I certainly don't want a man in my life.

I cross the kitchen in my scruffy fake-fur slippers, pivot, and return. He probably just wants to smoosh it in my face that he signed Stick Woman rather than me. Men can be so sensitive at a tongue being stuck out at them.

But maybe he does want to discuss a crossover from

Farnsworth to Intrepid. After all, I would bring considerably more readers to the table than Birgitta Roth. Too, in stealing me from Farnsworth, he'd score big against his alienated family. Has to be some value there.

"Just call him!" I mutter. "Pick up the phone and get it over with."

I reach to the handset, snatch my hand back, reach again. "Blast!" I tap my front teeth with a Mystic Maroon polished nail.

It's Friday. If I don't call him today, it will be Monday before I can do it.

Craaack . . . nibble . . . nibble . . .

"Aah!" I wrench my hand away from my mouth. The nail of my right index is ragged.

I bit it. *Bit* it!

Not since my mother broke me of the habit twenty-five years ago have I indulged myself. First stammering, now nail-biting. That's it! I am *not* calling Nick Farnsworth. If Noelle wants to, fine, but not me. The man is downright dangerous.

The rapid thud of footsteps on the stairs precedes Morticia's entrance.

"You all right, Ms. Sinclaire?" my personal assistant asks as she rounds the corner.

Though the young woman has worked for me a year, I'm still jolted by her appearance. I curl my fingers into my palm and lower my arm, slow to conceal the guilty pleasure of my teeth. "Of course I'm fine, Angel— " her real name—though the moment we met, I privately dubbed her Morticia. "Why wouldn't I be?"

She halts three feet away, shrugs. "You screamed."

I did, didn't I?

And over a chewed fingernail.

"I . . . uh . . . thought I saw a mouse."

Her black-rimmed eyes widen and glossy black lips tilt. "Which way did it go?"

Probably thinking of keeping my imaginary beast for a pet. Or concocting a potion out of him. These gothic people are definitely on the side of strange, and Morticia is no exception. Twenty-two years old, long-legged figure clothed all in black, pretty face powder-pale for dramatic contrast, she raises her heavily penciled eyebrows.

I shake my head. "Probably just my imagination."

Disappointment lines her brow, but before she can voice it, I ask, "How's it going upstairs?"

It takes her a few moments to get over pining after the little rodent, but she eventually sighs. "Finished the filing, almost done with the correspondence; now it's on to your mailing list and newsletter."

As usual, she's on top of everything, and I wonder how I ever survived without her. If she could just write the books for me . . .

"You sure it wasn't a mouse?" She twists a strand of long black hair around two fingers as she peers around me into the kitchen.

I shrug. "Never know, but if it was, he's gone."

"He? You think it was a male?"

Gritting my teeth, I say, "I honestly don't know, Angel."

"But it *was* a mouse?"

"Don't know that either." I step from the desk to the sink.

"But you said—"

"Some hot water?"

"Sure," she mutters, following me.

As I pull two cups off the shelf, I catch sight of my nibbled nail and realize that, for once, the circumnavigation of "Point A" to "Point B" with Morticia had a positive effect in that it made me forget about my nail. My beautiful nail.

I slip a cup under the hot water dispenser, fill it, and hand it to Morticia.

She doesn't notice, as she's busy scanning the floor for the mouse. How long before she lets this one go?

"Here." I thrust the cup forward.

She accepts it. "Thanks."

As I dispense water into my cup, she lifts the hem of her above-knee skirt, reaches into the black leather holster strapped to her thigh—à la Laura Croft—and removes a tan-colored tea bag. No sooner does she plop it in the water than her cup wafts a scent that always makes my eyes water—licorice, ginger, sage, and something I don't care to identify.

I gulp, remove a bag of good old English Breakfast tea from a canister, and bob it up and down in my cup.

"Oh!" Morticia croons. "What happened to your nail?"

Tea sloshes over the rim of my cup onto the tile. Feeling as if I've been caught doing something obscene, I mutter, "I . . . well . . . I . . ."

"Ah! You're a nail-biter!"

"I am *not* a nail-biter."

With a sympathetic shake of her head, she says, "Believe me, Ms. Sinclaire, I know a bitten nail when I see one." She sets her stinky tea on the counter and holds up her hands. "See these?"

As if anyone could overlook her black claws.

"They're artificial."

Reeeeaallly?

"And you know why?"

Hmm, why?

"Bitten to the quick—every one of them. And I used to get so nervous, I even bit off the artificial ones—especially when Iggy took me to see a horror flick."

I nearly spit out a mouthful of tea. Morticia nervous over a horror movie? Yes, despite her morbid makeup and clothes, she's really quite nice, but why the death's mask getup if she can't handle horror? It's not her boyfriend, Iggy. I know—I've seen him. And what a shock that was! A well-groomed computer nerd, spectacles and all.

"But I overcame my habit," Morticia continues. "Would you like to overcome yours?"

Feeling as if I'm watching an infomercial, I glare at her. "I don't bite my nails, Mor—Angel."

She wags a finger. "The first step to overcoming a problem is to admit you have one."

Yeah. And didn't it work wonders for my writer's block, I silently bemoan the love scene to which I have yet to give birth.

"Thanks for the advice," I say. "Now I'd better get back to work."

She sighs as I carry my tea past her. "I'm here for you when you need me, Ms. Sinclaire."

And even when I don't. I do *not* bite my nails! "I appreciate that," I say as I round the corner and start up the stairs. Shortly, I enter my office and lower my cup to the desk. It's the second time this morning I've engaged in the ritual, and I have yet to get past it. With every intention of succeeding this go-around, I reach to pop the button on my darkened monitor. But then my fingernail comes into view.

Won't do. Won't do at all.

A minute later, I'm upstairs rectifying the problem. I mean to do just the one nail—honestly!—but when I notice imperfections in the polish of the others, there's no choice but to go all the way. Of course, by the time I finally drag myself back to the computer, my tea is lukewarm. Only one remedy for that.

As I step from my office, Morticia appears in the doorway of the office opposite mine.

"I know I reminded you about—" She breaks off as her gaze falls to my fingers wrapped around the cup. "Ooh, gorgeous color. What's it called?"

Telling myself I have no reason to feel guilty, though the

emotion threatens to turn me beet red, I casually lift my other hand for her to better see. "Eve's Sin."

"Mmm. Love it."

"What did you remind me about?" I ask before we once more get stuck on the topic of my nails.

"Your book signing," she says with such innocence the name "Angel" comes to mind before "Morticia."

I groan. "Forgot. Tomorrow afternoon, right?"

Sheesh! The last thing I need is to spend time promoting my new release when I should be concentrating on my next.

"Nope, today."

Morticia again, the little vamp.

"Five o'clock 'til seven," she says.

"Barnes & Noble," I grumble.

"Yep. Sure you don't want me to accompany you?"

She asks every time, and I always decline, though it certainly hasn't stopped her from popping in at some of the signings. Fortunately, she usually shows after the bulk of my readers have drifted away clutching autographed books like some divine treasure. Thus, the number of readers scared off by her appearance is minimized.

"Thank you, but I'll be fine," I say, though I'll be far from fine with this deadline nipping at my heels.

For once, Morticia looks relieved. "Iggy will be glad to hear that. There's a special preview of *Lord of the Dark and the Deadly* this evening."

Far be it for me to deprive them of a romantic evening. "Enjoy, then."

"Thanks." She starts to turn away. "Oh! Almost forgot. Your mother called—said she was returning your call."

I perk up. Though I've been trying to reach her to confirm Stick Woman's revelations about Dick, I've had no luck. Wondering where I might have been when she finally phoned, I ask, "When did she call?"

"This morning. I got her message off the answering machine."

"Must have been asleep," I mutter.

"Sorry I didn't mention it sooner."

I sigh. "Don't worry about it. I'll call her back."

Morticia nods and disappears inside her office. Almost immediately, she starts pounding at the keyboard.

One hundred words a minute, two errors, I recall the typing statistics that jumped off the application her employment agency sent. Of course, when she appeared for her interview with a parole officer in tow, I'd been certain it was a mistake. A terrible mistake. The parole officer had calmed me with assurances that she was a good kid who had been caught only the one time with a controlled substance. An hour later, she accepted the position of personal assistant. Life is so weird.

I glance at my watch. Ten thirty, which gives me roughly six hours before I have to catch a cab to the book signing.

Prim pops up. *So plunk your rear in the chair and write that love scene!*

What? Improper protests. *Gotta look your best. Just the right outfit and accessories can mean the difference between selling a hundred books and three hundred.*

"Or ten and twenty," I mutter. It happens, you know. Just because I'm a best seller doesn't make me immune to dead signings. And I just hate those. Makes me feel like a wart. Stacks and stacks of my latest release and back-list books and not a devoted reader in sight.

Well, at least you'll look good, Improper urges.

Don't do it, Prim warns.

"To heck with it!" Abandoning my love scene, shrugging off the call to my mother, which can wait a while longer, I climb the stairs.

You'll be sorry.

Maybe the cream suit. Or the black—very slimming, especially paired with the white shantung blouse.

"Oh, Ms. Sinclaire, I just love your books," a sixty-something woman gushes, "especially your Highland series."

Highland series—six or seven books back. The second was my first to make the *New York Times* Best Sellers list. It had climbed from the eighth slot to the third before coming down from the high. I still get warm and fuzzy thinking about it.

"Tell me— " the woman leans conspiratorially forward, and

I lift my pen from the book to meet her gaze. "Do you think Jamie ever got over Laurel?"

Jamie? I keep smiling as I search backward for a clue about the character I created. Or did I?

"I mean, a love like that . . . "

Like what? What is she rambling on about? I never wrote a hero named Jamie. However, I do vaguely remember Laurel.

She sighs and presses a hand to her heart. "A love like that comes along only once in a lifetime."

She's waiting for a response, so I nod. "I know. Believe me, I know." I glance past her at the line of readers waiting for an autograph, hope she takes the hint, and return to the book I'm signing for her.

"Well?" she says.

My hand jerks, and the signature trails off the page. "I . . . er . . . " I look up. "Yes, he got over her, but it took a special woman to free his heart."

She gasps. "Who? Tell me."

Groan. Not the first time a reader has breathed life into a beloved character, wanting the lowdown on him or her as though they're more than bits of imagination congealed into what I call POPOs—people on paper only.

Suddenly, she throws up her hands. "Christina! Of course, Christina—the chambermaid. I knew there was more to them than just friends." She grins. "You sly one."

And suddenly Jamie returns to me—the blacksmith of *A*

Highlander's Promise. Not even a secondary character. Had maybe a dozen lines throughout the book.

I pop a glossy bookmark in the book. "Found me out," I say, and hand the book to her.

She sighs contentedly and grips the tome with reverent hands. "Thank you, Ms. Sinclaire. I can't tell you how relieved I am."

"You're welcome, Ruth. Have a wonderful evening. Next?" I glance past her to a svelte woman dressed in a black designer suit.

Reluctantly, Ruth steps aside and the other woman takes her place. I sign three books for her—my new hardcover and two books released in paperback last year. And so it goes for an hour and a half—thanks to my well-chosen outfit, I tell myself to minimize guilt over having never made it back to my love scene. Sacrifices . . . sacrifices . . .

The line finally thins as seven o'clock approaches, and I begin to relax. Almost there, then I can . . .

What? Go home and write the unwritable?

"To 'Jillian,'" a pretty voice speaks above my head.

I look up, smile. Pretty face, too. "Jillian." I pull a hardcover from a wonderfully diminished pile. Shortly, she trots off toward the café.

At ten to seven, the line dries up. With a sigh, I sit back.

Well done, Adda. Well done.

The young man assigned to ensure my comfort during the signing appears. "Another chai latte, Ms. Sinclaire?"

"No, thank you, Rupert." No need to tell him I'm about to

pop. Nine more minutes and I can make a lock-legged dash to the restroom.

"Wow!" he says with a jerk of his head that causes his dreadlocks to bounce. "You nearly sold out."

I feel a jolt of pride as I scan the table. I've still got it!

"You know, I assisted Ms. Roth with her signing last month, and I think she sold maybe two dozen books," he says. "But then, you're a *New York Times* Best Seller."

'Nuf said. Secretly pleased, I busy myself straightening the remaining books so he won't see my smile.

"But she is a rising star," he generously excuses Stick Woman's low sales.

Has been a rising star for eight years. Honestly, how long can one cling to such outdated distinction?

"Of course," I say.

Eight minutes to go.

"I'll be back at seven," Rupert says and scoots away.

The reason for his abrupt withdrawal appears a moment later—black, pleated slacks, leather belt. Another husband forced to fetch "one of *those* books." Poor wife is probably stuck at home with their brood of kids.

Keeping my gaze low—husbands of romance readers tend to hate eye contact, as though for fear of being identified in a line-up—I pick up my pen.

He slides the hardcover toward me.

Nice hand . . . nice nails. Reminds me of—

"Autograph only," he says.

My heart stops.

Can't be!

I look up.

It is.

Nick Farnsworth's eyes slide through me like warm chocolate through a sieve, and suddenly I feel naked without my sunglasses. What is he doing here? And asking for an autograph after I stuck my tongue out at him?

He raises an eyebrow.

"Autograph only?" I croak.

He nods.

I look down, turn the book around, and flip to the title page with quivering hands. It's the caffeine in the chai lattes, I tell myself as I push the pen across the paper.

I slam the book closed, slide it toward him, and look up.

He's frowning. Why?

He opens the book and places it in front of me again.

What's his problem? A moment later, I nearly shriek. I signed his name! Worse, I dotted the "i" in Nick with my signature mini-heart. Wishing I could slink between the pages of the book, I mutter. "Oops . . . sorry," and reach for another hardcover.

"This one will do," he says, all deep and rumbly. "Just sign beneath."

"Oh." I grip my pen, add 'To:" in front of his name, then my autograph. "There you are, Mr. Farnsworth." I hand the book to him, and his fingers brush mine.

Shudder . . . shiver . . . quake . . .

Stop it, Adda! You're embarrassing yourself! I lower my hands to my lap and out of sight.

"Thank you," he says, and that left cleft of his appears.

Flip. Flop. My heart feels like a fish out of water, and the automatic reply of "You're welcome" cleaves to the roof of my mouth like peanut butter. So I nod.

He glances at his watch—not a Rolex, though I don't doubt he can afford one. Frugal, then? Unlike Dick who went through my advances like a pig through popcorn.

"Done at seven?" he asks.

"Er . . . yes."

He looks toward the café. "Join me for a drink, then."

"Why?" I blurt, and am so horrified I nearly clap a hand over my mouth.

He considers me, then leans forward, presses his hands to the table, and says, "You didn't return my call, Ms. Sinclaire."

I stare into his eyes—the color of dark chocolate—and start salivating. I *love* dark chocolate—with nuts . . . caramel . . . coconut . . . nougat . . . thick black lashes . . .

Shameless! Prim reproaches.

You go, girl! Improper encourages.

"I . . . " I moisten my lips, and his eyes lower to the tip of my tongue. I whisk it back inside and too late realize the resemblance to a snake. "I've been incredibly busy, Mr. Farnsworth."

"As have I," he says with a flash of annoyance. "Which is why it's inconvenient for me to be here tonight." He straightens and glances at his watch again. "Will you or will you not join me in the café?"

Of all the arrogance! *I* didn't ask him to come! I open my mouth to tell him so, but a woman appears over his shoulder. Beaming, she steps to the side and plops a brown paper shopping bag on the table. It sounds heavy, meaning there are probably a dozen or more Adda Sinclaire books inside. Thus, she's one of two things: a devoted fan who has hauled out her collection of books for autographs, or a bookseller hoping to rake in the bucks by offering autographed copies for sale.

Ignoring Nick Farnsworth, I size up the woman. Dressed well enough, hair a bit untidy, eyes sparkling. But what most tells on her are her clasped hands. They're trembling.

"Excuse me, Mr. Farnsworth," I say, "but it's almost seven, and this young lady would like some autographs."

She steps around him. "No, I wouldn't." She digs into the bag and, a moment later, plops a twenty-pound manuscript in front of me. "I thought you might have time to discuss my book with me."

Oh. One of *those*. My smile falters, but I paste it back in place as she starts rattling on about plot devices and multiple points of view. There's usually one at every book signing, sometimes more. They gush over an author, never mention a single one of the author's releases by name, pitch stories, and ask for advice on how to get published. After the author has generously coughed up beaucoup bucks' worth of *free* advice, they walk away without purchasing a thing.

I glance at Nick Farnsworth. He's watching me with an arched eyebrow. And in him I see my rescuer.

"I'm sorry, Miss— "

"Handel." She thrusts out a hand. "Olivia Handel."

I shake her cool fingers. "I'm sorry, Ms. Handel, but Mr. Farnsworth and I have an appointment, and it is . . . " I look at my watch. " . . . seven o'clock. However, if you would like me to sign a book for you, I'd be more than happy."

She looks at the meager selection, as though considering one, and guilt starts to creep over me.

"Nah." She wrinkles her nose. "I don't read those books."

Redeemed! But how I hate the bad rap women's fiction gets—as if it's substandard. As if love is a four-letter word. Well, you know what I mean.

She shakes her head. "Sci-fi reader *and* writer." She hefts her manuscript, drops it in the bag, and stiffly strides toward the sci-fi section.

I meet Nick Farnsworth's gaze. "Welcome to women's fiction, Mr. Farnsworth."

He tucks the hardcover beneath his arm and nods toward the café. "I'll be waiting for you." He strides away before I can protest.

Blasted man! He knew I was bluffing—that I had no intention of joining him. I sit and stew a few minutes, consider walking out on him, and in the end grab my purse and turn toward the café.

Rupert and I nearly collide.

"All done, Ms. Sinclaire?"

I nod. "A fine signing, Rupert. Mind if I ask for you when my next book hits the shelves?"

He blushes beneath his dark complexion. "I'd consider it an honor, Ms. Sinclaire."

I could almost hug him, especially considering that during my last two signings I was attended by a peak-faced geezer who peered over his glasses at me with a mix of disdain and boredom.

"Would you . . . " He picks up my new release. "Would you sign one for me?"

I smile. "Of course." I set the book on the table and grab my pen. "What name should I inscribe? Your girlfriend's?"

"No—mine."

"Wonderful." It does happen. In fact, there are more male readers of romance than any would admit. Of course, maybe he's just being kind. "To Rupert," I say as I brandish my pen, "for a wonderful evening at the B&N." I top each "i" in my name with a mini-heart, snap the book closed, and hand it to him.

"Thank you, Ms. Sinclaire."

"You're welcome. Good night."

Bladder urging me to stop at the ladies room before joining Nick Farnsworth, I hesitate. But then he'll think I've gone off to powder my nose for him.

Hmmph! I can hold it. Patting a hand down my outfit in

an attempt to smooth two hours' worth of wrinkles, I start toward the café.

A couple dozen people are scattered among the tables, but Nick Farnsworth comes immediately to notice, dark head bent over my book. He looks up as I near, stands, and pulls out the chair beside his. Though tempted to pull out the chair opposite, I set my purse on the table and slip into the seat. After all, when's the last time a man pulled out a chair for me?

A moment later, he resumes his seat. "Impressive list of quotes and reviews," he says, tapping my book.

I glance at the page of praise, which continues on the next. "Thank you. So, Mr. Farnsworth, what is so urgent that you had to inconvenience yourself by attending my signing?"

Sheesh, I should have visited the ladies room!

"Nick," he says, turning those dark chocolates on me.

He wants me to call him Nick? Even as I question his motive, I'm once more turning to goo.

"Coffee?" he asks.

Just the mention of it relaxes my bladder, and I have to squeeze hard to hold it. Good for the glutes, though.

"No, thank you."

He tilts his head and once more zaps me with his x-ray vision. "You're not what I expected," he finally says, and I'm sure I know exactly where he came by his expectations—Stick Woman. Of course, I didn't brighten the image with my scene at the restaurant, which I'd brilliantly finished off with a childish gesture. And for which I really ought to apologize.

I will, I silently promise in an attempt to shut up Prim before she puts in an appearance.

"Not what you expected? How is that?"

He lifts his cup of java and takes a drink. "You work your readers well, including the . . . difficult ones."

His delivery is so smooth, the meaning nearly slips past, but I wrestle it around and stare it down. He was spying on me! Lurking behind some book display and watching me long before he put in an appearance. Did I do anything embarrassing? Roll my eyes at a reader's back? Bite my nails?

"Thank you," I say, as there's really nothing else to say. And Lord knows, it's hard to form coherent thought when I should have visited the ladies room!

"Are you well, Ms. Sinclaire?"

Does he know? Am I wiggling too much?

No.

Tap-dancing beneath the table?

No.

Teeth swimming?

Possibly.

"Excuse me." I stand and rip past him.

Ahead, the restroom sign is visible above the bookshelves. Feeling like a rat chasing cheese through a maze, I wind among boxed stationery, paperbacks, hardbacks, audio tapes, and CDs. But the cheese isn't waiting at the end of the maze. A bright yellow sign is, which states that the ladies room is temporarily closed for cleaning.

Oh no, it's not!

I step over the sign, thrust the door open. And nearly body slam a couple entwined near the stalls.

I screech to a halt as they jump apart.

Ah, young love . . .

Not!

Late twenties, early thirties. Certainly old enough to know better. And how desperate can one get? A public restroom! Yuck!

"Sorry to interrupt your romantic getaway," I mutter and shoot past their flushed faces into a stall.

When I step out, they're gone, along with the yellow sign. I rework the maze toward the café, half expecting Nick Farnsworth to have made an exit, but he's still there. Certain I would return, was he?

He stands at my approach, and once more treats me to the chair ceremony.

"Better?" he asks as he resumes his seat.

Hoping he thinks nausea was my problem, I nod. "Much, though I thought you might have cleared out by the time I got back—busy as you are."

"And leave your purse unattended?" He glances at my bag on the table.

Completely forgot about it. However, my embarrassment quickly turns to horror. Did he go through it? Discover minute details about me from my checkbook, credit cards, amount of cash, lipstick, four shades of nail polish? Squashing the impulse to grab my purse, I say, "Thank you for keeping an eye on it."

He inclines his head.

"So, why are we sitting here, Mr. Farnsworth?"

"Nick," he reminds me. "And may I call you Adda?"

He wants to call me Adda! And the way he says it—drawing out the first syllable as though savoring it! Trying to appear nonchalant, though it goes against every tingling fiber of my being, I say, "That's fine."

He smiles, showing his full complement of white teeth, and I'm so grateful I'm seated. No way my knees would hold.

"I want to discuss your future with Intrepid."

Business. Oh, what I wouldn't give—

Stop it!

I raise my eyebrows. "And what future is that, Mr. Farnsworth?"

"Nick."

"Okay . . . Nick."

"I want you, Adda."

Oh . . . my . . . word . . . What a line! Slightly crude, but—

He's talking business! Prim bursts my lovely bubble.

"Why me?" I manage.

"Because you have one of the strongest male points of view I've seen in women's fiction—as does Birgitta Roth."

Just had to ruin the moment by equating *that* woman with me! I smile tightly. "Then you've read one of my books."

"All of them, including this one." He taps the hardcover. "Your agent sent an advance reading copy to my senior editor."

"Oh. You're very thorough, Mr. Farnsworth."

"Nick," he clips, "and yes, I am. I believe it's best to know the dregs of one's business dealings."

"Dregs," I murmur. A far cry from the images evoked by "I want you, Adda."

"My, you do know how to flatter a girl, Nick." As in rhymes with Dick.

His mouth curls. "And you know how to turn a man's head."

The tongue. He's talking about the tongue. Heat flushes me, and I just know I glow red to the tips of my ears. Should have gotten the apology out of the way earlier.

I draw a deep breath. "You probably won't believe this, but I don't normally go around sticking my tongue out at people. It was a . . . rough day."

He stares at me.

I shrug. "So I apologize."

"Accepted." He lifts his cup and drains the last of his java. "Now back to business." His gaze narrows. "Are you ready to cross over to Intrepid?"

What would Noelle want me to say? *How* would she want me to say it? Don't want to appear too eager. Nor too greedy.

I moisten my lips, and he once more focuses on my mouth with an intensity far beyond the interest of business. "I leave such matters to my agent, Nick, but I will say that if the terms are right,

I could be enticed."

He spreads a hand atop my book and absently caresses the binding's edge.

I swallow—hard. Imagine being jealous of a book cover!

"What about your loyalty to Farnsworth?" he asks.

Guilt swamps me, and I resent it. Deeply. I've been in this game long enough to know how publishing works—and exactly where a publisher's loyalty lies. Not that I blame them. They are in the business of making money. But what I resent most is *this* man posing such a question—as though I'm about to commit a treasonous act. As though I'm boiling up something nasty in my little cauldron, which he would never consider stirring up himself. Hypocrite!

It's just as well, though, because it brings me back into line. My attraction to him dissolves completely—well, almost. "*My* loyalty to Farnsworth?" I snip. "*Mine*?" I snap. "What about yours, Mr. *Farns . . . worth*?"

His jaw tightens and lids narrow. "*I* am not at discussion here, *Ms. Sinclaire*."

Good. We're back to last names.

"I am simply trying to determine what it will take to bring you over. *If* I bring you over."

Obviously, I struck a sore spot in reminding him of his own defection. I struggle between making tracks out of the café and what Noelle would want me to do. I can just hear her now—flapping her bat wings, screeching about the mess I left her to clean up. And am I ever tempted to mess it up even more! But I won't. I'll behave.

So what to say to smooth out the wrinkles? Should I apologize?

"Mr. Farnsworth," I try. "I . . . "

He's not looking at me, his attention captured by something past my shoulder. "Your editor has arrived," he says.

Feeling as though I've been doused with ice water, I glance around. It *is* Kathryn, and she's scanning the bookstore as she makes her way toward the café where I sit consorting with the enemy.

"Oh no!" I hunch my shoulders in hopes she won't notice me. "What's she doing here?" She *never* comes to my signings. Coincidence?

"I asked her to come."

I sit up straight. "Are you crazy?"

His ugly brown eyes—and I mean *ugly*—return to me. "Not at all, Ms. Sinclaire."

As I stare at him, it hits me. I've walked straight into a trap. Seven figures! Yeah, right! Alienate Farnsworth Publishing, and he thinks he can pick me up for a song. *That* is where this is heading.

"I see," I say. "Perfectly."

"No, you don't, so let me explain."

Delay tactics to give Kathryn time to catch me with him. I shove my chair back. "Good evening, Mr. Farnsworth."

He's rising, but I sidestep and head opposite the direction of Kathryn. Desperately hoping to slip away before she catches sight of me, I veer right, then left, and gain the cover of a book display. I give myself to the count of ten, then shoot toward the front doors. At last, I step out into a dusky night jam-packed with cars, blaring horns, and frazzled New Yorkers. As I seethe over Nick Farnsworth, I notice a yellow cab parked at the curb—a major miracle on a Friday night, let alone any night—

Not! I realize, noticing the illuminated "off duty" sign on the roof. I sigh. Nothing I can do but hail a cab—which, of course, could take some time. I step to the curb, but before I can stick out a hand, another closes around my upper arm. I jerk around, ready to unload on the pervert who has hold of me, but Nick Farnsworth is not your everyday pervert.

I snap my gaping jaws closed. If he's come to apologize, he's wasting his precious time. Of course, tell that to my wayward attraction, which kicks in as I stare into his semi-shadowed face.

"Yes, Mr. Farnsworth?"

He releases my arm. "Your purse," he says, and extends it.

My . . . purse? Groan. Did it again. What must he think of me? Not that I care!

I pluck it from his hand. "Thank you."

He nods, then steps to the cab parked at the curb, opens the door, and gestures for me to enter.

I raise my eyebrows. "It's off duty," I say, surprised it escaped his notice.

He ducks his head in, says something to the cabbie, then steps back and waves me in. "He'll take you wherever you want to go."

He will? Not too proud to pass on a miracle, I step past him. "Thank you," I say as I slide into the back seat. As I feel around for a seat belt, he leans past me—so close I can smell his cologne and, beneath it, the faint male scent of salted perspiration.

Oh my, my, my.

He's talking to the cabbie, but his words are lost on me as I try to deal with insides that are flip-flopping all over the place.

Drawing back, he meets my breathless gaze. "Good evening, Adda."

First names again.

He straightens and closes the door.

I don't look behind as the cab muscles its way into traffic, but I have the feeling he's watching me drive away.

A half hour later, the cab pulls up in front of my townhouse, and I reach into my purse for my wallet.

The cabbie, a distinguished, gray-haired man, looks around. "I've been paid, ma'am."

Really? I didn't see Nick Farnsworth pass him anything.

"Good evening, ma'am."

Dazed, I climb out. As I mount the steps, fumbling for my keys, the cab pulls away. Not until I step into the foyer and flick on the light do I hazard a look at my right hand. Three nibbled nails in dire need of repair.

Dirty, rotten Nick Farnsworth!

● ● ●

"I didn't think it was all that important to mention it, dear," my mother says in that chipper voice that rarely varies regardless of the situation—and which makes me gnash my teeth.

I flop onto my back to stare at the glow-in-the-dark stars that dot my ceiling. Though I turned off the light only five minutes ago—after two hours of trying to convince my hero to consummate the marriage and half an hour searching for relief from writer's block amid the pages of Josh's little black book—the stars have begun to dim. Like my career?

I take a deep breath. "Not important? How do you figure that, mother?"

"You *are* divorced, dear."

As if I need a reminder of Dick's betrayal! And was that accusation in her tone? "Silly me," I mutter.

"Hmm?"

"Nothing. Nothing . . . at . . . all." I sigh. "So he's in Houston?"

"Um hmm."

Pulling teeth. . . . "And that means he and Birgitta . . . ?"

"It would seem so, dear."

"Seem so?" I nearly shriek. "Mom, you and Donna talk every day, and all you can tell me is it *seems* to be over between Richard and that . . . that— "

"Don't say it, Adda!"

I roll my eyes. "Answer the question, mother."

She harrumphs. "How would you like it if I disclosed to Donna your conversations with me?"

"But I'm your daughter!"

"One must have principles, dear. Remember: Character is

who you are when no one is watching."

I slam the handset to my chest, take a bite of my pillow, and muffle my scream of frustration in the polyfil depths.

"Adda? Adda, Adda, Adda!" my mom chirps as I pry the handset from my chest.

I grit my teeth. "I'm here, *Mom*."

"So," she says, "have you written anything good lately?"

Oh, why did I call? What am I? A masochist? Noting the ceiling stars have grown dimmer, I say, "Just another best seller."

A copy of which I sent her, but which is likely shoved to the back of a shelf.

"Nothing to brag about," I tell her.

"Oh," she groans sympathetically, "I'm sorry, dear."

And that's my mother. Or maybe I was adopted. Or switched in the hospital nursery. Or maybe this is all just some twisted dream . . .

"Well, at least you're out on your own and paying the bills," she consoles in her own, special way.

And I feel *so much better*. "At least," I say, then yawn loudly. "It's late. I'd better hit the sack."

"All right, dear." *Smack, smack, smack*.

Refusing to return the kisses she sends across the telephone line, I say, "Love you, too. 'Night." I punch the off button, toss the handset into the wide, open space beside me, and wish the bed wasn't so big and gapingly empty. Should have bought a twin.

FOUR

Four-and-a-half weeks to go, and I'm no nearer to resolving my love-scene dilemma. My career is definitely on the skids. Of course, it doesn't help that Noelle is starting to agree with me. But then, she's been moodier than normal since I gave her an overview of what happened after the book signing with Nick Farnsworth. Said I'd handled it wrong, wrong, wrong! What does she know? *She* wasn't there.

As for my editor's appearance at the bookstore, on that Noelle had become thoughtful and concluded it meant Nick Farnsworth was not only after me, but Kathryn. And as my editor accepted the invite, she must be interested. If true, it casts Nick Farnsworth in a somewhat better light.

I sigh, force my thoughts from *that* man to my three-month extension. Noelle says Kathryn hasn't returned her phone call. Unusual, for she's usually very conscientious. Perhaps she turned down Nick Farnsworth? If so, what if she saw me sneaking out? What if he briefed her on our conversation? Did he flaunt my purse before chasing after me?

I groan.

An Arnold-esque voice throbs above my head, yanking me back to the present. "No pain, no gain," Ludwig lectures. Arms and legs trembling in an effort to support my body at push-up pose for the required sixty seconds, I glare at the mat.

"Suck it in," Ludwig reminds me.

Grateful the sitting room is too small for him to unfurl his whip, I pull my abdominals back toward my spine as a drop of perspiration beads on the end of my nose. "How much longer?" I croak.

"Umm . . . "

I hear a loud, crackling sound made by a straw sucking up the last bit of liquid—no doubt one of those banana-berry yogurt smoothies he whips up when we meet at my townhouse rather than the gym. Thoughtless brute!

Realizing I haven't given Ludwig a nickname, I momentarily consider "Brute"; however, Ludwig is a Ludwig. No adjustment required.

"Five seconds," he says, and begins to count down after one more ear-splitting suck.

At last, I collapse on my mat.

"One more set of sit-ups," he says.

I shake my head. "I've done my quota for the day." I'm not going to be sucked into an extra half-hour of his outrageously expensive time.

"Leg lifts?" he suggests.

"No."

"Butt squeezes?"

"No, Ludwig." I roll onto my back and slide my gaze up his muscle builder's bod. Pausing on the whip that hangs like a lasso from his waist, I smile. "I've had enough, thanks."

He sighs, shakes his head pityingly. "We are not making the kind of progress I like, Ms. Sinclaire."

Struggling onto my elbows, I look down my leotard-clad body. Nothing at all to be ashamed of—anymore. "I'm more than happy with my progress," I say. No more overhangs, lumps, or bulges. Everything toned and lean.

He makes a sound of disapproval, turns, and strides out of the sitting room on legs as big around as tree trunks. Well, maybe that's an exaggeration, but the man's five-eleven frame is one solid mass of muscle.

As I begin my cool-down stretches, I hear the whir of the blender. As usual, he's whipping up one to go. I only wish he would return my glasses. Last month I had to purchase a new set of twelve. When he leaves, I'll be down to six.

He reappears a few minutes later and corrects a calf-and-hamstring stretch—both of which I was doing correctly. Needs to justify his rate, I suppose. If I weren't so afraid of slipping back into the old me, I'd give him the heave-ho.

Legs shaky, I stand and eye his smoothie. "Hope you saved me some."

He smiles that big, toothy smile. "Always."

Pity he never thinks to pour me one. Of course, there would

probably be a charge for that. I step past him and tramp to the kitchen.

"Gotta go, Ms. Sinclaire," he calls as he heads toward the door.

"Don't forget to return my glass," I shoot over my shoulder.

"You bet."

Um hmm . . .

Dumbbell strikes dumbbell as he heaves his duffle onto his shoulder, then the door opens and closes.

I pour a glass of the remaining smoothie. And what a reward! As berry- and banana-flavored ice chips hit the back of my throat, I slip down the cabinet and settle my hot glutes to the cool tile. Perfect.

For the next quarter hour, I sip at the smoothie and try very hard not to think about *The Gifting*, which hangs heavier around my neck with each passing day. Then I hit bottom—as in no matter how high I lift and tilt the glass, not another drop to drink. I set it on the floor beside me, clasp my hands around my shins, and prop my chin on my knees.

Okay, I should shower and go directly to my office.

Absolutely, Prim agrees.

Not, Improper disagrees. *Spend the next eight hours reading and rereading your measly sentences like you did yesterday?*

"Hey, I added a word or two," I snarl, and grimace at the realization I'm talking to myself. Not that it's unusual. Lots of writers talk to themselves when they're working through a story. In fact, Joyce Kuchner—better known as "Puffer"—gave a workshop a couple years back, "Codependent Self-Talk: Keeping the Relationship Alive."

I smile. Puffer—a gossip, gabber, slouch, slob, ashtray klepto, nonstop smoker, and, above all, friend.

We've known each other since before I was published, having met at an Iowa chapter of Women's Fiction Writers shortly after the release of her sixth book. She had invited several unpublished authors to lunch, and I sat gape-mouthed as her raucous laughter, crude jokes, as a pack's worth of cigarette smoke swirled around me. I couldn't remember ever being so embarrassed as I had that day with every other patron staring at our table with disgust. In no way does Puffer personify the image of a romance writer, and not one of those staring at us would have believed that the path between her mind and pen could be transformed into something stunningly beautiful. Indeed, *no one* writes romance better than Joyce Kuchner, and if she would only take her writing seriously, she could climb out of mid-list and set up house on the best-seller lists.

I shake my head, still unable to reconcile that the woman who became my mentor—who red-inked my first manuscript until it looked like a crime scene—languishes in the dust of my success. But she's happy there, refusing to be budged no matter how much I talk up my agent and editor.

"Not every writer wants to be where you're at, missy," she said the last time I pushed. "No, ma'am, won't have anyone telling me to get a life like I'm always telling you."

She had a point—a painfully sharp one. Despite the mouth-watering gratification bestowed by one best seller after another, there is a price to be paid for my success. Fortunately, I'm usually too wrapped up in my stories to rue my relationship with the printed word that takes precedence over all other relationships. Unfortunately, loneliness has a way of slipping through the cracks.

Feeling the sharp prick of Puffer's point, I shake my head. Writing is safe. It doesn't lie. Doesn't cheat. Doesn't steal. Of course, it does nag. And bicker. And at times it can be unbelievably . . . frustratingly . . . obstinate!

On that note, my thoughts return to *The Gifting*. Eyes beginning to sting, I open my lids wide and draw a deep breath through my nose. I will *not* cry. Will not!

Sob!

I bury my face against my knees as tears begin to flow. "I hate writing!" I gasp. "Hate . . . hate . . . hate it!"

Whatever possessed me to become a writer? Why, oh why, do I torture myself like this? What was I thinking?

And so I let out my agony until I have no choice but to stop or suffocate. Plugged up to the roofs of my sinuses, I grab a towel draped over the sink and blow—a fairly useless endeavor.

Eyes sore and puffy, throat achy, I clamber up from the tile floor and lean against the counter. What am I going to do?

"Don't start on me!" I snap before Prim answers.

Improper sniggers.

"Cork it!" I straighten.

Maybe Noelle's right. Maybe I should pull out *Wings of Love* and rework it. If only there were someone I could talk to, someone who might understand—

Puffer! With a sputter of hope, I retrieve the cordless phone and punch in the long-distance call to Iowa, from which I moved four years ago after signing my first six-figure deal.

I hold my breath as the phone rings once . . . twice . . . three times. . . . On the tenth ring, accepting she's either out or under deadline, I sigh.

"Yeah?" a voice rasps as I start to lower the handset.

I slam it back to my ear. "Joyce! It's me—Adda."

She hacks without covering the handset, then clears her throat loudly. "How the *bleep* are you, missy?"

"I . . . I . . . "

I hear her take a long draw on her cigarette.

"I . . . "

"That bad, hmm?" She hacks again and I wince.

"Yeah."

"What is it this time?"

I unload on her, telling her everything, beginning with my date with Jake Grainger proceeding through Nick Farnsworth to my bitten nails. On and on I moan and groan while she listens patiently. Finally, I draw a shuddering breath and wail, "My career is over!"

Silence. She's thinking—conjuring advice sure to lift me out of this darkness. I wait, and in the breathless silence hear . . . the patter of little keys.

"Joyce!" I cry. "Have you heard a word I said?"

"Two or three times now," she mutters around the cigarette I envision dangling from her pinched lips.

"Joyce!"

"Just doin' a bit of editing. Don't take much brain, you know." She takes a noisy drag of her cigarette.

Though tempted to slam the phone down, I counsel calm. "So what do you think?"

Another long drag.

Though her keyboard has gone silent, I have the sneaking suspicion she's reading through some scene.

"Joyce?"

"Hmm," she murmurs, and loudly blows out smoke.

I swear I can smell it through the handset. "Joyce, would you turn off your computer and put down that disgusting cigarette!"

"Can't."

"Why not?"

"Already turned off the computer, and it's a cigar I'm suckin' on."

"Cigar?" Oh, gross!

"Yep, decided to take the plunge last winter and haven't regretted it since. Good smoke those Cubans make."

"Remind me not to sit at your table at the national conference," I mutter.

"Not goin'."

I jerk. "What? You always go."

"Not this year."

A national conference without Puffer? Unthinkable! She's the mainstay of "The Good, the Bad, and the Ugly" as she calls the threesome we've become when we get together: me, the Good; her best friend, Jackie Hingle, the Bad (she writes "sensual" romance); and Joyce Kuchner, the Ugly. Momentarily forgetting my dilemma, I shake my head. A conference without Joyce would be like a heroine without a hero, peanut butter without jelly—

Suddenly, dread descends. Is she sick? What if she has lung cancer?

"What's up, Joyce?" I ask, unable to keep a tremor from my voice.

She takes another drag on her cigar, and anger seizes me such that if I could reach through the phone and rip the executioner from her lips, I would.

"Daughter's gettin' married that week," she says.

"Oh." I sink to the edge of a bar stool, lower my face into a hand. Only Felicia getting married—Felicia whose name suits her about as well as a rabbit coat suits Liz Taylor. "You scared me, Joyce."

She cackles, and I realize that was her intent.

Wearily, I say, "So Felicia is getting married again." I attended her second and third marriages, but missed the fourth a couple years back.

"Yeah, the little tramp," Puffer grumbles. "Chose that week just to spite me."

It's selfish of me, but I have to ask, "Think you'd be missed if you opted out?"

"Oh, she'd notice, sure as *bleep*." Another long drag. "Then she'd make me suffer for the next twenty years."

"What about your nomination for Best Short Historical?"

"Probably get passed by like I did last year . . . and two years before that." She hacks out a cough. "As for *your* award, I'd like to be there, but it ain't as if I haven't seen you take home a few of them gold curly-cue thingamajigs."

Honestly, I hadn't even considered my own nomination for Best Long Historical, but I do feel suddenly hollow knowing she won't be there for my big moment—if it comes. I remind myself that the instant one starts believing one is a "shoo-in" is the instant one topples flat on one's face.

I shake my head. "And the workshop you were presenting?"

"*Faking Chastity in the Wild Wild West*? Canceled it."

"Our loss," I mutter.

"Yeah. So, about your— " She hacks again, one of those rumbly, bubbly ones.

I grimace. "You okay?"

She clears her throat. "Nothing another good puff won't cure." A long draw and a contented sigh later, she says, "All better. So, about your love scene . . . "

"Yes?" Hoping for revelation, I hold my breath.

"You're gonna have to take up smoking, missy."

I groan. "Is that the best you can do?"

"It's all in the smokes. Trust me on this. Nothing will clear and relax your mind faster."

"Nor faster lead me down the path to cancer!"

She shrugs. No, I haven't switched point of view. It's just

the place where she would do that eyeball-rolling, one-shouldered shrug of hers. "Still got that pack of cigs I gave you at last year's conference?" she asks.

"Of course not!" I tossed them into the first trash can I met.

"Guessed as much. Well, then, run out and get some. Best to start with menthols—"

"No."

Another shrug. "Suit yourself, but that's the only way I know of to deal with blockage."

I wrinkle my nose. Only Puffer could make a writer's ailment sound intestinal.

"So watcha gonna do, missy?"

Should I tell her of Noelle's suggestion? "Well, I . . . "

She hacks again, and I hold the phone away until it quiets. "Remember the proposal for my option book that got rejected?"

"Yeah. Great story."

"Noelle thinks I ought to chuck *The Gifting* and turn in *Wings of Love* in its place."

A long silence ensues, but I don't hear her deep inhalations. Did I lose the connection?

"Joyce?"

"I'm here."

"What do you think?"

"Not a bad idea—assuming you finished the story."

"I did." Not only had it been an act of defiance, but of denial. Though a proposal typically consists of a synopsis and the first three chapters, which makes it easier to abandon and move on to the next project if a publisher rejects it, I'd refused to dump my hero and heroine.

"*Bleep*!" Puffer yells.

I startle. "What?"

I hear her whacking at something, then she mutters, "Burned another hole in my chair."

I could strangle her.

I hear the creak of her chair as she settles back in it. "Well," she says, "if you're not gonna take up smoking, I suppose that's the best alternative."

I bite my lip. "But is it lead title material? I wrote it years ago while in mid-list."

She laughs—a cross between a bark and a cackle that's strangely comforting despite its ability to earn her the evil eye. "Missy, you just pull it out, bring it up to standard, and in no time you'll have yourself another best seller. Guarantee it."

"Think so?"

"Mmm."

"Then maybe I'll do it."

Once more I hear the patter of her keyboard. I guess this is where we part ways. "I'll miss you at the conference," I say.

"Same here."

"Thanks for lending me your shoulder."

"Anytime. Oh! While I've got you . . . "

"Yeah?"

"I'm plotting my next book. You think a cross-dresser would fly in Regency England?"

Leave it to Puffer.

"Secondary character, of course," she clarifies.

"What's his motive?"

"No motive. It's just who he is—a bona fide cross-dresser."

"Oh. Well . . . have you asked your editor?"

"Yeah, but you know Liv—so backlogged she'll take any proposal as long as it entails very little editing."

That's Liv, all right. Wholeheartedly throws herself into every new author she buys, so much so that her tried-and-true mid-listers are pretty much left to fend for themselves. Always searching for the next sensation when she has a stable full of potential best sellers from which to choose. Go figure.

Puffer hacks, sniffs loudly. "What do you think, missy?"

"I'll wager it's never been done. Will probably gain you a whole new audience."

"Along with a new genre of fan mail," she says with enthusiasm.

Honestly, the mail is likely the reason she writes. She adores it and still answers each letter personally. No telling how many hundreds of pen pals she's made over the years. Testament to their numbers, dozens always show up at her signings and conferences. And to see and hear them, one would think Puffer has been friends with them since grade school. The woman is amazing.

"So go for it," I say.

She cackles. "I knew you'd back me."

I frown. "Against whom?"

"Jerry."

Her husband, a spectacled, mild-mannered nonsmoker one would never expect to be paired with a woman like Puffer. And the envy of every one of her friends, as he's that rare beast of a man who absolutely and unconditionally adores his wife.

"What are Jerry's objections?" I ask, curiosity piqued by the fact he's hands-off where her writing is concerned.

She sighs. "Says he's not ready to come out of the closet."

I nearly drop the handset. "What?"

"Yeah—afraid it will tip off his buddies. Not that they read my books, mind you."

So, then, Jerry . . . oh . . . wow . . . I lay my head on the counter, roll my eyes up into my head. "I didn't know, Joyce."

"Sheesh!" she rasps. "You're not taking it hard, are you?"

"I . . . well, it is a bit of a shock."

"Hah! You don't know Jerry. Remind me to show you a picture of our trip to Fiji last year when he donned a grass skirt and—"

"I get the picture, Joyce." I lean back on the stool. "Guess I'd better get upstairs and pull out *Wings of Love*."

"You go, girl," she says, which sounds so weird coming from a sixty-year-old woman.

"Thanks again, Joyce."

Hack, hack, hack. "No problem."

"Bye—"

"Adda?"

I frown. Usually, the only time she calls me by name is when something serious is coming down the pipe. "Joyce?"

"About Jake Grainger . . . "

"What about him?"

"He's a boy in a man's body. You'll have to look farther afield if you're ever going to live what you write."

I sigh. "Believe me, I'm very aware he's younger than me."

"I'm not talking age, Adda. It's more than that."

"I know. You can be assured I'm not thinking of turning our one date into a lifelong commitment."

She's quiet a long moment, then asks, "Were you attracted to Nick Farnsworth?"

I slip right off the bar stool. If not that I'd hooked a foot around the leg, I might have managed to get my balance, but down I go, throwing out a hand to break my fall—and managing to crack another nail as I land flat on my back.

"Oh, man!" I lift my hand to stare at the ugly tear.

"Adda? You okay, Adda?"

I grope for the handset where it skidded to the right. "I'm okay," I say, pressing the phone to my ear.

"What happened?"

I shrug. "Broke another nail."

"Huh! Thought you might have fallen or something."

I rub my backside. "Gotta go, Joyce."

She cackles. "Not gonna answer my question, hmm?"

With shrill innocence, I say, "About what?"

"Nick Farnsworth."

"Oh. Am I attracted to him? Hardly. The man is way too pompous for my taste."

"Uh-huh," she murmurs knowingly. "You know, I met him once."

I blink. "You did?"

"Yeah, when I was first published and he was still with Farnsworth Publishing—right before he went through that nasty divorce."

He's divorced . . . "Really?"

"Yup. He was at a conference—not in the capacity of an editor, mind you. Vice President of something or other. Anyway, he was sitting alone in the hotel restaurant, dozens of women authors ogling him, so I invited myself to join him."

Surprise, surprise.

"Know what he did?"

"What?"

"Pulled out a chair for me."

I swallow the lump forming in my throat.

"So over eggs and grits I pitched him a couple of stories. Said he was only there to learn more about the genre, but gave me his card and told me to send the proposals to his senior editor. Of course, I never got around to it."

That's Puffer for you.

She drags on her cigar. "Pompous or not, the thing is this:

Nick Farnsworth is a *man*, not a boy."

You're telling me. "So?"

"So, missy, a *man* is what you need. Jake Grainger might be a good kisser, but he isn't going to fill any of your empty places."

Suddenly aware of those empty places, especially the one at my center, I sit up and press a hand to my chest. Though my heart thumps steadily, it feels deserted.

"Only so long you can run on fumes," Puffer says.

Is that what I've been doing? Is that the reason I can no longer write a love scene?

"Adda?"

"I—I'm here."

"You understand what I'm saying?"

"I think so. Some of it."

I hear her drag on her cigar and realize it's the first in a while. "The rest will come," she rasps.

Will it? The possibility that it won't nearly makes me cry again. "Thanks, Joyce," I say past a tightening throat. "I appreciate your advice."

"Prove it."

"Hmm?"

"Next time Nick Farnsworth comes around, be nice—and just maybe he'll be nice to you."

Clearly, she's not talking simple courtesy. "I am *not* interested in Nick Farnsworth."

"And I'm the good fairy. Talk to you later, missy."

Click.

I pull the handset from my ear and press the power button. "Nick Farnsworth," I mutter, staring at the ceiling. "Nick Farnsworth." Not a chance.

Trying to not think about all of those empty places Puffer mentioned—and there are more than she knows—I roll to sitting and stand. As I return the handset to its base, I glimpse the book I pressed beneath the phone book. The little black book, intentionally placed there in hopes of rectifying the warp caused by the snooze I took in the middle of it.

Wasn't one of Josh's issues loneliness? I stretch out a hand. Maybe—

Or maybe not.

I jerk my hand back and am on the verge of turning away when Prim puts in an appearance.

Can't hurt, she whispers as though fearing Improper will hear.

"You think?" I whisper back.

Umm hmm.

Despite my lack of faith and understanding, there is something strangely comforting about that book. Something that draws me to it. "No, it can't hurt," I say—too loudly, for in the next instant, Improper appears.

The big yellow book, she attempts to sway me. *Everything you need is in there—psychiatrists, psychologists, astrologists, numerologists—*

I lunge forward and, in my fervor, cause the phone book to slam to the floor.

Where it belongs, Prim assures me.

I snatch up the little black book and, telling myself Noelle need never know I'm not pounding at the computer, return to the sitting room and curl up in a corner of the love seat.

Under "loneliness" Josh references Matthew 28:20. Ah, the red print, which conveniently signifies actual words spoken by Jesus. Strangely, every time I read red words, I get this warm, fuzzy feeling.

"And surely I am with you always," I read, "to the very end of the age." Sounds good, but if I should get to a point where I believe all this about Jesus, would he really be there for me? Assuming, of course, he actually exists.

"I hope you do," I whisper, then proceed to look up the other passages listed under loneliness. Though each offers hope for those who are empty, it's the first I return to—because of the red words. Wondering at the context, I back up and read the entire paragraph in which the passage is embedded. Interest piqued further, I back up some more and continue to back up until I reach the crucifixion upon which Josh and Dustin told me salvation hinged. Though touched by Jesus' cruel death, it's too heavy for me, and I once more take cover in looking over Josh's issues.

"Success," I muse. "Now that one sounds upbeat." Turning to Proverbs, I read, "Commit to the Lord whatever you do, and your plans will succeed."

Really? But how do I do that? Especially when I don't know God much beyond the few exposures to him as a child when my mother searched for something she never found. Not that she didn't believe in God. She simply concluded that God was a personal matter, and the Church, with all its hypocrisy, was an unlikely place to get to know him. Of course, our turbulent home was an even less likely place. And yet, somehow, my older sister, Molly, found God. But that's another story.

I sigh, read the passage again, and actually consider praying.

You don't know how, Improper discourages.

Prim makes a sound of disgust. *How hard can it be?*

And so I look left . . . then right. . . . Concluding I have nothing to lose in the emptiness of my home, I clear my throat, clasp my hands atop the little black book, and close my eyes.

"Uh . . . God . . . "

Hmm.

"Dear God . . . "

Sounds like a letter.

"Hey, there!"

Lacks respect.

"Oh, God . . . "

Makes me sound like a TV evangelist.

"God, it's me . . . um . . . Adda Sinclaire . . . "

Not that he wouldn't know that. I think . . . I hope . . .

Exasperated, I unclasp my hands, close the book, and drop my head back. "Just help me. *Puhleeease.*"

FIVE

Two days, six hours, fifteen minutes to deadline—not counting the three-month extension I told Noelle to nix. *Wings of Love*, retitled *The Gifting*, its hero and heroine renamed Philippa and Robert, is ready. I think. . . . I hope. . . . I pray. . . . Well, sort of—still haven't gotten that prayer thing down, but doing better.

With a flutter of excitement that's building toward an OOB—out-of-body experience—I pat the 550-page manuscript in front of me. In my opinion, there is very little in this world that compares with such an accomplishment. Forget that the manuscript will soon come back with editing suggestions, forget that once changes are made I'll have to pore over galley proofs and suffer through the work of some overzealous copy editor. After four solid weeks of adding, cutting, slashing, burning, tweaking, and fine-tuning—all of which allowed me few nights of more than four hours of sleep—I have birthed *The Gifting*!

I only hope Kathryn doesn't realize I stole into the nursery and switched babies . . .

Humming, I push up out of my chair, fit rubber bands around the hefty little tyke, and plop it in the box just as Morticia pops her head around the doorway.

"Courier will be here in five minutes, Ms. Sinclaire."

Beginning to float up . . . up . . . up . . . I smile. "Great." I lower the lid on the box and turn, holding it out to her. "It's all yours."

She steps into my office and accepts the package. "I'll take it downstairs," she slurps around her newest self-inflicted body-pain acquisition—a tongue bob that glints from the depths of her mouth. I just don't get it . . .

"Thanks," I say, feeling as though I'm happily hovering above my own head. Man, it feels great!

"That was your agent who phoned a while ago," she calls over her shoulder. "Wants you to call her ASAP."

Ugh! My option book? Beginning to sink back into myself, I say, "I'll do that," and settle into my chair. As Morticia pads down the stairs in her bare feet—to preserve her recently painted toenails—I look at the phone. Has Noelle heard back from Intrepid? After receiving a high six-figure, three-book-contract offer from Farnsworth three weeks ago, she turned around and delivered the proposal to the editor at Intrepid with whom she'd been speaking before Nick Farnsworth butted in. And not a word since.

Putting my OOB on hold, I sigh. Obviously, Intrepid is no longer interested. Nick Farnsworth is sitting on the proposal with no intention of going to bid. In fact, I wouldn't be surprised if he signed Birgitta Roth just to spite me.

So should I call Noelle? Ruin a day otherwise destined to greatness?

She said as soon as possible, Prim reminds.

Soon is relative, Improper counters.

True. The last time I asked her to return my call ASAP, it took her two days. Of course, she'd been vacationing in Paris.

"And I'm vacationing now," I mutter. In anticipation of my OOB, I close my eyes.

Shortly, the doorbell rings. It's the courier. He and Morticia converse longer than usual, and I imagine them comparing body piercings—believe me, I've seen the young man, and if anyone leaks, it's him.

The door closes.

"Ah," I breathe as my baby is sent out into the world. Here comes the OOB. Any moment now . . . any moment . . .

Call her, Prim pleads.

Forget about it! Improper snips.

I grunt. It's no use. As long as Noelle hangs over me like a vulture, I can't enjoy the moment.

"It's me," I say when her assistant patches me through a minute later.

"'Bout time," Noelle gripes.

I bite my tongue. Don't say it. Don't—

"I can't begin to express how much your support means to me, Noelle," I drawl.

"The least I can do," she gives back.

I scowl.

"Finish up the manuscript?"

"Courier just picked it up."

"That's a relief."

Yeah, I'm sure she's been losing sleep over the second half of my advance. Wonder what she'll buy with her fifteen percent?

"Why the ASAP?" I ask.

"I've heard from Intrepid."

My heart jolts. "Okay . . . ?"

"Nick Farnsworth wants to meet with you."

"He does?" I squeak.

"He does," she purrs, and I know she's salivating over what fifteen percent of seven figures will buy her.

"Then he wants to make an offer," I tentatively conclude.

"That's rather obvious, isn't it?"

I frown. "Did you speak with him, Noelle?"

"No—his assistant."

"And what, exactly, did she say?"

She heaves an ugly sigh. "That he wants to meet with you."

"That's all?"

"Darling, what more do you need?"

Is she right? Of course, why else would he request a meeting? "What about the editor—the one you've been working with? Will she be there?"

"Didn't I tell you?"

I grit my teeth. "No."

"Moved to another house last week—Gentry Books."

My first publisher. "But didn't she recently move from Heart Core to Intrepid?"

"Sure did."

A house hopper, then, which is the reason a wise author doesn't alienate her editor—even when she changes publishers. Never know when "a woman scorned" might morph into your next editor. Baaad news!

"I'm not surprised, really," Noelle continues. "Nick Farnsworth would *never* have hired her. The little twit simply isn't up to his standards."

I prop the phone between shoulder and ear and examine my Divine Pink nails. Five weeks without contact with Nick Farnsworth has done wonders for them. No more chips, cracks, or nibbling. "But why does he need to meet with me when I have you?"

"If there's one thing you'll learn about Nick Farnsworth, Adda, it's that he takes a personal interest in his authors."

I certainly hope so, Improper breathes.

I lower my hands. "Surely he doesn't intend to take up editing."

"Can't imagine, though I wouldn't be surprised if not a single word makes it into print without passing his inspection."

Stomach beginning to knot, I imagine all manner of clashes with the man—beginning with my inability to produce another work of fiction for which I've been paid an unconscionable advance.

What if I block again when it comes time to write the love scene for my new proposal?

"Maybe I should stay put," I say, unable to keep panic from my voice. "Farnsworth Publishing has been good to me."

A long, dead silence follows, indicating Noelle's vocal cords have seized up. If she dared speak, her manicured voice would be reduced to a squeak. Finally, she trembles, "I'll kill you, Adda. I swear it."

Heard that before, though never with quite so much conviction.

After another long silence, she draws a deep breath. "You've arrived, and if I have to, I'll drag you kicking and screaming to the top."

I would smile at her analogy if I weren't so riled.

"Still there, Adda?"

I lean back in my chair and loudly plunk my feet on the desktop.

"Listen to me," she snaps. "You're not going to mess this up. I'll die before I let you do that."

That could be arranged.

"Adda?"

I heave a loud sigh.

"What am I, Adda?"

Best to not respond.

"Your agent, that's what I am!"

Not to mention the one who's keeping me from an awesome OOB.

"And your friend," she adds on a last, desperate note.

It works. Not that I truly believe she's a friend; however, something tells me *she* genuinely considers *me* a friend. And I feel sorry for her. If I'm what she considers a bosom buddy, her life is shallow. Of course, I'm not exactly oozing with friends myself, am I?

Panged by the admission, I find myself reflecting on a recent venture into the little black—rather, the New Testament. "Love one another," Jesus said. At the time of the reading, it seemed sensible and easy, and yet it isn't. Far easier to cloak one's feelings in nonchalance and sarcasm. Safer, too.

"Adda?"

Wondering if I should turn left or right, I bite my lip. In the end, I trample my pride and veer right. "I'm here," I say, "and I . . . um . . . want you to know I'm grateful for your friendship, Noelle."

"Then you'll meet with Nick Farnsworth." It's a statement, not a question, and once more spoken in a meticulous voice. Her world is right again.

Wish mine were. I did the right thing, didn't I? If so, why do I feel used?

"Come on, Adda, stop zoning out on me!"

I sigh. "Yeah. I'll meet with Nick Farnsworth."

"Seven thirty, then."

My jaw drops. "Huh?"

"Seven thirty."

"*This* evening?"

"Of course—at Cristoforo's."

Cristoforo's. An old bitterness churns through me.

"And don't be late," Noelle says. "He's very punctual."

I close my eyes, grip a hand over my face. "*This* evening?"

She heaves a sigh. "Don't go to pieces, Adda. Pry your little butt out of the chair, get upstairs, and pick out something sexy to wear."

I scowl. "Sexy? I thought this was a business meeting."

I hear her tapping a pen. "Whatever it takes to get what we want, Adda."

We.

"You're a lovely woman in a tight little package," she continues, "so put it to work for you."

This is *not* what Jesus was talking about! I drop my feet to the floor. "I am *not* sleeping with Nick Farnsworth!"

"I didn't ask you to sleep with him. All I'm saying is to use your looks to your advantage. You've got them, so why not flaunt them? Besides, don't tell me you haven't noticed what a good-looking man he is. Think of the evening as a . . . reward . . . a celebration of the completion of yet another best seller."

I can't wait.

"You *are* familiar with Cristoforo's, aren't you?"

"Never been there, though I know where it is," I say, remembering the first time I heard the name. My first editor had taken me to lunch at a Chinese dive when I'd flown into New York for a conference years back. The place had been so filthy I'd been afraid to eat anything other than steaming hot egg flower soup—not exactly how one envisions a working lunch with a New York editor.

To drive in the nails, my editor had nearly turned somersaults when the bill arrived. "Look at this! Thirteen dollars and fifty cents. You're my cheapest author date ever." She had laid down her platinum credit card. "Took two of our best-selling authors to Cristoforo's last night—*the* place to go—and between the three of us, we racked up a bill of $350. Tip excluded!"

Never had the line between mid-lister and best seller been so miserably clear. And for the first time, I'd been envious. So envious it had driven me to reach for what lay beyond my grasp. So envious I'd gotten hold of it. And yet, even though I can now afford to eat at Cristoforo's, I have never set foot inside. Strange . . .

"Think Kathryn will show up again?" I ask.

"I doubt it."

"She still hasn't said anything to you about seeing me with Nick Farnsworth?"

"Not a word. In fact, I was going over Suzie Klinehopper's new contract with her this morning, and she didn't even mention you."

Suzie, another of Noelle's best-selling authors. A real sweetheart who writes humorous contemporary romance, though you'd never guess she has a single funny bone in that dowdy little body that cranks out a baby every year or so. Just thinking about her causes a warm feeling to rise from my turmoil. Though our lives are too different for us to support a friendship, we often e-mail each other. If I ever get to the place in my life where she's at—adoring husband and children—I don't doubt she'll welcome me to her inner circle. Of course, I'm not getting any younger, so the chances—

"Gotta go," Noelle says.

Realizing I've been staring out the window at the townhouses on the opposite side of the street, I blink. "All right."

"Call me tonight when you get home." She laughs. "Unless you're not alone."

"Noelle!"

Another laugh and she hangs up.

I drop the handset into its base and glare at the inanimate object. Its little green light stares back.

"Of course I'll be alone," I mutter and glance at the clock. I have barely four hours before I catch a cab to Cristoforo's. Plenty of time. More than enough.

I push out of the chair and tramp from my office. The smell hits me before I reach the stairs, and I look down to see Morticia climbing the steps with a cup of pungent tea.

Swallowing hard, I say, "I'm calling it a day. You can, too, if you'd like."

She steps to the landing. "Celebrating, hmm?"

I grimace. "Something like that."

She shrugs. "If you don't mind, I'll finish out the day—need the money."

I nod. "Fine with me."

As she steps past, I hear what has become disturbingly familiar these past weeks—the scratch and squeak of Doodles the Rat. Actually, he's a mouse, but a rat by any other name . . .

"Almost there," Morticia assures Doodles with a pat to the holster beneath her skimpy skirt.

I shake my head and start up the stairs toward my bedroom. I still can't believe I let her talk me into allowing her to bring that little rodent into my home. I despise all things small and creepy and crawly, and every time I walk into her office and see Doodles camped out on her shoulder, nesting in her hair, it's all I can do not to screech and climb on something. What *was* I thinking?

I enter my bedroom, but rather than go straight to the closet and rummage through outfits for my dinner date with Nick Farnsworth, I head for the bathtub. It's still not too late for an OOB, and maybe I can tap into it while submerged in lavender bubbles with flickering candlelight. If I don't linger too long, I should have plenty of time to change my nail polish. Good plan.

I'm late, and the crazy thing is I can't say whether or not it's intentional. After all, Noelle did warn me to be on time, and I do have tendencies toward passive-aggressiveness. Just as likely, though, the faulty plumbing is to blame. And Doodle's disappearing act, which had Morticia scrambling room to room calling, "Come to

Mommy, sweet 'ums," while I crouched atop my dresser. And of course, I mustn't forget the run in my last pair of black hose. Even so, I might still have made it on time, but Divine Pink polish didn't cut it, and nude hose with a black skirt suit simply didn't have the desired effect. So I changed my nail polish to Power Red and had the cabbie stop at a corner drug store so I could run in for a pair of hose. Should have known his insistence that I pay up front meant he wouldn't be waiting when I emerged.

But I'm here now, having dragged on my hose in the back seat of another cab. I glance at my watch as the doorman opens the door for me. Quarter past eight. Might Nick Farnsworth have given up and left? Half hoping, half dreading, I halt at the realization of where I am. Cristoforo's. *Finally*.

I sweep my gaze around the marble-and-granite lobby, which boasts beautifully framed artwork, lighted glass sculptures, enormous fresh flower arrangements, and black leather settees upon which carefully coifed ladies and gentlemen await their tables.

Wow. I've arrived. Really, truly arrived. Feeling as if I'm floating through a dream, I move toward a black lacquered podium attended by a maitre d' who stiffly surveys me from beneath raised eyebrows.

"I'm with the Farnsworth party," I say, halting before the podium.

He glances at his reservation list. "That would be *Mr. Nick* Farnsworth?"

What an obtuse question. Of course, there might be another

Farnsworth here this evening—

My thoughts grind to a halt. Might one of Nick Farnsworth's alienated family members—as in my *current* publisher—be here? Remembering my editor's appearance at Barnes & Noble, I take a step back. Surely he wouldn't pull that one again. Would he?

"Mr. Nick Farnsworth?" the maitre d' repeats.

"I . . . " I switch my purse to the opposite hand, force a bright smile. "Is there any other Farnsworth?"

The man frowns. "Your name, miss?"

Refused the bait. For a moment, I contemplate walking out, but Improper plops down on my shoulder and tells me I'm being paranoid. As Prim is strangely silent, I assume the two are in agreement.

"Adda Sinclaire," I say.

"Ah." The man's eyebrows jaunt higher. "Then Mr. Nick Farnsworth it is." He plucks up a leather-bound, gold-tasseled menu and steps from behind the podium. "Lovely to have you with us this evening, Ms. Sinclaire. If you'll follow me."

He leads me past a partition wall of etched glass and into a dining room hung with glittering crystal chandeliers and set with linen-covered tables and plumply padded chairs.

Suddenly self-conscious, I pluck at the collar of the white blouse beneath my jacket, then reach behind to assure the hem of my skirt didn't get caught in the waistband of my hose. Whew!

As I follow the maitre d', I scan the tables in search of lurking Farnsworths. However, despite all that glitters, the dining room is dimly lit and its uptown patrons more shadow than form. Does that mean that if I can't see them, they can't see me?

Get a life, Improper quips.

"I'm trying," I mutter as I realize Cristoforo's clientele is largely comprised of couples, many of whom have their heads bent near each other. Of course, some of the patrons are suited up for business, and one of the tables ahead boasts a gaggle of girlfriends.

A pity to waste the romantic ambience on them, I muse. Forgetting my own reason for being here, I curl my nails into my palms as a delicious shiver courses my spine. How long since I've been wined and dined in a place like this?

As the maitre d' leads me around the "girlfriend" table, one of three young women meets my gaze. She's a pretty thing in red—perhaps twenty—with a mantle of sleek black hair swept over one shoulder. Her large, dark eyes are set on either side of a perfectly shaped nose and punctuated by a mouth slightly too wide for her pale, oval face. And she's all the more stunning for the mismatch. Making a mental note to fix Snow White's face on a future heroine, I step past.

At the next table, a couple is bending near and a moment later kisses. My heart flutters longingly—until the couple parts, and I recognize Jake Grainger. As in the cover model whose kiss did nothing for my writer's block. As in formerly Gorgeous. As in Louse! And the woman? It's Mary Creekmore, an editor at Sift Publications. So, the randy little self-promoter is drumming up business on the other side of publishing. No wonder he hasn't called. Not that I've missed him calling, mind you. Lousy two-timer!

Grateful neither of them looks up as I pass, and that their coffee cups and dessert plates evidence they won't be at the restaurant much longer, I quicken my steps to catch up with the maitre d'.

Shortly, he halts before a table against the wall. "Here we are, Ms. Sinclaire."

And there stands Nick Farnsworth. Something glitters in his dark eyes as our gazes meet, something that makes me forget all about Louse. Then Nick is pulling out my chair.

Feeling strangely tingly, I lower myself. As he pushes me in, he leans down and his warm breath fills my ear. "I'm pleased you could make it, Adda."

No man has ever spoken my name like that. I gulp, look around. His face is so near I would only have to shift slightly to press my mouth to his.

Lips curving, he straightens and crosses to his chair.

Ooh! Did I almost do what I think I almost did?

The maitre d' sets the menu in front of me. "Bart will be with you in a moment. Enjoy your dinner, Mr. Farnsworth . . . Ms. Sinclaire." He turns away.

Flushed with heat that feels as though I fell asleep on the beach without sunscreen, I lower my head and busy myself with staking out a campsite for my purse. When I've cooled down sufficiently to look up, Nick Farnsworth is watching me.

"I hope you'll forgive me for being late," I say. "It was a deadline day."

He picks up a glass of what appears to be club soda, a slice of lime caught between ice cubes.

I shrug. "You know how that goes—rush, rush, rush. And every time you turn around, there's Murphy's Law just waiting to dump you on your— "

I'm babbling!

He raises an eyebrow.

I flash an apologetic smile and pick up my napkin.

"But you met your deadline." His voice thrums across the two-and-a-half feet separating us.

I settle the napkin in my lap, and when I look up, I nearly go to goo as his incredible dark eyes sink into mine. "Certainly did." I attempt a confident smile, though it feels as though my confidence has slipped down around my ankles. Of course, the way my day has gone, that might be my hose.

Beneath the table, I lift the hem of my skirt. No, the hose are still there.

Gaze unflickering, Nick Farnsworth takes a swallow of his drink.

Sheesh! How *does* he do it? And why am I allowing it? It must be the restaurant—all these couples fawning over each other. Love in the air . . .

I take a deep breath. "So is it just the two of us this evening, Mr. Farnsworth?"

He lowers his glass. "Just the two of us."

Never have five words sounded so suggestive . . .

"No surprises," he says. "And please call me Nick."

I hesitate over the temptation to wrap my tongue around his name, but in the end wave a dismissing hand. "Why, exactly, did you want to meet with me?"

He looks up as our waiter appears.

The mustached man smiles at me and inclines his head. "My name is Bart. I will be your waiter this evening. May I get you something from the bar, Ms. Sinclaire?"

He knows my name . . . Obviously, the maitre d' told him. Or Nick. I glance at him—Nick of the gorgeous chocolate-colored eyes, left cleft, broad shoulders, long-fingered hands. Nick—

Just listen to yourself! Prim snaps. *How did the man suddenly go from being Mr. Farnsworth to Nick?*

"Adda?" Nick prompts.

I really wish he wouldn't say my name like that. It does weird things to my insides.

"Um . . . " I look to Bart, follow his gaze to the wine list. Though I rarely indulge, not only is Cristoforo's the kind of place that goes hand-in-hand with fine wine, but Nick will surely order a glass for himself. I smile. "Your House Zinfandel, please."

He nods and looks to Nick. "Another club soda and lime, Mr. Farnsworth?"

"Yes." Nick opens his menu.

I blink. Just club soda? Strange.

"As you wish, Sir." Bart strides away.

"Have you eaten here before?" Nick asks without looking up.

So he wants to dine before getting down to business. Of course, I did keep him waiting nearly an hour. He's probably starved.

"No," I say, opening my menu. An instant later, the prices jump out at me, and I nearly slam the cover shut. So this is how my first editor and two of her best-selling authors racked up $350 in one evening. "Any suggestions?" I ask.

Nick looks up. "What are your preferences?"

Oh, silvering jet-black hair, dark chocolate eyes, left cleft, shoulders out to here . . . oh my! Improper sighs.

Bad, Adda! Bad! Prim scolds.

"Um . . . " I scan the menu, shrug. "Prime rib—always a favorite."

"Except when served with horseradish," Nick says.

Heat flushes me, hairline to throat. How did he know about that? Sure, he had witnessed the humiliating scene at The Ivories, but he couldn't possibly know the cause. Could he? Unless he was watching me before the incident . . .

I tuck my chin lower and pretend an interest in the menu. "Not one of my favorites," I mutter.

To my relief, he lets it go. "The herb-crusted prime rib is excellent," he says, "but you'll need a doggy bag."

For a dog I no longer have, thanks to Dick. However, no matter how much I miss Beijing, I've declined visitation as it would mean subjecting myself to Birgitta Roth. No way I'm setting foot in her hive.

"I also understand the filet mignon is good," Nick says. "At least, Birgitta Roth enjoyed it."

Well we can wipe that option off the list! Hating that it hurts so much to learn he's been here with enemy number one, I clench my hands in the napkin.

Calm down. Get a grip. You are not jealous!

I look up. "Then you bring all your prospective authors here?" I try to say it casually, but it comes out shrill.

He finishes scanning the menu and meets my gaze. "Actually, you're the first."

For a moment, relief washes over me. But what about Birgitta? If she wasn't here with him for the purpose of business—

Jealousy isn't green. It's red, as in Santa Claus move over! I declare, next time I won't settle for just one hunk of that witch's hair!

Appetite in sharp decline, I stare at the man opposite.

He stares back with mock innocence, then drains the last of his club soda.

I try to pull back, but I've gone into a nosedive. "What needs to be discussed with me that can't be handled by my agent, Mr. Farnsworth? And why tonight? And why here when you could be out enjoying the evening with—" I smile, falsely bright. "Oh, I don't know . . . Birgitta Roth?"

Amusement traces the corners of his mouth. "I assure you, Adda, my relationship with Ms. Roth is strictly business."

He said *Ms.*—and seems sincere. Have I made a fool of myself? Again? But how—

"*All* of my dealings with authors are strictly business."

All? Feeling like a balloon with a fast leak, I force a smile. "Which is exactly as it should be." Still, I'm dying to know how he knew Birgitta enjoyed the filet mignon. Of course, maybe he's just covering for a slip of the tongue. Perhaps he and Stick Woman really are—

Eeew! Somehow, that's even more repulsive than Birgitta and Dick.

"White Zinfandel, Ms. Sinclaire."

A glass appears in front of me, and I look up to see Bart standing alongside the table. "Thank you," I murmur.

He inclines his head. "May I tell you our specials this evening?"

As if I could eat. . . . "Yes, of course."

The man folds his hands before him, settles into his shoulders, and reverently details the preparation of a multitude of dishes with expensive names. Of course, not once does the price pass his lips.

I can't stand it. The frugal side of me, which more often than not haunts clearance racks, settles for Chicken Oscar. As everyone knows, dishes prepared with chicken are almost always cheaper. Fortunately, I like chicken, and it better fits my calorie-and fat-conscious regimen than red meat.

"Decided against the prime rib," Nick says as Bart departs with our order.

I shrug. "The chicken sounded better."

He lifts the club soda Bart brought and drinks deeply—the

most innocent thing in the world, though he manages to make it look exciting. As he lowers the glass, his gaze flicks to the left and settles on something.

I turn my head and catch Snow White of the "girlfriend" table looking at Nick. Her gaze slides to mine, but she abruptly breaks the contact and turns to a young woman who wasn't present when I arrived. Caught! Caught making eyes at *my* date. The little flirt!

I look back at Nick, but there's no trace of guilt on his face. Of course, flirtation is probably everyday fare for him.

I draw my shoulders up with a deep breath. "Mr . . . um . . . Nick, why am I here?"

He folds his hands on the table. "Your trilogy. I want it for Intrepid."

Oh, thank goodness. I think . . . "I'm . . . pleased to hear it. You do know Farnsworth Publishing has offered on it?"

"I do, and I'm prepared to outbid them."

Trying very hard not to jump out of my shoes, I grip my wine glass as Noelle's words, *You've arrived*, soar through my head.

"Providing, of course, you're willing to do things my way."

I come back to earth with a thud. Don't like the sound of that, nor the sudden steel in his eyes. "Your way?"

"My way."

So he wants to shape and mold me into his image, does he? Take away my voice like that nitwit whose slash-and-burn editing resulted in a three-star rating for *Whispers in the Night*. And which had nearly been the end of me. Never again.

I release my glass for fear of snapping the stem, press my palms to the table, and lean forward. "Mr. Farnsworth— " Hearing my voice rise, I lower it. "I have fourteen books in print—soon to be fifteen—and the last eight hit the best-seller lists big-time. Believe me, that didn't happen because I allowed my publisher to bully me into doing things *their* way. I've put in my time, earned my way through the ranks, and no one— "

Something warm settles over my left hand, and I drop my chin to stare at the long fingers covering mine.

Oh . . . my . . . he's touching me. Nick Farnsworth is touching me!

You are one deprived woman, Prim drawls.

Exactly. My black suit feeling suddenly restrictive, though it isn't, warm, though it's cut from a light fabric, I look up and catch a disturbance in Nick's eyes that makes me realize he's just as unnerved by the gesture. So much for "strictly business."

He pulls his hand back. "Are you going to walk out on me again?" From the level depth of his voice, I wonder if the startle in his eyes was imagined.

Managing a breath past taut vocal cords, I clasp my hands before me. "I probably should."

He considers me, then settles back in his chair as though completely at ease.

Wish *I* were . . . With effort, I uncurl my toes.

"Hear me out?" he asks, and I watch him pick bread from a

bowl that wasn't there minutes earlier. Bart has come and gone, and I was too aflutter to notice. *Never* has a man affected me so—not even during the early days of Dick's courtship when I'd been a dewy-eyed sophomore in high school, and he'd been the most popular senior boy. What is wrong with me?

"Still thinking about it?" Nick asks as he butters his bread.

I come back with a start. "Yes, I—I'll hear you out." Stuttering again. Just peachy. I curl my fingers into my palms for fear I'll be nibbling my nails next.

Nick gestures toward the bowl and takes a bite of bread with strong white teeth.

I hesitate, then pick out a piece and set it on the plate that appeared with the bread.

"I don't presume to be a writer," he says, "but I know the difference between garbage and sensation." He takes another bite and, a short while later, says, "*You* are sensation, Adda Sinclaire."

I stare at him as that goo feeling returns en force. And, on my granny's hairnet, I swear I can't remember what, exactly, set me off a minute ago.

"You write and rewrite history in a manner few can match," he continues, "staying true and yet bending enough to transform fictional characters into living, breathing people."

The ego massage is like none I've had. Not even my most zealous fan who writes me five-page letters can compare. Of course, the woman *is* sixty-some years old, portly, spectacled, and has a bit of a moustache. Whereas Nick . . .

"As I mentioned the last time we met, your male characters are your greatest strength," he says. "They're the reason I want you—"

Wants me.

"—for Intrepid."

Intrepid. Oh . . . yeah. My male characters. I do them well, not only according to Nick Farnsworth, but fans and reviewers who give me high marks for insight into the male psyche. What I wouldn't give if that insight translated into real life . . .

Nick leans forward, chandelier light dancing in his eyes. "What Intrepid plans is to tap into your strength and others' and do for men what publishing has been doing for women for the past thirty years."

My wine glass is halfway to my lips before a huge question mark lands smack between my eyes. "I don't understand."

He smiles. "Beginning next summer, Intrepid will repackage select women's fiction for men."

I stare at him. "I still don't understand."

He takes another bite of bread and keeps me waiting as he chews it down. "If we come to terms, your trilogy will not only be published for women, but men—different cover, of course, possibly an alternate title, A. Sinclaire versus Adda Sinclaire, more male point of view, more plot intensive."

Realizing my jaw has dropped, I snap my teeth closed.

This time it's Nick who doesn't seem to notice Bart's appearance or the salad he sets in front of each of us. Light continues to dance in Nick's eyes, but there's something else. He reminds me of one of my heroes standing over his mortal foe ready to gut the miscreant.

"The male readership of women's fiction has grown steadily since its authors started pushing the envelope," Nick continues, "and Intrepid feels there are millions more men who would eagerly come over if the perception of women's fiction could be altered to better reflect a man's world. Equally as important, the repackaging has the potential of wooing those women who typically shun romance. And there will certainly be many of your current following who purchase both editions."

He raises an eyebrow, and I realize he's waiting for a response.

"Oh," I say. "That's . . . really . . . interesting."

He flashes both rows of teeth and laughs—a deep, sensual sound that vibrates between us. "Somehow, I don't think you're impressed."

I suppose I should be, but his proposal broadsided me. Not that I'm unaware of the male readership. Indeed, I receive quite a few letters from men—and not all from prison inmates.

I pick up my fork, stab a frilly piece of lettuce, and pop it in my mouth. Unfortunately, it's of the bitter variety, and I didn't catch any dressing on it. I almost grimace, but in the event Nick assumes I'm choking as Noelle did over the horseradish, I force it down. Of course, the Heimlich might actually be a pleasant experience with Nick . . .

"No comment?" he prompts.

I poke at another piece of lettuce drizzled in bleu cheese. "I'm still digesting it," I mutter, and in the next instant snort as the double entendre hits me.

Oh, very ladylike, Adda, Prim sneers.

Once more flushed with embarrassment, I look up.

Nick is still smiling—a lazy smile that reveals only the top row of teeth.

My toes curl again. "It's a . . ." What to say? "It sounds like an ambitious project." I shake my head. "But how—"

"Two editors."

"Two?"

"The usual, and the second who edits and shapes the book for the male audience."

"I see." Not really.

"Do you?" He pushes his salad aside.

I do the same. Rabbit food is for rabbits. "I'm listening."

He leans forward. "The male edition is where we do things *my* way, Adda."

"And what way is that?'

"You'll work with a male editor who—"

"You?" the word pops out of my mouth like an overinflated speech bubble.

His gaze flickers. "At the outset, perhaps."

Ignoring Improper's appreciative growl, I say, "How much editing are we talking about?"

"Once you understand the effect Intrepid wishes to achieve, likely little more than what you're accustomed to."

Once I understand.

I take a sip of wine without realizing I've done so until its subtle sweetness piques my taste buds. "You said more plot intensive." I set my glass down. "What about the romance?"

"It will be there, but in smaller doses. For instance, if you have a scene where your heroine is going about daily life, we might shorten it or cut it altogether and instead look in on the hero who would normally be working behind the scene to . . . say . . . thwart your antagonist. In other words, more show than tell with your hero, and more tell than show with your heroine. But the same story."

"Same story," I say, "but two different books."

"Essentially, which means your trilogy would require a six-book contract with separate advances for each book."

This is starting to sound good. Still, there's the sizable grey area about the male edition. Sure, I get inside the hero's head often, but to shift my focus to him? What if I'm not capable of doing it?

"Are you interested?" Nick asks.

"I . . . "

"Finished, Ms. Sinclaire?"

Bart has returned. I nod and sit back as he clears away my salad plate.

He collects Nick's as well, says something about our entrees, and turns on his heel.

Nick watches him go, and I nearly miss his gaze once more

settling across the room.

Snow White. And this time I catch sight of her before she swallows her smile. The little flirt!

"Well?" Nick says.

I look back at him, and from the firm line of his mouth, one would never guess he's contemplating adding another name to his little black book.

Down, Adda. Down! Prim warns.

Up, Adda. Up! Improper counters.

I clench my hands to keep from flicking them off my shoulders.

I am *not* jealous.

Well, maybe a little bit.

I put my chin up. "Does my agent know about Intrepid's new line?"

"No. You're the first—outside of Intrepid."

I'm flattered, until Stick Woman's smug, fishy face returns to me. "You're telling me you didn't discuss this with Birgitta Roth at your recent 'strictly business' meeting with her?"

Irritation rumples his brow, and I have the overwhelming urge to smooth it away. "You're the first, Adda."

And he has no intention of letting me in on Birgitta, even though he equated her writing with mine the last time we met. I still haven't got over that.

I break off a piece of bread and pop it in my mouth. What should I say? The concept *is* appealing, but I'd be a fool to not recognize the risk. Sure, I have a faithful following who would rush out to buy the first edition, but if the second fails . . .

It could have long-term effects on my reputation from which I might not recover. There are numerous writers who boast staggering sell-through numbers and write far better books than those currently on the shelves, but who can no longer get a publisher to touch them with so much as a four-figure contract. They've been hung out to dry—all because of one little mistake. Of course, if I block again, it's all rather moot.

Fear ripples through me. It *could* happen.

"Think about it," Nick says, and nods at the plate Bart lowers before me.

Though my insides churn at the prospect of my next love scene, I'm struck by a smell so delicious I'm suddenly hungry. I look to my plate and nearly gasp. Not that I haven't seen frou-frou before, but this is astonishing. Painted on an oversized canvas of white porcelain, glistening asparagus spears top a golden chicken breast, which is topped by a crab meat mixture, which is topped by parsley-flecked Béarnaise sauce. And it doesn't end there. Wild rice and bulgur hugs one side of little boy Oscar, while slices of papaya sprinkled with edible flower petals kiss the other side.

Shoot! I'm so deprived even my food is starting to have more fun than me.

I glance at Nick's plate. His thick porterhouse isn't exactly a work of art, yet it manages to be more appealing—rather like an attractive man alongside a gorgeous woman. One requires mere presence to make an impression, the other beautiful clothes and tons of makeup. Men and red meat have it so easy.

"Something wrong?" Nick asks.

I jerk. "Uh . . . no . . . it looks wonderful." I pick up my knife and fork and, with silent apology, cut into Oscar. As the bite melts in my mouth, I watch Nick slice into his steak, and I start to salivate. I love red meat—and men who eat it. I nearly sneer in remembrance of Dick who went over to the other side. During the last two years of our marriage, he converted to vegianity—or whatever you call it. How I'd grown to hate the smell of beans, rice, and steamed veggies!

Suppressing a shudder, I return to my plate for another forkful of real food.

Two bites later, Nick says, "I've been keeping an eye on your latest release."

Why that should make me tingle, I don't care to examine. I look up. "Have you?" A silly question, but I want to hear all about it.

"Three weeks in the number one slot," he obliges. "Impressive."

I frown. "You didn't say, 'for a romance.'"

Holding my gaze, he carries another piece of steak to his mouth and thoughtfully chews it through before responding with, "One thing you'll learn about me if you come over to Intrepid, Adda, is that I take the romance genre very seriously."

"Ah." I smile. "A man after my own heart."

He arches an eyebrow. "You think?"

Unsettled by his response to an expression so cliché it warrants little to no notice, I avert my gaze and assure myself that the fluttering at my center is merely a form of indigestion—albeit ticklish.

"Actually," he says before I can form coherent thought, "it's your books I'm after."

I look up from my plate. "Of course it is." I am *not* disappointed. But, oh, how I wish those chocolates of his were of the milk chocolate variety rather than the dark. "So . . . um . . . do you come here often?" *Oh, Adda, you can do better than that!*

A half smile turning his lips, he once more applies himself to his steak. "I've been here once before." He sinks his fork into another piece of severed meat.

"Oh."

From this point forward, our conversation degenerates into a halfhearted discussion of favorite restaurants, the weather, and books we're currently reading—rather, books *he's* currently reading, as no way am I admitting my growing fascination with Josh's little black book. It's simply not . . . politically correct. And the last thing I want is for Nick to rethink signing me on at Intrepid.

Near the end of the meal, I catch him and Snow White going at it again. In an attempt to calm my roiling, I recall the promise I made myself to never again *publicly* yank another woman's hair from her head.

And don't forget this meeting is strictly business, Prim throws a carrot into the pot. *It's your books he's after.*

Thereby, no right to be jealous.

I'm not. I'm not.

After some time, Bart clears away our plates and tells us he'll return with coffee.

Nick settles his forearms to the table. "Any questions about Intrepid's plans?"

Dozens, but the moment his eyes capture mine, the questions scurry away. I chase after them and drag one back by the tail. "If you're shooting for next summer, won't that be tight getting the first book of my trilogy to press? After all, I've only written five chapters."

"When can you have the first draft of the entire manuscript to me?"

Trying to not think about the possibility of another block, I say, "Minimum of four months—and that's pushing it."

"Which leaves seven months for editing."

"And artwork," I remind him, "and marketing."

"Much of which can be done while you're finishing the first draft."

True, though it's rare for a publisher to put the cart before the horse. They're all so cautious. "All right," I say, "but we'll be editing two books—one extensively, it seems. And all the while I'll be on deadline with the second story in the trilogy."

"Which is the reason Intrepid wants to space your books nine months apart."

I stare at him. A three-month buffer? Better than I could have hoped.

"Think you can work with that?"

"Yes," I say, slightly breathless. "Yes!"

He smiles. And I just love it when he does that.

Moisture pooling in my mouth, I swallow for fear of drooling and say, "What kind of publicity does Intrepid plan?"

"Print, radio, the Net, and—if the board approves—television."

"Television?" Wow.

"I assume you're interested."

It shows, does it? Noelle would not approve. I sit up straighter. "I am."

"Good."

A flash of red draws my gaze, and I look around. That little flirt . . . that little vamp . . . has risen from her gaggle and is moving toward us on long legs and two-inch heels. No doubt about it, she's headed for us—rather, Nick.

And of all the gall, he's rising to meet her.

I am *not* jealous—just appalled that an old goat like him is encouraging a young thing like her. I don't have to look any closer to know the minx is half his age. Half! I'll bet he's twenty-five years older than her twenty-something.

The next thing I know, she's embracing Nick. Oh, for goodness sake! The randy old rat is giving it back.

I frown. Maybe they know each other?

He draws away, though one hand remains at her waist. "Enjoying yourself?"

I grit my teeth. I'll just bet she is. After all, she's probably looking at sugar daddy number umpteen!

"I am," she says in a level, faintly husky voice. She flips her dark, sleek hair over her shoulder and hands him something. "There's the damage."

Without a glance, he sets it on the table, and I see it's the check for her table—$270!

She leans forward and pecks his cheek. "Thanks, Dad."

SIX

dda Sinclaire,” Nick says, “I’d like you to meet my daughter, Sophia—Sophia, Adda Sinclaire.”

Suddenly, Nick doesn’t look the old geezer, and Snow White sheds a few years herself, especially when she beams at me. She still has a teenager’s glow. Seventeen? Eighteen?

“Ms. Sinclaire—” she steps toward me as I rise and offers her hand. “Pleased to meet you.”

The mystery of the other Farnsworth party solved, I numbly slide my fingers across hers. “A pleasure to meet you, Sophia,” I say, searching for a resemblance to Nick, “and call me Adda.”

She releases me and clasps her hands at her waist. “I’ve read every one of your books.” Her sweet voice flecks me like gentle rain. “You’re my favorite author. Well . . . you and John Steinbeck.”

And how does one respond to that? John Steinbeck is “literature,” and not even an act of Congress would convince the “literary” world that women’s fiction is so esteemed. Ask my mother, who continues to press me to stop messing around and get down to writing a “real” book.

"I'm flattered," I say.

An awkward silence follows, but Nick fills it. "You and your friends are off?"

Snow White nods. "Okay if Roberta spends the night?"

"Sure."

Snow White lives with her dad? Or does she bounce between parents?

"Fawkes will see you and your friends home, then," Nick says.

Fawkes? Must be his chauffeur—probably sitting in one of the sleek black limos outside.

"Nice to meet you, Ms.—Adda," Snow White says.

"And you."

She looks to her father. "See ya." She flashes a smile, winks, and swings away.

What was that about?

Nick lowers to his chair. "Sophia's off to college this fall," he says as I sink into my chair.

"She's lovely."

"Yes, she is."

He adds a splash of cream to the coffee that materialized as so many things have done this evening.

"When I told her I was having dinner with you," he says, "she insisted on changing her plans in order to meet you." He smiles across his coffee cup. "She's an avid reader of romance, so when I mentioned Intrepid's plan to stretch its women's fiction division in new directions, you're the first author she recommended."

Then I have Sophia Farnsworth to thank for an opportunity sure to be the envy of fellow writers. Of course, I'm sure Nick Farnsworth already had an idea of who he wanted for the new line. "I'm pleased she enjoys my books."

"Could I persuade you to sign her copies?"

I nearly drop the creamer. "Of course."

"This evening?"

A thrill goes through me, raising goose bumps along my arms and legs. I glance at my watch. "It's 10:30."

"Early to bed, are you?" His lips tilt appealingly.

The goo is back. I shake my head. "Actually, I'm a late nighter. This . . . evening will be fine."

I'm going to Nick Farnsworth's home, I realize with sudden trepidation. Of course, it's not as if anything can happen with two teenage girls under the same roof.

A quarter hour later, two checks totaling $500 settled, Nick retrieves my purse—would have forgotten it again!—grips my elbow, and guides me out of Cristoforo's and into a waiting cab. We sit side by side, thighs nearly touching as the driver whisks us in and out of relatively light traffic toward the address Nick gave him.

Something hangs in the air between us as we exchange light conversation, and I wonder if he feels it as strongly as I. Knowing that if I don't place my mind elsewhere I might melt, I draw a deep breath and look out the window.

Ten minutes later, the cabbie pulls up in front of one of Manhattan's tallest buildings—one I immediately recognize as housing the headquarters of Intrepid Publishing. Not Nick's home, then. And I'm relieved.

Sort of.

Nick hands me out of the cab, pays the driver, and leads me into the lobby, which is deserted except for a pair of security guards.

In unison, the men acknowledge Nick. "Good evening, Mr. Farnsworth."

He answers them by name as we head toward the elevators. Shortly, he punches a number in the elevator control panel, and when the doors close I find myself alone with the most attractive man I've met outside my imagination. As we're whisked upward, I catch myself playing the elevator nerd by watching the floors count up.

I look to Nick, hands slung in his pants pockets, gaze resting on the elevator doors.

"Almost there," he says.

Shortly, the elevator slows. As the doors swish open, Nick gestures for me to precede him.

I step into Intrepid's dimly lit lobby with its gleaming wood walls, floor-to-ceiling view of the city, and immense framed prints of the covers of its best-selling authors. Impressive, but understated compared to Farnsworth Publishing, which goes the extra ten miles to boast its success. Somehow, I don't think Nick misses marble floors, luminous brass fixtures, suede sofas, and the monstrous aquarium filled with exotic fish.

"This way," he says, stepping around me.

I follow him past a reception desk and down a wide hallway. Doors on either side are fitted with black placards engraved with the names of editors, several of whom I do not recognize. Of course, those are likely the editors for Intrepid's other lines—mystery, sci-fi, western, horror, self-help, etcetera.

At the end of the hallway, he pushes open a door marked "Nicholas Farnsworth, President," reaches inside, and flips on the light.

The office is not as large as expected, but it's a good size, and its sparse but tasteful furnishings lend an air of masculinity.

"So this is where Nick Farnsworth conceives his ambitious projects," I muse.

"Occasionally." He proceeds to the credenza behind his desk, which is piled with paperbacks and hardcovers. "Here they are," he says of a familiar pile of books.

They're all there, I realize—including my latest. I halt alongside him. Trying to not sense him across the inches between us, I flip to the title page. And there's the autograph, complete with a heart-dotted "Nick." Blushing in remembrance, I say, "You'd like me to add Sophia's name above yours?"

"No, she has her own copy. As she's reading it again, I'll have to get it to you later."

What every writer lives to hear—their book is a keeper to be read and reread. To be cherished above others that end up getting passed around and eventually are tattered, battered, dog-eared, and fit only for the wastebasket.

"You can sit at my desk," Nick offers.

I look around and find he has once more pulled out a chair for me—a sleek tan leather job. "Thank you," I say, and turn back to retrieve the books; however, he's already scooped them up. And that's when I notice the names of the authors to whom the other piles belong—Mona Wales, Peggy Bird, Renee Zealan, Jeanne Matriarch, Shannon Sweet, and Birgitta Roth. All known for their strong heroes. With the exception of the latter, I'm in excellent company. Unfortunately, it's true about one rotten apple spoiling the bunch.

I set my purse on the desk in clear sight, where I won't be able to miss it, and lower to the chair, of which I'm keenly aware last held Nick. Just as I'm once more aware of the fit of my suit. Too warm. Too restrictive. I unfasten the three buttons of my jacket, and as I start to shrug out of it, Nick leans over and slips his hands inside the lapels to assist me. His fingers graze my collarbone, then shoulders.

"Thank you," I strangle. As he crosses the office to the coat rack alongside the door, I lower my chin and smooth my blouse in an attempt to inconspicuously blow cool air up my warm face.

Oh . . . my . . . gosh! I pull my hands away to stare at the dark outline of my bra beneath the thin, white blouse. I didn't! I did . . . Somewhere between Morticia's "mouse on the loose" and the discovery I had a run in my hose, I strapped on a black bra.

I look up as Nick hangs my jacket on a coat hook—impossibly out of reach. A groan rises, but before it can betray me, Nick turns. In a futile attempt to hide my fashion faux pas, I scoot nearer the pile of books and hunch my shoulders.

A few moments later, he leans against the desk alongside me and hands me a pen.

I accept it—a bit too hastily—and flip to the title page of the first book. Deciding that the more simple I keep it the sooner I can retrieve my jacket, I write, "To Sophia" and sign and date beneath.

Book after book, Nick hovers over me, and I just know he's staring at my bra strap visible through my blouse. Still, I continue to take the extra moment to dot each "i" with a heart, though it feels increasingly juvenile.

I close the last book, and as I set it atop the teetering pile, a name jumps at me from a slip of paper tucked beneath the edge of Nick's desk blotter—Kathryn Connell. The phone message, dated today at five forty-five in the afternoon, says simply, "returned your call."

They're still talking, then. About bringing Kathryn over to Intrepid as Noelle surmised?

Though I know it will brand me as nosey, I have to know. I tap the capped end of the pen to the slip. "It looks as though you need to return my editor's call."

"So it does."

I look up and around.

His gaze is unreadable—or almost. Once more, I glimpse steel there.

"I did offer to explain that to you," he says.

As I'd been in the process of making a hasty retreat to avoid running into Kathryn. I lean back in the chair so I don't have to crane my neck so far. "So you did. Does the offer still stand?"

His eyes harden further, and I'm certain he's going to refuse, but then his gaze flicks lower. A moment later, he returns to my face and the steel is far less in evidence. "It does." He settles a thigh to the edge of his desk "Kathryn and I—"

Not Ms. Connell.

"—go back years."

Oh, really?

"I hired her while I was still at Farnsworth Publishing. She was fresh out of college, top of her class, and ambitious. Within six months she moved from assistant editor to editor, and a year later was promoted to senior editor." He crosses his arms over his chest. "Kathryn is one of the best editors I've come across, and though I've tried before to lure her away from Farnsworth Publishing, she's always turned me down—until now." His gaze travels down me and up again, and the last of the steel in his eyes evaporates. "If you come over to Intrepid, Kathryn has agreed to follow."

I stare at him as his words unfold a possibility not previously considered. My ego teeters. "Then it's Kathryn you really want?"

That slight smile of his—at once attractive and irksome—

curves his mouth. The big lug is enjoying my deflation!

"No," he says, "I want you, Adda. *And* Kathryn. I assure you, your price is too high to gain *any* editor. Thus, I'll make do with one or the other of you. Or both."

I feel better. I think.

"Or neither," he adds and nods at the credenza where the other authors' books are piled. The man doesn't put all his eggs in one—too cliché. How about . . . he doesn't put all his tobacco in one pipe?

I push the chair back, stand, and step to the credenza. "So if we don't come to an agreement, who will you approach next?"

"They've all been approached," he says at my back, "though, as I said earlier, you're the first to know the details."

Well, duh. You did run into him and Stick Woman at The Ivories, Adda! Unfortunately, this means I might soon be in the same boat with her. The possibility is almost enough to make me turn down Intrepid, but that would give old Birgitta a better chance of dragging herself up out of mid-list. Can't have that, now, can we?

I survey the other books. Seven authors. Nick says he wants me, so who are the others?

I glance over my shoulder and find him watching me closely. "I don't suppose you'd tell me who the others are likely to be?"

He lifts an eyebrow. "Don't care to keep company with Birgitta Roth?"

I gulp. How does he know? Am I that transparent? Did it

show when Stick Woman dragged me to his table? Did—

"Word is that the two of you got in a catfight a few years back during a conference."

My insides sink, and I turn back to Birgitta's pile to hide the color flying across my face. Though I'll be forever grateful to the discreet hotel personnel that the incident didn't make the papers or tabloids, it was too much to hope Nick Farnsworth hadn't heard of it. After all, it had spread rapidly among women's fiction writers and become the headliner for many online chats. Unfortunately, the speculation over the cause of the catfight had turned fact when Dick and I divorced shortly thereafter, and he and Birgitta made no attempt to cover their living arrangements. Nick surely knows about that as well.

I draw a deep breath, shrug. "It's true," I say as flippantly as I can manage.

"True also that you pulled out a handful of her hair?"

Throwing embarrassment to the wind, I turn to him. "Remind me to show it to you sometime."

Both eyebrows go up.

I laugh. "Just joking." None of his business that Birgitta's bottle-dyed hair—dark roots and all—is pressed between my divorce papers. Man! Do I have issues, or do I have issues?

He straightens and takes the single stride to the credenza. "Mona Wales—contemporary," he says, "Jeanne Matriarch—Civil War era, and Shannon Sweet—fantasy."

Did I hear right? Did he pass over Birgitta Roth?

"Providing we come to terms," he adds.

Then there's yet the possibility she might squeak through. "I consider myself in good company," I murmur.

"Glad you approve."

I pick *The Love Bounty* from atop Birgitta's pile, a book released shortly after my divorce. Tacky title. Tacky cover. Though I never so much as cracked the spine to peek inside enemy territory, the book stands out due to its top reviews and reader acclaim—which had sickened me considering her writing should so improve with Dick in her bed. In fact, one reviewer went so far as to write that *The Love Bounty* narrowed the gap between Birgitta's writing and mine. And I *had* felt Stick Woman panting at my heels. Fortunately, her next book had once more put me way out in front. Perhaps the novelty of her affair with Dick had worn off?

The Love Bounty also stands out for its cover art, and I grin as I spot the hero's third ear amid his long, flowing hair. Rumor has it the artist intentionally added it in retaliation over a money dispute with the publisher. Funny thing is, though the little stunt ought to have seen him blacklisted, he suddenly became one of the most sought-after cover artists. Who'd have thunk?

"Her best work," Nick says.

I look up, and he's so near I can clearly see the lines at the corners of his eyes, but most intriguing are those alongside his mouth. I nearly sigh. The man has absolutely no business getting so near me.

"I've heard that," I say.

"You haven't read it, then?"

Not in this lifetime. Or the next. "'Fraid I haven't had the time."

He takes the book from me, and as he flips it open, I notice slips of paper protruding from between the pages. "Despite your differences," he says, "I think you'll agree that Birgitta is a talented writer."

Again, not in this lifetime.

He passes the book back. "Read that passage."

Do I have to? Gritting my teeth, I begin to plod through a scene where the hero is alone in the stables agonizing over feelings for the heroine. Though tempted to yawn, a short while later I have to agree with Nick. It is good—and familiar, strangely enough. Have I read it, after all?

"You're right," I begrudge. "It's well written."

He reaches to the book again and, as I continue to hold it, flips to the next marker.

My, he smells good, though cologne is definitely not responsible.

The next passage is also impressive—and familiar—as are the following two, each offering incredible insight into the male psyche. Hmm . . . ?

"Unfortunately," Nick says after once more prompting me to concur with his assessment of Birgitta's talent, "despite the number of books published since, she has yet to repeat what she accomplished here—close, but not near enough."

I set the book down and shrug as I turn to Nick. "Some stories simply bring out the best in a writer—book of the heart, and all. Maybe this was hers."

"Perhaps."

I stare at Nick. He stares back. I stare some more. He stares some more. Then his eyes lower, and I'm relieved until I follow his gaze.

With a squeak, I cross my arms over my chest in an embarrassingly pubescent attempt to conceal the outline of my bra. To worsen matters, my elbow connects with a pile of books, causing them to tumble to the floor between us. The other piles shift and teeter, but hold.

"Sorry," I gasp as Nick bends down, and I drop to my haunches to gather up the books. A moment later I go cross-eyed as our foreheads connect with such force I land on my rear.

He grips my shoulder. "All right, Adda?"

I lift my hand from my hairline to peer at him where he's dropped down in front of me. Even though he now has four eyes, two noses, two mouths, and one more ear than *The Love Bounty's* hero, he's still the most attractive man I've met.

Grimacing, I nod. "You?"

He smiles. "Hard head. Ask anyone who's ever worked for me."

Still, there's a bright red spot—well, two at the moment—on his own forehead. Without thinking, I reach up and touch it. And he jerks beneath my fingertips.

"Not a good idea," he rumbles.

His rejection stings, and I snatch my hand back. "Neither is that." I nod my chin at where he grips my shoulder.

Though I expect him to release me, after a long pause he merely flexes his hand on my shoulder. "No, it's not."

Confused, I look up. His face is once more singular, and a crooked smile is in place that makes him look surprisingly boyish.

"Perhaps not 'strictly business,'" he murmurs.

Does he mean what I think he means? Holding my breath and his gaze, I feel his hand leave my shoulder and trail my collarbone to the base of my throat. Though my lungs urge me to splurge on a refill, I'm too afraid of losing the moment. Air or no air, it's perfect just the way it is.

Though his gaze has yet to flicker, his head lowers toward me and I feel his breath on my lips. I part them and, in doing so, sip air enough to sustain me through what's sure to be the kiss of a lifetime.

Nick doesn't disappoint, though he surprises. Rather than demanding, his mouth lightly covers mine as though to test it, and he doesn't press me to the floor.

With a murmur, I curve a hand around his neck to draw him nearer. He deepens the kiss, the intensity of which causes me to startle. And my foot to strike the credenza. A moment later, the remaining books topple.

Leave it to Adda . . .

Nick grunts and loosens my mouth as he's jolted by what is

surely a hardcover hitting his head, but like a true hero, continues to shield me and bears the brunt of the onslaught. He grunts twice more, and I wince. Not until silence settles around us do I creak my lids open to discover Nick's face above mine.

"Sorry," I croak.

"You should be grateful," he says with regret that carries a tremendous punch, "not sorry." He straightens and looks down at me. "I know I am."

Ouch. Double ouch.

He extends a hand, and though I'm pained by his words, I accept his offer and a moment later stand before him — thoroughly flushed with embarrassment. What *was* I thinking? Did I really allow that to happen? And why does he — a red-blooded man — appear to regret it more than I? Fighting for composure, I lower my chin and, with one hand, smooth my skirt, with the other, tug at my blouse.

"You might want to straighten yourself while I pick up this mess," he suggests.

I look up, and he nods to a door across the room.

"Good idea," I mutter. I grab my purse and, with as much dignity as I can muster, sidestep a conference table and cross the room. Suppressing a groan that's been climbing steadily up my throat, I close the restroom door behind me and lean back against it.

Warned you, Prim sneers.

Did not, Improper snipes.

Did too.

Did not.

"Cork it," I grit between my teeth and push off the door. I cross to the sink above which an oval mirror gives back my sorry reflection. And let the groan loose. Fingering my lips which, though lipstick is in scarce evidence, present a rosy red—a perfect complement to the knot on my forehead—I growl, "Klutz," and open my purse.

I linger too long in collecting myself—a good quarter hour—but after what happened, I need every minute to face Nick again. Fortunately, he doesn't come pounding on the door to hurry me along as Dick would do. When I finally step from the restroom—lipsticked, powdered, fluffed, buttoned to the throat, head high—Nick is sitting behind his desk with the air of one completely at ease. As though he and I didn't just have a meeting of the mouths on the floor between desk and credenza. The big faker!

He looks up from the papers he holds, and I'm surprised to see he's wearing glasses—small, light wire frames that practically disappear into his face. But rather than make him appear older, they somehow impart a youthful streak that causes my heart to toss.

In the next instant, he lowers the papers to his desk, pulls off his glasses, and stands. "Ready to go?"

Behind, the books have been restacked in their respective piles on the credenza. I've always loved and respected books—careful to not crack spines or dog-ear pages—but at the moment I could set the lot of them on fire.

"Ready," I say, and head for the door.

With long strides, Nick reaches it first and pulls it open.

I lift my jacket from the coat rack and am grateful when he makes no attempt to assist me into it. In silence, we walk past Intrepid's offices. Not until we're ensconced in the elevator and starting down does Nick speak. "I apologize for what happened."

Unfortunately, I open my mouth well in advance of my mind. "Don't apologize." I meet his gaze. "Nothing happened that I didn't want to have happen."

He wasn't expecting that, as evidenced by a flicker of surprise.

Ugh.

Hey! Your heroines don't play coy, and neither should you, Improper objects to my sinking feeling. *You liked that kiss. Admit it.*

I did. I *really* liked it.

And just where do you think it would have led if you hadn't kicked the credenza? Prim argues indignantly. *That's right! A place you don't want to go again.*

No, I don't. At least, I *shouldn't* want to go there. Dick was one time too many.

"Regardless," Nick Farnsworth finally says, "I assure you it won't happen again."

What next leaps off my tongue, Adda Sinclaire would *never* say, but the words catch air before I realize the source. "Call it my *strong* male point of view, but I believe it will happen again."

Improper! You little imp!

With more than a flicker of surprise, Nick stares at me.

To my tremendous relief, the elevator doors swish open. Lunging forward, I leave Nick behind. *At least I managed to unsettle the suave Nick Farnsworth*, I tell myself in a lame attempt to find some good in my departure from acting the "lady." But it doesn't work, and that sinking feeling sinks deeper. What must he think of me? That I'm a loose woman? That I'm game for whatever it takes to make it to the top?

I cringe.

Not good, Adda.

In fact, bad. Really bad.

But nothing happened, I try to defend myself, only to question the reason nothing happened. Why didn't Nick try to take advantage of me like so many men would have done? Is there something wrong with him? Or is it me? Perhaps I'm too old for his taste . . . not thin enough . . . too tall . . . dull . . . clumsy . . .

Hmm. That could be it.

Halfway across the lobby, Nick draws even with me, nearly causing me to startle.

Keeping my gaze averted, I focus on the security guards who give me the nod before bidding Nick a good evening.

When we step out into a Manhattan midnight, two cabs are waiting, and I realize Nick must have called for them while I stalled in the restroom.

I head for the nearest one, but Nick says, "Take the first."

As if it matters.

With a sigh, I veer toward the cab indicated. As I grab for

the door, Nick reaches past me and his chest brushes my shoulder. Awareness shuddering through me, I duck into the back seat.

Nick closes the door, steps forward, and says something to the cabbie. The man answers, then Nick steps back as the cab slides onto the road.

He's watching me go again, I realize. And for some silly reason, my eyes water and nose pricks. In an attempt to set my emotions straight, I give my head a shake, only to catch the cabbie watching me in the rearview mirror. His eyes are kind, and I sense he wants to ask if I'm all right—not your typical New York cabbie, I assure you—but he looks forward again.

I take a deep breath and recite my address.

"Yes, ma'am." He puts on his blinker to turn left.

Sinking back into the surprisingly comfortable seat, I stare out the window as the night faces of shops, bars, and restaurants blur into a single, moving mass.

"You're home, ma'am," the cabbie says as he pulls up in front of my townhouse.

Scooting forward, I peer at the meter only to find it isn't running. I meet the cabbie's gaze in the rearview mirror. "How much?"

"Paid up, ma'am."

Just as before following my meeting with Nick at the B&N. Well, at least I can cover the tip—which I didn't think to do the last time. I unzip my purse and close my fingers around my wallet.

"Gratuity as well, ma'am."

Nick Farnsworth thinks of everything.

"Good evening, ma'am."

"Thank you," I murmur, and step from the cab.

Ten minutes later, I crawl into my big, lonely bed and try not to think about what happened in Nick's office. Try not to imagine him also lying awake. Of course, if he is, I'm sure he's promising himself "it" won't happen again. And despite my declaration to the contrary, something tells me it's a promise he'll keep. After all, Nick Farnsworth is a man in control.

SEVEN

ackety hack hack hack!

I wince.

Puffer clears her throat. "You had dinner with Nick Farnsworth, and you're only now telling me about it?"

Sheesh! We're talking one week. I never should have mentioned it. "Sorry, it's just that I've been swamped with revisions."

Not! Three days after Kathryn received *The Gifting*, she called and was positively enthusiastic—a reach for Little Miss Tight Lips. The revisions were so minimal she'd said she would handle them herself. My previously rejected manuscript redeemed! Crawling out of the slump of Nick Farnsworth, I'd thrown my arms wide and allowed the long-awaited OOB to take me away. What a day!

"Revisions, huh?" Puffer grumbles and draws deeply on her cigar.

And I know she knows I'm lying.

"Well," she says, "were you nice to him, missy?"

As much as I regret what happened between Nick and me, I go all warm just thinking about that kiss. "Too nice," I mutter and gasp at the realization I spoke aloud.

The patter of Puffer's keyboard ceases. "Oh, ho! It's like that, is it?"

"Joyce!"

"I want to hear all the details."

"No!"

Hack hack. "Come on. I'm in the middle of a love scene and could use a little inspiration. Give over!"

"Gotta go, Joyce."

"Your place or his?"

"Neither! We went to his office so I could sign— "

"His office? Yo!"

"Joyce, I'm going to hang up on you!"

She chortles. "Bet your face is as red as a full-blown diaper rash."

The image her words evoke cause me to splutter, snigger, then giggle as outrage puddles around my feet. "Redder," I admit. "Steam's rising off it."

She guffaws, and despite the crudity of her laughter, I'm warmed. I really love the old crone.

"Better kisser than Jake Grainger, I'll bet," she says.

I flip onto my back and stare at the ceiling above my bed. "Yeah. Wouldn't have thought it possible, but what a kiss!"

"Go on."

"That's it, Joyce. Really. There's nothing to go on about."

Puffer groans. "Thanks for the inspiration, Miss Goody Two

Shoes." She hacks again, and I hold the phone away until she clears her throat. "So what did you do? Knee the poor guy in the middle of your kiss?"

She knows me too well, but no way am I going to admit to what actually happened. "We . . . uh . . . let's just say we came to our senses."

Nibble, nibble—

I jerk my hand from my mouth and scowl at the damaged nail which, fortunately, is limited to a ragged tip. Unfortunately, the Copper Top polish will have to be overhauled. But then, I didn't like it anyway.

"Come on, missy," Puffer prompts. "I could use a good laugh."

I almost refuse, but then shrug. A good laugh is the least I can do for Puffer who has stood beside me for so many years. "All right, then, here goes—I bumped the credenza and caused a tower of books to rain down on him."

But she doesn't laugh. "Oh, missy."

Imagining her shaking her head and staring at the glowing tip of her cigarette—make that, cigar—I murmur, "Yeah."

"So, you gonna pick up where you left off? Or have you already?"

I scowl. "We haven't—and we're not going to. It was a mistake. And one that's *not* going to happen again."

"Oh, I think it will."

I open my mouth to protest, but those are the exact words

I flicked at Nick and to which he gave no response. Feeling the fool I've felt a hundred times since confidently assuring him it *would* happen again, I say, "Uh, so how are Felicia's wedding plans coming along?"

Fortunate for me, the change of topic clicks. "The snooty little twerp wants me to wear pink. Can you imagine? Me? Pink?"

Envisioning Puffer in a fluffy pastel creation, a cigar clamped between her teeth, I laugh.

"Naturally, Jerry loved it," she continues. "Went on and on about it being my color—wouldn't shut up until I suggested *he* wear it. 'Course neither he nor Felicia thought it was funny."

I frown. "Uh . . . does Felicia know . . . ?"

"No, but maybe her wedding could double as a coming out."

"Joyce!"

"Ha-hah!" she cackles, then spits, "Pink!"

I sigh. "I can't imagine."

"*Bleep* right, you can't!"

"So what are you going to tell her?"

"Already told her I ain't gonna wear pink, but she ordered the dress anyway."

I sit up. "So you're stuck."

"You know me better than that, missy." A long, harsh draw on her cigar. "Way I see it, I've got two options—either gain fifteen pounds over the next three weeks so the thing won't fit—"

"Won't happen."

Puffer is the scrawniest shriveled prune, though certainly not from lack of sustenance. I've seen her at buffets, and believe me, no matter how much she shovels in, it doesn't add an ounce to her skin and bones.

She sighs. "Yeah, that's what I'm afraid of."

"What's the other option?"

"Ashes," she touts, triumphant. "Guaranteed to burn a nice fat hole through prissy pink chiffon."

I grimace. "Felicia won't like that."

"Sure won't, but accidents happen." *Hack hack*. "Think I should do it in front of her?"

I imagine Puffer wiggling her scrabbly eyebrows and almost feel sorry for Felicia. Though Felicia is entirely unlikable, it couldn't have been easy growing up with Puffer for a mother.

"No," I say, "you're not a good enough actress."

She grunts. "Yeah, probably right."

"Maybe you should just grin and wear it. It is only for a few hours, after all."

There's a long silence. Might she actually be considering it?

Clickety click click clack.

Nope, she's writing. "I'll let you go, Joyce."

"All right, missy. Give my regards to Nick next time the two of you have at it, huh?"

"Good-bye, Joyce!"

"And have a grand time in Tahoe."

I grimace. "I'll miss you, Joyce."

"Me, too. Bye."

I drop the handset on the mattress and consider the conference slated for the end of August. Up until Puffer backed out, I'd actually looked forward to it. Now . . .

I sigh and check my watch. Ten fifteen. Enough procrastination. Time to pull out the keyboard and give it a good bang. Trying to not think about Noelle's seven-figure phone call, which will surely come today after Farnsworth Publishing and Intrepid shoot it out over me, I lower my feet to the floor and stretch left and right. My short shirt rises above the waist of my drawstring pants, exposing abs neglected since Ludwig began his two-week vacation ten days ago. They'll go to flab again if I don't watch it. Promising myself I'll do a hundred sit-ups later, I spread my ponytail and pull the band tight to my head.

"Ready or not." I trot from my bedroom and am halfway down the stairs when the doorbell rings.

Morticia steps from her office to the landing below. "I'll get it," she calls.

I shrug. Better her than me. One look at her, and whatever unsuspecting salesman has come calling will go running. How on earth did I ever live without her?

As I settle into the chair in front of my computer, I hear a familiar voice.

"Is Ms. Sinclaire in?"

"Sure is, Ms. Parker," Morticia lisps around her tongue bob. "She's in her office."

What's Noelle doing here? Worry wringing my gut, I stare at my hand frozen before the computer's power button. But then I remember the last time she appeared at my townhouse—to deliver the glad tidings that I had made my first appearance on the NYT. Now, surely, it's to deliver news of my first seven-figure deal.

With a gurgle of excitement, I jump out of my chair and bound down the stairs.

As Noelle turns from Morticia, I grin expectantly. "Well?" I halt before her.

With a tolerant smile, she glances at Morticia who's gnawing on her black-painted lips in anticipation of Noelle's news.

Though I don't mind Morticia's presence, it's obvious Noelle wishes to speak with me alone. "Got the mailing list updated?" I ask Morticia.

"Took care of it yesterday."

"Good. Um . . . how about the newsletter?"

"Waiting for your approval, Ms. Sinclaire."

She doesn't get it. "Oookay. How about the—"

"How about you give Ms. Sinclaire and me a few minutes alone," Noelle clips with a saccharine smile.

Morticia startles, and I see hurt flash in her eyes. "Oh, of course." She turns and hurries up the stairs so fast an outraged squeak issues from her holster.

Noelle gapes. "What the *bleep* was that?"

"Doodles, her mouse."

Disbelief contorts her face. "Mouse?"

If I weren't all prickles waiting for her news, I'd prolong her horror. I nod. "She totes him around in her holster."

Noelle closes her lids a long moment, draws a deep breath, then pops her eyes wide. "A mouse in a holster?" she punctuates each syllable. "What holster?"

"The one under her skirt."

Her mouth twists as though she's sucking a lemon. "Why do you put up with her? I'd have fired her little— "

"I like her, *and* she's good at what she does."

Noelle shakes her head. "If you ever hope to fit into New York, you're going to have to learn to deal with people like her."

"I deal with her just fine."

"Not the way I see it."

I smile tightly. "Sorry, but rudeness was not part of my upbringing."

"Well, it was part of mine." With a sniff, Noelle heads toward the kitchen. "Coffee brewing?"

Making faces at her back, I follow. "Nope. How about tea?"

She glances over her shoulder and rolls her eyes.

"Bottled water?" I offer, counseling patience though what I really want is to grab her by the lapels and make her spit out whatever she came to spit out.

"Whatever," she says with a flip of a hand.

As she settles on a bar stool, I open the refrigerator.

From the sigh she heaves as I set a glass of ice and dollar-a-bottle water in front of her, my offering is substandard.

Surprise, surprise.

I lean back against the sink counter and cross my arms over my chest. "Okay. You didn't come across town merely to insult my assistant and drink cheap water. Where do we stand?"

Glug glug glug. She sets the bottle on the counter, lifts the glass, and takes a sip. All the while avoiding my gaze.

Foreboding slithering in, I uncross my arms. "Noelle?"

She grips the glass with both hands and meets my gaze. Her eyes are moist, and I swear I've never seen them like that. "We didn't hit the seven-figure mark, Adda."

My partially digested breakfast bagel tosses about. "Okay," I say in a trembling voice, "but we will, right?"

"Not this go around."

"What do you mean?"

"The bidding's over—was over before it began."

Shaking my head, I step around the counter. "But Farnsworth Pub—"

"Refuses to bid."

"What?"

She gulps another mouthful of water. "Wiped their hands clean of you the moment I told them who they were up against."

With a sickening lurch, the heart goes out of me. Vengeance dies hard, and it seems I'm caught in the middle. I wouldn't be surprised if Nick Farnsworth banked on this happening.

"Okay." I stare into Noelle's misery and realize she wanted this as much as I. Perhaps more. "There are other publishers, right?

Others you can approach?"

"There are, and you're definitely a hot commodity. But . . . " her voice trails, and she shakes her head.

"But? What? What's the problem?"

"They haven't been primed. It's not likely any are prepared to talk seven figures on such short notice."

I frown. "Are we in a hurry?"

She meets my gaze. "We're under deadline, Adda. Nick Farnsworth wants your answer, or he goes elsewhere."

As in Birgitta Roth?

"How long do we have?"

"Monday."

Three days out, and as it's Friday, it might as well be one. I sink to the stool beside Noelle. "What's the plan?"

"We accept Intrepid's offer, which, considering they're not going to bid, is quite generous—and more than Farnsworth Publishing was prepared to offer outside of a bid situation." She names a high six figure that is twice what my last books commanded. Very respectable, utterly enviable, and not too far off the seven-figure mark. Still . . .

Honestly, my disappointment is not rooted in greed. It's more about reaching the next level, ringing the bell, joining a group of elite writers. And once more I have to admit my whole identity is wrapped up in writing—as Puffer has warned me for years. There is no "me" outside of it and no one with whom to share anything on a meaningful level. No husband, no child, not even my mother, who thinks I write trash. As for my father, the thrice-divorced bum became interested in me only after I hit the big time following his fifteen-year absence from my life. Though I was a little slow to catch on, and it cost me $10,000, I finally rid myself of him.

Of course, there's my sister, Molly, but we had a falling out nine years ago, and our relationship has been strained ever since. So strained that I have yet to meet the instant niece and nephew she gave me when she and her husband adopted six months ago following years of infertility. Funny thing that . . . now they're pregnant.

A "God thing," my church-going sister called it during the sixty-second phone "conversation" we had at our mother's insistence. I called the pregnancy coincidence—which offended Molly and instantly returned our disapproving mother to the line. Though I regretted my comment, I had shrugged it off and not let it bother me much. Until now.

Must be all that red ink I've been reading, not the least of which is a passage Josh underlined, highlighted, and starred—Jesus' warning that the evil in a person's heart flows out of their mouth.

Evil . . . was that what made me callously discount Molly's "God thing?" For certain, it hurt her.

The acknowledgment causing me to twinge—apparently one of the side effects of reading the words of Jesus—I find myself wishing I had kept my mouth shut. Instead, I widened the divide between us. And suddenly I realize how much I miss my sister—how much I wish I had patched things up years ago. Now it's probably too late. To my surprise, a tear slips down my cheek and splatters on the counter between me and Noelle.

"Oh, Adda," Noelle moans.

Having forgotten I'm not alone, I look to her and realize she's been watching me.

Eyes bright, she shakes her head, drops an arm around me, and begins to sob in a very un-Noelle-like manner.

She thinks it's the money I'm upset about . . .

"I'm sorry I didn't see it coming," she burbles. "Seven figures . . . seven figures."

It would have been her first as well. Awkwardly, I pat her shoulder. "It's just money."

"Just money!" She pulls back. Her face is mottled though her makeup remains intact.

"Just money," I repeat. "We'll hit the nut next time. It'll give us something to shoot for."

With a scowl, she slides off the stool. "You really belong on a farm, Adda." Jerkily, she straightens her suit coat.

I stand. "A farm?"

"Oh, never mind." She tugs at her lapels and plucks at her pleated pants.

Having never seen her so frazzled, so un-New Yorkish, I step forward and brush her hands aside. "Next time," I assure her as I straighten the collar of her green blouse. "We'll get there next time."

She stares at me, then heaves a sigh. "Yeah." As she turns and starts for the door, I call, "Make Intrepid jump through a few hoops, won't you?"

She halts, and when she looks over her shoulder, there's a glint in her eyes that even Nick Farnsworth would have difficulty staring down. "Oh, you bet I will. Anything in particular you want?"

"Two hundred author copies of each book would be nice, and cover art *approval*." I was given cover consultation with Farnsworth Publishing, meaning I was allowed to offer input. Of course, nothing I suggested was given the slightest consideration.

"Done," she says. "Anything else?"

For the moment that I allow it, Nick Farnsworth rises before me. I shake him off with a jerk of my head. "I leave the rest up to you—whatever you can wrangle out of them."

Noelle is back, as evidenced by the predatorial flare of her nostrils and curl of her upper lip. "I'll send the contract by courier as soon as Nick Farnsworth and I come to terms—probably Monday."

"I'll be waiting." I follow as she steps into the entry hall. "Thanks for delivering the news, Noelle."

She pulls the door open. "Sorry it couldn't be better."

As the door clicks closed, the phone rings. I'm contemplating a hot tea when Morticia appears above.

"Phone call, Ms. Sinclaire—Jake Grainger."

Well, fancy that. After all this time, Louse—formerly known as Gorgeous—is calling. Burn out on the editor, did he? Probably wants to take our one "date" to the next level. And, for a moment, I'm tempted to accept his call, but I know it won't make Nick Farnsworth go away. I am one sick puppy.

"Take a message," I say. "I'm going to the gym."

Morticia bites her lip, and I know she wants to ask about Noelle's news. "But I thought today was a writing day."

"*Was*—" I wrinkle my nose, "—but I think I'll celebrate my switch to Intrepid Books by giving myself a day off."

Her face lights. "Intrepid won the bidding war!"

"Um . . . sort of. I'll explain later." As I start to turn away, her enthusiasm falls flat, and I'm struck by how easily I dismiss her and how much it must hurt. Guilt—red ink-induced, no doubt—washes over me. But rather than puddle at my feet, it sticks, pointing out how much I've hardened since Dick's betrayal and the resulting divorce. Though years past I concerned myself with others' feelings, now I more often brush them aside. For protection, I tell myself, but that doesn't excuse my shrug-and-carry-on behavior and how it affects those around me. And which significantly narrows the gap between Birgitta Roth and me—

I startle at the comparison between myself and that woman. Did I really think that? Did that come from me? Aha! It must be Prim. In fact, I'm certain of it. Though she's usually pretty direct, she seems to have changed her tact. And I wouldn't be surprised if my forays into Josh's favorite New Testament sayings is behind it. Improper is *not* going to be happy, especially with the comparison between Birgitta—

"You all right, Ms. Sinclaire?" Morticia asks.

I am different from Birgitta Roth, I tell myself. I am! Aren't I? Ouch. This soul-searching hurts.

A moment later, a hand touches my shoulder, and I'm surprised to find Morticia standing before me. "All right?" she asks.

As I focus on her face, I start to shrug, but the concern replacing her disappointment stills my shoulders. I'm doing it again — the easy shrug and carry on.

Well, not this time.

"Actually," I hear myself say, "I'm not all right."

Her penciled eyebrows rise. "Anything I can do to help?"

It's not an empty offer. She really means it. And that she should care makes me smile. "Yeah, there is something you can do."

Her face starts to brighten again. "Anything — just name it."

"Have lunch with me — my treat."

It's as if I handed her a double-scoop ice cream. "Really? I'd love to!" Despite her startling makeup and clothes and the numerous earrings marching up her ears, she suddenly looks pretty. "When?"

"Now." To heck with the gym. "We'll walk down to the corner café."

With a squeal of delight, she does an about-face and hurtles down the stairs.

I grab my purse, and she follows me outside into a stifling August day.

Upstairs, Louse is stuck on hold.

EIGHT

ye," he rumbled, his voice causing sensation to spiral through her. "Now breathe."

That's it . . . that's it . . . yes . . .

Click click. Thud.

Elianor did not realize she held her breath, and for several moments questioned whether or not it was true. It was, and when she parted her lips to draw air, his mouth settled on hers—

"The captain has requested that all loose items be stowed in the overheard bins—" a flight attendant chirps over the speakers, "—and all electronic devices be turned off."

Blah blah blah blah blah.

I poke my nose above the screen of my laptop and look left to the blessedly empty seat beside me, and right to the elderly passenger across the aisle. Coast is clear—

She said "stow it," Prim warns.

They don't really expect you to close up shop in the middle of a love scene, Improper argues. *Not now when the words are flowing.*

It's true. Despite our kiss gone awry, I have but to remember

Nick's lips on mine, and suddenly my hero and heroine are off and running. Of course, who's to say how long I'll be able to draw on the memory before I'm once more sucking fumes . . .

I nibble the inside of my cheek and eye the computer screen. Surely no one will notice if I just—

"Excuse me," a chipper voice sounds to the right.

I look up at the flight attendant—Perky, as I dubbed her the moment I boarded. Though I know what she wants, the long day has made me testy. Up at 4:00 a.m. to get to La Guardia to catch my flight at 7:00, followed by a three-hour layover in Dallas, and now a three-and-a-half-hour flight to Reno. Of course it doesn't end there. There's still the drive up to Lake Tahoe. Looong day.

"Yes?" I ask, all innocence.

Perky's smile falters, but she props it up with a flash of teeth. "The captain has requested that all electronic devices be turned off and stowed until we're in the air."

I moisten my lips and, with apology, ask, "Has it ever really been proven that electronic devices interfere with the operation of a plane?"

Façade slipping, Perky leans forward. "It's the law, miss."

In an attempt to get back on her good side—hopefully she has one—I turn my mouth toward her ear and say, "I know, but you see I'm in the middle of a very important scene—"

"You're a writer?" She draws back and meets my gaze.

With a hopeful smile, I say, "Yes."

"Published?"

Can always count on that question. I nod.

"What kind of writer?"

"Romance writer."

She blinks, and the interest which had begun to displace annoyance disappears. "Oh." Her eyebrows arch. "One of *those*."

Meaning she's one of *them*—literary snobs who are too sophisticated for monogamous relationships and happy endings. Telling myself I have no reason to be ashamed, I grit my teeth. "You . . . uh . . . have a problem with romance writers?"

With a tightening of lips, Perky bends nearer and, before I realize what she intends, jabs my laptop's power button. "Not anymore."

I gape as my screen goes black. She didn't do that. Surely I imagined it. But the paragraphs written since my last save have disappeared—vanished into the black hole of "off."

I look up. "You've got to be kidding."

Perky straightens and, with a superior shake of her head, says, "Nope."

"It wasn't saved." My pitch rises, causing others in first class to look around.

She shrugs. "Ill-gotten gains . . . "

In an attempt to dispel Improper's panting in my ear, I give my head a shake. "Look, Perky— "

"Buckle up," she says, and turns to the elderly gentleman across the aisle.

Deep breaths, Prim counsels. *That's it. Calm down. It's only a few paragraphs. And it's not as if you didn't deserve—*

Whaaat? Improper shrills.

I give my head another shake. Sheesh! The more I read the New Testament, the more Prim thrives, especially with these backdoor tactics that not only have me comparing myself to Birgitta Roth but accepting the blame for Perky's ill-mannered behavior. Not that I didn't incite—

Aargh!

"We'll have to stow your case in one of the overhead bins, sir," the flight attendant says, pointing to the elderly man's baggage, which is strapped into the seat beside him.

"Eh?" He lifts his head from a book.

She bends near. "I'm sorry, sir, but we have to— "

"Eh?" He tilts his ear toward her, and I catch sight of a hearing aid.

She puts her hands on her thighs, bends nearer, and repeats herself.

He nods, smiles at her with an appreciative gleam in his eyes, and passes the case to her.

Perky checks his bin. Finding it full of pillows and blankets, she does an about-face. Her eyes flick coolly over me as she pops open the overhead bin. "Buckle up," she percolates again.

Grudgingly, I grope for the seat belt.

As she attempts to lug the case up, I hear someone rise behind me. Likely a misguided knight in shining armor. So where was he when I struggled with *my* carry-on? As he steps alongside, I heave a sigh and bend my head to locate the seat belt.

"Why, thank you, sir." Perky's voice is suddenly husky.

Umm-hmm.

As I secure the belt, the bin clicks closed and the knight murmurs something in a tone that curls my toes. Deep voices are a weakness of mine, as evidenced by Dick. And Nick.

Curious, I look up, but the knight has resumed his seat and once more Perky is smiling falsely bright.

"Tray in the upright position," she says with a pointed look at mine.

"Silly me," I say. As she hovers, no doubt to make certain I follow the rules, I close up the laptop, fit it in its case, and fold the tray away.

"Better?" I look up.

She's smiling—a beautiful smile—but it's not for me. It's for the knight. And no doubt, he's giving it back. She flicks me a dismissive look and flounces toward the cockpit.

I blow a breath up my face, stirring my limp bangs as I drum Raspberry Rose nails on the armrest. True, we'll be airborne soon, and I'll be able to bring out my laptop, but the muse is with me now and I'm itching to get back to Barak and Elianor in their tent in the woods. Of course, first I'll have to recreate what Perky sent hurtling into that gaping black hole.

Fifteen minutes later, I eagerly power up and wait for my desktop to boot. Blue flashes across the screen and the neat rows of icons pop into place. Only to disappear.

Huh? I stare at the blackened screen. Nothing. I pop the power button again, but the laptop remains unblinking.

"Battery," I mutter. Fortunately, I have a backup. Unfortunately, the laptop is just as unresponsive a few minutes later.

"Come on," I say and flip the power button off and on again. Still nothing. Nada. Zero. Zip. Zilch.

Off . . . on. Off . . . on. Off . . . on.

"Oh, poop!" I grumble.

The elderly gentleman snaps his head around and glares at me. Obviously, his hearing aid works just fine and his "Eh? Eh?" was merely a ploy to draw Perky nearer.

I try the power button one last time. No good. Either my computer has died—likely the result of Perky's pecking finger—or Morticia forgot to recharge the spare battery. Hoping it's the latter, I snap the laptop closed, plunk it in its case, and dispense with the tray.

"Now what am I supposed to do?" I mutter. Maybe read?

Thoughts turning to my recent purchase of the Bible, I grimace in remembrance of what should have been a fifteen-minute side trip but turned into a two-hour ordeal. Of course, it didn't help that the bookstore clerk was even more ignorant of Bibles than I. Left to slog it out for myself, I stood dumbfounded before shelves of Bibles in all sizes and colors—not to mention versions. By the way, I now know what NIV stands for, and all I can say is thank goodness Josh's friend chose that version for him. Don't think I would have made it past the first sentence if I'd had to plod through "thee" after "thou" after "thy" of another version.

So now I have access to both the Old and New Testaments. Unfortunately, because of the certainty I would be writing during the flight, I packed the Bible and Josh's New Testament in my luggage.

I heave a sigh and singsong, "What to do?"

A few moments later, something brushes my shoulder and a woman says, "Try this."

Frowning, I look around and there, in the crack between the seats, protrudes a notepad and pen.

Oh. She must have heard my muttering and, helpful darling that she is, wants to solve my problem.

She wiggles her offering, and I dutifully pull it through. Not that it will be of use, as I do my composing on the computer. Still, I should thank her—plus, it will be an excuse to take a look at the foolhardy knight.

I release the catch on my seatbelt, turn, and lever up to peer over the seat back. "Thank you," I say, only to feel my eyes bulge as Sophia Farnsworth comes to focus.

"You're welcome," she says.

Gulp! Where did Snow White come from? How—?

She must have boarded late in Dallas when I had my head buried in my laptop. Of course, if *she's* on the plane . . .

I slide my gaze left, and there sits Perky's knight—Nick Farnsworth in the flesh.

If I weren't so mortified, I'd be tingling. He's been behind me all this time—sitting in on my exchange with the flight attendant and listening in on my battery dilemma and subsequent muttering.

What did I say? Something embarrassing? Oh . . . yeah. Among other things, "poop."

"Hello, Adda," he says, chocolates gazing at me through his glasses. From the slight curve of his mouth, I wonder if he's remembering the kiss I'm remembering. Or perhaps he's simply amused.

I force a smile. "Hello, Nick. I . . . didn't see you there."

"Hmm," he murmurs deep, and I silently kick myself for not recognizing it was he who aided Perky—or at least not considering the voice belonged to him. After all, he's slated to introduce Intrepid's new line at the conference.

As a dry-mouthed silence gathers between us, I glance at the papers on his tray. "I see you brought your work with you."

"As did you." He cocks an eyebrow. "Computer problem?"

"Battery—I hope." I look to Snow White and find her looking from her father to me—watching us as though she might otherwise miss something.

She smiles at me. "Think pen and paper will do?"

I haven't the heart to tell her they won't. "Um . . . yes. Ideal replacements. Don't know why I didn't consider it myself."

"Great!"

"Well—" I glance at Nick and find he's returned to his papers, "—I'd better get to it." I lift the pen and pad. "Thanks again, Sophia."

As I start to lower to my seat, she says, "Thank *you*."

I pause. "Hmm?"

"For signing my books."

"Oh. It was nothing." Unless, of course, one counts what followed behind Nick's desk. And I certainly do. Does Nick?

I look to him. He's watching me again, and something in those chocolates tells me he's remembering what he vowed wouldn't happen again. And it makes me warm all over.

I give a tight smile and lower to my seat.

During the next five minutes, Perky passes through first class taking and delivering drink orders. I ask for a bottled water, and with barely a flicker of acknowledgment, she scoots past.

"What can I get you, Mr. Farnsworth?" she asks, obviously having checked the passenger roster in the almighty quest for a man.

"Club soda with lime," he says.

And call me Nick, I mouth.

But he doesn't offer.

I smile. *Hah!*

Nick's daughter orders a bottled water, and Perky moves on.

"May I join you?"

I look up, and there stands Nick, long legs encased in denim, the sleeves of his white shirt rolled up to reveal muscled arms.

I jerk up from my relaxed slouch. "Of course." I lift my computer case from beside me and shove it under the seat. "There you are."

He looks at the vacated seat, raises his eyebrows.

"Oh . . . right," I mutter. Though it's roomier in first class, it would still be a squeeze for him to get past me. Not that I wouldn't mind the squeeze . . .

I slip over, and he settles in my warmed seat.

"I have something to show you," he says, unfolding the tray and opening a folder on it.

Then this isn't a social call. Shoot!

"Mock-ups." He hands me an art board.

Though our fingers don't contact, a thrill goes through me at the near touch. I lower my gaze to the art board and realize *this* is the cover art approval Noelle negotiated—though only for the women's edition of the book. I stare at the sketch of a medieval man and woman in the foreground. Whew! Not a bodice ripper, not even a clinch. Though the heroine stands near the hero, the hero keeps his hands to himself as the two gaze into the distance—their future. An imposing castle is the backdrop. Very nice, as is "Adda Sinclaire" at the top in large letters. The title—*Feud: The Abduction*—lies beneath in smaller letters. I smile. An author has made it big when her name takes precedence over the title.

"I like it," I say, lifting my gaze to Nick's. My, he's good looking! In fact, he gets better looking each time I see him. "It's very . . . " I swallow, smile, " . . . romantic."

His eyes lower to my mouth, and I groan inwardly at not having reapplied lipstick. "I'm glad you approve." He looks back at the folder.

Is that all there is to cover art approval?

He hands me another art board.

The first thing I notice is my name. "Adda Sinclaire" has been reduced to "A. Sinclaire" and is in smaller print *beneath* the title. Though I twinge on that, it makes sense—at least, the "A." part. This, obviously, is the men's edition.

"We decided the titles for both editions should remain the same to prevent reader confusion," Nick says, and it strikes me how often he says "we" where others say "I" to the exclusion of others who might be owed credit.

"A good decision," I say, and frown over the artwork. It's simple, verging on dull. Three shields are lined up vertically, each denoting one of the three families involved in the feud. A sword intersects two of the shields, and I realize it represents the joining of those two families through marriage in the first book. No, not dull. Deep.

"Clever," I murmur.

"Then you also approve?"

Nick is leaning in, and when I look up, he's so near everything else dissolves. Feeling myself slipping into him, I return my attention to the art board. "So," I say, slightly winded, "I have approval on this one as well?"

"No. *I* do, but I am interested in your input."

I keep my gaze lowered, as it's the only way I can think halfway clear with him so near. "I appreciate that." I touch the sword hilt and trail a finger down its length. "As I said, it's clever."

And men do love swords. I tap the art board. "Embossed?"

"That's the plan."

"And a good one." Wincing at my doofus response, I hand him the art boards.

As he returns them to the folder, Perky reappears.

From her pursed lips, it's obvious she's put out at finding us together. "Your club soda and lime, Mr. Farnsworth." She sets the glass in the depression of his tray.

He looks up. "Thank you."

She smiles at him, though with less enthusiasm than earlier. When she turns her attention to me, her mouth goes flat. "Your water." She passes me a perspiring bottled water and a glass of ice.

"Thank you," I say, adding beneath my breath, "Perky."

As she sashays away, Nick looks around. "Perky?"

I shrug. "It fit when I first boarded." I clamp the bottled water and glass between my thighs and reach for my tray. "I did, however, hit the mark with the ticketing agent." Remembering the twin gobs of flesh that skimmed the man's collar, I grin. "Jowls."

"Ah." Nick reaches past me to assist. "I know exactly the one." As we lower the tray, he asks, "Do you make a habit of giving people nicknames?"

I place my glass in the depression. "Actually, I don't give it much thought. It just . . . comes to me."

He lifts his club soda. "Tell me some others."

Surprised by his interest, I tilt my head. "Okay. There's my mentor and critique partner, Joyce Kuchner. She's Puffer—and very dear to me."

"I know of Kuchner—met her quite a few years back."

Remembering Puffer's accounting of that meeting, I smile. "She's a talented writer."

"Give me another."

"My personal assistant, Angel, is Morticia." I wave a dismissing hand as he starts to frown. "Don't ask. Then there's my editor—Little Miss Tight Lips—"

"Kathryn."

Oops, forgot they knew each other. "You don't think it fits?" I say with apology.

He takes a drink of club soda. "Actually, it does fit." He stares at me over the rim of his glass. "What of Birgitta Roth?"

My smile jerks at *that* woman's name on his lips.

"Surely she hasn't escaped your private amusement," he presses.

I start to stretch my smile again, but his words sink deeper. "Private amusement." It sounds . . . mean. Catty. Un-Bible-like—if that's even a word. Too late wishing I hadn't given Nick Farnsworth a guided tour of my head, I grudgingly reply, "She would be . . . uh . . . Stick Woman."

He considers me, then inclines his head. "So everyone's fair game?"

Ugh. Makes it sound like an assault. But then, in a way it is, even if only for my "private amusement." And there's that guilt again, courtesy of my interest in Jesus' life and teachings. I smile sheepishly. "I suppose." Now for a change of topic—

"What name have you given me?" he asks.

I blink. "You?" And in that instant, I realize I haven't dubbed him. Of course, I *have* dubbed his eyes—chocolates—but he doesn't need to know that. "You . . . " I shake my head. "You're just Nick." A name that fits quite well.

He lowers his glass. "Really? Just 'Nick'?"

Where is he going with this? And how do I get him off the topic? "Just Nick," I say again.

"Should I consider that an honor?"

An honor? It's then I realize that my nicknames are derogatory—at least, the ones I related to him. Is it too late to tell him I dubbed his daughter "Snow White"? Or that Jake Grainger is better known as "Gorgeous"—

Uh, not a good example. And mustn't forget Jake is now "Louse." Of course, there's my friendly mail lady, better known as—

"Should I?" Nick asks.

Should he . . . ? Oh. Hating what he must think of me and promising myself to take a long, hard look at my "private amusements," I shrug. "I don't know. *Do* you consider it an honor?"

He holds my gaze a long moment, then tips a smile. "I suppose we'll have to wait and see."

And what's that supposed to mean? What it sounds like? A fluttering in my chest, I unstick my tongue from the roof of my suddenly dry mouth and avert my gaze. Catching sight of the bottled water between my thighs, I pull it free. And freeze. The thighs of my light blue capris are damp, the darkness spreading outwards as though—

It looks as if I've wet myself! I jerk my gaze to the bottled water. Bad enough it was perspiring when Perky handed it to me, but it's also developed a leak. By design?

I look up and catch Nick looking down. "Leaky bottle," I squeak, and grab my wisp of a napkin. Hoping to avert his attention as I blot at the moisture, I ask, "So, did you sign the other three authors you wanted?"

He hands me his napkin. "I did—Jeanne Matriarch, Shannon Sweet, and Mona Wales."

Forgetting my damp capris, I look up. "Oh? No Birgitta Roth?"

He removes his glasses and slides them into his shirt pocket. "Not for the new line."

Relief sweeps me, only to return on the wave of what he leaves unspoken. Hoping against hope, I say, "Not for the new line. Another, then?"

"As a matter of fact, yes. We've signed her for Intrepid's historical romance line—two Westerns."

Feeling my lips tighten, I look to the bottled water, uncap it, and pour the water over ice as I draw a deep breath.

Hold it in, Adda, I counsel as I set the bottle aside. *You have the coveted position. Smile.* But I can't. It's bad enough being in the same line of work as the woman who stole my husband, but to share the same publisher? To see promotions for her books plastered in the backs of mine—and vice versa? To attend the same author–publisher functions? To be thrown in her path more than I am already?

"I think we can grow Ms. Roth," Nick continues. "Tap her strengths and broaden her range."

Get a grip. I press my nails into my palms in an attempt to distract my heaving emotions. *Even if he knew every sordid detail of what happened between you and Dick and Birgitta, he couldn't possibly understand the scars.* Sure, Jesus says, "forgive" and "love one another," and it sounds wonderful, but how does one apply it to real life? Real betrayal? Real hurt? Real anger? How does one peel away the scars and leave no trace of the hurt? How does one trust again?

"From your silence," Nick says, "I assume you don't approve."

Realizing the reflection on New Testament readings has eased my roiling somewhat, I blink at him. "Hmm?"

"You don't approve."

Ah, Stick Woman—er, Birgitta Roth. With an attempt at levity, I say, "I guess that all depends on whether we're talking cover art or Ms. Roth."

He arches an eyebrow.

I force a laugh. "Don't worry, if she gives me reason to relieve her of another skein of hair, I'll be careful to do it in such a way Intrepid won't be scandalized by feuding authors."

Though he smiles wryly, his voice is all seriousness when he says, "Give me your word on that?"

He doesn't trust me. But then, with my "private amusements" and inability to hide my dislike of Birgitta Roth, I haven't exactly made a good impression, have I? Yes, I want to be a better human being. Yes, I'm exploring the New Testament, but given enough provocation, would I really be able to "turn the other cheek"? Simply walk away? I don't think I'm there yet—certainly not near enough to risk being made a liar.

With regret, I meet Nick's gaze. "I give my word that I will do my best to avoid any behavior that might reflect poorly on Intrepid."

To my relief, his chocolates don't give rise to censure. Rather, he says, "Then your best will have to do."

And I'm unsettled in a way I don't understand. As I stare into his eyes, the silence stretches . . . and stretches.

Then, abruptly, Nick rises. "I'll let you get back to your writing."

My . . . ? Oh. Forgot about that. Feeling as if I've been caught playing hooky, I retrieve the pad and pen his daughter loaned me. "Yes, lots to do," I say. Then, fixing a look of concentration on my face, I open the pad and bend my head to it. "See you at the conference."

A few moments later, I hear Nick lower to his seat behind me. Shortly thereafter, Perky is on him like a fly on—

Well, you know.

I sigh. So what to do with the hours that stretch before

me? I fan the pages of the notepad. Drum my fingers on it. With the capped pen, tap out a tune which earns me a glower from the elderly gent. Doodle a border of vining flowers. Consider folding a paper airplane. Stiffen when a certain flight attendant sashays by with an over-the-shoulder, eyelash-batting glance at Nick.

Tempted as I am to let my resentment of Perky dig deeper, I determinedly turn my energies to the long, hard look I promised to take at my nicknaming habit. Considering the alternative—exploring the thousand and one things one can do with a notepad—now seems as good a time as any. So let's have a look-see. I uncap the pen and jot down *Perky.*

Louse

Stick Woman

Little Miss Tight Lips

Morticia

Puffer

I lower the pen and stare at the list of names, which is hardly exhaustive. "Private amusements," Nick called them, and he's right. Though I haven't come across anything in the New Testament that specifically forbids such, it's there "between the lines," isn't it? True, Little Miss Tight Lips, Morticia, and Puffer are more forms of endearment, but they're not without sarcasm. As for Louse, Stick Woman, and a half dozen others that come to mind, the names are hardly kind. And the acknowledgment makes me feel like a heel.

That's it! I'm giving them up. Washing my hands—and mind—of them. Justified or not, they're out of here! Don't know if I'll ever advance to the "love one another" part Jesus went on and on about, but it's a start. Yep, no more private amusements.

With a flourish, I rip the paper from the notebook and crumple it. Voila!

"Not going well?" a dulcet voice asks.

Having forgotten about my neighbors, I startle. "Uh . . . " I rise just enough to meet Snow White's gaze over the back of the seat. "Just a bit of writer's block."

Ugh.

Did I really say that?

"Sorry if I disturbed you."

She smiles sweetly. "Not at all."

Before sliding back down in my seat, I steal a glance at Nick and find him looking at me over the rims of his glasses. And those chocolates of his go right through me.

Stomach aflutter, I settle in my seat and look to the paper balled in my fist. No more private amusements, I remind myself in an attempt to avert my thoughts from the man at my back. No more Stick Woman, Louse, Stick Woman, Perky, Stick Woman, Puffer, Stick Woman, Little Miss Tight Lips, Stick Woman, Morticia, Stick Woman, Snow White—

I frown. Surely Snow White can stay. After all, there's nothing derogatory about it. Nor "chocolates." Not even a hint of sarcasm. I nod. Snow White stays. As does chocolates. Definitely *chocolates.*

● ● ●

Could be worse, I tell myself as I look to Stick . . . uh . . . Birgitta Roth who plunks down right beside Nick. Worse in that she could have plunked down beside me.

Snow White, sitting on the other side of her father, peers around him and frowns. Obviously, she's just as put out that Birgitta and her pal, Regency writer Denise Pinch—previously known as Prune for her perpetual scowl—invited themselves to ride up to Lake Tahoe with us. Not that I had any intention of joining Nick and his daughter, but the alternative was unappealing. One of the buses chartered to pick up the conference attendees from the airport had broken down, resulting in a minimum two-hour delay. Though it's only two in the afternoon, it's five o'clock in New York. That, combined with tedious travel makes for a weary day, and I can't wait to collapse on a bed.

Fortunately, a limo was waiting for Nick. When Snow White invited me along, I jumped at the chance to join them. Now I almost wish I could jump out. And I just might if Denise doesn't blow her garlic breath elsewhere. I scoot a few inches to the left as the driver closes the door.

"Lovely to see you, again, Adda," Birgitta lilts.

Will this day never end? "And you, Birgitta." I show some teeth, falling just shy of baring them.

She leans forward. "Word is that your bosom buddy, Joyce Kuchner, won't be attending the conference this year."

Feeling my teeth begin to bare, I press my lips inward and nod.

"Tsk. Tsk. Tsk," Stick Woman—oops—shakes her head as the limousine pulls into traffic. "Very hard on you, I'm sure."

She's pushing it, and with each push the scandalous scene between us in the hotel lobby becomes less of a deterrent. I heave a dramatic sigh. "I imagine I'll find a way to survive—always do." I flick my gaze to her forehead that shines from behind wispy, dyed blonde hair.

And I just can't help myself. "So tell me, Birgitta, who does your hair these days?"

Her eyes widen and her plastic smile takes a nosedive.

Score! Feeling Nick and Snow White's gaze, I look elsewhere—unfortunately, that happens to be Denise.

With pursed mouth, the woman's eyes flick between me and her sidekick. "Heard you left Farnsworth Publishing," she finally says.

"Word gets around, doesn't it?" I say.

She chuckles—a real strain for her. And one that blasts me with garlic. "Sure does, especially the juicy stuff." She winks at Birgitta, and I'm reminded of the "juicy stuff" that went around when Dick moved in with her pal.

"Decided to go over to Intrepid with Birgitta, did you?" Denise nods at Nick.

There's no "with" about it, but I grind my teeth and murmur, "I've signed with Intrepid."

Denise harrumphs. "Nice work if you can get it."

Snow White catches my eye and gives me a sympathetic smile.

Time to turn the topic. "So, Sophia," I say, "your father tells me you're off to college this fall. Starts soon, doesn't it?"

Birgitta seizes up, obviously shocked to learn I'm privy to Nick's personal life. Of course, I wasn't angling at that. Some gems just fall right in one's lap.

"Actually, I've decided to postpone college a semester," Snow White says.

I frown. "Really?"

"Yeah." She beams. "I've been doing a lot of praying—"

Praying?

"—and have decided to go on mission instead."

"Mission?"

She bobs her head with such enthusiasm I'm reminded of one of those cute little dashboard pups. "With my church. A group of us college-bound teens have decided to put higher education on hold a semester and go to Ecuador to help build churches."

Oh. Wow. Then—

"Ooh!" Birgitta coos. "I didn't know you were spiritual, Nick."

I glance at him and, from the wry tug of his mouth, guess she missed the mark. More than willing to allow her to be the one to stumble over herself, I clamp my mouth shut.

"Sophia and I are Christians," he says.

Something at my center leaps. He's a Christian, meaning he owns a Bible—like me. However, unlike me, he's probably read it cover to cover and understands every word of it—

That doesn't mean he lives it, Improper attempts to deflate me. *Forgiveness, even when you're the one who hasn't wronged—Hah! Love one another, even when the "other" doesn't deserve it—yeah, right*!

But if it *were* possible, imagine life without all this pent-up hurt and anger. . . .

Coming out of my musing, I realize the limo is strangely silent, as though Nick Farnsworth's revelation was actually some deep, dark confession. Considering the company we're in, it might be. I glance at Birgitta and almost laugh at the stiff smile she's trying to fit to her lips, then Denise who's simply staring at Nick.

However, in the next instant, she laughs. "Imagine that—a New York City Christian." She shakes her head. "A bit of an oxymoron, if you ask me."

Nice one, Pru—er, Denise. Maybe you should have swallowed that one. However, as much as I dislike the woman, I can't help but feel a bit sorry for her. I look to Nick for his reaction and am surprised to find his wry smile has turned to one of amusement.

Snow White sits forward. "Not at all," she says without offense. "There are a lot of Christians in the city." She sweeps her gaze to me, lifts her eyebrows. "Of course, it's our own fault that we're not more visible."

What? Does she think *I'm* a Christian? Are those raised eyebrows my cue to 'fess up? I almost wish I could, but it would be a lie, and so I smile. "Um . . . so when do you leave for this mission thing of yours?"

Mission thing! Ugh. If that doesn't clue her in, nothing will.

She returns the smile and leans back. "Next weekend."

"Excited?" I ask, afraid she might give me the eyebrows again.

She gathers a deep breath, nods. "And a little scared."

Nick covers her hand with his. "It will be a wonderful experience, Soph."

Soph. Aww, isn't that sweet . . .

He smiles. "A new chapter, hmm?"

His gentle reassurance touches me, and it's all I can do to not puddle on the spot. She doesn't know how fortunate she is to have a dad who loves her.

"And a new chapter for you," she says, wrinkling her nose at him. When she returns her gaze to me, there's a gleam in her eyes. "First time in eighteen years Dad will be alone."

I blink. Surely she's not giving me the go ahead? Especially as I missed my "fellow Christian" cue—by a long way. Or maybe she knows something I don't. Maybe Nick *is* interested in me . . . Perhaps he's confided his attraction for me . . . But then, what about what happened in his office?

It hits me then. Maybe he actually lives a Christian life. Heck, even I know the Bible's take on fornication—as in THOU SHALT NOT! At least, not without a wedding band firmly in place.

Down, Adda, down! Prim returns, riding the exclamation mark. *Nick Farnsworth is off-limits. You do NOT want to go there again. I repeat—*

Says who? Improper gives a dissenting snort.

Says Adda Sinclaire, as you well know. You were there the day she signed the divorce papers. Remember? YOU advised her against selling her wedding ring to benefit charity.

And she took my advice, just as she's going to do now.

I wince in remembrance of my wedding band, the sale of which wouldn't have contributed much to charity—or so I convinced myself to justify the juvenile behavior for which I opted in the end. Amazing how many flushes it took for that skimpy little piece of gold to finally disappear from the bottom of the toilet bowl. And every day that it lingered only made the pain of Dick's infidelity worse.

Feeling the ache begin to rise—a terrible reminder of what could happen if I get into a relationship again—I concur with Prim. Nick Farnsworth is off-limits. Besides, as much as my ego would like to use his Christianity as an excuse for him putting on the brakes in his office, everyone knows Christian men sin just like any other. Thus, I'm more likely to blame for his rejection than religion. He simply didn't want to pursue a relationship beyond that of publisher–author.

Finally getting that smile of hers in place—albeit a bit crooked—Birgitta leans forward and, in reaching past Nick, brushes against him. She pats Snow White's knee. "Now don't you worry about your father, dear. Men are resilient, and I'm certain Nicky—"

Nicky?

"—will have plenty to keep his mind off your absence."

In her dreams!

Snow White looks down at the claws covering her knee, then to her father. They exchange a look.

"Thank you, Ms. Roth," Nick says.

With a barely perceptible startle—surprise at the use of her last name?—Birgitta pulls back.

"Nicky" indeed! I settle back in my seat.

"Anyone attending the cocktail party this evening?" Denise asks. Unfortunately, she turns her head toward me, along with her breath.

Eyes burning, I say, "Only if I can pry myself out of bed."

"And that, of course—" another blast of garlic, "—depends on who's sharing it with you." She jabs me with an elbow and winks. "Heard you and that model—what's his name? Oh, Jake Grainger. Yes, heard the two of you are quite the item."

Oh . . . my . . . I look up to find Nick staring at me, a muscle convulsing in his jaw and something—disappointment?—in his eyes.

"I suppose the two of you will be rooming together?"

And I was actually feeling sorry for Prune—*that* slip was intentional.

I look right. Snow White's eyes are wide with surprise and . . . hurt?

"Quite a few years younger than you, isn't he?"

I look left. Birgitta is smiling like the Cheshire cat.

Pull yourself together, Adda, I tell myself. *Nothing happened between you and Jake. A kiss, that's all. You have absolutely nothing to feel guilty about.* I force a smile, look around. "I'm afraid you heard wrong." Refusing further explanation, I slide a hand in my purse and pull out my trusty metal tin. "Altoid, Pr—er, Denise?" I flip the lid back.

She eyes the dusty mints, makes a face. "No, thanks—never touch the stuff."

Now why doesn't that surprise me? I look to Snow White, Nick, and Birgitta. "Any takers?"

Nick's daughter searches my face as though to ascertain the truth of my disclaimer about Jake, leans forward, and picks one of the "Curiously Strong" mints from the tin. Neither Nick nor Birgitta takes me up on the offer.

I pop one in my mouth, snap the lid closed, and sink back in the seat.

Well, isn't this cozy? Must be how a fly feels in a spider's web. Wishing the blasted computer worked so I could duck behind it, I close my eyes.

Crunch! And that's about how long mints last before I chew them down.

It doesn't take long for Birgitta and Denise to strike up a boastful conversation for the benefit of Nick. They drone on and on about awards, print runs, sell-throughs, and fan mail—pumping up their accomplishments for all they're worth. And I'm almost embarrassed for them.

Throughout the ride up the mountain, I stay behind my lids, struggling to keep my face impassive when threatened by a scowl, a smile, a roll of eyes — or a gag when Denise's breath pumps my way.

But then Snow White exclaims, "Look, Dad, there's the lake."

I open my eyes. Having only seen Lake Tahoe on posters and postcards, I'm unprepared for the breathtaking scene.

"Wow," I breathe.

Suddenly, the view is snatched away by a curve in the road. Forgetting whose presence I'm in, I scoot nearer the window in anticipation of my next sighting. I'm not disappointed. "Look at that!" I exclaim, nearly bouncing in my seat. "Look how blue the water is! And the mountains! The big ones still have snow at the tippity top! Have you ever seen anything like it?" Mouth stretched as wide as it's ever stretched, I look around at the others.

"A dozen times," Birgitta drawls with a roll of her eyes.

Oh . . . right . . . forgot about her and Denise. I plop back to earth — a globby mass of juvenile silliness.

Nick's gaze flicks from his daughter to me, but the condescending amusement I expect to see is absent. There's something else, and though I can't name it, I have the peculiar feeling he in no way disapproves of my enthusiasm. So there!

Denise pokes me in the arm, and I feel a terrible sense of loss as I look from Nick to her.

"My, Adda," she says with airs that fall far short of her breath, "one would think you've never seen a lake."

I bristle. "Not like this one."

"You really must get out more often, Adda, dear," says *Stick Woman*. Habits are *so* hard to break.

I sigh. Though her words are barbed, they're true. I *should* get out more. Just as I have no one with whom to share my life, I have few experiences to draw upon. True, all my books are set in England, Scotland, Wales, and France, but everything I know about those countries I gleaned from books and travel videos. Adda the Hermit. Adda the Recluse. Adda the Loner.

"It is beautiful," Nick says, his deep voice filling the limo. "Every time I see it, it's like the first time."

I jerk my head around, but his gaze is fixed on the scenery.

"I quite agree," Birgitta pipes up. "Nothing like it in the world!"

Going through the mental motions of sticking a finger down my throat, I wonder what Dick saw in her that wasn't in me. I roll my eyes, but when I come back around, it's to find Nick looking at me—smiling that half-smile of his. Then he winks.

Goo alert! Goo alert! And there's only one thing for it if I'm to avoid making a further fool of myself. I close my eyes again and feign a snooze.

By the time the limo pulls up in front of our hotel, I'm fairly recovered from my near swoon. With a pat to my hair and a tug to my top, I plop my sunglasses on and duck to emerge from the limo behind Snow White.

Nick, having climbed out before the driver made it around, releases his daughter and hands me out after her. It's a mistake. I know it the moment his warm fingers curl around mine. Still, I thrill to the pricks of awareness that rise across my body.

"Have a nice nap?" he murmurs as I step to the concrete.

I meet his gaze through the dark tint of my sunglasses and remember the last time I looked at him from behind shades—at the restaurant shortly after retching across the table. "I wasn't napping," I murmur back.

His mouth tilts. "I know."

Then he can see through eyelids as well . . .

"Equal attention, here!" Stick Woman calls from behind.

"Yeah," Prune echoes.

Wondering if there's a twelve-step recovery program for name-aholics—this self-imposed reform is harder than expected!—I allow Nick to pass me in the direction of Snow White who has stepped from beneath the valet canopy to peer up at the soaring hotel–casino.

I flick my gaze over a dozen guests who appear to have arrived just ahead of us: romance writers, several of whom I recognize. We exchange nods as I cross to Snow White. "Impressive, hmm?" I say, halting alongside her.

She lowers her chin, and a smile drapes her mouth. "We grow them bigger in New York."

I chuckle. "We do, don't we?"

"Watch the tapestry!" Stick—aargh!—Birgitta's voice grates on the air. "Watch it!"

I look around. She and Denise are hovering over the poor

driver as he extricates what appears to be a two-week supply of luggage for a four-day conference.

Sheesh! If there's one thing I can't stand, it's luggage-totin' mommas.

Me? Years ago I discovered the power of UPS. No mad rush to the baggage carousel to wait eons for one's cache to show. No pushing, no shoving, no lost luggage. Mine goes straight to the hotel. And just in case something goes wrong in shipping, my wheeled carry-on covers me for the first day or so. It's all rather ingenious, if I say so myself. And I don't share that with just anyone. Let Birgitta and Denise duke it out with their luggage!

Snow White and I return to the limo where Nick is passing several bills to the bellhop who has loaded our luggage onto an opulent brass cart.

I remove my carry-on and pull the handle up. "I can take it up myself," I say.

"Is *that* all you brought?" Birgitta asks.

All innocence, I look down. "This? Uh-huh." I smile, flutter my lashes, try to ignore the twinge to my conscience. "How much did you bring?"

Her lids narrow and right eye begins to tic.

Yes, folks, she weaves, she feints, she completes the pass! Score one for the lovely Ms. Adda Sinclaire!

Nick catches my eye, and I beam at his disbelief.

When we walk into the lobby a short while later, I'm still congratulating myself on the fine shade of red that does absolutely nothing for Birgitta's complexion. Thus, I don't see *him* coming until he's almost on top of me.

"Adda!" Jack Grainger flashes his cover-perfect teeth.

Oh . . . my . . .

His arms enfold me. Right before he swoops down and plants a kiss on my mouth, I catch sight of Nick and Sophia where they've halted ahead.

"Heard wrong, did we?" a gloating voice says as Louse draws back.

Score one for Stick Woman.

NINE

Buck up, Adda.

I'm trying. I'm trying. Standing before the full-length mirror in my suite on the twelfth floor, I run my hands down the silk skirt of my calf-length evening dress. It feels good, fits good, and looks good. But I feel like . . . doo-doo.

Though I hadn't looked at Nick and his daughter again after the shattering appearance of Jake (note: have made a fresh start in eliminating "private amusements"), I felt them watching me. While standing at the registration desk, Jake hanging at my elbow and murmuring gibberish that might be interpreted however anyone wished it to be, I'd felt them at the next counter. Riding up in the elevator, I felt them at my back and was grateful I'd not only managed to shake Jake in the lobby, but that Stic—er, you know who—and her pal were waylaid by a glitch in their reservation. Even when I'd stepped from the elevator and the doors closed behind me, I felt Nick and his daughter continuing up to their floor, and was sure they were saying nasty things about me.

They surely believed they had caught me in a lie, and I couldn't blame them. It *had* looked as if Jake and I were an item, and from his behavior, it was obvious we were on friendly terms. How I'd longed to shout, "It was just dinner and a kiss!" but I wouldn't be believed and would only make a fool of myself. Besides, it's not as if anything is at stake here, is it?

I push a stray tendril back into my upswept hair.

Forget that Sophia Farnsworth was sending out matchmaking signals. Forget that Nick is at least somewhat attracted to me. Forget the kiss in his office. Forget it all! Nick Farnsworth is off limits. He doesn't want a relationship, and *I* certainly don't want one. Right?

Right.

Er . . . right!

I hold up my hands, give a nod to Burnin' Love nail polish, then grab my little black purse and slip the strap over my shoulder. Westward ho!

As I pass through the sitting room, the pantyhose I tossed off earlier catch my eye where they hang from a chair-side lamp like a scene from a bad flick. Worse, the darker nylon of the built-in panties loudly proclaims them to be of the tummy-control variety. I nearly do a U-turn but shrug off the impulse to put them away. After all, it's not as if I'll be bringing anyone back to my room later this evening.

I cross to the door where the open UPS box that contains my luggage blocks my exit. I push it to the side and, in doing so, dent the polish of my pinkie.

"Oh, *maaan*!" I consider repairing it but somehow beat the

urge and pull open the door.

The ballroom is humming like a hive when I enter five minutes later. Hoping—praying—I won't run into Jake . . . or Nick . . . or Sophia, I head for the bar. I'm halfway across the room when a murmur rises from a group of women.

"That's Adda Sinclaire."

"Is it really?"

"*New York Times* Best Seller."

I smile. As few published writers would allow themselves to be overheard ogling, my guess is that they're a group of unpubs—as in unpublished writers.

"Have you read her latest?"

"Ooh, it's wonderful!"

My shoulders ride higher, and I'm infused with an air of confidence.

"Wonderful?" another scoffs. "I couldn't get past the first chapter."

Whoosh. The air goes right out of me.

"Really, Shelly? I loved it."

Bless you, my child.

"So did I."

With a snort of disgust, Smell—Hah! Caught myself before a new nickname could fully form—*Shelly* says, "Are we talking about the same book here?"

Thankfully, I quickly move out of earshot. Nodding and smiling at writing acquaintances, I near the bar.

"Adda!"

A hand touches my shoulder, and I look around.

A short, slender woman peers up at me. Do I know her? She seems familiar. Fortunately, she's wearing a name badge: Elizabeth Carp, Heart Core Publishers.

I smile inwardly. She's either newly published, or clinging to her mid-list status, as the ones who wear badges to an evening function are either unpublished, recently published proclaiming their new status, or die-hard mid-listers who lack confidence. Those who don't wear them are confident mid-listers, or best sellers who, by nature, are easily recognized by their fellow writers. Of course, some are just plain forgetful. I didn't say it was an exact science. . . .

"You probably don't recognize me," the woman says. "Elizabeth Carp, Manhattan Women's Fiction Writers."

Oh. Oh!

"I know," she says. "It's me under all those pounds—lost forty-five so far."

"You look great!" I remember her now—the treasurer of our local chapter. As I haven't attended for the past eight months, I had no idea she had gone on a diet.

"I appreciate that," she says. "Amazing what a first sale can do for one's self-control and confidence."

It is amazing, though not unusual. An unpublished writer makes a sale, and suddenly it's makeover time. Of course, publicity photos are a big motivation. "Congratulations on your sale," I say.

"Thanks." She reaches up and absently tugs on a pendant

suspended from a silver chain.

I glance at it. Glance again. It's a cross. Meaning she's a Christian? Of course, I've seen Morti—Angel wear crosses, and I doubt she's even heard of the Bible.

"Haven't seen you at the meetings in a while," Elizabeth says.

I blink myself back to her, grimace. "Deadlines." It's the standard excuse, but painfully true. More true, however, is the possibility Birgitta might put in an appearance at one of the meetings. I shrug. "They're real killjoys."

Elizabeth laughs, and I'm struck by how pretty she is. "Well, I finally understand the meaning of deadlines myself." She taps her name badge. "Signed a two-book contract with Heart Core two months back."

I smile. "Congratulations—and welcome to the world of publishing."

"Thank you."

"Who's your editor?"

"Genie Paola."

Ugh, that stuck-up—

"She's wonderful," Elizabeth says.

"Hmm." I decide not to burst her bubble—allow her to enjoy the fantasy for as long as it lasts, which won't be long if Meanie Genie's reputation is anything to go by. And for the record, *I'm* not the one who gave her the nickname.

"I'm happy for you," I say.

She takes a sip of what appears to be Coke. "I've decided to quit my job so I can write full time."

Uh oh. The romance writer's maxim is: Don't quit your day job. And for very good reason. First-time authors command very little advance and don't see royalties for at least a year, and when royalties finally kick in, it's usually at a dribble. Then, of course, who's to say if the publisher will offer another contract? Though I should probably just smile and congratulate her again, I can't. "Are you sure about that?" I ask. "I mean, it's a pretty big risk."

"Positive," she says with a confidence I hope doesn't betray her.

"Remember the workshop I gave the group a few years back about the stages of a writer's life?"

"I know, I know." She waves a hand. "But I'm going to beat those odds."

And how does one argue that without sounding the doomsayer? "I bet you will," I lie. Not that I think she won't make it. It's just not an easy road. "Well, I'm off to get myself a drink."

"Nice to see you, Adda."

"And you, Elizabeth."

"Let's have lunch sometime."

I look over my shoulder. "Love to." And I mean it. "Call me." I smile as I slide into line at the bar. The plump, mousey Elizabeth would never have asked me to lunch, but Elizabeth, the published author, does so with confidence.

A half-hour later, packed into a circle of published writers, which includes Puffer's . . . *Joyce's* best friend, Jackie Hingle—the

"Bad" in "The Good, the Bad, and the Ugly"—I sigh at the drone of voices. It's not the same without Joyce. It's flat . . . tedious . . . and all I can think about is sneaking back to my room without being accosted by Jake. Shortly after ordering a Perrier and lime at the bar, I'd caught sight of him—and from his questioning brow and craning neck was certain he was looking for me. I'd slunk away only to bump into Jackie who had squealed with delight and dragged me into a group of writers.

I rise to my toes. Jake is easy to spot. Not because he's one of only a few dozen males among hundreds of women, and not because of the women trailing him like puppy dogs. The eye-blinding flashes of blue are a dead giveaway. Authors—published and unpublished—are unashamedly snapping photos of the man who has graced numerous covers and borne names such as Grit the Gunslinger, Rurik the Viking, Sir Tristan the Knight Errant, Trey the Millionaire Entrepreneur. Etcetera, etcetera, etcetera.

Coast is clear—except for Nick who catches my eye as I visually map my route across the ballroom. When did he come in? And *why* does he have to be stationed between the two sets of double doors?

I force a smile, but he doesn't smile back. Holding my gaze, he speaks to a woman on his right.

I lower to my one-inch heels. No prob. It's not as if he's going to intercept me. I'll just . . . walk past him.

"What's up?" Jackie hisses in my ear.

"Huh?" I look around.

She rolls her huge eyes. "I just told the best joke of the evening about the worst lover I ever had, and everyone laughed but you."

And that's why Jackie is the "Bad" one of our triangle, which is not really a triangle, but a "V" with Joyce at the point connecting the three of us. Sure, I like Jackie, but that's the extent of it.

"Sorry I missed it," I say, glancing at the others who are now exclaiming over a rumor about a merger between two of the smaller publishing houses.

"I'll bet you are," Jackie mutters and gives me a punch in the arm. "You're such a stick-in-the-mud."

I rub my arm. "I know, which is why I'm going to call it a night."

She wiggles her heavily penciled eyebrows. "And may I ask with whom?"

Great! The rumors are flying—or else Joyce told her about my date with Jake. I shake my head. "No one, and especially not Jake Grainger."

She chuckles huskily. "That's not what I hear."

I scowl. "Surely your mother told you to not believe everything you hear."

"She did, but she was naive."

I step back. "Good night, Jackie."

She flutters her fingers. "Nighty night."

I'm stopped a few times as I edge through the crowd, which is starting to thin as the attendees filter off to answer the call of the slots and tables. As I skirt Nick and the group of women gathered around him—among them, Shannon Sweet and Jeanne Matriarch—I avert my gaze.

Suddenly, a clear path opens to the door, but as I head down it, Little Miss Tight—er, Kathryn!—appears.

"Adda!"

I halt. "Hey!" I'd forgotten my former—and future—editor would be here.

A moment of silence follows—awkward because she and I have yet to address my move to Intrepid or her own pending defection.

"How are you doing?" I finally spit out.

"Good. You?"

I nod. "Good."

She adjusts the collar of her elegant suit dress. "There's something I need to talk to you about."

Great. However, as much as I'd like to make my excuses and catch up with her later, it's best to get it over with. "Okay?"

"It's about *The Gifting*."

Ooh. Did she discover my switch and bait? I take a deep breath. "What about it?"

She steps closer. "Farnsworth has given your lead spot to another author."

"What?" The word shoots out like an arrow.

She nods.

Dread fills me as I recall what happened to another author several years back. The publisher that the author was leaving had printed the last book of her contract, but had stripped it of lead title status, moved its release back fourteen months, and slotted it for the dead of after Christmas. Needless to say, the book's sales were greatly diminished.

"Lisa Leatherman," Kathryn says.

I know the author who bumped me. A good writer, but not yet lead material. I clench my hands. "And *The Gifting*?"

She shakes her head. "Slated for this January."

The dead of after Christmas. However, a moment later, I'm struck by the second offense. "*This* January? As in five months?"

"That's right."

"But that's impossible! That's five months ahead of schedule. What about marketing? What about cover art?"

"Exactly."

I close my eyes as anger quivers through me. Farnsworth Publishing is going to trash my book. They're going to send my baby out into the world half-naked. They're going to lose money just to rap my knuckles for leaving them. Well, not *just* for leaving them but for going over to the enemy, Nick Farnsworth. Of all the petty, low-down, rotten, nasty, vile—

"I'm sorry, Adda."

I open my eyes only to realize they're moist.

"I tried," she says and shakes her head. "I think they got wind I'm also leaving."

I draw a shaky breath. "I appreciate that you tried. Really."

"Are you going to be all right?"

"Yeah. Of course." Another deep breath, but it doesn't prevent my eyes from stinging. "Thanks for telling me."

"Sure." Then Kathryn does something of which I would have sworn she was incapable. She hugs me. "It's a nasty business, Adda. If you're going to survive, accept it and give as good as you get."

I nod dumbly. Though I know she just imparted a nugget of wisdom I shouldn't shrug off, I'm too angry . . . too disgusted . . . too dejected . . . too weary. "Thanks, Kathryn."

She pulls back. "If you want to talk— "

"Hey! How about letting me in on some of that," Jake Grainger's voice comes at me from behind.

Not now. Please not—

He comes around and hugs me fiercely.

I gnash my teeth. "Let go, Jake."

He chuckles. "What's the magic word?"

The *bleepity bleepin'* magic word! He's a boy, I remind myself of what Joyce said, and that couldn't be more apparent than at this moment. Thus, I'm obliged to go easy on him.

"Please, Jake, I'm tired and— "

He hugs me tighter. "Come on, Adda, what's the magic word?"

I tried. I really did. I turn my mouth to his ear. "You either take your hands off me, or I'll put a move on you that will make it next to impossible to walk out of here upright."

He startles and pulls back. "A bit touchy, are we?" Though he tries to make light of it, I can see he's unsettled.

"Yes, *we* are." I step back and glance at Kathryn who watches us through narrowed lids.

A sudden smile wipes away Jake's discomfort, and he leans forward. "Maybe you just need a little lovin', huh?" He wiggles his eyebrows, and I wonder what ever attracted me to him.

Praying no one past Kathryn heard his proposition, I smile tightly. "I don't think so. Good night." Congratulating my self-control, amazed I didn't go extreme on him, I step past.

Outside the ballroom, the steady *whirr, ker-ching*, and *ding-ding-ding* of the casino can be heard—the noisy lament of money down the drain. It's calling to the romance writers, as evidenced by the steady trickle who have escaped ahead of me.

Determined to hold in my rumbly bubbly boiling—at least until I make it to the elevators and find an empty one to carry me to the twelfth floor—I grit my teeth and grip my purse. As I near the bank of elevators, a hand clasps my shoulder.

"Ad—"

I don't wait for the rest of Louse's cajoling, don't even think about the impulse that whirls me around and snatches my hand up and back. I just do it. "I told you, 'no'!"

And, oh . . . no . . . it's Nick. Nick's temple that suffers my swing. Nick's blood that springs from an inch-long gash caused by the metal clasp of my evening bag.

He releases me and touches his temple. A moment later, he and a dozen other people stare disbelievingly at the blood on his fingers.

And like a fish out of water, I open and close my mouth—searching for something to say. "I thought . . . I didn't mean . . . didn't know . . . I . . . "

Mouth grim, eyes like steel, Nick's lids narrow as the buzz begins.

"Did you see that?"

"Did you see what she did to him?"

"Isn't that Adda Sinclaire?"

"A lover's quarrel?"

"Nick Farnsworth of Intrepid—the new president."

"Isn't she dating that Grainger hunk?"

Suddenly, I'm floating in tears, and a sob has me by the throat. This day has been too much.

Just as I'm about to put the finishing touches to making a fool of myself by bawling, Nick grabs my arm and pulls me toward the elevators. One opens as we near and emits a half-dozen badged romance writers who start their own buzz at the sight that greets them. Nick pulls me into the empty elevator. A few moments later, we head up.

He releases my arm, and I lean back against the wall as he pulls a white handkerchief from his jacket pocket.

It takes a few swallows, but I find my voice. "I'm sorry," I croak, keeping my gaze lowered. "I thought you were— "

"Grainger," he rumbles. "I know."

So he witnessed Jake's unwelcome pursuit . . .

Blotting his temple with the handkerchief, he captures my

gaze with those steely eyes. I look quickly to the elevator panel. Floor twelve is lit, meaning we're heading to my room. Meaning what?

Meaning he's being a gentleman by assuring you safely reach your room, Prim says.

Who are you kidding? Improper sneers.

I'm with Prim. No way is Nick Farnsworth interested in anything beyond an escort, especially not after I clubbed him. More than likely, he merely wishes to berate me in private.

As the elevator eases to a stop, I push off the wall and square my shoulders to hold against whatever he intends to say before he whisks himself back to the party.

The doors part, and he gestures for me to step out. Surely I'm not getting off that easy?

I cross the threshold and Nick follows.

Ooh la la, Improper proclaims.

Not! Prim pops off. *Off-limits! Off-limits! Off-limits*!

Now what? Does Nick actually intend to enter my room and let loose on me there?

As we traverse the corridor, I hide my nervousness by digging longer in my purse than necessary. Before the door of my room, I finally produce my card key and fumble it into the slot. Nothing. No green light. No soft click. So, out and in the card goes. Nothing. Out and in . . .

"Adda!" Nick slides his hand over mine and relieves me of the card key. With a twist of his lips, he turns the card and inserts it right side up.

Heat flushing me to the roots of my hair, I step into the suite and flick on the light. Nick follows and the door closes.

Swallowing hard, I look around at him where he stands in front of the door, a dribble of blood at his temple.

"Oh!" I say, and nearly trip over myself as I head for the bathroom. When I return with a cool washcloth, Nick is standing before one of two armchairs in the sitting room outside the bedroom.

I toss my purse—the little perpetrator—on the opposite chair and halt before Nick. "Here," I say, leaning in, "let me—"

"No." He pulls the washcloth from my hand. "Let *me*."

I take a step back. "Of course." I've caused enough trouble as it is.

He blots his temple and glances at the stained washcloth.

"Does it hurt?" I ask. "Would you like an aspirin?"

"No and no." He drops the cloth atop the chair-side table.

I take a deep breath. "I'm really sorry, Nick. If I'd known it was you I would never have . . . "

His eyebrows rise.

"Um . . . not to say I should have done it to Jake . . . "

He stares at me, and I realize the steel has gone from his eyes.

"It's just that . . . well . . . it was bad timing."

Very bad. Remembering Kathryn's news that started it all, I bite my lip as emotion flurries through me.

"Kathryn told me about *The Gifting*," Nick says.

I startle. "She did?"

"It's the reason I wanted to speak to you outside the ballroom."

I frown. "Really?"

"I'm sorry about what happened, Adda. However, I can't say I'm surprised."

"Why?" I ask, bitterness edging my voice. "Because you would have done the same?"

He shakes his head. "I left Farnsworth Publishing for a multitude of reasons, and that was one of them."

I sigh and rub my forehead where a dull ache has started. "I just wish someone would have warned me."

"Would it have made you rethink your move to Intrepid?"

Would it have? Would I have wimped out to maintain the status quo? I look up. "I don't think so. I just wish I had been prepared."

"Then I should have warned you." His voice is deeper than moments earlier.

Once more, attraction shoots through me, and from the flicker in his chocolates I know he's in its grip as firmly as I. But I'm the one who has to make the first move, I realize. Dare I?

Off limits! Prim cries.

I hear a loud smack and guess Improper has knocked her adversary upside the head.

As I moisten my lips, Nick follows the movement. Though it may be against his will, it appears he *is* attracted to me. Nick Farnsworth, a man, not a boy like—

"Jake," I say. "I . . . I should explain."

Nick's mouth tilts. "Yes, you should."

Never before have I had to explain one man to another, and the awkwardness causes my mouth to go dry. "It . . . " I shrug. "It was a mistake—the date, I mean. We had dinner and he came back to my place—" ooh, didn't need to add that detail, "—and he . . . uh . . . fell asleep in front of the television, believe it or not." I'm babbling. Must . . . catch . . . my . . . breath. "Short of a kiss," I rush on, heedless of my own good advice, "nothing happened."

Nick takes a step closer, causing my mouth to go drier. With a pop, I unstick my tongue from my palate.

"Adda," he says low.

I raise my gaze to his. "About tonight . . . " Does he have gorgeous eyes or what? "Jake just doesn't understand 'no.'"

Nick curves a hand beneath my chin and tilts it up. "*I* understand it." He lowers his gaze to my mouth. "I'd like to kiss you again, Adda. If you're going to say 'no,' you really should do it now."

I've gone to goo again, and it's only a matter of time before I melt at his feet.

"Are you going to say it?" he asks again.

"No," I breathe. "I mean—" I stamp my foot. "No, I'm not going to say 'no.'" I cock my head. "Does that make sense?"

"Perfect sense." He lowers his head.

"Um." I pull back a space. "About . . . Birgitta . . . ?" After all, I told him about Jake.

His brow furrows, reminding me of our first meeting at The Ivories when I'd so longed to explore the grooves there, the tiny lines at the corners of his eyes, his lopsided left cleft—all just fingertips away.

"Birgitta?" he says.

It's stupid. I know it is. After all, he shows no sign of interest in the woman beyond her writing ability. Indeed, his behavior toward her borders on disdain. Still, after what happened with Dick . . .

Resisting the urge to dip a fingertip in his left cleft, I say, "At Cristoforo's, you told me Birgitta recommended the filet mignon. As you said I was the first prospective author you had brought there, I just wonder where you came by her recommendation."

"Ah." His eyebrows rise, and the cleft deepens with a suppressed smile. "You want to know if she and I dined there for a purpose *other* than business."

I shrug apologetically.

"No," he says, and as if that's explanation enough, his mouth closes in on mine.

"Then?" I press on.

He grins, and I realize he's enjoying this. "I should come clean, hmm?"

"That's the idea."

"All right. The day you and I dined, Birgitta Roth dropped by my office to inquire about Intrepid's marketing program. Thus, she was present when I asked my assistant to reserve a table for two at Cristoforo's. And that's how I ended up with the filet mignon recommendation."

"Oh."

"Satisfied?"

Returning his grin, though I doubt it makes me look as appetizing as it does him, I lower my gaze to his lips. "I sure am."

With a throaty chuckle, his mouth closes over mine, and I fall into him. The kiss we share turns out to be better than the first, which is the reason I'm surprised when it doesn't go any further. Just a kiss. But, then, maybe that's why it's so good. Then it's over, though not abruptly like the first time. Nick eases back, and when I open my eyes, his face is only inches from mine.

"You know, of course," he says in a deep, dark voice, "this is a bad idea."

It is?

Feeling suddenly uncomfortable, guessing I'm about to be rejected again, I say, "Very bad—mixing business with pleasure. Yes—" I nod. "Bad." Then out of my mouth pops what should remain a thought. "But I would do it again."

He stares at me.

I stare back—waiting for his own admission, but it doesn't come.

Hating the silence and the fool it makes me feel, I pop my chin into the air. "And you would, too," I say with confidence I certainly don't feel.

His face is all seriousness, and I steel myself for his disclaimer.

"Yes, I would," he says.

"Oh . . . my," I murmur before I catch sight of my tummy-control pantyhose flung over the lamp beyond him. Eek! But surely he hasn't noticed them. Surely . . .

His head lowers, blocking my view of the hose. Embarrassment overriding sense, I determine there's only one thing to do. So, as Nick kisses me, I slide a hand up and over his shoulder and . . . reach . . . reach . . .

If I can just grab them and drop them to the floor, he'll never notice. Pressing nearer Nick, I wiggle my fingers and brush the silken material.

Close, but no cigar. So I reach some more.

Got them!

Though I intend to ease them from the lamp as inconspicuously as possible, I feel Nick hesitate. Desperate for the tummy controls to make a quick exit, I wrench the hose leg.

With a teeter and a lurch, the pantyhose pull the lamp down toward us.

I gasp, and Nick yanks me aside. A moment later, the lamp hits the floor.

Still holding me against him, Nick looks to the lamp, and when he returns his gaze to me, his chocolates aren't chocolate any more. "It was you again, wasn't it?" he says, gruffly.

Too late, I release the evidence of my guilt.

He eyes the hose on the floor beside us, shakes his head. "First books, Adda—"

Just had to bring up the incident in his office . . .

"—then your purse—"

Not going to forget the case of mistaken identity, then.

"—now a lamp!"

I wince.

"What were you trying to do?"

I bite my lip. "My hose . . . they were . . . um . . . on the lamp." I sigh. "I'm sorry, Nick."

He steps back.

Nice one, Adda! Improper sneers. *Just had to ruin the moment. Again*!

It's over, then. What man in his right mind would risk injury to have any kind of relationship with me? "I'm really sorry, Nick. Don't know what I was thinking."

"Neither do I," he says, then heaves a sigh. "I'd better go." He glances at his watch. "I have an early morning meeting."

Right . . .

He bends and, to my horror, picks up my hose and hands them to me.

Wanting to slither down a hole, I attempt to will the heat from my cheeks and take the hose from him. As he straightens, lifting the lamp and returning it to its place between the two armchairs, I ball the hose and clasp it in my hands behind my back.

"Adda?"

Here it comes. I draw a deep breath and give him my gaze. "I know," I say, "bad idea—very bad idea."

He stares at me, then says, "If you're free tomorrow afternoon, I'd like to take you sailing."

I nearly choke on my spit. "Oh! I . . . "

"Are you free?"

My head bobs up and down like a pogo stick. "Yes," I finally manage with as little dignity as I can muster. "I'm free. Er . . . what time?"

He's smiling. "I'll meet you in the lobby at 12:30."

"Perfect," I say, breathless.

He leans in, brushes his mouth across mine, then turns away. I'm all dewy-eyed as I watch him cross the room — until I realize the box alongside the door has caught his attention. Great! First the hose, now the UPS box. Not good.

He looks across his shoulder.

I offer an apologetic shrug. "Caught," I say. "So, are you disillusioned?"

"Very."

For a moment I believe him, then he grins. Whew!

"I suppose I'll just have to accept there's no such thing as a perfect woman," he says with mock regret.

I sigh dramatically. "The very conclusion I've reached about men."

"Because of your ex?"

His question jolts the playfulness right out of me, and all I can do is stare.

He raises an eyebrow. "Richard, isn't it?"

Trying to shake myself back to a semblance of nonchalance, I laugh. But it's not a real laugh — rather, one of those achy things that lurches up out of a person's throat.

"That's what his mother calls him," I say, "but I prefer Dick." And it's all I can do to not roll my eyes at having once more indulged in what he calls "private amusements." Of course, as "Dick" is a proper nickname for "Richard," it's not quite the same thing as "Stick Woman," is it?

Nick considers me, then says, "I perfectly understand your feelings, Adda."

It's how he says it, as much as what he says, that impresses me with his sincerity—as if he truly does understand. But as though realizing this, he looks away.

What did he just allow a glimpse of? Did something in his past find an echo in mine? Did his ex cheat on him? Lie to him? Betray everything sacred between them? Heavy sigh. Perhaps one day he'll tell me.

He glances at the box again, only to take a closer look that causes him to frown. As he reaches down, I almost groan. What embarrassment will I have to explain away now? I prepare myself for granny undies, a bra, or some feminine hygiene product, only to be startled by the book he lifts out. Vaguely aware I've dropped the hose, I stare wide-eyed at the Bible. For a moment, I'm embarrassed, but then I remember the revelation in the limo. Unlike Noelle, Nick Farnsworth is not going to give me grief over it. I hope.

Questioningly, he looks across the room. "You didn't say you were a Christian."

Is that accusation in his voice? Confusion? "That's because I'm not. I mean—" I shift my weight. "I believe in the whole God thing, and Christ certainly seems feasible, but . . . " Babbling again. Why didn't I simply play along? Score a few points for sharing his beliefs?

And set yourself up as a liar, Prim reproaches.

As Nick waits for me to spill the rest, I bite my lower lip, scratch my head, toe the ground, heave a sigh, and shrug. "I'm searching, and so far the New Testament seems to meet my needs."

He nods. "I appreciate your honesty, Adda."

Score!

"You're certainly an interesting woman." He returns the Bible to the box and grips the door handle. "Good night."

"Good night," I say, almost breathless.

A moment later, the door closes. A thrill building inside me, I stare at it, then toss myself into the armchair and squeal. To heck with the workshops I planned on attending tomorrow afternoon—The Taxable Writer; The Ultimate He-Man Scene; and Me, Myself, and My Editor. In fact, to heck with the morning workshops as well. Among other things, Momma's gonna need a brand new coat of paint. I lift my hands and give a nod to my nails. Yup. Lots to do before my sailing date with Nick.

I push out of the chair and am one step from the bedroom when I screech to a halt. Sailing date . . . as in on the water? As in on a boat? As in lurch, lurch, dip, barf?

"Oh, no." Wherefore art thou Dramamine?

TEN

o far, so good.

Smiling, I roll to my stomach.

"How old are you?" Snow White asks.

I lift my head and look across at her. She's also on her stomach, but has pushed onto her elbows and is staring at me over the tops of her sunglasses.

Needless to say, I was disappointed to discover she was coming along on my sailing date, but I've gotten over it and enjoyed her company. I lever onto my elbows and clasp my hands. "Thirty-five."

"Hmm. Dad's forty-two." Then, almost to herself, she adds, "Seven years difference."

"Seven years," I echo. That isn't much, is it? After all, women mature faster than men.

"Do you like my father?"

I blink. "I . . . well . . . yes, I do."

She considers me. "I'm glad."

She's glad? Then I pass inspection? I look across the deck to where the sailboat's steering wheel stands unmanned. Throughout the sail to Emerald Bay, I'd watched Nick behind the wheel and marveled at the ease with which he managed the boat. On occasion, he had called his daughter to assist with the sails, but otherwise it was all Nick—Nick's chocolates squinting against the sun, Nick's silvered dark hair sifting in the wind, Nick's tanned hands turning the wheel, Nick's muscles flexing as he pulled on one sail line and loosened another. Confident in the Dramamine that held embarrassment at bay, I'd pined away over the captain of *The Second Chance*. Then he had to go and drop anchor in the bay to prepare us a snack in the galley below.

"Time to toast the other side," Snow White says. Smiling, she turns onto her back and begins to fit her CD player's ear buds.

"What are you listening to?" I ask, also turning to my back.

"A new Christian rock band."

Christian rock? Really?

"Here— " she offers me one of the ear buds. "Have a listen."

I hesitate.

"The group's really good."

"Okay." I fit the bud and am shortly surprised by the tunes that leap into my ear. "Wow."

"Uh-huh." Snow White readjusts her one ear bud and relaxes into the deck. "Keep listening."

Wondering if her father told her about my "whole God thing/feasible Christ" speech, I give over to the music. Surprisingly, some of the lyrics are familiar, and I'm confused until I realize they're from the Bible. Who would have thought a person could rock out to Bible sayings?

"Dad likes you, too, you know," Snow White murmurs.

I remove the ear bud and turn my head to meet her gaze through her sunglasses. Though I'm tempted to ask the reason Nick likes me, as it's obviously not for my grace, I merely smile.

"And so do I," she says. "You're . . . different."

Ugh. Usually when people call someone or something "different" in that halting, uncertain manner, it's not intended as a compliment.

Feeling the boat dip gently beneath me, I ask, "How is that?"

She shrugs on her towel. "You're real."

"Real?"

"Not plastic—like some of the women he dates. You know the kind—not a hair out of place, glossy red smiles, bulimic figures, claws for nails."

I glance at my hands. Three Alarm Fire polish glints at me from oval-tipped nails. A good length. Hardly claws—at least, not in my estimation.

"My mother was plastic, too," she continues, returning me to last night when Nick asked about Dick.

I perfectly understand your feelings, he'd said as though he truly did—as though he's no stranger to the worst kind of betrayal.

Needing to scratch the itch of curiosity, I ask, "Do you see your mother often?"

"Never," she says, painfully matter-of-fact.

"Oh. I'm sorry." And I am.

"Sometimes I am, too, but most times not."

If I itched any more to know about Nick's past, I'd have fleas. "Why?"

She turns onto her side and props her head in a hand. "Though I wasn't supposed to know, my mother relinquished all rights to me in exchange for enough money to keep her in style for the rest of her life."

Ouch.

"Oh."

"Dad had to sell his shares in Farnsworth Publishing to pay her off. And *that's* where the ill will between him and his family came to a head. My uncles pounced—gave him thirty cents on the dollar."

Sounds like Peter and Damian Farnsworth. Though I've met them only once, stories abound of their ruthless exploits in the publishing business. "Why didn't your father sell outside the family?"

"That's just it. Years earlier he signed an agreement that stated he could only sell within the family."

"Wow." I turn onto my side to face her, and my stomach does a flip-flop. Assuring myself the discomfort is merely a result of hunger, I ask, "Who told you all this?"

She smiles tightly. "My mother. Sent a letter several years back and unloaded on me after Dad refused to give her more money. Needless to say, he was not happy."

Then he knows she knows. It must have been a cruel truth for a teenage girl to learn. "I'm sorry, Sophia."

An uncomfortable silence settles between us, and as much as I'd like to know more about Nick's ex, I decide against delving deeper.

"Do you know my uncles?" Snow White asks.

I shake my head. "Not personally."

"Me neither. Had they been attending the conference, I assure you Dad wouldn't have allowed me to tag along."

Hardly surprising considering their fallout. "What about your grandfather?" I ask. Though the "old man" retired years ago and left his sons to run the business, he's far from hands-off. In fact, I've run into him at the publishing office a couple of times—once, literally, as in coming fast around a corner and colliding with six feet and some inches of glowering behemoth.

Snow White scowls, and I note the fleeting resemblance to her grandfather. "I have lunch with my grandmother once a month, and occasionally he shows, but it's all very strained."

"He sided with your uncles against your father?"

"Let's just say he didn't take a stand." She sighs. "A prime example of age and treachery transcending youth and talent."

"Then your father's the youngest?" The words are out before I realize the foolishness of them. After all, I've seen his brothers, and they are definitely years ahead of him.

"By eight years," Snow White says, "whereas there are only

two years between Peter and Damian."

"So your father doesn't have any contact with his brothers?"

"Oh, he has contact all right—in the business arena." She sighs. "Though he's forgiven them for taking advantage of his situation—"

Forgiveness. Then he's mastered that particular Christian virtue?

"—he's determined they will never again get the better of him." Unaware of the side trip I just took, Snow White shrugs. "Thus, when the opportunity arises, he outdoes his brothers."

Her words nearly slip past, but something causes me to pull them back for a closer look. I frown. "Outdoes his brothers—such as stealing authors away?" Though I'd known my defection would be a feather in Nick's cap, I believed his offer of a contract was grounded more in my writing ability. Maybe not . . .

Snow White bobs her head enthusiastically, but suddenly stills. "Only if the author is 'top of the crop,'" she clarifies, "or has the potential to be. Dad's too astute to let emotion bypass business sense."

True. According to a bit of shameless research I've conducted, just about everything he's touched since leaving Farnsworth Publishing has gone platinum.

I sigh. "Think there's any chance he and his brothers will reconcile?"

She grimaces. "Perhaps, but I'm not holding my breath."

I nod. "Fair enough."

"Telling our family secrets, Sophia?" Nick asks. And there he stands—legs spread, hands on hips. A veritable feast of inspiration for any romance writer. Fortunately, he's *my* inspiration, and I can hardly wait to put it to good use with a nail-pounding session at the computer.

Recovering before me, Snow White says, "Only the ones that won't land us in prison."

"Ah." He nods, the movement drawing my gaze to the small gash at his temple over which a thin scab has formed. "Then don't let me interrupt."

"Too late." Snow White gains her feet with the grace of a ballerina. "Sea rations ready, Cap'n?"

"Ready," he says with a grin that would endear him to me were he not already endeared. "Adda?" he prompts.

With the grace of a steel worker, I jump up. Big mistake! Not only do I lose my footing on the rock-a-bye-baby deck, but my stomach lurches. Oh . . . no . . .

Nick saves me from the first fate by catching my arm as I go down, but there's no salvation from the second. Fortunate for him, he recognizes the signs and hustles me to the railing. And so with raging humiliation, I succumb to motion sickness.

● ● ●

Though I'd like to blame it on Dramamine failure, I'm the culprit. One to two tablets every four to six hours the package instructed, and I would have been perfectly fine had I taken the pill a half-hour before boarding the wicked little skinny dipper. But *noooo*. I'd taken it two-and-a-half hours before boarding with my late breakfast, in the event the pill upset my stomach.

Nick and Snow White had been understanding, and while I'd waited for my second dose of Dramamine to kick in, the two had stayed near. Feeling somewhat better, I had snoozed, and upon awakening discovered we were almost back at the dock. Thoughtful Nick had motored across the lake rather than set the sails.

Now, insides swaying to and fro as I cross the lobby between Nick and his daughter, all I can think about is how wretched I must have looked hanging over the railing, not to mention how I *still* look. The last thing I need is—

"Adda, dear, are you well?" Birgitta Roth calls above the clank and clunk of slot machines.

E-gad! Has she been staking out the lobby waiting for me? Or maybe it's Nick she was waiting on? Hmm. Not content with relieving me of a husband, now she's—

"Next stop, the elevators," Nick says, taking my elbow and steering me toward the bank of golden doors where a dozen hotel guests are surging forward to claim an elevator that has emptied. Unfortunately, the doors close before we reach them. Worse yet, Birgitta has followed us.

I groan as she appears before us, and she blinks wide as though I belched.

"You look awful, Adda. Sick?"

I press my shoulders back. “Just a bit tired.”

“Oh, that’s a relief.” She smiles, revealing something green—spinach?—between her front teeth, and looks left and right of me. “Nick . . . Sophia.”

They nod.

“So, Adda,” she returns her gaze to me, “what on earth has wrung you out?”

I hesitate, uncertain as to whether or not Nick would want me to reveal our little excursion.

“I took Sophia and Adda sailing this afternoon,” he answers for me, and I’m so grateful.

Her smile puckers. “Really?”

“Really,” Nick says and steps forward to punch the elevator button.

Feeling Birgitta’s beady gaze, I smooth a hand over my hair and ask, “Enjoying the conference, Birgitta?”

She affixes a pasty smile. “You know how these things are. Ten boring workshops for every halfway stimulating one.” She heaves an oh-so-weary sigh. “Of course, most are geared toward the unpublished writer. Old news—all of it.”

And don’t you sound like a snob? Wondering what’s holding up the elevators, I say, “Sorry to hear that.”

She shrugs. “*C’est la vie.*”

Unable to suppress a roll of my eyes, I duck my head and give the elevator button another jab. Of course, it’s already lit, and my little distraction only serves to make me look like a simpleton.

"Think you'll be up to attending the publisher's banquet this evening, Adda?" Birgitta asks.

And ruin the evening for her? I look around. "Wouldn't miss it for anything." After all, it wouldn't do for Intrepid's launch author to be a no-show. And what a surprise when she learns about the new line for which she was passed over.

Her mouth tightens as she attempts to disguise her disappointment, but I'm allowed only a moment of satisfaction before my conscience is twinged. Though I reason that, after what she stole from me, I have every right to gloat, I'm twinged again—rather, pricked. And hard!

"I just need to rest up a bit," I mutter.

A moment later, the doors of an elevator swoosh open, and I turn with Nick and Snow White toward it. Grateful my legs are beginning to feel like my own again, I step into the elevator alongside Nick.

Unfortunately, the doors don't close fast enough to cut off Birgitta's parting shot. "Thought you'd like to know, Adda—Jake Grainger has been asking about you all day."

And I felt bad about gloating.

Though thankful I explained Jake to Nick last night, I cringe at what his daughter might think. As the elevator begins its ascent, I look past Nick to Snow White. Lips compressed, she stares at the panel of numbered buttons, and the air between us is as tense as it was yesterday when Denise asked if I was rooming with Jake. Well, at least Nick . . .

I slide my gaze to him and find him watching me, a question creasing his brow. Though he smiles a moment later, it's a tight smile, and I know he's wondering if I told the truth, the whole truth, and nothing but the truth. Doing my best to not take offense, I remind myself of the insight he allowed last night. If his ex *did* cheat on him, he's not likely to trust women easily—which would explain why he never remarried. And it's not as if I can't relate.

The elevator's ascent is interrupted once to admit an elderly woman. Gnarled hands clutching a bucket brimming with quarters, she flashes her dentures and hobbles to my side. Shortly thereafter, my floor number lights up.

I step out. "Thank you for an enjoyable afternoon," I say, meeting Snow White's gaze, then Nick's. "I guess I'll see you at the banquet."

Nick nods, and the elevator doors close as I turn and head toward my room.

"Stick Woman!" I mutter as I shove a hand into my purse. "Prune!" I jerk my card key from the depths. "Louse!" I halt before my room and insert the key.

I know . . . I know . . . I've fallen off the wagon again. I'm not perfect. And habits are *so* hard to break.

With a deep breath, I press the handle and push the door inward. And there, center of the table, is a vase bursting with roses. I stare at the profusion of greenery, white baby's breath, and pink buds. Pink. Why pink?

Hoping . . . praying they're from Nick, I step forward and

halt as paper crackles underfoot. Wondering if the envelope slipped under my door is related to the flowers, I retrieve it and pry the flap loose. The card inside is as tacky as tacky gets—a cutesy print of a man and woman's flung-off clothing trailing down a hallway toward a bedroom. With a sinking feeling, I open the card.

Wear the little black dress. I'll pick the movie this time. Your hero, Jake

Why is he picking on me? A hunk like him can't possibly lack for female company. Surely our one kiss and viewing of *Pride and Prejudice* can't mean more to him than that? After all, soon thereafter he was at Cristoforo's with that editor. And that was no peck on the cheek he gave her. So what am I to do? How to make him understand it's over—that I'm not merely playing hard to get? That—

That's it! He isn't accustomed to being turned down. I've usurped *his* prerogative and he can't handle it. I sigh. I suppose I'll have to stop avoiding him and have a heart-to-heart.

Shaking my head, I step into the room. As the door closes behind me, I cross to the flowers and drop Schm . . . Jake's—see, I'm trying—card to the table. From the center of the arrangement, I pull the pick and remove the itty-bitty card.

Sorry I can't be there tomorrow. Think pink when you're receiving your award. As for me, I'll be molting in scads of chiffon. Love ya! Joyce.

Though I'm touched by her confidence in my book, my smile is for the image of her sitting in a garden chair with pink chiffon poofed up around her scrawny figure—hopefully minus cigar burns. I sigh, missing her ten times more than before.

Grateful for her levity, I tote her card to the bathroom and slide it under the mirror's edge where I can grin over it while I bring order to my appearance.

I look at my reflection, which isn't as bad as expected. Color has returned to my cheeks, my mascara didn't smear, and the sunscreen I slathered on before the boat ride has kept the freckles at bay. Still, there's work to be done. I glance at my watch, and turn my gaze to my nails. Lots of work to be done. Unfortunately, I have only an hour and a half before the banquet.

Blowing a breath up my face, I reach for the nail polish remover and ponder which shade of polish to apply—Aphrodite Red or Cherry Moon?

● ● ●

The banquet hall is abuzz as I ascend the stage and cross to where Nick stands behind the podium from where he unveiled Intrepid's new romance line.

Telling myself I should be accustomed to the spotlight by now, I halt alongside the projection screen, which is lit by a montage of Intrepid's authors and the covers of their latest releases. Dodging the overwhelming urge to chew a fingernail, I clasp my hands before me and, for an unguarded moment, wish I were more like my ex who is as comfortable before hundreds of people as I am in my townhouse with only my fake fur slippers for company.

It'll be over soon, I tell myself as the other authors who have signed with the new line are called to the stage. And as Nick informed me, Birgitta Roth is not among them. I look to where she sits in full-blown misery and imagine how much worse she'll look should I receive the award for Best Long Historical romance at the luncheon tomorrow. And there goes my conscience again. Prick, prick, jab!

Never have I been more conscious of my thoughts and how . . . well . . . how spiteful they can be. *Never* have I felt less like the good person I used to consider myself. Someone really ought to stamp the cover of Bibles with a list of the possible side effects of reading Jesus.

Shortly, Nick closes his presentation, and applause fills the room. As I descend the stage behind the other Intrepid authors, I glance over my shoulder.

He's following, and when he smiles, my knees go to goo. Fortunately, I look forward in time to prevent missing a step that would have sent me flat-faced and spread-eagled on the floor. Lucky break.

As one more publisher has yet to present, we return to the Intrepid table where I resume my seat across from Nick. Though it's a nice view, I'm envious of Birgitta who laid claim to the seat on his left while I was upstairs blowing on my nail polish. On the other side of him sits Snow White.

Can't have everything, I console myself. Must leave a few crumbs for Birgitta Roth. Not that she left any crumbs for me when she swept my husband off his feet.

Hoping Nick's smile meant he'll join me after the banquet, I reach for my glass of water.

"Really?" Birgitta exclaims, and I look up to see her claws on Nick's sleeve. "*This* evening?"

What about this evening? I look from him to her, from her to him.

He inclines his head. "This evening," he confirms whatever he's confirming.

"Pity you're not staying for the remainder of the conference." Birgitta thrusts her lower lip forward, affecting a pout more suited to a runway model. "You'll miss the awards luncheon tomorrow."

He's leaving. *This* evening.

As though feeling my distress, Nick glances at me.

I force a smile.

"You *do* know I'm up for Best Short Historical romance, don't you?" Birgitta mewls on.

Please, Lord, let Joyce win. Pretty please!

Nick looks back at Birgitta. "You mentioned it."

At least a dozen times, I'll bet. As I entertain the scathing thought, I notice my hand is frozen alongside my glass. Hoping no one noticed, I grip the glass and take a sip.

Why didn't Nick tell me he was leaving before the end of the conference?

Since when does he answer to you? Prim ribs me. *Despite the way he looks at you . . . the way he kisses you . . . there's not much more to your relationship with Nick than there is to your relationship with Jake.*

Ouch.

But there *was* something more, wasn't there? Maybe something urgent called him back to New York, and he just hasn't had the chance to tell me. Or maybe I'm wearing rose-colored glasses.

The introduction of the final publisher returns me to the present, and I blink Nick and Birgitta back to focus only to find their attention turned to the editor at the podium. However, Snow White is looking at me.

Though my mouth feels as taut as a rubber band, I stretch it into a smile. And am thankful when she returns the smile. Not that Jake Grainger is forgotten, I'm sure. And he's somewhere out there in the sea of faces that crowd the banquet hall—waiting to pounce at the most inopportune moment. Well, at least after this evening Nick won't be here to witness Jake's unwelcome attentions. Small consolation.

Shifting into defense mode, I tell myself I have no reason to be hurt that he hasn't mentioned his early departure, that I know the score as well as he does, that what I feel for him is nothing more than infatuation, that what *he* feels for *me* is nothing more than infatuation, that he's just another man, that I don't need another man, that I have better things to do with my time, that it's all for the best.

Yes, all for the best. I am perfectly content being footloose and fancy-free. Perfectly.

Liar.

• • •

A knock.

I lift my head from where I sit cross-legged beneath the sheet I pulled over me a half hour earlier when I set up camp in the middle of the bed. Bathed in the silvery blue light of my laptop's screen, I stare at the impossibly thick Bible that lies open across the keyboard.

Could it be Jake come in search of that little black dress? Though I've promised myself I'll set him right, my hotel room at ten o'clock at night is hardly the place or time. Of course, it might be Nick. In the ensuing enthusiasm for Intrepid's new line, which had seen us surrounded by published and unpublished authors, he and I didn't have the chance to talk. Thus, I'd taken as much of the hoopla as I could stomach and retreated to my room.

Another knock.

Telling myself Nick is likely on his way to the airport, and chances are it's Jake, I duck from beneath the sheet and slip off the bed. I pause a moment to smooth my knee-skimming T-shirt, the front of which is emblazoned with: *Proceed with caution: contents highly flammable*, then hurry from the eerily screen-lit bedroom into the darkened sitting room. No sooner do I press my face to the door to peer out the peephole than the one in the corridor slips from view.

"Shoot!" A flash of white is all I have to identify my caller.

Don't do it, Prim cautions.

Surely it's Nick, Improper tempts.

So? You're wearing a T-shirt!

My struggle lasts all of two seconds. I fumble the deadbolt back, pull the door open, and pop my head around the door frame.

You really are pathetic, Prim taunts as Jake pivots around.

A slow, are-you-ready-for-this? smile lifts his mouth. "Hey."

"Hey . . . Jake."

Pathetic with a capital P.

I grip the door frame tighter to keep from slapping at my shoulder. "I thought you were someone else."

"Oh?" He saunters forward.

I angle the lower half of my body behind the wall to obscure my bare legs, and wedge my upper half between door and frame. "Listen, Jake, I . . . "

He reaches up and releases the top button of his white tuxedo shirt. Not good. A moment later, he halts before me. "Room service," he says with a throb in his voice that nearly makes me laugh.

"Jake, I— "

He lays a finger to my lips and lingeringly draws it downward.

Though what I really want is to swat his hand away, it would require me to let go of the frame or door and thereby grant him access to my room.

As his finger trails my chin, I say, "I've been meaning to talk to you— "

Ping! a distant elevator announces its arrival at the twelfth floor.

And just my luck, its occupant will be none other than Nick—Of course he had to leave early, didn't he? Suddenly grateful for his absence, I try again. "Look, Jake—"

"I sure hope there's a little black dress under this thing." He eyes my T-shirt.

Patience on the edge of harsh words, I shake my head. "'Fraid not."

He leans against the door frame and slides his finger down my neck. "We'll make do without."

I tried. Releasing the door, I grip his hand before he can hook it in the neck of my T-shirt and am oh, so tempted to bend his finger back and drive him to his knees. "Listen, Jake—"

For once, it's not Jake who interrupts, but a movement to the left. Peering past his shoulder where he continues to lean against the door frame, I see someone come around the corner.

Nick Farnsworth.

No! If my life were a book, critics would rip it apart. *Contrived*, they'd say. *Suspend disbelief!* As for me, I think it's best summed up with one word: *doomed.*

An instant later, Nick slows as his gaze settles on the scene before him, but he doesn't halt. Jaw hardening, lids narrowing, he keeps coming.

Unaware we have company, Louse—surely I can be forgiven the relapse—lowers his head toward mine. "Adda—"

"I apologize for the interruption," Nick says as he nears.

With a long sigh, Jake looks over his shoulder.

Realizing my hand's still on his, I snatch it back. And just in time as he pushes off the frame and turns to Nick.

"Mr. Farnsworth." He thrusts a hand forward as Nick halts before him. "Jake Grainger. A pleasure to meet you, Sir."

Schmooze time, and here I stand in the doorway wearing a T-shirt and guilt three sizes too big.

To my surprise, Nick shakes Jake's hand. "And you, Mr. Grainger." He pulls his hand back and looks past Jake. "I know the hour is late, Ms. Sinclaire—"

Has he reverted to last names for Jake's benefit? Or mine?

"—but there's a marketing matter I need to discuss with you before I return to New York."

Jake steps aside, and it's all I can do to not clasp my arms about me as Nick catches sight of my T-shirt.

I shrug. "Sure—"

"That's my cue," Jake says and glances over his shoulder at me. "Let's hook up later, hmm?"

"We'll have that talk then," I say in a feeble attempt to clarify the situation.

Jake nods and sidesteps Nick, and I watch until he disappears around the corner. With dread, I look to Nick.

Darkly handsome in jeans and a black T-shirt, he raises an eyebrow.

I moisten my lips. "I . . . heard you were leaving this evening."

"I am."

"Oh. Problem at Intrepid?"

His eyebrows gather. "Unless you care to conduct business in a hotel corridor, you should probably ask me in."

Business.

"Uh . . . right . . . of course." I open the door wider, and his arm brushes mine when he strides past.

As the door swings closed, the sitting room is once more thrown into near darkness—the only light being that which filters through from my computer in the bedroom.

As Nick turns toward me, I feel a hand up the wall and fumble the light switch on, only to feel my eyes pop wide as the light above the table illuminates the flower arrangement.

Surely he won't think . . . He might. But they're pink. Pink! Still . . . perhaps he won't look around.

Hoping my nervousness doesn't show as much as I feel it, I shift my gaze to Nick.

Hands shoved in his pockets, he stares at my *Proceed with caution* shirt, then slides his gaze down my bare legs.

Could be worse. Had I slipped on my satin nightie as I was tempted to do, there I would have stood wearing more skin than garment as Jake attempted to seduce me.

With a tight smile, Nick looks up and peruses my face, which, I realize, is devoid of makeup—thankfully. After all, what woman arranges a tryst and foregoes camouflage?

So . . . no nightie, no makeup. What further proof that Jake's visit was not by invitation?

Nick frowns, and I realize he's looking at my hair.

Becoming aware of the static electricity imparted by the sheet I dragged over me and my computer, I groan inwardly. No nightie, no makeup, but bed-tousled hair. . . .

"What . . . um . . . marketing matter did you wish to discuss?" I ask.

He shakes his head. "No marketing matter."

"Oh. Then . . . came to say good-bye?"

Maintaining his distance, he says, "Actually, yes."

And there was Jake. Though what I really want is to explain his presence at my door, and I sense it's what Nick is waiting for, I hear myself ask again, "Problem at Intrepid?"

He considers me, nods. "Distribution."

Then something unexpected *did* come up. "I imagine you'll have it straightened out in no time."

"Perhaps."

The tension is killing me. "I've been working on the new manuscript." At least, that had been my intent before the Bible pulled me in. I jut my chin toward the bedroom.

He looks around, and I nearly yelp when his gaze pauses on the flower arrangement, then the card beside it. Jake's tacky card that I had every intention of tossing.

"Glad to hear it," he says. Then, to my horror, he crosses to the table. "Nice flowers," he murmurs, though it's the card that holds his attention.

Panic flies through me. "My friend, Joyce Kuchner, sent them in anticipation of the awards luncheon." I take a step toward him. "Good old Joyce—ever the optimist."

Going from very bad to incredibly worse, he pulls his hands from his pockets and flips open the card to Louse's—I give up. "Louse" it is—suggestive inscription.

"Persistent," he murmurs, then turns to me. "Perhaps you ought to try a tact other than simply telling him 'no.'"

My mind has gone so blank, my mouth so dry, I can only stare.

With finality, he inclines his head and starts for the door.

So that's it? This is where we leave it—him thinking I lied about Louse and me standing mutely by like a total doofus? Not!

I step between him and the door. "I can explain about the card. And Jake—why he was here."

He halts and looks down on me. "I know why he was here."

O . . . kay. "And you would be right, but not if you believe I invited him—or wanted him here."

A muscle spasms in Nick's jaw.

"There was a knock, and I thought it was you coming to say good-bye," I continue, hating how desperate I sound. "When I opened the door— "

"Adda." He shakes his head. "It's not necessary." He shifts his jaw as though to ease the tension there. "Though I'll admit I was disappointed to see Grainger at your door—jealous, in fact—I have no right." To my surprise, he steps closer and tilts my chin up, and though I sense what's coming, I thrill to his touch. "We're not committed to one another. Far from it." His thumb brushes my bottom lip. "I'm attracted to you, and it's obvious you're attracted to me, but we both know it won't work—as much because of my past as yours."

When was the last time I felt as though a part of me were dying? When I discovered Dick's adultery? Close, but somehow this feels worse. Feeling a lump rise in my throat, and realizing I'm about to make a fool of myself by crying, I swallow hard and press my lips inward.

"Sophia's waiting in the lobby," he says. "We're catching the red-eye out of Reno."

I pull a deep breath. "Then you'd better go, hadn't you?"

He searches my face and, to my surprise, lowers his head. The kiss is brief, but long enough to know it will only make his "so long" hurt all the more.

"For luck tomorrow," he says, and releases my chin. He steps around me, and a moment later, the door closes softly behind him.

Doused in achy silence, I lay fingers to my lips, close my eyes, and remember Nick's kiss. A kiss that, in no uncertain terms, said "have a nice life."

Ouch.

ELEVEN

Done it again—completed a book to top all previous books. As I stare at the final word of *Feud: The Abduction*, I point my index finger, take a deep breath, and punch the period.

It is done. Finished. Over. The End!

And here comes my OOB. I flop back in my chair, lift my face toward the ceiling, and close my eyes as the out-of-body experience transports me to distant realms.

Yes . . . yes . . . mmm, yes . . . oh, yes.

This is good!

Throughout, the phone is silent, the doorbell is silent, my assistant is silent. Not a single interruption. And so I wallow, savoring every moment that won't come again until I finish the next book.

Later, as the last of the waves lap me, I sigh and open my eyes. Life is good. Doesn't get better than this. And as further testament, my most prestigious awards atop the bookshelf shine down on me. Best Short Historical Romance, Best Romance of the Year, Best Medieval Romance, Best Short Historical Romance (again), Best

Long Historical Romance . . .

Staring at that last, the ripples of exaltation ebb as I flip back five months to the awards luncheon in Lake Tahoe. It had been bittersweet to hear my name announced, but I had smiled, smiled, smiled as I ascended the stage and accepted the award. Not even Birgitta Roth's loss of Best Short Historical Romance to Joyce eased my ache.

But I'm over Nick now. Have been over him for months, weeks, days, hours, minutes. And I owe it all to yellow Post-it notes, an unexpected, if not unconventional, form of self-therapy. Pleased with the outcome, I look to the dozens of sticky papers that border my monitor's screen. Those on the left are covered with rows of tally marks to mark the passage of days, while those on the right are covered with relevant sayings—make that Scripture—which I've encountered during my exploration of the New Testament and my trials within the Old Testament. The latter causes me to wrinkle my nose. HEAVY stuff, complete with exhaustive lists of descendants who bore this son and bore that son—all of whom had names that no one in their right mind would try to pronounce. Still, there are some interesting parts to the Old Testament, chief among them the prophecies of Jesus' birth, life, and death, which as far as I can tell, line up with the actual events in the New Testament. Almost as interesting is "Song of Songs," which focuses on two lovers. Talk about racy! And so distracting that, at the time of the reading, Nick kept popping into my—

But he's a distant memory now. Yep. Distant. Very distant.

Waaay out there. Though I'll likely have to deal with him again when work begins on the men's edition of *Feud*, this time it will be strictly business. And providing I'm not hit with another debilitating case of writer's block, my future relationship with all men will be strictly business. Fortunately, Nick's kisses provided plenty of inspiration for my love scenes—not to mention the tear-jerker scenes.

As for my private amusements, they're under control—at least with regards to those dear to me and those I've forgiven. And no, Birgitta Roth is not among the forgiven; however, I am determined to desist from all thoughts of "Stick Woman" and, eventually, pardon her. Even if it kills me. Thus, I have every reason to be content. And I am. Really. Truly. In fact, the last good cry I had was for the cover of *The Gifting*.

I grimace. This past Halloween, Farnsworth Publishing sent two dozen cover flats in advance of the book's release. With bated breath, I opened the envelope and, for the first minute or so, simply stared at the atrocity that was to bear my tiny name—previous Farnsworth releases having boasted ADDA SINCLAIRE in letters three times as large. *The Gifting* had been sentenced to a bodice-ripper clinch, the kind of cover that gives romance books a bad name and affords us no respect. Yep, Robert and Philippa are slobbering all over one another, and in front of a waterfall that had no part whatsoever in my story. But at least in that there was some consolation in seeing my name made less conspicuous.

It gets better, though. Turns out the cover was a recycle,

the artwork having been commissioned years earlier for an author whose first book was her last. Thus, *The Gifting*, released two weeks ago, bears the distinction of being the only one of my books whose back cover blurb faces out on my bookshelf. The front covers of all others proudly face forward.

Fortunately, as the book's insides do not reflect its outside, it received glowing reviews. Of course, if not that the ARCs (advanced reading copies) are sent out to reviewers so far in advance of the book's publication that they sport a plain cover bearing little more than the author's name and title, the story might be different. Reviewers are human, after all, and not immune to judging a book by its cover.

As for the best-seller lists, *The Gifting* is a no-show, as Farnsworth Publishing cut off its long wooden nose to spite itself by underprinting me by . . . oh . . . a few hundred thousand. It hurts all right, but the good news is that I have both halves of my hefty advance. Therefore, if the book doesn't earn out its entire advance, which it can't possibly do with its current print run, it's Farnsworth whose shorts get eaten.

See, if one digs deep enough, one can find something good in something bad—very bad, very, very bad.

Still, I do hope Farnsworth will get over its tizzy and order a second print run to meet the demand. But who knows what evil lurks in the hearts of publishers? And if I let it eat at me anymore, I'm going to retch.

"All right, then!" I slap my hands to the chair arms. "Let's print this puppy out."

Shortly, the printer sets to humming—a sound even more thrilling than the click and thud of the keyboard. I have given birth!

As the pages eject one atop the other, I peer at my desk calendar. Right. A talk at two for the local chapter of Women's Fiction Writers. Though I've been attending the meetings these past months and have become close with Elizabeth Carp, the newly published author I reconnected with at Lake Tahoe, it's the first time I've been asked to present. And strangely, I'm looking forward to it. So it's roughly two hours before I catch a cab, which means . . .

I splay my hands. Though the polish at the tips of my nails is worn from the morning's marathon writing session, my nails are otherwise intact—as in no nibbles. Put that nasty habit behind me when I put Nick behind me. Of course, I was able to do so only after nibbling all ten down to the quick. And *that* was when I started marking off days on Post-its.

But no more. And to prove it . . .

One by one, I pull the yellow notes from the left side of my monitor, tear them in half, and toss them in the wastebasket. Ah, sweet closure!

As for the Scripture, it stays. Since Elizabeth Carp invited me to her church months back, I've learned even more about God and Jesus—much to my agent's dismay and my assistant's confusion. Not that I'm a Christian. Yet. Faith, or rather, faithlessness, holds me back. Believe that God really sent his son to endure such a horrific death for *me*? That *his* sacrifice—not mine—is enough to forgive my sins? That just being a good person won't get me into heaven? That if I give up control of my life and accept Christ, the Holy Spirit will come to live in me?

I don't know.

Still, the more I read the Bible, the more I attend church, and the more time I spend with Christians, the easier it is to believe it's all true. So maybe . . .

The phone rings, and I startle when caller ID pulls up the name S. Farnsworth; however, an instant later I realize it's Snow White. Although she's called twice since Christmas, we have yet to speak, as I've missed her previous calls—intentionally, of course, as I can't bear the prospect of any mention of Nick. And I should walk away from this call, too, but when her voice comes across the machine, I pick up.

"Hi, Sophia."

"Adda! Good to hear your voice."

"And yours."

"How are you doing?"

"Great. And you? How was the mission?"

"Awesome! Totally awesome. I'll tell you all about it when we get together."

Not much chance of that. "I'd love to hear about it." And I really would.

"Then let's do it!"

"What?"

"I'm heading off to school soon. Let's get together before I leave."

"Uh . . . "

"Doing anything tomorrow night?"

"As a matter of fact, um . . . " Though tempted to lie in order to keep as much distance between my heart and Nick as possible, I can't. "No," I change course. "I'm not doing anything."

"Then how about dinner?"

Sounds harmless enough. "Sure."

"And a movie."

"Oh." I like Snow White—very much—but the last thing I need is a girlfriend whose father happens to be Nick Farnsworth. Of course, it's not as if he'll be joining us, is it? "Just the two of us?"

Do I detect hesitation?

"Just the two of us," she says.

Surely my imagination . . . "All right."

"Great! I'll pick you up at six."

"Oh, that's not necessary. I can meet you somewhere."

"Nah, I'll come get you."

I shrug. "Okay. My address is— "

"I have it. See you at six." *Click.*

Frowning, I lower the handset to its base. How did she get my address? Through Intrepid? Do they even have my home address? Everything goes through Noelle, doesn't it? I ponder the curiosity a bit longer, then lift my hands and sigh over my nails.

So what's it to be? Very Vamp or Hearty Heart—just two of the new colors that caused my polish collection to swell to seventy-four following my return from Lake Tahoe.

Leaving the printer to its magic, I step to the landing and glance into Angel's office as I start up the stairs. She's nowhere in sight, meaning she's probably in the kitchen turning a scary combination of carrots and various other produce into thick, pulpy juice—her latest thing, as evidenced by her complexion's orange tint. Believe it or not, that myth about too many carrots causing an orange "glow" in some people isn't a myth after all.

I take the last of the stairs two at a time and am a foot inside my bedroom when I'm stopped by the sight of black-hosed legs and spiked boots poking out from beneath my bed.

Either I'm hallucinating, or that's Angel. I squeeze my eyes closed, open them. What—

"Come on, Sweetie," she croons, voice muffled by the dust ruffle. "I won't hurt you."

Huh?

"You like cheese, don't you?"

No. No. NO! "Angel!" I shriek, "What's going on?"

The sound of a skull striking wood is followed by a groan, then, "Come back, little one."

And there I stand as a gray dust ball streaks from beneath my bed—gray, not white like Doodles. I scream, jump aside, and flatten myself against the wall as the whiskered and tailed rodent hurtles through the doorway and down the stairs.

Heart whacking at my ribs, I stare at the threshold. A mouse. There is a mouse in my house. On the loose.

Angel emerges and sweeps back her long, black flyaway hair. "Ms. Sinclaire," she exclaims with a smile ten miles wide, "you were right!"

Slowly, I peel myself off the wall. "Right? How so?"

She rises and, with all the enthusiasm of a child about to recount a trip to Disneyland, says, "Remember last year when you thought you saw a mouse in the kitchen?" She waves the wedge of sixteen-dollar-a-pound Camembert cheese she used to entice the rodent. "It really was a mouse!"

Not!

"I was working away, when I saw movement out of the corner of my eye." She pops the cheese in her mouth and says around it, "There, in the doorway, sits this cute little mouse, and it's staring at me and Doodles with this really sad expression."

Uh-huh.

"Like it wants someone to play with."

This girl obviously doesn't read body language, even when it's pouncing on her. I gnash my teeth, hold up a finger. "I have only one thing to say."

She smiles expectantly.

"Exterminator."

Her jaw drops. "Ms. Sinclaire!"

I shake my head. "Look, Angel, though I can't stand creepy crawlies, I agreed to allow Doodles into my home—providing he wasn't given free run—but I draw the line at wild, disease-ridden rodents."

"Disease-ridden? But—"

I wave a silencing hand. "Get an exterminator out here today. Understand?"

Bottom lip trembling, she gives an affirmative jerk of her head.

"Good." I take a deep, calming breath. "Now, about the manuscript—when it finishes printing out, I want a copy couriered over to my agent and one to Kathryn Connell, my editor at Intrepid. You can handle that?"

Eyes glistening—making me feel like such a meanie—she nods.

My decision stands. I will *not* be swayed. "All right, then, I'm going to get ready for my meeting."

Nose reddening, she stiffly steps past me.

This has got to be how parents of teenagers feel when they come down on their children. But I will *not* be moved. Go tough love!

Oh . . . maaan . . .

"Angel?"

She jumps around, and I know she knows she's gotten to me. "Ms. Sinclaire?"

"I don't care how you do it—be it exterminator or you catch the little intruder yourself—but when I return from my writer's meeting, I expect that rodent to be gone from my home."

With a teary smile, she says, "It will be, Ms. Sinclaire. I promise." She takes a step forward and, before I can avert her intention, throws her arms around me. "You're the best."

An ear-piercing squeak erupts between our chests.

"Aah!" I yelp and jump back.

"Oh, Doodles," Angel laments, "I'm sorry, baby." And as I watch, the white mouse pokes its head up above her scooped neckline and turns its beady little eyes toward me with such accusation I'd hang it by its twitching whiskers if it didn't require a certain amount of proximity.

"Take care of the problem, Angel," I say in a voice that quivers all over the place.

She strokes Doodles' head. "You can count on me, Ms. Sinclaire. Which reminds me—all the arrangements have been made for your jaunt to Martha's Vineyard next week."

The getaway I've been promising myself since I moved to New York. Of course, I never intended to visit in winter, but what the heck. "Thanks," I say.

"No prob." She scoops Doodles into her palm, kisses his nose—eew!—and bounds out the doorway and down the stairs.

Weak-kneed, I look toward the bathroom. Though fairly confident no part of me came into contact with Angel's rodent, there's only one thing for it—a full-body scrub beneath the hottest spray I can handle without melting away.

● ● ●

"Let me get this straight," I say as delicately as possible, "your hero, a six-foot-four, two-hundred-and-some-pound alpha male spends the entire first chapter relating his past to a canary that's perched in his peach tree?"

Carol, an unpublished writer, nods enthusiastically, "Clever, hmm?"

Dare I be more direct? I glance at Elizabeth who has paused with a celery stick halfway to her mouth. An apologetic smile and shrug is the only aid she offers.

Back to Carol who is happily gnawing a buffalo wing. Wishing I hadn't accepted Elizabeth's offer of an early dinner as payment for the talk I gave—I'd thought it would just be the two of us—I reach deep. Real deep. "Yes, clever, and certainly an unusual means of delivering your back story, but it strikes me as a bit . . . out of character for the manly hero you've created."

She sweeps her tongue across her top and bottom lip, removing the glow-in-the-dark buffalo sauce there. "You think?"

"Just a thought." I pick a fried mozzarella stick from the assorted appetizer platter.

Brow bent, Carol munches down another wing before acceding, "You may be right. What if it were a . . . " She looks up and left, then right. " . . . a cat? Or a dog?"

"Or a human being?" I suggest and snap my teeth on the breaded cheese.

"Nah." She wrinkles her pert little nose. "That would mean dialogue, and I'm no good at that."

"Oh."

Pretending an interest in the print behind me, Elizabeth begins chewing her celery with vigor.

Thank you, Elizabeth—Elizabeth who is rarely at a loss for words in the singles' Sunday School class I've been attending with her.

So, how to help Carol? Providing, of course, she isn't beyond help. . . . "Then you'd say that—"

My cell phone rings, causing me to startle. And send thanks heavenward for the reprieve. "I'll be just a moment." I flip open the phone. "Hello?"

"Ms. Sinclaire, it's Angel."

Hoping she's calling to tell me the mouse problem is resolved, I say, "Hi, Angel. Any luck?"

"Yep. Caught the little guy."

"Great!" I smile at Elizabeth and Carol. "And you put him where?"

"In a box. On my way home I'm going to drop him at Central Park."

Then she hasn't taken it into her head to adopt the rodent. That's progress. "Good idea," I say.

"I thought you'd like it."

"Thanks, Angel."

"Welcome. See you tomorrow." She hangs up.

I close my cell phone and look to Carol, who's expectantly waiting for me to resume the conversation interrupted by Angel.

"So narrative is your strength," I say.

She nods, deposits another grisly set of bones on her plate. "Definitely."

"So what are you going to do about the dialogue between your hero and heroine?"

She plucks another wing from the platter. "Already worked that out."

"How so?"

"My heroine—Jesse's her name—is deaf."

Tempting. Very tempting, and if I weren't so determined to prevail against my nicknaming habit, I'd give in and label Carol right here and now. Instead, I draw a deep breath. "Um, what kind of romance do you read?" Maybe she doesn't . . .

"All kinds."

Okay. . . . "So romance is your favorite genre?"

"No."

Now we're getting somewhere.

"But that's not to say I don't love it. I do!"

Maybe not.

"However, my favorite genre is self-help books—the 'Men Are From Mars' variety. I'm a psychology major, you know."

Didn't know, though should have guessed. I reach for a loaded potato skin.

"So what do you think?" Carol asks. "Have I got a viable story?"

I take a bite of the potato skin and chew it slooowly.

"It's definitely unique," I finally say. "Really pushes the genre's boundaries."

"Which is what editors want, right?"

Or so they say. I set the uneaten portion of the potato skin on my plate and clasp my hands on the table. "Dialogue is the heart of fiction, Carol, especially in a romance. It's your hero and heroine's primary mode of communication whereby they express their innermost feelings and desires. To top it off, good dialogue makes for a fast pace, which is really what our readers want—a breathtaking, seat-of-your-pants ride."

Her face has fallen right down to her britches. And I feel like a heel.

"You don't like it, then?"

"I'm not saying that. It's an interesting premise, and some editor may fall in love with it, but where do you go from there? What about the next book? If you want to write romance, eventually your hero and heroine have to talk to one another—not to mention your secondary characters."

Realization rises on her face. "I hadn't considered that."

"Listen, Carol—" I pull a cocktail napkin toward me. "There's an excellent online workshop called, 'The Power of Purposeful Dialogue.'" I pen its web address and push the napkin across the table to her. "I think it might help strengthen your dialogue."

"Oh!" Elizabeth finally jumps in. "I took that workshop last year. It was great."

Thank you, Elizabeth.

Carol stares at the napkin a moment before slipping it in her purse. "Maybe I'll give it a try. That, or write a self-help book instead."

She said it, not I.

As she reaches for another wing, I catch Elizabeth's gaze. She shrugs again. I shrug back.

TWELVE

"Uh, where are we?" I peer out the cab window at an immense old warehouse converted into specialty art galleries.

"Dinner and a movie," Snow White says as she opens the cab door. "Come on up." She steps to the sidewalk.

Suspicious, I hang tight until she pokes her head back inside the cab, "Come on, Adda."

Wondering what she's up to, I slide across the seat and join her on the sidewalk, where I drop my head back to survey the top two floors of the warehouse with their numerous glass panes reflecting "twilight's last gleaming."

Snow White loops her arm through mine. "If you're worried Dad's here, don't. He's out of town."

Then it *is* his loft she's brought me to. I meet her sparkling gaze. "Bad idea, Sophia."

"Look," she says, "we'll order Chinese takeout and pop in a movie. What harm is there in that?"

What harm when it's taken all these months since the conference at Tahoe for the rumors over my involvement with

Nick to die down? True, much of the speculation was merely annoying, but some had been downright ugly, replete with insinuations about publisher "casting couches." Fortunately, as the rumors have had nothing to feed on since, they've become old news. Which is exactly how I want to keep it. I draw a deep breath. "I shouldn't be here, Sophia."

"Sure you should," she says, then calls over her shoulder, "Thanks, Fawkes."

Fawkes? How does she know the cabbie's name? And why does it sound so familiar? She tugs me forward. "Come on."

I dig in my heels. "Look, Sophia— "

"Please." She bites her lip beseechingly, and I suddenly feel like Grumpy to her Snow White.

I sigh. "All right."

She beams.

Dragging my feet, I accompany her into the common entrance where we pass several darkened galleries on our way to the elevator. Shortly, she drags the gate of the elevator closed, and we begin a lurching ascent.

"Here we are," she says when we reach the loft. With a clamor, she pushes the gate back, and we step out. She has her keys ready, and a few moments later I enter the lair of Nick Farnsworth.

The door closes behind me, and Snow White flips a switch that casts light across an expanse of patterned cement floors, tastefully painted walls hung with art, and, ahead, the windows I spied from the street.

"Welcome to our home," she says.

"It's lovely."

She steps past me. "Dad did a lot of the restoration and remodeling himself."

I'm surprised, but then again, I'm not. It doesn't take a leap of imagination to picture Nick in jeans and T-shirt, a hammer in hand. Whew! Best not to let that image linger too long. "He . . . uh . . . owns the entire building?"

"Yep." She steps farther into the loft, and I follow. "Bought it years ago when it was a dilapidated warehouse with few prospects other than a wrecking ball." She turns a corner, and the room opens up into an enormous living area strewn with dark brown leather chairs and sofas, rustic tables, and throw rugs. But what catches my eye is a wall hung with framed pictures of all shapes and sizes. Drawn to it, I find myself gazing into the private world of Nick and Sophia Farnsworth.

There's a much younger Nick cradling a dark-haired infant, her tiny hand grasping his thumb; a proud-looking Nick holding Sophia's hand as she toddles alongside; a wide-eyed little girl blowing soap bubbles through a wand; a close-up of her smiling wide to show off missing front teeth; a pig-tailed girl pounding nails into a two-by-four; Nick in tuxedo with his preteen daughter; a teenage Sophia kicking a soccer ball; a black-and-white of Nick and her walking along a beach. Then there's the Nick I first met nearly a year ago, dark temples touched with silver. An arm around Sophia, who's wearing a high school graduation cap and gown, he smiles at the camera. And there's no mistaking his fatherly pride.

Sophia, the young woman, draws alongside me, surveys the pictures, and sighs. "I had a wonderful childhood, Adda." She adjusts the graduation picture, meets my gaze. "My dad's one-of-a-kind. Men like him don't happen very often."

I know what she's trying to tell me and, for an unguarded moment, wish it were possible, but her blessing can't be mine. I force a smile. "You're very fortunate, Sophia."

Her brow gathers, and I know she sees the strain in my face. However, she suddenly smiles. "And to top it off, the man can cook!" She turns away. "So what do you think of the loft?"

Though it really doesn't matter what I think, I say, "It's impressive."

She nods. "Dad calls it his nest egg, but I call it his therapy."

Wondering if it's any more effective than Post-it notes, I say, "Oh?"

"Yeah, a project this size tends to take one's mind off of life's rude awakenings."

She's talking about her mother—his ex—I realize. "I imagine so," I murmur.

Obviously none the worse for having grown up motherless—a credit to Nick—she steps away. "Make yourself at home while I call in our order. Anything in particular you like?"

"Umm . . . Moo Goo Gai Pan's always a winner."

"Can do." She disappears through a doorway.

Discomfort continuing to dampen my appreciation of her

home, I glance one last time at the wall of pictures, then to the open flight of stairs that leads to another floor where, doubtless, the bedrooms lie.

I dig my nails into my palms. I definitely should not be here. Not with Nick's presence seeping from every pore of every wall.

"Food will be delivered in half an hour," Snow White says when she reappears a couple minutes later carrying two glasses, one of which she passes to me. "Hope you like lemonade."

"Yes, thank you." I wrap stiff fingers around the perspiring glass and lower to the leather sofa. "So tell me about your mission trip."

With a flash of teeth, she drops down beside me. "Thought you'd never ask." She takes a sip of lemonade, sets her glass aside, and draws her legs up as if to settle in for a long while.

And strangely, I don't feel dread at the possibility it might be a long while.

"Though honestly, it was the hardest thing I've ever done," she says, "it was also the most fulfilling."

She launches into details of the flight to Ecuador, their arrival, the long drive to the outlying village, the villagers' enthusiastic reception, the living conditions rank with poverty, the children who trailed them everywhere, the hard work of erecting a church, then on to the next village.

The food comes, the food goes, and throughout the retelling, Snow White's hands fly, eyes sparkle, and smile brightens my world. How I wish I had what she has. True, I'm learning more about God and what following Jesus might mean, but I'm nowhere near the belief and understanding that this young woman, who is almost half my age, exudes. I envy her—in a good way.

"And there you have it!" She drops her head back against the sofa and shakes it. "It was incredible, Adda. God's hand was everywhere. Especially on the children."

I look to the photos on the sofa table that mostly depict children—some with Sophia. Though the majority were taken during her Ecuador mission, she had shown me some from other missions taken during the summers between her high school years. When my gaze falls upon a group of pictures that show Nick and Sophia on a mission to Mexico, my heart tosses.

"So, have I worn you out?"

I turn back to Snow White. "Not at all. In fact, I'm feeling quite inspired."

Without blinking, without apology, she says, "Do you know Christ, Adda?"

I've been asked it before. First by the Bible-carrying youths who appear on my doorstep—among them Josh—then Elizabeth, and most recently some of the more bold members from church; however, this time I don't quell or scramble for an excuse. Remembering how moved I was this past Christmas when I finally "got" the meaning of Christmas, I say, "I'm beginning to know him, but I'm afraid I have a long way to go."

I see her shoulders ease, next her jaw, and realize she was holding her breath. "Not as far as you think. Several years ago,

Dad was probably where you are right now, and then I decided to take my first mission trip. At first he refused to allow me to go, but when he realized how much it meant to me, he agreed, but only if he chaperoned." She nods at the pictures. "Until then, he was mostly skeptical. When we returned a month later, he dedicated his life to Christ."

I frown. "You mean you were saved first?"

"Um hmm. A school friend kept after me until I finally agreed to go to church with her."

Just like Elizabeth kept after me . . .

Snow White sighs. "It was the most incredible experience. Of course, once Dad accepted Christ, the experience became even more incredible. Though it hasn't been easy for him to let go of the past, and sometimes he messes up and does things he did before becoming a Christian, most times he has this incredible peace about him."

Feeling my throat tighten and eyes sting, I swallow hard. "That . . . that's great."

Snow White sits forward, regards me a moment, then rises. "I'd like to give you something."

Curious, I watch her cross to a small writing desk where she pulls out a notepad and pen. Over the next couple of minutes, all is silent as she jots something down. When she returns, she smiles encouragingly and hands me a piece of note paper.

"When you go home," she says, lowering beside me, "look those up, and I believe you'll find you're closer to God than you think."

I scan the Scripture references she penned, most of them familiar—in particular, Romans 10:9; however, I don't have the heart to tell her I'm already acquainted with the Scriptures Josh listed under "Salvation." Nor that what holds me back more than anything is relinquishing control of my life. I'm just not ready.

I look back at Sophia, smile. "Thank you."

"Welcome," she says. "Now for that movie I promised." She slaps her hands to the leather sofa, stands, and crosses to a glass-fronted cabinet. "Mind if I choose?"

I fold the paper, slide it into my purse. "Not at all."

"Then *Pride and Prejudice* it is."

"Ooh, one of my favorites," I say, only to mentally slap myself upside the head. "Uh, that runs some five hours, Sophia."

"Uh-huh, and don't you just love every minute?" She steps to another cabinet that encases a large, flat-screen television and various components.

I glance at my watch and go pop-eyed at the realization I've been at the loft for over two hours. "I really wasn't planning to stay that long, Sophia."

She slides the first of two DVDs into the player. "Well, let's just see how it goes, hmm?"

It's been months and months since I've seen it, I reason as I settle back in the chair. In fact, my last viewing was with Jake Grainger.

Shortly after Snow White joins me, the opening credits brighten the screen and light heartfelt music resounds around the loft. Over the next two hours, I attempt to immerse myself in Jane Austen's classic tale of love found, love lost, and love redeemed, but thoughts of Nick persist in pulling me back to the present. Nick who somehow makes his presence felt despite his absence. Nick who is a new Christian. Nick whose faith has given him a peace I envy.

Nick. Nick. Nick.

When the first DVD reaches its end, Snow White doesn't ask, and I don't protest, when she inserts the second. I am simply too exhausted. Thus, it seems the most natural thing in the world is to curl my legs under me and cuddle a big, fat pillow. Beside me, Snow White does the same.

A half hour later, feeling pleasantly snug, my lids droop. And that's all she wrote. . . .

• • •

I hear myself murmur something and, wondering what it was, open an eye. The darkened room is slow to take shape, but when it does I jolt upright, causing the blanket draped over me to slip.

Realizing I dozed off, I scowl. Aww—missed the best part of the movie!

I look beside me, but Snow White is gone. To bed? Pushing a hand through my tousled hair, I lower my feet to the floor and stand. "Sophia?"

No answer. I look around the room and focus on a digital clock that rudely announces the hour of 1 a.m. Ugh. Though tempted to return to the sofa and worry about getting home in the morning, I cross to the stairs. "Sophia?"

Silence. And so I begin the ascent. As the first room at the top of the stairs proves empty, I move to the second and feel my hand up the wall for a switch. Light illuminates the bedroom that, doubtless, belongs to Nick. Although I know I should beat a hasty retreat, I take in the relatively simple furnishings that exude an air of masculinity, which makes my mouth feel enormously dry.

I flick the switch and turn away. "Sophia?" I call softly as I approach the last room. I turn the handle and push the door inward, but as I reach for the switch, the moonlight coming through the window illuminates the still figure in bed. For a moment, I consider waking Snow White, but there's no need. I'll just call a cab and let her sleep.

Gently, I pull the door closed and turn back toward the stairs. As I reach the landing, a door closes below and my heart slams up my throat.

Dear God! A burglar?

Light floods the living area and firm footsteps tread the cement floor only to falter. A moment later, the reason appears in the heart-stopping person of Nick Farnsworth.

Oh . . . no . . .

Peering up the stairs where I stand frozen, he lowers his suitcase to the floor. "Adda," he says tightly.

I gulp.

He stares at me, making me uncomfortably aware of my

flyaway hair, rumpled blouse, and bare feet. And envious. Though the late hour has had an effect on him as well—unbuttoned collar, loosened necktie, rolled-up sleeves, and hair that looks as if it's been raked through—he appears none the worse for it. In fact, he looks incredibly yummy.

"Makes sense now," he murmurs, glancing at a piece of paper he holds.

I frown. "What?"

"The note Sophia left."

Oh, dear. I run my tongue around my lips. "Your daughter invited me for dinner and a movie and I . . . well, I guess I fell asleep. I didn't know you were returning tonight."

His chocolates slide up me.

Wishing I didn't look so rumpled, I nip my bottom lip. "She assured me you were out of town."

His eyebrows rise. "I was."

Then she hadn't lied—well, not exactly. The little matchmaker! "Oh," I breathe. Mustering composure, I force my feet forward and step from the stairs to where Nick stands.

He hands me the note that reads, *Just talk to her. And don't blow it. Love, Sophia.*

Warmth flooding my face, I fake a shrug and look up into his handsome face with its one-in-the-morning shadow that makes my palm itch to feel its rasp.

Oh no, I'm caving. Can't cave. Must . . . be . . . strong. "Well, at least someone around here knows what they want," I say, only to have my words punch me between the eyes. Did I really speak that thought aloud?

Through narrowed lids, Nick stares at me with those dark chocolates. "A rather enviable position to be in, I'm sure you'll agree."

Did *he* just say that? He did—slammed Jake Grainger right back in my face. Oookay. I step past him to the sofa and slide my feet into backless sneakers. "I believe that's my cue to leave," I say, stepping forward.

He looks past me. "Your purse."

Mercy! What *is* my problem? Making no attempt to hide the roll of my eyes, I turn back and scoop it up. "Would you mind calling me a cab?"

He shrugs up his coat and pushes his hands into his pant pockets. "That won't be necessary. I'll drive you home."

Ooh, not good. As much as I want to hug the space between us, I tell myself the Post-it-notes therapy wasn't for nothing and force myself to cross to where he stands. "Thank you, but a cab will suffice."

With a stern frown, he says, "It's after one in the morning, Adda."

I almost laugh. "Look, I'm not your daughter."

He stares at me, and something flickers in his eyes. "No," he says, deep and dark, "I would never mistake you for her."

What have we here? Improper muses.

Nothing, I tell myself.

Zero. Zip. Zilch.

I look over my shoulder at the door. "I really should be going."

"I'll drive you."

I jerk my head around. "No!"

Both eyebrows go up.

"I mean, I don't want to impose. Uh, obviously you weren't expecting to go out again and I—" cut with the verbal diarrhea, Adda! "—wouldn't want to keep you from getting your rest."

"You're not. Let's go."

"Well . . ." I bite my lip. "If you're sure."

"I am." He steps past me and his shoulder brushes mine, causing my senses to catch their breath. And my Post-it-notes therapy to shudder. *Thank you, Sophia.*

In silence, we ride down in the elevator and enter a garage where I expect to see a Porsche, a Corvette, a Jag, a BMW—something fast, flashy, and oozing with male hormones. However, the door he opens for me belongs to a five-passenger Lexus sedan. Nice. But not your everyday bachelor-trying-to-impress-women car.

I smile. Unlike Dick—er, Richard—and so many others, Nick's identity isn't wrapped up in a piece of shiny metal. Not that I'm surprised. "Nice car," I murmur as he slides in beside me.

"I like it," he says, glancing at me.

A few moments later, an enormous garage door rolls up, and he pulls out into the alley behind the warehouse.

Settling in for a drive that shouldn't take more than ten

minutes in the light traffic, I prop an elbow to the door and cup my chin in my hand.

"I understand *The Gifting* has received outstanding reviews," Nick says some minutes later.

Keeping my gaze straight ahead, I force a smile. "It has, though you'd never guess it from its absence from the best-seller lists."

"Underprinted."

I nod. "Grossly."

"And no plans to print more."

Though I'm still smarting from Farnsworth Publishing's backhand, I shrug. "No surprise, really."

"No."

And that's it. End of conversation until he pulls up in front of my town house. As I feel for the door handle, Nick asks, "Have you wrapped up *The Feud*?"

I look into his dimly lit face. "The first draft landed on Kathryn's desk yesterday afternoon."

"Good. I look forward to reading it."

I draw my hand farther down the door and hit upon the handle. "Well, thank you for the ride." With a tug, the door opens out onto the sidewalk. "And I'm sorry for the inconvenience."

He grips my upper arm. "Adda."

I jerk at his touch, and he releases me.

"I apologize for Sophia's interference," he says. "She likes you and seems to think . . ."

I wait for him to finish the sentence, but he doesn't. And

doesn't need to. I smile tightly. "Bummer, huh? There's just no accounting for taste—or should I say youth?" I sigh. "But give her time and maybe she'll come around." Ooh, that sounded bitter. But it can't be unspoken. Swinging my feet to the sidewalk, I unfold from the car.

"Good night, Nick." I push the door closed and, feeling him watch me walk away, ascend the steps of my town house. Only as I slide the key in the lock am I struck by the realization I didn't tell Nick where I live—that he knew. Of course, so did Snow White. Sheesh! Is nothing sacred?

Though tempted to glance over my shoulder, I face forward, turn the knob, and let myself in. As I lean back against the door, I hear Nick's car pull away. I sag. He still has a hold on me, and I hate it. I want him out of every little crevice he's seeped into. But how do I manage that when even his name makes me weak at the knees?

THIRTEEN

*essage from: Noelle Parker, Monday, the 23rd : Call Nick Farnsworth.*

Message from: Noelle Parker, Tuesday, the 24th: Call Nick Farnsworth.

Message from: Nick Farnsworth, Wednesday, the 25th: Call me.

Message from: Nick Farnsworth, Thursday, the 26th: Call me.

Message from: Noelle Parker, Friday, the 27th: Call him, bleep it! And just where the bleep are you?

I sigh, fan the sheaf of "urgent" messages that Angel shoved at me the minute I walked in her office. Some welcome home. Returned from vacation all of five minutes and I'm bombarded by reality. Not that I didn't know about the calls, as I checked in with Angel several times from Martha's Vineyard, having intentionally left my cell phone behind. Of course, I know I shouldn't have ignored the messages, but at the time saw no reason to spoil my vacation by calling *him*. After all, he'd encroached on my R & R enough as it was, especially during my walks along the deserted beach.

Remembering the gray days and chill air that swept in from

the ocean, I shudder. Whatever possessed me to visit Martha's Vineyard in winter? Not only was it dreary and frigid, but it was downright dull. Still, something good came of it, as the lack of activity and resulting solitude found me time and again turning to the Bible. Not only did I finally finish the New Testament and poke around the Old—sans lists of descendants!—but I had plenty of time to contemplate Snow White's Scriptures. Of course, on those nights when sleep eluded me, I'd had plenty of time to contemplate her father.

But I *am* over him. There's just this . . . residue. Nothing I can't handle, though.

"Gonna call him?"

I startle, blink Angel to focus where she peers at me across her desk. "Later," I croak. Avoiding looking at Doodles, who's curled in a mess of hair on her shoulder, I crumple the phone messages and drop them in her wastebasket.

"Love his voice," Angel says.

"Hmm?"

"His voice—Nick Farnsworth's." She gives a little shudder. "Deep and oh so yummy."

Though I attempt to turn back the green-eyed ogre named jealousy, it takes a firm hold of me.

Over him, are you? Improper puts in a special appearance, having been absent for some time.

Am too, Prim sniffs—another special appearance.

I shrug. "His voice? Hadn't noticed."

Ugh. Little white lies are harder to control than whoppers.

"Well I noticed his voice," Angel says. "And when I saw him—"

"You saw him?"

"Um hmm."

"He was here?"

Her black-lined eyes pop wide. "Oh! No! I'm talking about the full-page article in yesterday's paper." She throws her arms wide as though to brag on the size of a fish. "*Nick Farnsworth: A Man in Perpetual Motion*." She lowers her arms. "Of course, you probably didn't get the paper."

"No," I say as evenly as possible, though I declare I'm having heart palpitations. "You . . . uh . . . didn't happen to keep the article?"

"Sure did. It mentioned you, after all."

It did?

She swivels around in her chair and pulls open a file drawer. "Said you were lead author for Intrepid's new line." In her usual, efficient manner, she locates the clipping, unfolds it, and hands it to me. "It's all there."

He certainly is. I stare at the grainy, full-length picture of *him* standing alongside his desk—the same desk behind which we kissed—

Stop it! Stop it now! Hoping my hands don't start trembling, I look lower. Center of the article are four small publicity photos captioned: "*Nick Farnsworth's new leading ladies—Mona Wales,*

Shannon Sweet, Jeanne Matriarch, and Adda Sinclaire."

I'm listed last. . . .

Don't take it personally, I tell myself. He had nothing to do with the article's layout.

Or perhaps he did. . . . Maybe an attempt to further disassociate himself from the rumors over our involvement?

"Isn't it great?" Angel says.

I startle. "What?"

"The article."

"Oh. Yes. Great." I fold and tuck it beneath my arm. "Time to unpack." I heft the large duffle I dumped on the floor of her office and shoulder it. As I turn away, the phone rings. "If Ludwig shows early," I toss over my shoulder, "have him *whip* up a batch of smoothies."

"Right, Ms. Sinclaire." A moment later, I hear, "Adda Sinclaire's office. Angel speaking. How may I help you?"

Her delivery is so smooth and professional—despite a slight slur around her pierced tongue—no caller could possibly guess what's at the other end of the line. If they only knew . . .

Half wishing I had canceled the session with Ludwig, though I certainly need it after stuffing my face with gourmet cuisine these past five days, I start up the stairs.

"Ms. Sinclaire!"

I look around.

Angel's head pops around the doorway. "It's him," she says, beaming away. "Mr. Farnsworth again."

Something flutters in my chest, and I slap a hand to it in a feeble attempt to squash it. "Um . . . tell him I'm still out." Ooh. That was a lie, wasn't it?

Angel's smile dims. "Okay, but Ms. Parker is not going to be happy."

Despite my pricked conscience, I repeat, "Tell him," and continue up the stairs.

I *will* call him back. Eventually. Perhaps tomorrow—Saturday—when Intrepid's offices are closed. Or I could wait until Monday. Yes, Monday. Gives me the weekend to prepare myself for his "deep and oh-so-yummy" voice.

I step into my bedroom and dump the duffle, the unpacking of which can wait. "*Nick Farnsworth: A Man in Perpetual Motion*" cannot.

● ● ●

"And breathe out. That's it, Ms. Sinclaire. Now inhale as you go down."

I make a face at Ludwig where he's hunkered alongside me and, keeping my back flat, lower my chest to the floor for one blessed second.

"And up," he pounds away, "breathing out on the effort."

The burn! Arms beginning to shake, I grunt and barely elevate myself enough to straighten my arms. I'm dying. Dying!

"Good. One more set."

Toes teetering on the chair seat upon which I've elevated my legs to perform incline push-ups, I slowly lower my chest to the floor again. Don't know how I manage it, but I give him his final set. And collapse. "I hate you, Ludwig."

Grinning big, he rises to his tree-trunk legs and crosses to the table before the sofa where two smoothies sit. "That is good. It means I'm doing my job."

"No," I say, flopping onto my back, "it means I hate you. Simple as that."

He shrugs. "As long as you keep paying me." He takes a long drag on the smoothie.

I eye the other smoothie that has yet to pass my hot, dry lips. "Have mercy and give me some."

"Cool down first," he says, and I hate him double time.

Muttering above my breath so he'll hear, I work through the cool-down stretches as quickly as possible.

"Not so fast, Ms. Sinclaire. Start over."

I glare at him. "I will not."

He raises an eyebrow and pats the whip at his waist.

"Just you try it, Buster." I reach to my toes one last time.

"Uh, uh, uh." He shakes his head. "You haven't worked out in over a week. You're going to be sore. Now start over."

I pull my knees to my chest, give them a hug, and lean back on my hands. "No can do."

"It's for your own good, Ms. Sinclaire—and mine." He unhooks the whip. "You limp tomorrow, people say Ludwig doesn't take care of his clients."

In no mood to humor him, I say, "Don't worry. I take full responsibility and promise I won't short you the last ten minutes."

A determined glint in his eyes, he sucks down another mouthful of smoothie, then sets his glass on the sofa table.

Uh oh.

With a flick of the wrist, he cracks the whip, and it strikes the carpet alongside me.

It almost hit me! I glare at the black, braided leather that landed near my hand, then lunge for it.

Ludwig squeaks—yes, squeaks. "Don't touch the whip! Don't touch!"

I stand and, hand-over-hand, travel the whip's length toward him.

"Ms. Sinclaire," he protests with a tug that only pulls me nearer, "let go."

A few moments later, I'm chest to chest with him—well, chest to abs. "Look, you big lug—" I poke his tautly T-shirt-clad chest. "When I say 'no,' I mean 'no'!" Which is exactly how I handled Jake the last day of the conference at Lake Tahoe. And it worked. "Got it?"

Ludwig stares down at me, hurt flickering in his eyes. "Got it, Ms. Sinclaire. Now can I have my whip back?"

I am woman; hear me roar!

"Uh . . . Ms. Sinclaire?" Angel calls.

I look over my shoulder and . . . oh my . . . It's *him*. In the flesh. Perhaps a bit more silver at the temples, but as good-looking as ever. And he's staring at me as though he's not sure whether to laugh or leave.

"Mr. Farnsworth is here," Angel says.

I can see that. And here I stand, whip in hand, wearing a sweat-darkened two-piece that leaves no bump to the imagination. Ludwig, the Terminator, looms over me grasping the other end of the whip.

How's this for a headline: ROMANCE AUTHOR, ADDA SINCLAIRE, TO STAR IN THIS YEAR'S MOST PERVERSE FLICK.

I am a glutton for punishment.

"Mr. Farnsworth," I say, and am jolted by his name on my lips. Having sworn off speaking any part of his name as another form of self-therapy, it feels strange . . . kind of nice . . . actually good . . . bordering on wonderful.

You are sooo busted, Prim drawls.

I haven't succumbed to his first name, I defend myself. Of course, it's only a matter of time. In which case, there's always Post-it notes and tally marks. Not to mention Scripture. Lots of Scripture.

"Please, Ms. Sinclaire—" Ludwig's Arnold-esque voice resounds around the room. "Can I have my whip back?"

"Oh!" Fingers smoking, I release it and wrench my gaze from Ni—*him* to Ludwig. "Sorry." I step back. "Well, I . . . um . . . guess our session is over, hmm?"

Precious whip restored, he glares at me as he reels it in. "It's over."

Attempting to right my upended composure before I turn and face *him* again, I nod. "Thank you, Ludwig. It was a great workout."

Still glowering, he returns the whip to his belt and crosses to his duffle. With the usual clank of dumbbells, he hoists the bag onto his shoulder, then retrieves his smoothie.

And there goes another of my glasses—a small matter, considering who's waiting for me to turn around. Well, *he* can wait a few moments longer. Thankfully, my glutes are still in tip-top shape.

Sucking at his smoothie, Ludwig steps forward. Though I expect him to blow past me, he halts and, to my horror, pinches the exposed flesh between the top and bottom of my outfit. "Eat less," he says, jiggling thc handful, "move more."

Oh . . . my . . .

As though fully aware of my discomfort—and enjoying every moment—he grins. "I'll bill you." He steps past me. "Have a good day, Ms. Sinclaire."

I look heavenward, do the "why me" thing, then suck in my abs and turn. Avoiding *his* gaze, I look to Angel. She's also grinning, though I'd say it has more to do with the man beside her than my humiliation. "Angel, would you see Ludwig to the door?"

The grin dissolves. "He knows where it's at."

Accurate, efficient, and a hard worker, but as for

etiquette . . . "Humor me, hmm?"

She heaves a sigh and follows Ludwig from the sitting room.

And now for the matter that outweighs the loss of yet another glass. Wondering how much of my spat with Ludwig *he* overheard, I meet his gaze.

"You appear to have perfected your 'no,'" he says.

I blink. "My . . . 'no'?"

He raises his eyebrows. "The 'when I say no, I mean no' bit."

Ah. My assertive-slash-aggressive encounter with Ludwig over the whip, which had worked so well with Jake. I shrug. "All in the delivery, I suppose."

"Then you've been practicing?"

Was that an inquiry into my status with Jake? I shrug. "Practice makes perfect."

He stares at me.

Moving right along . . .

"Ms. Sinclaire?"

I look past his shoulder to where Angel has reappeared in the doorway. "Yes?"

"If you'd like, I can stay late and start on that mailer we discussed."

She's *never* offered to stay late on Fridays. In fact, though she works ten 'til five Monday through Thursday, she kicks off at three on Fridays — which is fast approaching. Too fast for her, apparently, and it can only be because of *him*.

"No thank you," I say. "Monday will be soon enough to start on it."

Her hopeful smile dissolves. "You sure?"

"Positive."

"All right. Just thought I'd offer."

"I appreciate that."

As she turns away, I shift my gaze to *him*. "I wasn't expecting you."

He looks me up and down. "I can see that."

Fighting the urge to cross my arms over my abs, which are actually in better shape than Ludwig would have him believe, I say, "Obviously, you caught me at a bad time."

Looking oh-so-good in a collarless white shirt and black slacks, he thrusts his hands into his pockets, and I realize how much I miss seeing him do that. Sounds strange, but there's something so . . . masculine about it.

"Unfortunately," he says, "it was either today or not for another two weeks."

Oh? He's going somewhere? Not that I care. Constantinople or Timbuktu would be better than here. Just hope I haven't used up all my Post-its.

"When I spoke with your . . . " The corners of his mouth tilt. " . . . personal assistant . . . "

His meaningful pause jolts me to an awareness of the situation, which, until this moment, went right over my head. Conjuring a vision of Angel opening the door to this suave, sophisticated man, I snort. And snort again as I recall his phone call earlier when I'd humored myself over the stark contrast between Angel's phone persona and reality—that no caller could guess what lay at the other end of the line, and if they only knew . . .

To my surprise, the tickle in me multiplies to giggles. Though I slap a hand over my mouth and lower my chin, my eyes tear and shoulders shake as bubbles of laughter pop from me. Bending forward, I'm struck by another vision: Doodles nesting in Angel's hair and chittering away as she opens the door to *him*.

"Adda?"

I hold up a staying hand. "Sorry." Another vision—Angel soothing the overwrought Doodles by easing him into the holster beneath her little black skirt.

"What is it?" *he* asks, advancing on me.

And to top it off, he walks in on me and Ludwig in the middle of our whip-induced tiff. I almost feel sorry for him.

"Adda?" His hand clasps my shoulder—the fastest cure for the giggles if ever there were one.

I draw a deep breath and straighten. "Oooh," I sigh long, meeting his gaze with moist eyes. "Forgive me. Something just . . . tickled my funny bone."

He drops his hand from me.

Shoot! Not that I'm interested in him. The goose bumps, flushed skin, and racing heart are all merely a case of nerves.

And you are the most pitiful woman in all of New York City.

"More private amusement?" he says, reminding me of my

confessed penchant for nicknames. And once more, I guess I'll have to own up.

I shake my head. "I was just imagining your reaction to Angel when she answered the door—a shock, I'm sure."

He continues to glower, but then—RED ALERT! RED ALERT!—a bit of the left cleft dimple appears. "Momentary only, as I recalled you had renamed your assistant Morticia. Thus, I was assured I was at the right place."

For one long, unguarded moment that wreaks havoc with these past months of self-therapy, I smile. And he smiles back, putting me at risk for totally and completely falling off the wagon. I look down. "So . . . you're here."

Well, duh!

"As I said, if not today, it would be two weeks before I could discuss your manuscript with you."

Get a grip, Adda. Breathe . . . exhale . . . breathe . . . I press my shoulders back and lift my chin. "Do you do this sort of thing often—make house calls to your authors?"

That smile of his that did a number on my self-therapy? It disappears faster than you can say "open foot, insert mouth." Oops. I mean—"Open mouth, insert foot."

"Never," he rumbles. "Though I would have preferred to discuss the manuscript with you over the phone or at my office, you've been impossible to reach all week. Thus, when I overheard you instruct your assistant to tell me you were out, it seemed the best avenue—if not the most inconvenient."

Groan. *Oh, Angel, dahling, remember that raise you were hinting at? We'll talk about it when you learn to use the HOLD button!*

Though I tell myself he neither needs nor deserves an explanation, I say, "Sorry about that. I returned today from a getaway and was in no mood to talk business."

Apology *not* accepted, if his steely eyes are anything to go by. "Then you make a habit of leaving town without informing others of your whereabouts?"

I blink. Just who does he think he is to question me about what I do with my personal time? Me—a writer who punches no time clock; a single woman who answers to no one?

And don't forget—a scorned woman who has sworn off men. Especially this one, Prim reminds.

I prop my hands on my hips. "My assistant knew how to reach me, and as far as I'm concerned, it was no one else's business." Which was exactly what I'd told Angel. And she had complied by informing all callers I was out.

"That's where you're wrong," he snaps. "When a publisher pays out the kind of advance Intrepid paid for your manuscript, it *is* their business—especially considering the magnitude of the project Intrepid is attempting to get under way and that *you* are its lead author. Of course, that's open to renegotiation."

When he puts it that way . . . Though what I really want is to go to the mat with him, I know he's right. I should have called. But I just . . . couldn't. I wasn't ready.

Peering up at him, I draw a deep breath and sigh. "Look, if

there's one thing I learned recently, it's never to mix business with pleasure—of any sort. I would think you had learned that yourself."

His mouth tightens.

"I'm sorry if my absence inconvenienced you," I continue, "but I believed that whatever you wished to discuss could wait until Monday."

He shifts his jaw as if to ease the tension. "There you're wrong, as well."

Then . . . ? Ooh. Doesn't sound good. Though I was confident *The Feud* was as near perfect as I could make it, maybe not. Squashing the impulse to chew my lower lip, I motion to the sofa. "Since you're here, we might as well get it over with."

"I'm glad you share my sentiment," he returns, then strides to the doorway, retrieves a black leather case, and, a few moments later, lowers to the sofa.

"So what's the problem?" I ask, coming around the glass-topped table to stand over him.

He sweeps his gaze up me. "Perhaps you'd like to change before we get started?"

I glance down at the two-piece, which despite Ludwig's attempt to humiliate me, fits pretty well. Perhaps too well for you-know-who's peace of mind. Enjoying the ego massage, I say, "Actually, I'm quite comfortable. However, if it makes *you* uncomfortable . . . "

Nostrils flaring, he says, "Not at all."

Liar, liar, pants on fire.

"Good, then let's get to it."

He opens his case and deposits my hefty manuscript on the table. "Male point of view," he says.

Hovering, I stare at the title page, which is crammed with numbered notes jotted in red. Reminds me of when Joyce red-inked my first manuscript until it looked like someone had died.

With dread, I sink down on the sofa beside him. "What about my male point of view?"

"There's not enough."

"Oh?" I drag my gaze from the manuscript and find myself staring into eyes that are waaay too close. Though I know I should be less obvious, I pop up and scoot down the sofa to put a respectable two feet between us.

Amusement lights his eyes, and I remember the first time I saw him after I upchucked at The Ivories.

"You're referring to the . . . um . . . men's edition," I say.

"Actually, the women's is what's at discussion here."

"The women's," I echo. The *women's*?

"Of course," he continues, "the revisions I'm asking for will carry over into the men's edition and be further expanded upon."

I shake my head. "I thought you only intended to get involved with the men's edition."

"I did, but considering what we're attempting to do with the new line—the risk involved—Kathryn thought I should handle this."

"Oh." The bottom threatening to drop out of me, I pull my

lower lip between my teeth. "That bad, huh?"

He hesitates, but instead of cranking the screw another turn, says, "Not bad. In fact, I believe this story has the potential to be your best."

Well, that's some consolation.

"However, to attain that status, it has to be reworked. Though the strong male point of view your readers have come to expect is evidenced throughout the first ten chapters, it falls short during the last eighteen."

I look down at my hands clasped in my lap. "Oh," I say again as I search for an explanation of how it might have happened. Post-Lake Tahoe, I realize. Post-*him*! Mentally bracing myself, I look up. "How much revision are we talking about?"

He angles his body toward me and, almost apologetically, says, "You'll be busy."

There are worse things in life. I blow a breath up my brow. "So male point of view is the only problem with the story."

"The *main* problem."

Then there's more . . . Averting my gaze, I catch sight of my smoothie where it sits on the table. Though it's lost its appeal, I lunge for it and snap my teeth on the straw.

Suck . . . suck . . . suck . . .

Were I alone, I'd assume the fetal position. Reluctantly, I lower the glass.

He raises an eyebrow as though to ask if I'm ready for the next round.

So I stall. "As it appears we're going to be here a while— " I start to rise. "Would you like something to drink?"

"Perhaps later."

Of course. He's having too much fun to stop now. "Okay." I drop back to the sofa. "Bring it on."

"Your love scenes."

I gape, and heat rises up my throat. "Excuse me?"

"Though Kathryn and I disagree on the extent to which they need revision, there are some changes I want made."

"What changes?"

"As Kathryn recently said about Birgitta Roth's submission, 'too many body parts.'"

Yuck. Determined as I am to forgive that woman, I really don't care to be equated with her. I shake my head. "What do you mean too many? Have I given my hero an extra hand . . . an extra leg . . . "

"As with your previous books, you need to leave more to the imagination, Adda."

Is this the Christian in him talking? 'Cause it sure can't be the man!

"I don't know what happened between your last book and this one— "

Doesn't he? *He* happened.

"—but it's off." He glances at the manuscript. "Your writing is strong enough to carry the book without falling back on sensationalism, which is what Intrepid bought—and what Intrepid wants."

I don't understand. "Uh . . . can you give me an example?"

He flips through the manuscript to the first love scene. "It starts here with the kiss." He taps a paragraph halfway down the page.

He's bothered by a kiss? Got to be kidding. Still, I read it through and am assaulted by remembrance of the kiss we shared in his office. Realizing I modeled my hero and heroine's kiss after that one encounter—hoping the man beside me doesn't realize it himself—I swallow hard. Regardless, I tell myself, there's nothing sensational about it. I look up. "You, of all people, have a problem with that kiss?"

Ooh, did I say that?

His brow lowers. "The kiss is fine, Adda. That's just where the love scene starts. Read on."

Just had to overreact. Man, am I jumpy! Wishing I could blame my flush of warmth on the workout, I gratefully return my gaze to the manuscript. Five minutes and three manuscript pages later, embarrassment at an all-time high, I force myself to sit back.

"Well?"

I meet *his* gaze. "My hero's just . . . adventurous," I say, lamely, though I silently concede he's right about the scene. I did go overboard. Far too much detail.

"*Too* adventurous," he says, more forcefully than I can handle at the moment.

Defenses going up, I raise my chin. "Unlike someone we know."

His chocolates darken. "More like Jake Grainger, hmm?" he

says in a cold, still voice, then sweeps his gaze over me.

That thing which pulses between us when we're together starts to throb. And for a moment, I forget the promise I made myself to not allow this to happen again. In short, I am *not* over him—may never be over him, ridiculous as that may seem—but I have my pride. Well, sort of.

I take a deep breath and pull back. "Perhaps it would be better if I changed into something more . . . suited to the purpose of your visit."

He inclines his head. "I agree."

I press to my feet. "It shouldn't take but a few minutes." I turn and, feeling his gaze, cross the room and step through the doorway. Out of sight, I pause at the base of the stairs and drop my chin to my chest. I can do this, I tell myself. If it takes two hours . . . if it takes five, I can get through this. But oh, how I wish I could just crawl in bed and pull the covers over my head.

Resignedly, I grab the stair rail and take the steps two at a time to the first landing.

"Ms. Sinclaire," Angel calls as I pass.

I stick my head in her office.

"Is he still here?" she asks.

The question is—why is *she* still here? But before I can jump on her crush over a man so far beyond her reach he might as well reside on Mars—of which I'm painfully aware myself—I squash the sarcastic rejoinder before it forms. "Still here," I say, then sigh. "It looks as though we'll be working on my manuscript a while.

Think you can rustle up some snacks to see us through?"

She jumps up so fast Doodles lets out a squeak. "You bet!"

I wrinkle my nose and nod at her thigh whence the sound issued. "Leave Doodles up here."

"Oh! Right!"

As she raises her skirt, I add, "And wash your hands."

"Of course!"

I turn and ascend the stairs to my bedroom. Twenty minutes later, five of which were spent beneath the stinging spray of the shower, I'm wearing gray sweat pants that go back to when I was two sizes larger and a navy blue slouch sweater, the sleeves of which extend past my knuckles.

I halt before the full-length mirror in my bedroom, turn this way and that, and give myself the nod. Nothing skimpy going on here, which ought to satisfy Prim. And infuriate Improper . . .

Patting my damp hair that I pulled back into a ponytail, I venture out of my sanctuary. When I step into the sitting room, I discover Angel and *him* alongside the table upon which a plate of cheese and crackers sits.

Wearing a lazy smile, he leans near to peer into her mouth. What the—

"What do you think?" she says, dropping back a step. "Get rid of it?"

He shrugs. "Does it make it difficult to eat?"

"Yes! And in case you haven't picked up on it, it causes me to slur a bit."

Great! I'm gone twenty minutes and she's consulting him about her pierced tongue. He's got to be crawling out of his skin. Or is that me?

"That's a decision you'll have to make yourself, Angel," he says, "but if it's causing you as much trouble as you say . . . " He lifts a shoulder.

"Yeah." She nods. "Tough decision. Hey!" She starts to lift her shirt. "Wanna see my belly ring?"

Past time I made my presence known. "Thank you for getting the snack together, Angel." I step farther into the room. "It looks great."

They turn to me, and there's no mistaking Angel's disappointment. "You're welcome, Ms. Sinclaire," she begrudges, smoothing her shirt. "Is there anything else I can get the two of you before I leave?"

I shake my head. "You've done enough." Far and away enough.

She sighs. "All right, then. I'll just call a cab and be on my way."

"Take mine," *he* says. "It's out front."

What? The cab's been waiting all this time? What is it with this guy and cabs?

"The driver will take you wherever you need to go," he says.

Angel beams. "Really, Mr. Farnsworth?"

He nods. "And call me 'Nick.'"

Nick. Nick. Nick, Improper chants, and I feel the hole I'm in sink deeper.

"Thanks, Nick," Angel says. "I appreciate it."

"You're welcome."

"Well, I guess I'll grab my jacket and Doodles and get out of your hair." She raises a hand and flutters a good-bye I've never seen before, then steps forward and past me as though I'm little more than a hat rack. Hmm. If not a pay raise, maybe a pay cut . . .

As her feet tread the stairs, I meet *his* gaze and, pretending everything is hunky-dory, spread my arms wide to display my change of clothes. "Better?"

His brow creases as he looks me up and down. "Worse, but then, that *was* the idea, wasn't it?"

"A good one, you'll agree." I cross to the sofa and lower to the edge. "Let's get started."

He comes around and seats himself, leaving barely a foot between us. But I can handle it now that I'm no longer scantily clad.

"Chapter eleven," he says, jumping right in. "Hero and heroine have just married under duress." He looks up. "Pivotal scene."

I nod.

"And all the insight you offer into your hero's feelings is through your heroine's eyes—*her* observations."

I frown. Did I really do that? If so, what was I thinking?

He flips forward through the manuscript and taps a passage marked "transition to hero's POV." "Here's where I want to see a shift in point of view."

I lean forward and skim the passage. To his credit, it's definitely the place to do it.

"A short, transitional paragraph will suffice, staying in your hero's point of view for the remainder of the chapter—roughly two pages."

I sit back. "That shouldn't be too hard."

He looks around. "It gets harder."

Surprise, surprise.

And so it goes for the next three hours as he picks apart my baby until I could scream. Not that he's off base. I'm humiliated, is all. Post-*him* or not, how could I have drifted so far from my fictional hero—that hunk of manhood who's been the only male in my life since Lake Tahoe?

By the time he returns to the shortcomings of my love scenes, I'm black and blue from all the blows he's landed to my ego.

An hour earlier, in hopes the floor would open and swallow me up, I slid to the carpet between sofa and table. But so far, the floor is not cooperating, and here I sit cross-legged alongside *his* legs as he searches out the next troublesome love scene.

Yawning, I look to the front windows, which have darkened with the arrival of night. I am soooo tired!

"Read this." He pushes a page in front of me.

Oh goody . . . I pull it nearer and scan to the paragraph where the redlining begins in the middle of my heroine's awakening.

So what is *his* problem? I look around. "And your point is?"

His eyebrows arch above wire-frame glasses that have

materialized since I last looked his way. "Suspend disbelief—to excess."

I blow a breath up my face. "Everyone needs a little suspension of disbelief—to excess."

He removes his glasses and sits back. "This isn't going to work, is it?"

Though I know he's referring to my love scene revisions, I'm reminded of when he dumped me. Emotions bouncing all over the place, I look back to the manuscript page and stare at all the red marks he made on it.

"No," I say, "it isn't going to work." With a resounding *thud*, I drop my forehead to the glass tabletop and stare at the blurred page beneath my nose until my eyes begin to cross and head to pound. With a groan, I lower my lids and sink into silence. Deeper . . . and deeper . . .

"Adda?"

Have I mentioned how sensuous my name sounds on his lips? "Hmm?"

"Perhaps we ought to leave the love scenes for you and Kathryn to hash out."

"Okay," I croak, sounding so pitiful I'd be embarrassed for me if I were him. But it can't be helped. I'm wrung out—nothing more to give. In fact, I can't think of anything that would induce me to move so much as an inch.

"Hungry?" he asks.

I sit straight up. "Come again?"

"Are you hungry?"

He's inviting me to dinner? Just like that? Despite everything? Of course, I'll have to decline. I think . . .

Oh, why can't he be a louse like Jake? Why does the mere hint of a smile . . . a glimmer in those chocolates . . . a shift in his tone . . . a tilt of his head . . . make my pulse react? What is it about Nick—

Aargh! He's supposed to be *he*, *him*, or *his*—not *Nick*. I have got it bad.

"Well?" he asks with a raised eyebrow.

Although Prim is shoving "no" up my throat, Improper reaches my lips first. "As a matter of fact, I am hungry."

He nods. "Like Japanese food?"

Not my favorite. "Depends on whether or not it's still moving when it hits my plate."

He smiles.

Helllloooo dimple!

"There's a nice little place not far from here." He stands. "Grab a jacket and we'll go."

I should turn him down, I know, but when he offers a hand up, there's no going back. I stare at his long fingers, remembering when they—

"Adda?"

"Oh!" I place my hand in his, and his fingers close warm and snug around mine as he draws me to my feet. And suddenly he's so near I can almost taste him. Not good.

I pull my hand free and step back. "Thank you," I say. "I . . . um . . . I'll just run upstairs and get my jacket and meet you at the door—" I wrinkle my nose as I catch sight of my slouch sweater and sweat pants. "Perhaps I ought to change."

"Don't," he says so abruptly there can be little doubt he's still attracted to me. Of course, I *am* biased.

I meet his chocolates. "Sure?" I sweep a hand down my front. "Next to you, I look like a slob."

"The restaurant is casual. You look fine."

Which is exactly how he prefers me. Wouldn't want to be tempted by a strappy little dress. "All right. I'll get my jacket."

When I return a few minutes later, his black leather case is at his feet, and he's lifting his coat from the rack beside the door. As he shrugs into the sleeves, he turns to me, and his brow gathers as he notices my jean-clad legs.

"A happy medium," I say, "casual without going grunge." And too bad for him if he can't handle clothes that flatter my figure.

As his eyes travel back up me, the phone rings.

I look over my shoulder toward the kitchen. "Probably my agent wanting to tongue-lash me for not getting back to you." However, when the answering machine kicks on, it's Joyce who calls to me.

"You there, Adda? Pick up if you're there." *Hack, hack, hack.* "It's important."

I frown over the urgency in her coarse voice.

"Need to take her call?" Nick asks.

I look back at him, considering. Probably just some problem with her editor. Or maybe her husband's coming out isn't going well. Perhaps—

"Okay, then," she says, and I hear her drag hard on what I hope is a cigarette and not a cigar. "Call me as soon as you get in, 'cause something's going down."

Click.

"Going down?" I mutter.

Strange . . .

"All right?" Nick asks.

"Uh . . . " I shrug. "I guess. I'll call her back later."

He picks up his case. "Let's go."

I start to follow, but in the next instant turn back around. "My purse. Let me just grab— "

"Do me a favor," he says. "Leave it."

I look over my shoulder, and the glint in his eyes reminds me of my penchant for forgetting my purse whenever he's near. "Uh . . . right." I grin.

Returning the grin—love that left cleft dimple!—he opens the door.

Trying not to go to goo, I tuck my chin into my jacket's collar in anticipation of the chill night air. Outside, I pause to lock the door. "The night you drove me home from your loft," I say, turning to face him where he awaits me on the steps, "how did you know where I live? Did Noelle tell you?"

"No," he says, and once more reaches a hand to me.

I hesitate, but in the end thrill to his warm flesh gripping mine. To my surprise, he doesn't loosen his hold when I reach the bottom step. And so, awaiting an explanation of how he discovered where I live, I walk beside him to the cab that's been waiting for hours, but he doesn't enlighten me. Doesn't need to, it turns out, for as I step into the back of the cab, the driver looks over his shoulder, and I'm struck by recognition.

"Fawkes," Nick says as he slides in beside me, "you've met Ms. Sinclaire."

I also recognize the name and, sifting backward, place it. The night we dined at Cristoforo's, Nick had told Sophia that Fawkes would deliver her and her friends home. Then when Sophia and I exited the cab at her home, she thanked the cabbie by name — Fawkes again.

The man smiles at me. "We've met, Sir. Informally, of course."

As in the distinguished, gray-haired driver who took me home following my rendezvous with Nick at his office all those months ago. And likely the same cabbie Nick arranged to deliver me home following my stormy exit from Barnes & Noble — which explains how he snagged an off-duty cab.

"Adda, my driver, Fawkes," Nick finishes introductions.

"Nice to meet you — again," I manage.

Fawkes inclines his head and looks to Nick. "Where would you like to go, Sir?"

"Arrigoto's."

"Yes, Sir." He shifts back around, puts the cab in gear, and pulls onto the road.

Nick is wearing one of his heart-thumping half-smiles when I look around. "So I have Fawkes to thank for informing you and Sophia of where I live." I settle back in the seat. "Or should I say blame?"

White teeth flashing in the cab's dim interior, he leans near me, and the outside of his leg brushes mine.

Be still my beating heart.

"That all depends on the outcome, doesn't it?" he says.

Telling myself he's referring to my book, I nod. "Everything depends on the outcome."

Adda, you philosopher, you!

FOURTEEN

"Don't know if I'll ever get used to this sushi stuff," I say, looking at Nick where he sits cross-legged on the opposite side of the low table.

He surveys me across the rim of his glass. "Much of it's an acquired taste."

I wrinkle my nose, point a Siren's Song polished nail at the raw slice of octopus before me. "*That* is one taste I doubt I will ever acquire."

"Tako," he says, "which is actually quite bland."

"And, therefore, not to be confused with a crisp corn tortilla filled with meat, lettuce, and cheese." I smack my lips.

He smiles. "No relation. But unless you try it, you're right—you won't acquire the taste."

Love that smile! "No thanks. I'll pass."

"Sure?" He reaches his chopsticks toward the lacquered tray that's scattered with the remains of an assortment of sushi—some good, some bad, some downright ugly.

"Absolutely," I say, eager to see the be-suckered thing disappear.

With a deft pinch of the chopsticks, he plucks it from the tray and pops it in his mouth. Don't know how he does it, but there's something sensual about the way he chews . . . and swallows . . .

Squelching the impulse to fan myself, I look to the tray. "Okay. California roll—good. Tekka Maki—marginal. Anago—eew!" I shudder. "Kappa Maki—good. Futo-maki—so-so. Noritama—bad. And . . . " I frown over two rolls brimming with bright orange pin-pricks. " . . . this is?"

"Flying fish roe."

As in caviar, the black variety of which I've tried and found less than palatable. "Pass again."

He shakes his head. "One pass only, and you've used it up."

I gape. "You never said anything about— "

"Not quite as adventurous as your love scenes lead one to believe, hmm?" He arches an eyebrow.

It's a challenge I can't pass up. Hoping the chopsticks don't slip and send little eggs flying everywhere, I pinch the roll of seaweed, rice, and roe, and dip it in my bowl of soy sauce. Look out stomach, here it comes . . .

Snap, crackle, pop, go the eggs—almost in tune with the plucky strains of the piped-in music.

When I look up, Nick's watching me, no doubt expecting a repeat of my scene at The Ivories. Determinedly, I chew some more, tell myself it's not so bad, and swallow. "Adventurous enough?" I ask.

"Getting there."

As I scowl, he scoops up a chopstick-full of wasabi — a light green mass which he earlier warned me was the Japanese equivalent of horseradish. Fortunately, it doesn't smell as bad. He stirs it in his soy sauce and sinks the last piece of Anago in it.

And once more I get to watch him chew and swallow.

"What is it?" he asks.

Realizing I'm staring, I avert my gaze and lift my cup. My empty cup. I reach for the teapot, but Nick gets there first. And, for a brief moment, our hands touch. As a current goes through me, I yank my arm back.

When I look up, his jaw is tense. As affected by my touch as I am by his?

The silence stretches until our waitress — a petite Japanese woman complete with kimono — slides the screen back and shuffles into our private dining room. She clears away the remainder of our meal, asks if we'd like another pot of green tea, and bows her way out.

"So," I say, guessing it's only a matter of minutes before she returns with the check, making my dinner date with Nick history, "Sophia has started college?"

"She has." He lowers his forearms to the table, leans in. "She told me she wrote you a letter of apology."

For her fruitless matchmaking efforts. "Yes, though it wasn't necessary." I shrug. "It's not as if she meant any harm. She was just . . . well, you know."

He nods. "She likes you."

"I like her, too. She's a lovely young woman." I take a sip of tea. "I imagine you miss her."

"I do. In fact, sometimes the loft is almost painfully quiet."

I peer into my cup. "I know the feeling," I murmur, and mentally bite my tongue at trampling my pride.

"Then you're not seeing anyone?" he asks.

Ooh. How did we end up here? And how do I respond? Truthfully and let him think I'm mooning over him?

"None of my business," he says, and I realize he's misinterpreted my silence—likely thinks Jake and I are still an item. "What about your family?" he continues as though unaffected by the tension. "Any living in the city?"

"Uh . . . my mother and sister live in Iowa—where I was born and raised."

"Do they visit often?"

I shake my head. "My mother dislikes air travel."

"And your sister?"

I sigh. "'Fraid, it's just me she dislikes."

He frowns. "A falling out?"

Something to which he can relate . . . "Of sorts." I frantically search for a way to turn the conversation.

"Recent?" he presses on.

I really don't want to go there. And why is he so interested? I gather a deep breath. "It happened nine years ago."

"That's a long time."

I run a finger around the rim of my glass. "Not as long as it's been for you and your brothers."

His face tightens. "True, but—"

Our waitress chooses that moment to return. Good thing *I'm* not the one tipping! She shuffles in and sets a small lacquered tray on the table.

"I'll give you the card now," Nick says, and removes a credit card from his wallet.

The waitress takes it, bows, and withdraws.

"Any chance you and your sister will make amends?" Nick turns the conversation back to me as the screen slides closed.

Thinks he's off the hook, does he? "Oh, we talk from time to time—try to be civil with one another—but there's too much strain there."

"Why?"

Yes, why? Because I have yet to say I'm sorry? Not that I haven't wanted to, but—

"Pride?" Nick submits.

Though my initial reaction is to scoff, I know it's true, and to deny it would only make me look like a liar. "It's hard to admit being wrong," I begrudge.

"About?"

I nearly drop my jaw. Just who does he think he is? My shrink? I'm *this* close to telling him it's none of his business when he offers a smile of encouragement. And I go to goo. "About my ex," I say.

He cocks his head, prompting me to continue.

"You really want to know?"

"I do."

"Why?"

He shrugs. "From a writer's work, I can usually ascertain the type of person he or she is, but you elude me, Adda Sinclaire."

Before I can think better of it, I lean forward, narrowing the space between us to little more than a foot. "Do I?" I shake my head. "And yet you have more material to work with than just my writing, don't you?"

There goes that muscle in his jaw again, and I could almost smile. Nick Farnsworth, the publisher, may want nothing to do with me outside of my writing, but Nick Farnsworth, the man, is still interested.

"Why does it matter—" I say, only to bite back my words when our waitress returns to set the little tray in front of Nick. A moment later, she withdraws and I begin again. "Why does it matter what type of person I am when we've agreed to maintain a strict writer–publisher relationship?"

"The better informed one is," he says tightly, "the more educated the decisions one can make."

Excuses, excuses . . .

"All right," I accede. "Let's see. . . . " I click my tongue as I consider the quickest route for the telling of my tale. "From early on, my sister, Molly, was dubbed the pretty one, and I was the smart one. Hence, she had the boyfriends, and I had the books. Then, when I was a sophomore in high school and she was a junior,

Richard DeMarco looked my way."

Nick's mouth curves ever-so-slightly.

"Though our mothers were the best of friends, he had never even looked cross-eyed at me. When he finally acknowledged I was alive, I was flattered . . . and enamored . . . and infatuated. My sister tried to warn me away—said the only thing he was interested in was my ability to improve his grades, so he wouldn't be benched for the remainder of the football season. Believing she was just jealous, I ignored her warning and tutored him. He kissed me a couple of times, while continuing to date other girls, and six months later went off to college without a backward glance."

I spread my hands, shrug. "To Molly's credit, she said very little about it, and spent the summer coaxing me out of my ugly duckling stage. A year later, she went off to college, and a year after that, I followed—where I once more met up with Richard."

Nick inclines his head for me to continue.

"At first, he didn't recognize me. Once he did, despite my sister's objections, we started dating—in between new tutoring sessions. Two years out of college, we were engaged. A year later, on the day we were to be married, my sister told me I was making the biggest mistake of my life—said her fiancé had seen Richard out on the town with his bachelor party and that he hadn't been wanting for female companionship. Of course, I refused to believe it and accused her of being jealous." Remembering the expression on Molly's face, I feel a pang in my chest. "I might as well have slapped her. But, less one bridesmaid, the wedding went on as planned. And . . . " I sigh long. " . . . we haven't been close since."

"Do you ever see each other?"

"The few times I've gone back to Iowa. Still, despite our mother's attempts to throw us together, we steer clear of each other as much as possible and rarely exchange more than obligatory words."

"Even after you and Richard divorced?"

"Even then." Nose starting to tingle, eyes to tear, I draw a deep breath. "Some things are better left alone."

Nick reaches across the table and picks up my napkin. "Some things, yes," he offers the folded linen, "some things, no."

I am *not* going to cry! Ignoring the napkin, I sit up straighter. "Oh? Are you presuming to offer me advice on family unity and harmony, Mr. *Farnsworth*?"

He lowers the napkin, draws back. "I assure you, *Adda*, my situation is a good deal more complicated than yours."

"In your opinion," I snap, though what he says is true. Nick's brothers stole from him, and despite the ill between me and my sister, we never intended to hurt each other. Big sister had simply been trying to protect little sister. And I had been too needy and infatuated to accept her protection.

"Well," I say, searching for greener pastures, "I've spilled my guts. It's your turn."

Nick glances at his watch.

"Equal time," I press.

He looks up. "It was my understanding Sophia filled you in."

"Bits and pieces only."

"There's not much more to it than that."

Dirty rat! "You mean, not much more that you want known."

He signs the receipt and returns his credit card to his wallet. "Perhaps another time, hmm?" Once more, he looks to his watch. "It's late, and I have an early flight to catch."

How convenient. Fine. Be that way. I don't care. Not one bit.

In an attempt to appear unruffled, I ask, "So where are you off to?" But then, with a saccharine smile, out of my mouth pops, "Or is *that* better left for another time as well?"

A smile the farthest thing from his own mouth, he meets my gaze. "Intrepid is expanding its operations in Sydney and London. I'll be a week in each city to oversee the process."

"Ah. You'll be busy, then."

He rises. "No more than you. Think you can have the manuscript revised by the time I return?"

Refusing to subject myself to a crick in the neck, I stand. "Two weeks is tight, but doable."

"Good." He shrugs into his jacket. "We'll begin revisions to the men's edition when I return."

With a disbelieving laugh, I say, "Not going to allow me to catch my breath, huh?"

"There'll be time enough for that later." He reaches for my jacket.

"Is that a promise?"

He opens my jacket and holds it for me—every bit as nice as having him pull out my chair. Actually better, I amend as I turn and slide my arms into the sleeves and he settles the jacket to my shoulders. Even through the material, I can feel him.

"Well?" I turn to face him.

"Does it have to be a promise?" he asks.

"Not really, but I *will* hold you to it."

"Of that I have no doubt." He gestures for me to precede him.

Shortly, we're side by side in the cab. Neither of us says a word as Fawkes negotiates Friday night traffic, and the silence lulls me into lowering my lids.

"Adda?"

"Hmm?" I creak open an eye, drop my head back, and there's Nick.

"You're home."

"What? Oh!" Realizing I dozed off against his shoulder, I straighten. "Um . . . sorry."

He hands me out of the cab and walks me to the door. When I fumble to fit my key in the lock, he takes it from me and, a moment later, pushes the door inward. "I'd ask to come inside for a few minutes," he says, warm breath clouding the chill air, "but . . . " He shakes his head.

I step into the foyer. "Don't trust yourself, hmm?"

Though I'm certain he'll deny it, he offers a slow smile that would cause Mother Teresa's brow to bead. "Actually, I don't."

Whoa, Nellie! I stare into those dark chocolates of his and hold my breath.

"Good night, Adda."

"'Night," I croak, gripping the door as he turns away. Going . . . going . . . soon to be gone . . .

"Nick!"

Two steps down, he looks over his shoulder.

"In answer to the question you wouldn't come right out and ask, Jake Grainger *is* out of my life—despite appearances, was *never* in my life. And as for the question you did ask, I'm not seeing anyone."

He turns fully around. "Glad to hear it."

He is? My stomach does a cartwheel.

Thrusting his hands in his pockets, he says, "Have dinner with me when I get back?"

Bring it on! Improper rejoices.

However, the ache I've felt since Lake Tahoe surges as a reminder of how much worse it can get. And so I defer to Prim. "Why?"

Nick looks down, and there's no mistaking his struggle. And so I stand there, telling myself to not hope, though the urge nearly consumes me. A moment later, he takes the two steps to the landing. "I shouldn't have come here," he says, looking down on me, "but it was the best excuse I've had."

Goo alert! Releasing my hold on the door, I say, "I don't understand." Actually I do, but I'm not letting him off this hook.

With a gruff sigh, he slides a hand up my jaw and pushes his fingers through my hair to grip the back of my head. "Yes you do," he says, and kisses me. And it's all I can do to not throw my arms around his neck.

But then, as abruptly as it began, it's over. He pulls back, and the cold night air rushes into the space between us. I open my eyes.

"Two weeks," he says, lowering his arms to his sides, "then we'll discuss what we're going to do about us."

"Discuss?"

He inclines his head. "The rumors will start again, Adda—none of which will reflect well on either of us."

He's right, of course, as evidenced by the speculation and insinuations following the writer's conference. Though I'd known they would get back to Nick, I had hoped there would be no repercussions for him that would make him regret our relationship any more than he already did. Obviously, there were repercussions.

And yet here he stands at my front door. There has to be some hope in that.

"You're right," I say. "We'll discuss it when you return." Forcing myself to step back, I begin to ease the door closed. "Good night, Nick."

"'Night, Adda."

As he turns away, I close the door, and it's all I can do not to run to the sitting room and watch from the window as he walks to the cab.

Two weeks, I tell myself, leaning back against the door. Two weeks and . . . who knows? But whatever happens, one thing is certain—Nick isn't over me any more than I'm over him. Life is definitely looking up.

Smiling, I push off the door and veer toward the kitchen to check the answering machine, only to draw up short. Nah. Nothing so urgent it can't wait until tomorrow—including Joyce and her mysterious message.

● ● ●

"Well, you took your sweet time getting back to me," Joyce huffs. "What about 'important' do you not understand, missy?"

"Sorry, Joyce. I got in late last night and went directly to bed."

"Well after what I've got to tell you, you may want to crawl right back under those covers, 'cause it ain't pretty."

Oh brother! Guessing it's going to be a long-winded conversation, I say, "Hold on," then plug my headset into the phone, fit the ear piece, and adjust the mouthpiece. "Okay, what's up?" I reach for the bottle of Sweet Betrayal nail polish. "Is Women's Fiction Writers demanding you return the award for Best Short?"

Gasp. *Hack, hack, hack*. "*Bleep* no! Just let them try."

That piece of plastic means more to her than her firstborn. Of course, that might not be saying much.

"Felicia, then?" I brush polish across the nail of my big toe.

"Felicia? *Bleep*, no! Though the little tramp *is* getting another divorce."

Surprise, surprise. That one lasted all of . . . what? Five months?

"Really ticked me off when she dropped that one on me." Joyce moans. "And to think I could have—should have!—been at the conference to accept my award. But no! I had to wear pretty boy pink. And you can imagine how that clashed with my cigar."

I'd rather not. Two toes down, eight to go. . . .

"'This time it's for real, Ma,'" Joyce mimics her daughter. "'A forever kind of love.'" Looong draw on her cigar. "*Bleep*!"

Four toes down, six to go. "Sorry to hear it, Joyce."

"Yeah. Well, I suppose it's a little thing compared to the fourteen-wheeler that's bearing down on you."

"Me?" Five down, five to go. "What is it?"

"Birgitta Roth is what it is. As in plagiarism."

My hand jerks, and polish slashes across the knuckle of my left big toe. "What?"

"You heard me. Plagiarism! Online chats are starting to buzz with talk of how much *The Gifting* resembles Roth's *The Love Bounty*."

She's kidding. *Has* to be kidding.

"Of course, you and I know you wrote it, but as her book came out years ago, it's being put about that *you're* the one who plagiarized."

I stare at the nail polish brush. "I'm not following."

"Well, you'd better, Adda, 'cause it's gonna get ugly."

Leaving the nails of my left foot unpainted, I return the brush to the bottle and lower my feet from the table's edge to the carpet. "Are you sure about this?"

"Yep. Had Jerry run down to the used book store to hunt out a copy of Roth's book."

Not that her one acclaimed book isn't still available in retail bookstores. Joyce just refuses to line the pockets of any writer she dislikes—even if the royalty on the sale of a new book amounts to all of thirty-eight cents.

"And it's true, Adda. Though she put your medieval hero and heroine in cowboy boots and stuck them in the hot desert, it's your story."

I shake my head. "That can't be."

"It is."

I'm trembling, I realize, and my heart is pounding up a storm. "You . . . read through both books?"

"Side by side, missy. Kept me up 'till three in the morning, but there's no doubt about it—you've been fleeced."

I unstick my tongue from the roof of my suddenly dry mouth. "No."

"Yeah."

A nervous laugh. "No."

"Yeah!"

I flop back on the sofa, raise my eyes to the ceiling. "No!"

"Get hold of yourself, Adda. This is bad."

I slap a hand over my eyes and drag it down my face. "But how could this happen?"

"Dick," she spits. "Been thinking about it, and it's gotta be him."

"Dick?"

"Yeah. He was foolin' around with the *bleep*, after all—sucking up to her in hopes of launching his career."

"But—"

"Okay, kiddo, here's the scenario I worked up. Let's say old Birgitta is up against a deadline. Time is tight as she's still anchoring the news, and it's either put out or get out. And here's Dick, her faithful lapdog who, at some time, has mentioned the manuscript your publisher optioned out of, and which you've drawered."

I envision it, and it's not a pretty sight—Birgitta's smug satisfaction at learning about my failure. . . . Richard and her laughing over it. . . .

"Adda?"

I blink. "I . . . uh . . . I'm with you, Joyce. Go on."

She draws hard on her cigar. "And so, with or without Dick's knowledge, the *bleep* gets hold of your manuscript and . . . walla!"

I'm sure she means, "voila." "But how, Joyce?"

"You tell me."

"I can't. I . . . don't know."

"Yes you do. Think, Adda!"

Beginning to feel sick to my stomach, I squeeze my eyes closed. How would Birgitta get hold of my manuscript? At the beginning of her affair with Di—Richard—while I was still in the dark about them? Maybe Richard brought her to our home and—

No. Perhaps I'm naive, but then as now, I can't imagine Richard bringing her to our home, especially when it was supremely convenient for them to meet at her place. But then how did she get hold of the manuscript? Did Richard steal it from my office and slip it to her? No. Maybe he downloaded it from my computer? No. Regardless of his infidelity, I just can't see him doing that to me. At least, not intentionally.

"Well?" Joyce prompts.

I swallow hard. "I don't know. This is too . . . sudden. Too shocking. Too— " my voice catches, "—ludicrous."

"Now don't go falling apart on me, missy. Buck up!"

"I'm trying." But the consequences are coming at me like bullets. What will my readers think? Publishers—past, present, and dare I say, future? Fellow writers? The media? Most of all, Nick? Will he believe me? Oh, God . . . I open my eyes and stare at the ceiling through a sheen of tears.

"We're going to need proof," Joyce muffles around her big, fat cigar. "Now tell me who all read the manuscript when you first finished it."

Proof. Yeah.

"You, of course— "

Totally biased.

"—Richard— "

Hardly on friendly terms, and possibly partners in crime with Birgitta.

"—my editor at Gentry Books—"

Who has since retired and hates my guts.

"—Noelle—"

Also biased, and won't want to touch this with a ten-foot pole.

"—and—" I laugh with a croaky sound that, under different circumstances, would be embarrassing. "Then there's me, Joyce. That's it."

"Bleep!" Hack hack hack.

"Yeah," I mutter. A pity party is starting to sound pretty good.

"Wait!" Joyce shouts. "When you signed with Noelle, didn't she shop the manuscript around?"

Nice try. "No. Told me to put it away for a while. Said I needed to start fresh and work up a new proposal."

"Bleep!"

So what am I to do? How do I defend myself? A sob bounces up my throat, and I gulp it down, but another follows and escapes.

After a long silence, Joyce says, "Wish I could be there with you, Adda."

"Me too."

"Don't worry. We'll get you through this. Now—"

"I'm sorry, Joyce. I know you want to help, but I can't think straight right now. I . . . " I press my lips inward and draw a deep breath through my nose. "It feels as if I've been hit by a train."

"Okay. I understand," she surprises me. "Look, take the day to pull yourself together, but be ready to enter the fray tomorrow, 'cause I guarantee I'm not the only one reading the books side by side."

I nod. "I'll do that."

"Up to a final word of advice?"

"What are you selling?"

"Get mad—real mad."

I can almost feel Birgitta's hair in my fist. I force a laugh. "That goes without saying."

"Good. Call me if you need anything or just want to talk."

"I will. Bye, Joyce—and thank you."

"Hey, what are friends for?"

Thank goodness I have one.

"Bye, sweetie," she grates.

Click.

I lower the handset, drag the earpiece from my ear, and stare at my clenched hands as emotions bounce all over my insides in search of a way out. I want to cry. To scream. To pound my fists. To kick something. And, yes, curse—to shout foul words until my throat is raw. But what good would it do? It won't make this mess go away. Certainly won't make Stick Woman—yes, *Stick Woman*!—go away. And what if God's listening?

God . . .

Should I pray? Would it help? I draw a deep breath and glance at the ceiling. "Are you listening?" I whisper past a throat so tight it hurts. What if he doesn't answer my prayer? Of course, what have I got to lose?

I clasp my hands against my mouth, struggle for a place to start, and in the end decide on one of the Scriptures I stuck to my monitor months back.

"All things are . . . "

No.

"I can do any . . . "

No.

"I can do all things through . . . "

Beginning to tremble, I unclasp my hands and croak, "No, I can't." And so, for the next hour, I stare into silence. Then the phone starts to ring. And ring. And ring.

FIFTEEN

WHEN NYT BEST SELLERS GO BAD

PLAGIARISM: ISN'T IT ROMANTIC!

FARNSWORTH PUBLISHING INVESTIGATES PLAGIARISM CHARGES

ADDA SINCLAIRE: WHAT WAS SHE THINKING?

Yes, I'm mad. Real mad. Gnashing my teeth, I sweep together the newspapers Noelle slapped down in front of me, come around her desk, and drop them in the wastebasket.

"This is bad," Noelle says.

I glare at her where she leans back in her fancy new chair—which her cut of my Intrepid advance likely paid for. "No kidding. So what are you going to do about it?"

She sighs. "We have to move carefully, Adda, especially now that Roth has come out with a statement."

Yesterday's paper—two days after Joyce's call. I huff, stalk to the windows, stalk back. "Outraged! *Her?* Outraged! Why, I could . . . " I snatch a handful of air and yank it for all it's worth.

"Calm down." Noelle holds up a staying hand.

"Calm down? This is my career we're talking about! My reputation! My life! *My* book! And that lying— "

Don't say it!

"SHE has the audacity to tell the world *she's* outraged over the blatant theft of *her* work?"

Noelle rolls her eyes. "I think I liked you better when you had your nose stuck in that cockamamie book."

I feel my teeth bare. "It's called the Bible." I lean near. "B-I-B-L-E." And it's not cockamamie, I almost say, but she may be right. After all, where is God now that I need him?

Noelle waves me toward the chair before her desk. "Please, Adda, sit down."

I step to the chair, drop into it, and jump back up. "I'm going to rip every hair out of her head, then I'm going to . . . to . . . "

"Adda!"

Huffing and puffing as though I've run a marathon, I meet her gaze.

"Sit!" she commands.

I glare at her, but in the end crumple into the chair, hang my head, and stare at my nails—every one of them bitten to the quick. "Dick doesn't return my calls," I say, foregoing all attempts to think of him as "Richard." "And when I finally get through to my old editor, she laughs and resorts to a cliché." Borrowing from Joyce, I mimic, "What goes around comes around."

"Which brings us to another favorite of the publishing world—don't burn bridges," Noelle reminds me.

As if I need a reminder! But how was I to know my Gentry Books editor would be fired after her cruel rejection of my manuscript sent me in search of a new publisher? *You simply haven't grown sufficiently in your writing for us to offer a contract on this proposal*, she'd written. What else was I to do? Work up a new proposal for a woman who had, from the get-go, made no secret she detested medievals and resented having me assigned to her? *She's* the one who burned the bridge!

I sink deeper into the chair, groan, and clap a hand over my face. "What am I going to do?"

"The papers want a statement."

Which is the reason Angel and I started screening all phone calls via the answering machine. I peer at Noelle from beneath the flyaway bangs that have escaped my ponytail. "And what do you suggest?"

"We give it to them—after I talk to Nick Farnsworth."

I sit up straight, looking, I imagine, like a dog begging for a bone. "Nick?"

Noelle nods. "I put a call into his office this morning. Hopefully, he'll get back to me before the end of the day."

"Think he's heard what's going on?"

She scowls. "What? You think the man lives under a rock? Of course he's heard. And I guarantee he knows more about it than even Kathryn."

And has to be counting his blessings that he exercised restraint the night he dropped me at my home. "What did Kathryn have to say?"

"Not a lot, but when I told her I had read your manuscript years ago, and that I was the one who suggested you submit it in place of your original proposal when you had your bout with writer's block, she loosened up. Said *The Gifting* certainly had your voice written all over it."

I sigh. "That's a relief."

"Not really."

I snort. "Well aren't you a ray of sunshine!"

"I tell it like it is."

And forget niceties! "Why do I have this feeling your bank account is flashing before your eyes?" I ask.

To my surprise, she flushes in remembrance of the words she let slip last year when she thought I was choking; however, she recovers soon enough. With a flip of the hand, she says, "Of course I ran the Richard/Birgitta affair scenario past Kathryn. However, though she agreed your ex's involvement with Roth is favorable to your defense, she said it isn't enough. We need proof, Adda. *Real* proof."

I could scream. "You told her my previous editor read the manuscript?"

"I did, but what use is that if the woman isn't willing to attest?"

She's right, and no doubt Dick is also turning his back on me. So what else is there?

"Did you pick up a copy of *The Love Bounty* like I asked?" Noelle says.

Stomach tossing at the thought of going into a bookstore to buy one of Stick Woman's books, I grimace. "Not yet."

Nicole pushes up out of her chair and comes around the desk. "Adda, if you're going to fight this, you can't stick your head in the sand and hope someone else picks up the pieces."

"I know, I know." I wave a dismissing hand. "But why don't you just loan me your copy?"

"I would, but it's at home. I was reading through it past midnight." To emphasize her sacrifice, she lifts a hand to her mouth and yawns.

I stand. "Then you leave me no choice but to put myself in harm's way by picking up a copy myself." Of course, maybe I could send Angel out for one.

"*If* you can still find one," Noelle says. "I understand they've become quite popular."

Can it get any worse? "Are we done?"

"For now."

I retrieve my purse from beside the chair and feel a pang of regret at not having forgotten it. If Nick were here . . .

I press my shoulders back. "Let me know when you hear from Nick Farnsworth."

"I will."

As I cross to the door, Noelle says, "Wear your sunglasses in the bookstore."

So no one will recognize me. "Of course," I say, and halt to slide them on my nose. Pasting a bright smile in place, I turn to her. "What do you think?"

"Lose the smile."

"Easy." Reverting to a glower, which has served me well these past days, I open the door and step out. As I close it, Noelle's receptionist looks up. "Holding up okay, Ms. Sinclaire?"

"No," I mutter, "but thanks for asking." At least not everyone believes I'm a fraud, a liar, a cheat. Or maybe they do. My royalties do help pay her wages.

I cross to the elevator and punch the button. It's a long minute before the doors swish open, and Elizabeth Carp steps out.

"Adda!"

So much for my disguise. Though I steel myself for the censure and contempt some authors have begun slinging over the Internet, she steps forward and gives me a hug.

Maybe she's been living under that rock I reserved for Nick—which would explain why she hasn't bothered to call. Of course, once she hears—

"I just heard this morning," she says, pulling back.

Oh. And she's not afraid to come within ten feet of me?

"I'm sorry I haven't been there for you." She smiles apologetically. "I would have if not that I'd holed up these past four days to meet my revision deadline—no phones, no faxes, no e-mail, no visitors." She bites her lip. "Sorry."

Is she for real? I shift my weight. "Um . . . what, exactly, did you hear?"

"Everything that's fit for gossip." She places an urgent hand on my arm. "But I don't believe a word of it, so don't think you have to explain anything to me—which is the message I left with Angel an hour ago."

I melt. Lowering my head so she won't catch the glitter of tears through my lenses, I say, "Thank you, Elizabeth. You don't know how much that means to me."

She pats my shoulder. "What can I do to help?"

"You've done enough already." Discomposed by her kindness and show of support, I draw a deep breath and look up. "So you're signing with Noelle?"

Allowing the change of topic, she smiles. "Yes, upon your recommendation. It still stands, doesn't it?"

I nod. "She's very good."

"Then she's handling this Birgitta Roth fiasco well?"

Is that what it is? A fiasco? Sounds so . . . trivial. "Better than expected," I say, and am so grateful Noelle exceeded my expectations.

"Good."

"Well, I won't keep you from your appointment," I say.

She nods. "I'll call you, hmm? Maybe we can get together after services on Sunday."

I smile sardonically. "Sure you want to be seen with me?"

She grabs me and gives me another hug. "Absolutely."

"You're an angel," I say as we pull apart.

She shrugs. "I aspire to give as good as I get, which reminds me—thanks for the advice about keeping my day job."

Glad she took it. "Sure."

She stares at me a long moment, opens her mouth as if to say something more, then snaps it closed.

Wondering what she thought better of, I say, "I guess I'll see you later."

"Yeah." Almost sheepishly, she adds, "Hang in there, Adda."

"I will."

As she turns toward the receptionist, I look to the elevator. It's headed back down. Well worth the delay because I feel better for Elizabeth's kindness.

I frown. If I didn't know better, I might believe divine intervention was responsible for us running into each other—a "God thing," as my sister, Molly, would call it. And maybe it *was* a God thing—

"Adda?"

I startle, peer over my shoulder. "Elizabeth?"

"I . . . " She shifts her weight side to side, then takes a step nearer and, in a hushed voice, says, "I don't do this kind of thing often, but I'd like to pray for you."

I can't hide my surprise. "Pray for me?"

She nods.

"Uh . . . " I glance past her, confirming that though we're hardly the center of attention, we are not alone. "Now?"

She nods again.

"Here?"

Another nod.

"I . . . " Though I know it's wrong, I can't help but be embarrassed at the prospect of her praying for me in public. And yet, the thought of being the recipient of her prayer causes something to glow at my center. Perhaps there's an empty stairwell where we—

Elizabeth lays a hand to my shoulder. "I really want to pray for you, Adda," she says, despite looking nearly as uncomfortable as I feel.

As I stare into her sincerity, my discomfort eases, and I find myself nodding. After all, if she's willing to go out on a limb, who am I to shake the tree? "I'd like that," I say.

And so, right there before the elevators, we bow our heads. Though Elizabeth's prayer for God to strengthen and guide me through this time of trial is short and simple, when she ends on "Amen," I feel as if I'm no longer alone.

"Thank you, Elizabeth," I say, eyes wet and nose a-tingle.

She nods, drags the heels of her palms beneath her eyes. "Any time." She gives her jacket a tug. "See you soon, hmm?"

"Absolutely."

I watch her walk away. Then, somewhat lighter of heart, I turn back and punch the elevator button. "A God thing," I murmur as I settle back on my heels. "Definitely a God thing."

● ● ●

I just know those beady-eyed cameras are watching me—following my every move.

From the cover of my sunglasses, I dart my eyes left and right, but no one appears to be paying me any notice. Probably waiting to spring the moment I enter the romance section.

Oh, please, let Barnes & Noble have a copy of *The Love Bounty*, I silently pray. It's the third bookstore I've tried—including a used one—and the book's sold out. If I have to sneak through any more doors . . . lurk in any more corners . . . tiptoe down any more aisles, I am going to scream. That, or resolve to give up my writing career and seek amnesty in some backward country that's never heard of Adda Sinclaire or Birgitta Roth.

I slow as I near the romance aisles, halt, and crane my neck to peer around an end cap. All's clear. Shifting my purse to the opposite shoulder, I make tracks down the aisle past the alphabetically arranged authors—the Es, now the Ls, the Ps, and finally the Rs.

"Rathbone," I mutter, and scan the shelf below, "Rimwit, Rogers, Rovings." Ooh, back up. Yep, there sits Birgitta Roth. I glance left over my shoulder, then right over my shoulder. Determining no one's watching, I reach to the pink-spined book—only to grab my hand back.

It's her latest release, and there are no others. Shoot! Looks like Barnes & Noble has been raided as well. I glance at the next section where S begins, but where there are usually a dozen or more copies of my titles, there's only a gaping space just like at the other two stores I sneaked into. Meaning . . . ?

Have the stores pulled my books? Or has bad publicity caused a run on them? Though neither portends well, I hope it's the latter which, if nothing else, will ring up the royalties. Gotta have something to live on in whatever country I end up in.

"Ms. Sinclaire?"

With a gasp of surprise, I look over my shoulder, and three feet away stands a familiar young man easily identified by his name tag—Rupert, who assisted with my last signing, and who I specifically requested for a signing slated for Valentine's Day. *If* it's still on . . .

"It *is* you," he says.

Don't look guilty, I tell myself. Act normal. Cooool. I step forward, extend a hand. "Nice to see you again, Rupert."

With obvious reluctance, he shakes my hand and almost snatches his cool fingers back.

Oookay. Looks like I've been weighed, measured, and found wanting. And it hurts.

"Uh . . . " He shifts his weight opposite and back again. "Can I help you find anything, Ms. Sinclaire?"

So how do I play this one? Slink away and hope he doesn't alert anyone to my presence? Or forget public opinion and get what I came for so I can get out of here?

Right.

I affix a smile my mother would be proud of and whip off my sunglasses. "I am so glad you asked, Rupert. You see, there's this vicious rumor circulating that my latest novel is a work of plagiarism—stolen from Birgitta Roth of all people."

He clasps his hands before him, shrugs.

"Anyway, I thought I'd better look into the matter myself and rustle up a copy of her one and only acclaimed book, which as you probably know, was said to be right up there with my books when it was first released."

Rupert clasps his hands behind him, shrugs again.

"Which, of course, started me thinking. If it's true *The Gifting* bears a marked resemblance to her work, she must have stolen my manuscript about the time she was stealing my husband right out from under my nose."

Poor Rupert. He doesn't look well. Wonder if his gut is churning as much as mine.

Though I attempt to pull up out of the nosedive into which I've put myself, I hear myself say, "Don't tell me you didn't hear *that* rumor?"

"Uh . . ."

I wrinkle my nose. "Well, you're pretty young, and it was a few years back, but I'm sure the papers will drag it out soon enough, and you'll learn all the sordid details—especially about the hair I wrenched from Ms. Roth's head at a writer's conference."

Rupert's eyebrows kink. "You pulled her hair out?"

I tap my forehead, nod.

"Wow."

I sigh. "Yeah, messy stuff, but what would you do if a

coworker, who's messing around with *your* girlfriend, starts passing around photos of the two of them—in front of you?"

He frowns, frowns some more. Then, with a shake of his dreadlocks, he says, "I'd probably do worse than rip out the dude's hair."

I sigh again. "And now to discover she stole more than just my husband." I shake my head and look down. "Is there no end to this nightmare?" Though I exaggerate for his benefit, the truth of it is that it *is* a nightmare. And how I wish someone would pinch me.

When I glance up, there's a sympathetic gleam in Rupert's eyes. "Gee, Ms. Sinclaire, I'm really sorry. This has gotta be tough on you."

"I'm handling it as best I can," I say and look over my shoulder. "So will you be ordering more copies of *The Love Bounty*?"

"You bet," he says with such enthusiasm my stomach turns. "Put in the order myself this morning—four cases."

Roughly two hundred books, courtesy of Adda Sinclaire, thank you very much. "When do you expect them?"

"Hopefully tomorrow—unless Ms. Roth's publisher has to go back to press."

Another print run, courtesy of Adda Sinclaire, thank you very much. "Think you could set one aside for me?"

He pops his shoulders back. "I can do better than that."

"Hmm?"

He wiggles his eyebrows, smiles. "I grabbed a copy before they were all snatched up yesterday. I'll give you mine."

I could almost cry.

"Wait here and I'll get it." He hurries toward the back of the store.

Two minutes later—and counting—I'm no nearer to getting my hands on the book when an elderly woman, complete with poofed blue-gray hair and a bumper-stickered walker, comes browsing down the aisle. Our gazes meet long enough for her to form a frown.

Uh oh. I jam my glasses back in place, scoot opposite, and nearly collide with Rupert as I start around the corner.

"Oops," he says, jumping back. "Sorry, Ms. Sinclaire. I didn't see you coming."

Does he have to speak so loud? I glance over my shoulder in time to see the woman's frown transform into an expression of surprise.

I look to the book Rupert holds. "So this is what's causing all the uproar."

"Sure is, Ms. Sinclaire."

I wish he'd stop calling me that. "Great." I almost snatch it from him. "What do I owe you?"

"Nothing. It's—" he shrugs, "—a gift."

My heart softens. Laying a hand to his arm, I give it a squeeze. "You're sweet, Rupert. I can't tell you how much I appreciate it."

The shuffle of sensible shoes and the bump of a walker alerting me that the elderly woman is closing in, I say, "I'd better be on my way," and step past him. "See you Valentine's Day, hmm?"

"You bet. Uh . . . actually . . . "

Oh. I look around. "Is there a problem?"

With a sheepish dip of his head, he says, "I planned on calling you."

"Excuse me," the woman calls in a trembly voice.

I grab Rupert's sleeve. "Is there somewhere private we can talk?"

"Sure." He glances at the woman. "I'll be with you in a minute, ma'am." Sensing my urgency, he steps ahead and leads the way across the store to a door marked "Employees Only" and pushes it open for me. As I step into a hallway, he says, "The problem is that there aren't any books for you to sign, Ms. Sinclaire."

Holding it together as best I can, I turn to him. "Farnsworth Publishing has ordered my books pulled, then."

"Just *The Gifting*—until further notice."

Ouch. Ouch. Ouch.

"But what about my other titles? I didn't see any on the shelf."

He brightens. "Sold out—curiosity, I guess."

Curiosity. Would I be totally out of line to hope it squishes the cat? "Well then, we'll just have to wait until this matter is cleared up."

"Yeah. I'll be rooting for you, Ms. Sinclaire."

"Thanks, Rupert." On that note, I pop *The Love Bounty* in my purse and leave him to deal with the elderly woman who, when I duck out, is heading for the "Employees Only" door.

Somehow, I make it out of the store unaccosted and, shortly, place myself at the mercy of a New York cabbie who's in more of a hurry to get me home than I. But it's lunchtime, and despite his persistence, traffic is sluggish. And so I take out the book and, with trembling hands, open to the first chapter. Though the names, setting, and medieval use of 'tis and 'twas have been changed to protect the guilty, in the span of two pages there's no mistaking it's my story. *Blatantly* my story. But I read on . . . and on, until my hands are shaking with an anger unmatched since the last time Stick Woman stole from me—and for which I *was* trying to forgive her.

Squeezing my eyes closed, I drop my head back against the seat. Forgiveness—hard enough when one is clear of the storm, but when in the eye of it . . . humanly impossible.

Unlocking my jaws, I look to the rearview mirror and catch the cabbie's gaze there. "Excuse me," I say, "we need to make a detour."

A quarter hour and two chapters later, he pulls up in front of Stick Woman's brownstone. "Can you wait?" I ask, handing him five dollars above the cost of the fare.

He accepts the cash and, in a heavily accented voice, says, "I come back for you."

Knowing the likelihood of him returning is next to nil, I mentally write off the five dollars as a tip and climb out. As he pulls away, I set my shoulders for the confrontation that lies ahead. A minute later, I'm at the front door, hand poised to knock.

Don't do this, Prim warns. *You'll regret it.*

Just one handful, Improper coaxes.

I close my eyes, take deep breaths of the chill air, and count to ten, but there's no turning back. I knock three times, which starts a dog barking—my Beijing, who's still imprisoned by Stick Woman. A moment later, I hear a voice and footsteps.

Knowing Stick Woman will look through the peephole before opening the door—*if* she opens it—I raise my chin.

Her footsteps halt on the other side of the door, and I stare at the peephole as she peers at me. Following a long pause, I hear muffled voices, meaning she isn't alone.

Beijing barks again, and Stick Woman's sharp command of, "Shut up!" pushes my hackles higher.

A moment later, the chain on the door rattles, the dead bolt clunks, and the door is pulled open to reveal enemy number one in bare feet and pink flannel pajamas.

"Well, well, well," she mutters, propping herself against the door frame and crossing her arms over her chest. "Look, Denise, it's Adda Sinclaire."

Should have known Prune would be here.

Stick Woman's sidekick opens the door wider to stand hip to hip with her buddy and, with great exaggeration, drops her jaw. "Well, I never!"

She's been chewing garlic again.

"And you never will," I say, "you bootlicking sycophant."

Behind, Beijing starts barking—a happy bark. Does he recognize my voice? It *has* been a few years.

"Sticks and stones . . . " Prune says with a superior wag of her head.

"Shut up, Beijing!" Stick Woman barks over her shoulder. And he quiets. Out of fear?

Though I hadn't thought I was capable of greater anger, it's on the rise.

With a smug smile, Stick Woman looks back around. "You surprise me, Adda, dear."

"Yeah," Prune says. "Of all the nerve—showing up on poor Birgitta's doorstep."

Poor Birgitta! I eye the "poor" thing's hair. All it would take is one lunge, and she'd be mine. Ten seconds flat, I'd have her in a headlock, ten seconds after that, another handful of hair. But this time I control myself. "*I* have the nerve?" I say between clenched teeth. "*Me*? Adda Sinclaire? The one from whom you stole the manuscript after you stole my husband? The true author of the book to which you gave the ultra-tacky title of *The Love Bounty*!"

As Beijing renews his barking, Stick Woman guffaws, looking so much like an emaciated cow I almost feel sorry for her. "I have no idea what you're talking about you poor, demented woman. But I assure you— "

Beijing's massively wrinkled head pops between Stick Woman and Prune.

Without thinking, I step toward him

"Get back, you stupid thing!" Stick Woman snarls, and bumps him with her thigh.

Beijing whimpers and withdraws.

Must get control of my anger. If I don't, I'll end up arrested for assault and battery. And it will all be Dick's fault—Dick who's never kept a commitment to anyone or anything. I draw a deep breath . . . and another. But in the end, what calms me most is remembrance of Elizabeth and the prayer she spoke over me. Strength and guidance for the trials ahead, she had asked on my behalf, and I'm bolstered by those words.

Telling myself I will get through this without resorting to aggression, I stand taller. "I'd like my dog," I say, which starts Beijing barking again.

"*Your* dog?" Stick Woman laughs. "Not according to the divorce papers."

I clench my hands at my sides. "If Dick isn't coming back for him, then I have every right— "

"No you don't." Anger coloring her an unsightly red, she looks over her shoulder. "I said, 'shut up'!" Beijing quiets and she looks back around. "By rights of abandonment, the dog is mine."

"Yeah," Prune says. "*Hers*."

Biting back a retort, I say, "You don't want him, Birgitta."

Her right eye tic starts up. "It's true the little beast is more trouble than he's worth, but I certainly wouldn't give him to you—a woman who has so grossly plagiarized my work."

Her work. *Her* work! If not that Beijing chooses that moment to once more thrust his head between the two women, I might forget I've sworn off acts of aggression—be on her like a fly on road kill.

I drop to my haunches. "Baby Beijing," I call, patting my thigh.

Before either woman can bump him out of the way again, he lunges forward, the press of his bulky body unbalancing Stick Woman who stumbles and lands on her bony rear.

I laugh at the tickle of Beijing's wet tongue across my face. He *does* remember me.

"You!" Stick Woman shrieks as Prune helps her up. "Get back in here, you stupid dog!"

I grab Beijing's face between my hands. "It's now or never. Wanna make a break for it?"

Slobbering like crazy, tail wagging so fast it's a blur, he barks.

"Let's go." I stand. "I'll see you in court, Birgitta." I turn away, and an exuberant Beijing falls in beside me as I traverse the sidewalk.

"Beijing!" Stick Woman shouts. "Get back here!"

He doesn't miss a step.

"Beijing!"

Though I pick up the pace in case she decides to give chase, I don't touch Beijing. Can't have anyone accusing me of stealing her dog, now can I?

"She's stealing my dog!"

Can I read this woman like a predictable novel or what? I look around. "You really ought to keep your dog on a leash, Ms. Roth. It's the law, you know."

She gapes.

I turn away only to snap my head back around. "Oh, and

you can just forget that whole forgiveness thing. I am *not* a saint."

She gapes larger.

The prick is coming, and though I steel my conscience, it's futile. As I turn into the chill wind, the prick finds its mark. Certain God is shaking his head in heaven, I wish there were some way to make him understand what I'm going through. Some way—

But he does understand, doesn't he? The difference is that he's God, and I'm human. A very hurt and betrayed human. Of course, not as hurt and betrayed as Jesus who still forgave . . .

I sigh. Life was so much easier before I got involved with the Bible. Wondering if it might not be better to set it aside until this crisis is past—if ever—I follow Beijing's lead toward home.

● ● ●

"You're not going to like any of it," Angel says as I dump a bag of cocktail kielbasa into a bowl.

"I don't expect so." Bowl in hand, I lower to the kitchen floor alongside Beijing. I offer a kielbasa, which he heartily accepts and swallows without chewing, and feed him half a dozen more before returning my attention to Angel. "So tell me."

She picks up the stack of phone messages retrieved from the answering machine throughout the day. "Farnsworth Publishing—wants you to return the advance for *The Gifting*."

Over my dead, maggot-riddled body. I feed Beijing another kielbasa.

"Heart Core Publishers—wants the name of your attorney."

In time. *All* in time.

"Augusta Tierney of Women's Fiction Writers—suspension of your membership is under consideration."

Boy, when the chips are down . . .

"Elaine Battalia, owner of Buncha Books in Panama City, Florida."

I remember her—did a signing in her store several years back. A true aficionado of romance and a gem of a gal.

"Uh . . . nah," Angel murmurs.

I look up. "What?"

She wrinkles her nose. "You don't want to hear this one."

That bad, huh? I make a face. "Can't be any worse than the others."

"It is."

"So shoot."

Grimacing, Angel reads, "You ought to be ashamed of yourself. I'm ripping the covers off all your books and returning them for credit. In the future, I will be more discriminating about thc romance authors who grace my shelves."

As if she knows anything about romance! For all I care, she can take her cubic zirconium personality and—

Beijing nudges my arm, reminding me he's waiting. "Next," I instruct Angel as I scoop up three more kielbasas and pop them into Beijing's drooling mouth.

"Oh, you'll like this one."

Just one . . .

"It's from your writer friend, Elizabeth Carp. It says, 'I don't believe a word of it. No explanation necessary. Just let me know what I can do to help.'" Angel offers a smile of encouragement. "Nice, hmm?"

Emotions so tight I don't dare speak, I jerk my head and put out a hand for the message.

Angel passes it to me. "A keeper, hmm?"

I read the message through, nod. "Anything else?"

Angel flips through a half dozen more. "Two other bookstores," she summarizes, "and the rest are newspapers wanting a statement or interview."

Deciding I'll pass on the sordid details, I say, "Then my ex hasn't returned my call?"

With a pitying shake of her head, Angel says, "Sorry."

I lower the bowl for Beijing to finish off the kielbasas, which he does in two gulps. "What about Nick Farnsworth?"

As Beijing stretches out beside me, settling his slobbering muzzle on my thigh, Angel props a hand on her hip. "Nothing. Bummer, huh?"

It's the way she says it—as though she knows the depth of my disappointment—that makes me look closer at her. "Bummer?"

"Well, yeah," she says with a contradictory shake of her head. "I may have more holes in my head than most people, but my brain doesn't leak." She grins. "I saw the way he looked at you and you looked at him."

Though I know I should squelch this before it goes too far, I hear myself ask, "And what way was that?"

"Those rumors last summer—about you and him—there was definitely something to them."

Knew I should have squelched it. Leaning my head back against the kitchen cabinet, I say, "Well, whatever there was to them, there is no more." Birgitta Roth made certain of that.

With the optimism of the young, Angel shrugs. "Maybe. Maybe not."

I wave her away. "Go, Angel."

"Okay, okay." She turns away.

"Oh," I call, "if a police officer comes knocking, don't answer."

She looks over her shoulder at Beijing who's snoozing contentedly. "Gotcha, Ms. Sinclaire."

As her feet pound the stairs, I stroke Beijing's head.

He opens his big, sorry eyes and wags his curly tail.

It's good to be loved! Even if only by a dog. I bend forward and hug him. "Looks like it's just you and me, Baby Beijing." For however long that lasts . . .

The phone rings, and I hold my breath as the outgoing message plays out.

"Adda, it's Kathryn Connell at Intrepid. I just received a call from Birgitta Roth—"

I release my breath, roll my eyes.

"—and she's very upset."

Can't imagine why. . . .

"Says you stole her dog."

Almost as big a lie as saying I stole her manuscript. Can I help it if Beijing followed me home? I sit back and consider the ceiling, which really needs to be repainted, doesn't it?

"Adda," Kathryn continues, "I know this is rough on you, but let's not make it any worse. I talked Birgitta out of calling the police, but you've got to return her dog."

Over my dead, picked clean-to-the-bone body. I rub the base of Beijing's right ear, then his left, which he absolutely loves. He moans, shifts, and raises his muzzle for me to stroke beneath his chin.

"Call me when you get in," Kathryn says. "I want this taken care of today."

Click.

"All righty, then," I murmur as Beijing's back leg kicks in time with my magical fingers. "Looks like it's time to go into hiding." But where?

The phone rings again, and the answering machine picks up. Though tempted to plug my ears and do the "la la la la" thing to block out any residual voice, I can't help but harbor hope it's Nick.

"Adda, it's Molly— "

Molly? Big sister Molly?

"—I need you to call me. It's about Mom."

My heart flings itself against my ribs, and a moment later

I'm scrambling across the kitchen floor with Beijing in lumbering pursuit.

"My number is 319— "

"Molly!" I shout, slamming the receiver to my ear.

A long silence, then, "Sheesh, Adda! You just about popped my eardrum."

"Is Mom all right?"

"Well of course she's all right—*now*."

"What happened?"

She sighs. "This whole plagiarism thing is what happened."

I wondered how long it would take to reach Iowa. Relieved that it's nothing serious—my life and career excluded—I lower to a bar stool, and Beijing comes alongside to lay his muzzle on my thigh again.

"Let me guess," I say, "Mom's connection to the scandalous Adda Sinclaire, author of trashy romance novels, has given her a bad case of hives." I lift my hand from Beijing to consider my nails—my short, ragged nails. "Or has she simply swooned?"

"Worse. Listen, Adda— "

"Ah! She's denounced me—cut me out of her will and forbidden anyone to speak my name." Submitting to Beijing's offer of a hand bath, I shrug. "Won't be the first time."

"Can I talk now?" Molly says with a note of irritation.

"Sure. Sorry."

"Look, Mom and Donna DeMarco got into it over this plagiarism thing."

I freeze. "You're telling me she and her best friend had words over it?" Meaning she was actually defending me? Taking a stand for her daughter against friend-to-the-end, Donna? *My* mom? About as believable as Dick's mom defending me. Well . . . actually, if I had to bet money on it, I might go with Donna.

"It was more than words, Adda."

Surely Mom didn't lower herself to raising her voice.

"They were rolling around on the floor of the public library, and before anyone could pull them apart, Mom borrowed a page from your book."

If it weren't so unbelievable, I might laugh at the image of two coifed and staid, sixty-year-old women locked in combat. I shake my head. "What page is that?"

"The one where you left Birgitta Roth without bangs for . . . what . . . ? Six months?"

I almost drop the phone. "No way."

"Yes way."

"Unh-unh. You're kidding."

Voice reflecting what might be a smile, she says, "Cross my heart."

The childhood expression echoing a time when we shared a room, a friendship, and Barbie and Ken dolls galore, I return to the conversation I had with Nick when I acknowledged my responsibility for the rift between me and my sister. And suddenly I have this overwhelming urge to fix what has been broken for too long.

"Adda?" Molly prompts.

Okay. Deep breath.

"You still there, Adda?"

Do it, Prim encourages. *Just do it.*

Too much water under the bridge, Improper says.

"Hellooo? I can hear you breathing."

Panting, more like it. I swallow hard. "Molly, I . . . I'm . . . "

"Yeah?"

"I . . . well . . . I'm . . . It's good to talk to you."

"Oh."

Yeah, "oh," Prim scoffs.

But what if she won't forgive me? That would hurt. A real blow to my—

Pride, Nick said. And he was right. It's what's holding me back. Just as it held back Mr. Darcy and Elizabeth Bennett of *Pride and Prejudice*. Is it too much to hope that everything will come right for me as it did for them?

With an exasperated sigh, Molly says, "Pull yourself together, Adda."

"Sorry," I blurt.

"It's okay. Now back to Mom— "

"No, I mean 'sorry'—as in 'sorry' sorry." Good one, Adda. Real eloquent.

After a long silence, Molly says, "For what?"

"You were right."

"About?"

Does she really not understand, or is she just trying to make this harder for me than it already is? Regardless, it has to be done. Wincing in anticipation of rejection, I say, "About Richard."

Silence. Is that good or bad? *Please, God, let it be good.*

"You were right about him," I piece the apology together.

I hear her draw a long breath. "I know."

Not exactly a sympathetic response, but at least she's still on the line.

"However," she says, "I wish I'd been wrong."

I blink, struggle against my tightening throat. "Me too."

More silence, which is my cue that our falling out is still far from reversed.

Oh, why didn't I just put this in writing! Determinedly, I put my chin up. "I also want to apologize for the things I said to you the day of my wedding."

"About my being jealous?"

"Among other things, but yeah. I know you weren't. I just—"

"But I was jealous."

Huh?

"You heard right."

"Really?"

"Did you see Mom strutting around proud as a peacock while I was dating Will?"

The man to whom she's now *happily* married.

"Did you see her throwing herself into my wedding arrangements?"

Too busy with mine.

"And at our wedding . . . "

She trails off, as it was only three months prior to her own nuptials that her relationship with me trailed off. In the end, we both lost bridesmaids over Richard.

"No," Molly says. "All that mattered to Mom was that you reeled in her best friend's son and the catch of the town."

It *had* seemed the highlight of Mom's existence. Never had she been happier or more proud than when I walked down the aisle on Dick's arm. Nor more shocked and disappointed than when we divorced. "And look who's laughing now," I mutter.

"No, I'm not laughing." Molly's voice shakes slightly, and I imagine her biting her lip as she does when she gets emotional, a habit which leaves her lower lip conspicuously devoid of lipstick. "I've never laughed over you and Richard. I meant it, Adda, when I said I wish I'd been wrong."

My throat tightens further as I try to hold in a sob. "Think you . . . " I swallow hard. "Think you can forgive me?"

More lip biting? "I would, but— "

But?

"—I put it behind me a long time ago."

"Really?"

"At least, as much as I could. I just didn't think it would go over well to call you up and say, 'Hey, I forgive you.'"

No, it wouldn't have. Besides being offended, I likely would have dismissed her forgiveness as just more of her church talk—the same as I'd done when she called her unexpected pregnancy a "God thing" and I called it "coincidence."

"I see what you mean," I say.

Molly sighs. "Look, Adda, obviously we have a lot to work through, but right now let's deal with Mom."

Ashamed at having set aside Mom vs. Donna, I say, "You're right. So . . . what happened after Mom pulled out Donna's hair?"

"The security guard from the bank across the street broke up the fight. Now they're considering filing charges against one another."

I wrinkle my nose. "When did this happen?"

"This morning."

"And what started it?"

"Mom says she and Donna were sharing the daily paper when Donna got all smug over an article that reported our local celebrity—you—were facing charges of plagiarism. Mom told Donna it was a pack of lies, that if anyone had stolen anything it was Birgitta Roth. Just like she stole your husband."

I startle, and Beijing cocks his head questioningly. "She's absolutely right," I say.

"That's what I figured."

Two more votes of confidence—just what I need. Hugging them to me, I say, "Go on."

"Anyway, Donna got all snotty and said the best thing that ever happened to Richard was when he met Birgitta Roth—said she'd done a heck of a lot more for her son than you ever did."

Richard, a full-grown man. Meaning I was expected to mother

him more than I'd done? Change his diapers? Spoon feed him? Wipe his nose? Amazing our marriage lasted as long as it did.

"By this time," Molly continues, "they're in each others' faces, voices raised. According to Mom, Donna pushed her, so Mom pushed back. Next thing she knew, they were on the floor, and that's when Mom pulled her hair out—gray roots and all."

"Whew," I sigh long. "That'll make the papers."

"You're telling me."

Trying not to think about how bad it could get, I ask, "So how's Mom?"

"Better than expected. She's resting now, but before she went to lie down she insisted on doing a little scrapbooking."

"You're kidding."

"Nope." Molly laughs. "You should see what she was able to do with Donna's hair—very creative."

Reminded of my own keepsake—Birgitta's bangs pressed between my divorce papers—I grudgingly acknowledge my mother and I have a lot more in common than I'd like to believe. And it makes me laugh.

Shortly, Molly's laughter joins mine and, despite all that is wrong in my life, makes me feel ages younger. When we finally sober, I know what I need to do.

"Molly," I say, "things are pretty bad here in New York, and I could use the support of my family. Any objections if I fly out and visit you and Mom?"

After a hesitation, which might be imagined, she says, "It'll do Mom good, and you'll finally get to meet Jack and Jinx."

"And the baby."

"In the tummy, if not the flesh," she quips. "Four weeks to go—unless baby decides to pop out early."

"Are you feeling well?"

"Feeling great."

Though I wouldn't have believed it possible to soar so high during such a low point in my life, I suddenly have wings. "I'll catch the next plane out. Pick me up at the airport?"

"Sure."

"Great! As soon as I know my time of arrival, I'll call."

"Okay."

Time to say good-bye, which is hard to do. "Bye, Molly."

"Bye."

"Um!"

"Yeah?"

"Thank you for calling."

After a long moment, she says, "I was worried about you."

Me? Then she didn't call just because Mom and Donna—

No. Not just because of Mom and Donna.

"That means a lot to me," I say. "More than you can know."

"Glad to hear it."

And so we ring off, and a quarter hour later tickets to Iowa are secured—one for me under my married name, Adda DeMarco, and one for Beijing under his alias, Jabba. We're out of here!

However, as I start up the stairs to begin packing, I'm struck by a possibility I've been too busy pitying myself to consider. I halt. Though I accepted that running into Elizabeth was a "God thing," what if this whole Birgitta farce is a "God thing"? What if this hurdle was placed before me to turn something bad into something good? It *has* been nine years since I turned my back on Molly. And it felt so good to talk to her sister-to-sister—as if a hole in my heart, which I pretended didn't exist, might finally heal. If not for Birgitta's plagiarism, Molly and I might be very old women before we spoke as we did today. If then . . .

Still, considering what lies ahead, it's difficult to be thankful for Birgitta's role in bringing us back together. Thus, I struggle for some time before I relent and retrieve my Bible from beneath the mound of sofa pillows where I stuck it upon my return from visiting Birgitta.

Kneeling, head bowed, I whisper, "If you're still there, God—if you can forgive me—I just want to say thanks." I squeeze my eyes closed. "Please see me through this mess."

A while later, I tuck my Bible into my carry-on bag and sit down to await the cab.

SIXTEEN

If I have to endure one more rendition of the catfight at the library, one more Barbie doll tea party, one more blast of the whoopee cushion, I will go INSANE!

As five-year-old Jack rolls on the floor, ecstatic over my latest encounter with the pink bladder my unsuspecting rump once more deflated, I rise from the armchair. "Very funny, Jack. Hah, hah."

He squeals and thrums his little feet on the hardwood floor. "Oh, Auntie Adda, you tho funny!" "Tho" for "so" since his stunt with an escalator went bad when he, his sister, and Molly picked me up at the airport a week ago. Minus two front teeth, he flops his arms out to his sides and smiles at me.

Sheesh, the little bugger is cute!

An instant later, he's on his feet. With a giggle, he retrieves his whoopee cushion and begins to huff and puff it full again.

Headline: AUTHOR-IN-HIDING, ADDA SINCLAIRE, TURNS UP AT MENTAL WARD

Which isn't too big of a leap, as my disappearing act seems to have made matters worse with the media. Fortunately, as a result of Molly's run-in with some journalists who badgered Mom for an interview, my sister brought me to Wildbend Cabin—a quaint place where she and her family occasionally spend weekends in blessed seclusion. *If* one can call blessed long days and nights with two active kids who 'no-it-all,' as in:

"Run along and play."

"No."

"Just give me a few minutes."

"No."

"Don't you think that whoopee cushion is a bit loud?"

"No."

"Can't you two just be friends?"

"No."

"I think Barbie and her friends have had enough tea for one day."

"No."

"It's bedtime."

"No."

Not that I don't treasure this opportunity to get to know my niece and nephew, but it's my seventh day as their play pal, pony, wrestling buddy, etcetera. Seven days! New York is beginning to look pretty good.

Mom sighs. "Adda, Adda, Adda . . . "

I look to where she sits on the couch with her head back and a cool washcloth across her brow. Hoping to appease her without opening myself to another indignant blow-by-blow that almost makes me feel sorry for Donna, I cross to her.

"I know, Mom." I lower beside her and pat her thigh. "And I can't tell you how much it means to me that you took a stand against your best friend."

"Best friend," she moans, rolling her head side to side. "Fifty-five years. Fifty-five!"

Next to my measly thirty-five, going on thirty-six. How does one compete with that?

"Grammy," Jack says, coming alongside, "lift your butt."

I snort—can't help it.

"Oh, Jack," Mom groans, "can't you see grandmother isn't feeling well?"

Wide-eyed and innocent, he nods, but says again, "Lift your butt."

I lean toward him. "Jack, honey, your grandmother—"

"Want her to lift her butt!" He stamps his foot.

Well, maybe he's not *that* cute. "Here, Jack—" I raise my rear. "Get me again."

He wrinkles his nose, shakes his head. "Want Grammy'th butt."

Mom moans. "Oh, my head. My aching head!"

"Pleathe Grammy." Jack begins to pry at the object of his desire.

"All right, Jack, all right." Mom leans to the side.

Jack shoves the cushion under her, and a moment later she wearily heaves her weight onto it. As the cushion explodes with a resounding rendition of Three-Bean-Delight, Jack bursts with laughter and doubles over. Two seconds later, the little imp is on his knees, two seconds after that, he's once more rolling around on the floor.

New York is looking better by the minute.

"Oh, Auntie Aaadda," little Jinx sing-songs as she enters the living room carrying a plastic tray complete with tea set. "Tea time!"

I sigh, pat Mom's thigh again, and rise. "Okay, sweetie—" deep breath. "I'm coming."

"Adda!" Molly calls from the kitchen.

I beam at Jinx. "Gotta talk to your mom, but I'll be right back." "Right back" *is* relative, isn't it?

Jinx's mouth droops and chin dimples with a pout, but at least she doesn't stamp her foot. Muttering something, she trudges past me toward the flowered table and chair set, which is three sizes too small for my adult legs and teetering "butt"—as Jack so indelicately puts it.

"Need anything from the kitchen, Mom?" I ask over my shoulder.

She groans. "Don't worry about me, dear. I'll be . . . fine." Heavy sigh. "Eventually."

My mom, the martyr.

I step into the kitchen. As Beijing rises from his orthopedically correct dog bed, a very pregnant Molly and her husband look up from where they sit at the table with the day's newspapers spread before them.

Molly smiles, and once more I'm swept with relief over our reconciliation. Though the first couple of days were awkward, we've begun to draw close again. Of course, the real ice breaker came when she learned of my interest in Christianity. Though I hadn't meant to say anything for fear she might pound her beliefs down my throat, a slip of the tongue has proven a blessing. Now I've added her Scripture suggestions for understanding salvation to Josh's and Snow White's—a very convincing list of reasons to join Jesus' team. So convincing that, if not for this anger over the injustice done me and fear of surrendering control of my life, I would.

"It's not good, Adda," Molly says.

I blink. "Hmm?"

She taps the paper in front of her. "Not good."

Oh. *That.*

"Give it to me straight."

As Beijing pushes up beneath my hand in search of a rub, Molly says, "They're not letting up. And they're not going to now that Birgitta Roth has agreed to that television interview."

Heard about it last night, and nearly vomited. Three days from now—prime-time Friday—it airs. And I'm still no nearer to digging myself out of this hole.

"In short," Will says with an apologetic twist of the lips, "you're being slaughtered."

I sigh, lower my head, and scrub Beijing between the ears. If only Nick would return Noelle's phone calls, but the only contact she's had with him is through Kathryn who keeps telling her to wait on the release of my statement to the press. Wait . . . and wait . . . and all the while I'm being sliced into cold cuts to be fed to the dogs.

The least Nick could do is call me, but every afternoon when I check in with Angel, she reports the same—silence. Of course, it doesn't help that the media have dragged out the rumors of our involvement and grossly expanded on them, complete with eyewitness accounts of improprieties that never happened. Get this—an interlude in a hotel elevator! It would be funny if it weren't so wrong.

Molly rises and comes around the table to drape an arm across my shoulders. "You know what you have to do, Adda."

I clap a hand over my face, groan. "Must I?"

"Well, you can stay here, lose more weight, and remain my kids' favorite plaything—which, as we both know, is wearing thin—" she gives me a squeeze. "Or you can put your head up, your shoulders back, and throw a swing into that skinny little rear of yours."

I peek at her from between my fingers. "Skinny? Did you say skinny?"

She laughs, steps back, and swats my rear. "Sure did."

I *have* lost weight, I know, but is it that noticeable? I lower my hands, peer down my front, then crane my neck to look at my backside.

"I'll make you a sandwich," Molly says and starts for the refrigerator with Beijing on her heels.

"Okay," I say, though I won't have the appetite to choke down more than a few bites—just like I haven't had the desire to exercise, apply makeup, fuss with my hair, or end my nail-nibbling. In short, I've gone to seed. All I need to complete the picture is a cigarette dangling from nicotine-stained teeth.

Will pushes up out of his chair and crosses to me. "Don't worry, Adda, it'll work out."

I try to smile. "You think?"

He winks. "Providing you take my wife's advice."

"I intend to." With a burst of conviction, I determine that, as part of my transformation from anti-active to proactive, I'll treat myself to a hot bath, pumice stone, makeup, and an all-out hair fest. As for my nails, a clip job to even out the ragged edges is about the best they can hope for.

I go on tiptoe and peck my brother-in-law's cheek. "Thanks, Will."

"That's mine!" Jinx screeches from the living room.

"Mine now!" Jack counters, and I hear him stamp his foot.

Molly turns from the sink and, with a weary smile, says, "Handle it, Will?"

He nods, steps back from me.

"Grammy," Jinx cries, "tell Jack to give it back."

My mother groans. "Now, Jack— "

"No! Ith mine!"

With an apologetic grimace, Will steps past me. "Still trying to get this parenting thing down," he mutters. "It's a lot harder than it looks."

"Jinx, dear," my mother pleads, "can't you let Jack— "

"No! The last time I let him use it, he broke it!"

"And I'll break thith one if you don't let me play with it."

All thoughts of my pamper session out the window, as it would mean passing through the middle of their argument, I watch Will disappear around the corner.

"Grammy!" Jinx whines.

"Grammy!" Jack mimics.

"Stealer!"

"Thtealer!"

Sheesh! Reminds me of the petty arguments Dick loved to drag me into. Dick who cheated on me. Dick who stole from me. Dick who left Beijing with Stick Woman. Dick who refuses to return my calls. Dick who would really benefit from a dressing down. Hmm . . .

"Double time out!" Will's voice rises above the bickering. "Jack—the chair by the window. Jinx, the stool by the door."

As with each time he intercedes, the moaning and groaning are reduced to a minimum, and in thirty seconds flat, silence reigns.

"It *is* a lot harder than it looks," Molly says behind me.

And it's going to get harder yet, I can't help but consider as I turn and glance at her bursting-at-the-seams belly. I meet her gaze. "I know, but the two of you are doing a great job."

She smiles. "We love them."

"That's obvious."

Eyes sparkling, she picks up a slice of multigrain bread and begins spreading a layer of mayonnaise. "Want to have a look at the articles before I trash them?" She nods toward the table.

Not really, but I should. "Okay." I cross the kitchen and lower to the chair Will vacated. As I read through the lies, my thoughts return time and again to Dick who could help me if I could just convince him it's in his best interest to do so. Thus, when Molly sets the sandwich and a glass of milk beside me, I hardly notice, as the rusty wheels in my head are beginning to churn out an idea. Even before it's fully formed, I nod. Head up, shoulders back, a swing in my skinny rear, I take control of my destiny.

First stop: Houston.

SEVENTEEN

"He's out?" I eye the sleek, red Jaguar that reclines two feet from me. "Really? Not expected back today?" I glance at his downfall—a placard on the cement wall that reads:

RESERVED
Richard DeMarco
All Other Vehicles Will Be Towed

"Get this message to him, will you?" I consider the cement slab overhead. "Tell him I'm in town, I need to see him, and I'm on my way to his office. However long it takes, I'll wait for him."

As the woman on the other end begins to babble about being unable to reach him, I say, "Thank you." Telling myself there's more than one way to flush out a snake, I flip my cell phone closed and begin counting as I peek from behind a cement pillar at the elevator doors across the parking garage. At ten-Mississippi, the doors slide open and three women step out. At forty-Mississippi, an elderly gentleman exits. And at one minute, thirty-Mississippi, out steps Dick. Briefcase in hand, he hastens across the parking garage toward the Jaguar.

He is going to die—just die!—when he realizes I've duped him. A nice change of pace.

As he nears, he begins fishing around in his pockets and is so preoccupied with what should be a simple task that he steps past the pillar without noticing me where I lean against it.

"Ah-hah!" He pulls keys from his jacket pocket.

Now comes the hard part—locating the correct key. He flips through them twice before grunting out another, "Ah-hah!"

The man has depth. Gotta give him that.

And now the really hard part—getting the key in right side up. And he doesn't disappoint. Of course, as Nick can attest, I'm not exactly a pro myself.

"*Bleep*!" he hisses and fumbles the key around. A moment later, the lock releases and he yanks the door open. Still clueless though I'm near enough to reach out and tap his shoulder; he tosses his briefcase in and slides behind the wheel. Following a repeat performance of the key debacle, the engine fires up and he pops the car into gear.

A smile in place, I lift a hand and do the ever-popular "girlfriend" wave.

As he begins to reverse out of his parking space, he glances over his right shoulder, then his left. And lets out a yelp that vies with the screech of his tires.

Confident in a knee-skimming leather skirt and fitted red

sweater, I push off the pillar and step to the car as he continues to gape. Smiling wider, I bend and tap the window.

No sooner does he blink himself out of shock than his face reflects struggle, undoubtedly over whether to reverse out of here as quickly as he can or spare me the time of day. Just in case he decides on the former, I'm prepared.

"Uh, uh, uh." I shake my head and show him the single key that fits my rental car.

He frowns.

With a flourish, I touch the key's jagged tip to his perfectly polished, unblemished door. Can't blame me for the scratch—or should I say gouge—if he backs up farther.

He reads the threat and lowers his window. "Adda. Uh . . . what are you doing here?"

I lean near. "You must not have received my message. Of course, I didn't expect you to, as you aren't in today, are you?" A little laugh. "Also, your receptionist has no way of reaching you. Imagine that—a big news station so financially strapped that its television personalities have to make do without cell phones. What, I ask you, is this world coming to?"

A flush crawling his lightly stubbled cheeks, he glances at the key, bites his lip, and says, "You're not really going to scratch my car, are you?"

I lean back a little and, with appreciative eyes, caress the Jag bumper to bumper. "This beauty?" Which my lump-sum divorce settlement in lieu of alimony likely paid for. I shrug. "That's really up to you, isn't it?"

He cranks his jaw left and right, then sighs, slides the car into first gear, and switches off the ignition. "Put the key away, Adda."

"Then you're inviting me to join you for a cup of Joe?"

He startles. "What?"

"Joe. You know—coffee. You still drink the stuff, don't you?"

He rolls his baby blues and says, "As a matter of fact, I don't. Causes premature aging, or haven't you heard?"

Same thing he said about meat years ago, and yet you'd never know he's five years younger than Nick. Not that he looks old—in fact, he looks pretty good with his day's growth of beard and dark, cropped hair with blonde highlights. As trendy as ever.

I shrug a shoulder. "Some things are worth a few wrinkles. So do we chat here in the parking garage, where any of your colleagues might pass by, or go some place a little more private?"

Naturally, I'm angling for elsewhere, as the last thing I want is to stick my head in the lion's mouth of the media—which I've risked by calling him at the news station. Though I didn't give the receptionist my name, I was required to identify myself to be put through to him. Thus, I'd said I was his ex. After five minutes on hold, the woman told me he was out.

So is it too much to hope she didn't make the connection to Adda Sinclaire when so many articles have mentioned Dick? Of course, even if she doesn't, I still have to worry about *him*. But surely his attempt to avoid me means he's more concerned with what Birgitta—his meal ticket to Houston—will think if he's caught consorting with the enemy than what could be a boost to his career if he's the one to root out the "Queen of Plagiarism," as I've been dubbed.

"Well?" I prompt as it becomes evident his latest struggle could drag on a while. Still, he refuses to get off the stick, so I begin tapping the key against his door.

"Okay!" he explodes. "Get in."

I sigh. "Don't know what I never saw in you, Dick."

Tight-lipped, he jabs a button that unlocks the passenger-side door.

Just in case he tries to pull one over on me, I trail the key a breath from his paint job as I circle the car. Shortly, I slide in beside him. "Where to?"

"Somewhere dark," he mutters and reverses out of the parking space with a screech of tires.

As the parking garage attendant raises the security gate, he says, "Have a nice day, Mr. DeMarco," then meets my gaze. "Ma'am."

Wishing I'd put on my sunglasses, I nod.

A moment later, Dick pulls onto the road. Silence descends as he forces his way into traffic, broken only when his jacket begins to chirp and twitter. He plunges his hand inside and pulls out a—

Fancy that, he does have a cell phone!

"Richard DeMarco speaking," he says with a deep inflection I remember him practicing over and over before job interviews.

"Uh . . . yes, sir. Umm . . ." His gaze darts toward me and back to the road. "That's right."

The silence that follows puts me on edge. Am I being paranoid, or does this smell like trouble?

"Of course," he finally says. "I understand." He flips the phone closed and glances at me. "I've got an interview scheduled for noon, so I can only give you a half-hour, Adda."

Is that what his call was about? Just an interview? Remembering other cryptic calls, which I later realized were from Birgitta, I nod. "It shouldn't take any longer than that."

Somewhere between the parking garage and the ten-minute drive, Dick's idea of "somewhere dark" takes the unlikely shape of a Starbucks—my favorite coffeehouse. I'd be touched that he remembered if not that gut instinct warns me he isn't here by choice. But even if something lies in wait, I can't turn back now—not when Dick may be all that stands between the truth and Birgitta's lies.

"So," I say, pushing my sunglasses on as we cross the threshold and join the queue to order drinks, "been too busy to return my calls, hmm?"

He shifts his weight opposite and back again. "Laying low," he mutters above the drone of some nasal singer piped in for our listening pleasure.

"What a coincidence. So am I." I make a face. "But you know that, of course."

I declare, the man is crawling out of his skin. But then, he *is* a snake . . .

"Uh, yeah," he says, "I heard."

"Hmm."

Scanning the overhead menu, he says, "The . . . uh . . . station keeps me busy."

"Really?"

"Yeah. There's . . . uh . . . a lot more to sportscasting than you'd ever guess."

"And you do a very good job."

Face brightening, an expectant light entering his blue eyes, he looks down at me. "You . . . uh . . . caught my show?"

I'd almost forgot how much he uses "uh" when nervous—which should have clued me in when he was messing around. "Yeah, I caught it." Smile. "Tuned in when I got to my hotel last night. And just when I was beginning to think Birgitta's news that you'd taken a job in Houston was a lie, midnight rolls around, and suddenly, there's my dear old ex."

His mouth twitches. "The . . . uh . . . midnight spot is temporary. The station has . . . uh . . . big plans for me."

"Oh, I'm sure." I nod. "Sure."

The woman in front of us steps aside, and the barista says, "May I help you?"

Dick, ever the gentleman, steps ahead of me. "Tall chai latte, please."

As if spicy black tea doesn't have caffeine.

The barista looks to me, "Are you two together?"

"Sort of," Dick jumps in, "but . . . uh . . . separate bills." He plunks down a five-spot.

Dick, ever the gentleman.

Shortly, a vanilla latte in hand, I cross to the window table he's chosen—a place that can hardly be called "dark" with the sun streaming in. Not surprisingly, he doesn't stand at my approach, nor pull out my chair. In fact, he barely spares me a glance before taking a swig off his chai.

I lower to the chair across the small table and lift my cup. "So, how long are you supposed to keep me here?"

His hand jerks, and a dribble of chai splashes onto the table. "Huh?"

I take a sip, glance out the window. "How long?"

"I don't know what you're—"

"Yes, you do. Your news station is sending out a camera crew, and your job is to keep me here long enough to give them the scoop."

He blinks. "How'd you know?"

Another sip. "I was once married to you, Dick. Remember? Despite some premature aging, you haven't changed all that much."

Ugh. Why did I say that? More flies with honey than vinegar, Mom always says, and here I am antagonizing him.

Mouth tight, he says, "Look, Adda, I didn't want any part of this. *You're* the one who called me at the office and announced you were my ex, then assaulted me in the parking garage and coerced me into coming here."

I snort. "Assaulted? Is that to be the headline on the afternoon news—QUEEN OF PLAGIARISM ASSAULTS EX?"

"I'm just saying you should have stayed away."

"Had you returned my calls, I would have, but—" I splay a hand, "—you left me no choice. So, were the garage security cameras my undoing or the attendant?"

He blows a breath up his face. "Both."

I sigh. "And so here we are."

"Here we are."

Over the next minute, the clock ticks away, dragging me closer to media exposure. With a deep breath, I lower my latte. "I need your help, Richard."

He raises an eyebrow. "What happened to Dick?"

I shrug. "Maybe it's just wishful thinking—" my throat tightens unexpectedly, "—but I really want it to be Richard across the table from me, not Dick."

He shifts in his chair. "I know what you want, Adda, but I can't help you."

Wishful thinking, then. Holding onto my composure, I slide the corrugated sleeve down my cup and up again. "Okay, but surely you can answer a few questions. After all, what else is there to keep me here until your camera crew arrives?"

He moistens his lips. "Depends on whether or not you're recording our conversation."

I lean back, sweep a hand down my front. "Notice any bumps or bulges that shouldn't be present?"

With a slight smile, he shakes his head. "Actually, you have fewer than I remember."

With false brightness, I say, "I'll take that as a backhanded compliment, thank you." No need to mention *his* infidelity was responsible for my weight gain all those years ago.

"You probably shouldn't," he says.

I double-take.

"What I mean is . . . uh . . . " He shakes his head. "You're too skinny, Adda. In fact, you look kind of . . . sick. Like you haven't been eating or sleeping well."

I clench my teeth into a smile. "Well, lies and vicious rumors tend to make one lose one's appetite. On the other hand, a cheating husband often has the opposite effect."

He actually has the grace to wince.

I plop my purse on the table. "Have a look and set your mind at ease."

He pulls it to him. After foraging through it and finding no recorder, he pushes it back. "Okay, you're clean. Wanna check me?" He leans back and opens his jacket.

"Not necessary. Remember, I have nothing to hide—unlike Birgitta Roth. And you."

His gaze narrows.

"All right, then," I say, "you'll answer some questions?"

"I'll try."

He'll try. . . . "I want to know how she got my manuscript."

He nods. "I thought you might."

Okay, we're getting somewhere. "Did you give it to her?"

"Of course not!" he exclaims as though I've insulted him in the worst possible manner.

"Then?"

He pulls a hand down his face. "Look, Adda, what difference does it make— "

"A lot!" I burst, causing a couple at a nearby table to snap their heads around. "To me," I add, lowering my voice. "It makes a difference to me."

"Why?"

I look at my cup. "All right, I'll ask it a different way. Did you bring her to our home? Did you— " Why do I suddenly feel close to tears? I draw a deep breath, toss my head up. "Did you sleep with her in our bed?"

To my surprise, he reaches across the table and closes his hand over mine. "No, Adda. I'm not that much of a scumbag. I never brought her to our home."

Nose beginning to tingle, I sniff and nod. "Thank you."

His thumb begins to stroke the back of my hand, and though it feels nothing like when Nick touches me, it's strangely comforting. "I never said I was sorry, Adda, but I am—sorry we ended the way we did, sorry I hurt you."

Am I dreaming? Is he apologizing? *Not in a million years.*

"It just wasn't working out," he continues.

I search his face. He looks real . . . I release my coffee cup, lower my hand beneath the table, and give my thigh a good, hard pinch. Yeow! "No, it wasn't working out," I agree.

Silence falls around us, and once more I become aware of the ticking clock. "So now all that remains to be told is how she got hold of my manuscript if she was never in our home."

"Yeah."

I cock my head. "Tell me. I know you know."

He releases my hand and sits back. "Adda, Birgitta's the one I have to thank for everything that's happened to me this past year. I'm finally a sportscaster in a big city, I'm making good money, and I'm well-respected. Richard DeMarco is somebody, whereas he was nobody before Birgitta. I owe her."

My emotions teeter. On one hand, I feel sorry for him; on the other, I'm outraged. Unfortunately, the latter wins out. "You owe her?" I snap. "What about me?"

He glances at the couple who are once more looking our way. "Adda, shhh—"

"Don't you shush me, mister! Who was it that tutored you through high school and college, so you wouldn't be kicked off the football team?" I jab a thumb to my chest. "Me."

"Adda—"

"Who ignored her sister's warnings about you and ended up alienating her for nine years?"

Another jab at my chest. "Me."

Hurt flashes across his face, giving him that sad, little boy look I once found so appealing. "Molly warned you about me?" He shakes his head. "I thought she liked me."

Thick as peanut butter.

"Who stood by you and supported your dreams job after job, none of which were—" I make quotation marks in the air, "—'the right fit'?"

Jab. "Me."

"Who uprooted and moved to New York so you could be where the action was?"

Jab. "Me."

Dick nods at the couple who are rising. "Adda—"

"Let them leave," I growl. "Who paid for your designer clothes, useless toys, and fast cars?"

Jab, jab. "Me."

With a groan, Dick puts his elbows on the table and his head in his hands.

"Who tossed pride and good sense out the window when you just had to be introduced to Birgitta Roth?"

Jab. Ow! That one hurt. "Me."

Dick's shoulders slump as another table clears out.

"Who endured the humiliation of your little affair? Me." Less the jab this time. "And who wrote you a check for a quarter of a million dollars to settle our divorce? Me! Adda Sinclaire-DeMarco, that's who!"

My breath is coming so quick and sharp I'm almost panting. "And you say you owe *her*? That . . . that—" ooh, it's coming and there's no holding it back, "—that Stick Woman?"

Dick jerks as though slapped. "Stick Woman?"

I stare wide at him. Then, with a resounding thud, I drop my forehead to the table. "Is that all you heard? Are you really so shallow?"

A long silence, then, "I heard everything you said, Adda. Believe me, I left no word unturned."

I look up, peer at him through narrowed lids. "And?"

He flips his hands palms up. "And you're right."

I am? I mean, he's actually admitting it?

"I owe you a lot, Adda."

Hope flutters in my chest, but I know better than to set it free—especially with regret reflecting in his eyes. I sit back. "But?"

He blows a long breath that stirs my bangs. "I'm too selfish to give up my gain—even if it is ill-gotten."

Uh-huh. "Then you really believe you'd lose your job?"

He pushes a hand back through his hair, nods. "*Her* connections, Adda. *Her* reference."

"But—"

He glowers. "She's said as much."

Surprise, surprise. "Then you've . . . talked."

"Yeah. She . . . uh—" he scratches his head, "—wants me to press charges against you for stealing my dog."

Beijing, who I left with my sister until things cool down. "And I suppose you'll accommodate?"

He shakes his head. "Actually, I told her I wouldn't—that Beijing is better off with you."

I'm touched. Too bad he doesn't feel the same way about my manuscript. "I appreciate it."

He shrugs. "Least I can do."

Sure is. I lift my cup, drain the last of my latte. "Well, looks like you have what you always wanted."

A frown troubling his brow, he considers his cup. "Yeah, though funny thing is that sometimes I miss what I had."

I blink. Surely he's not referring to me? Gotta be Birgitta Roth. Stake my life on it—until he meets my gaze. He *does* mean me . . .

"Do you ever miss us?" he asks and reaches across the table again.

I yank my hand to my lap before he can catch hold of it. Though I should savor hurting him—even though it doesn't compare to what he did to me—I can't. Thus, as gently as possible, I say, "Like you said, it wasn't working out."

His left cheek dimples, and I realize he's biting the inside of his mouth. However, a moment later he forces a smile. Tight though it is, I'm reminded of the smiles that caused my pulse to race and stomach to lurch when he needed me to get him through high school and college.

"No," he says with a sigh, "it wasn't."

"For the best," I say.

Yeah." He taps his empty cup on the table. "So tell me about this Nick Farnsworth. Is it true the two of you are seeing each other?"

"Not anymore."

He purses his mouth and shakes his head. "His loss."

My chest tightens. "Thanks."

A long silence follows, during which he looks out the window and scans the street. "Look, Adda, the camera crew will be here any moment. Why don't you get out of here and go back to New York?"

Pressing my lips inward, I glance out the window at the traffic. "Yeah, I think I will. You won't lose your job if I up and disappear, will you?"

"I'll be all right.

"Okay, then." I stand and sweep up my empty cup. "Bye."

As I start to turn away, he says, "Adda?"

I look around. "Dick?"

His brow rumples at my return to the shortened form of Richard. "If you really want to know how she got hold of your manuscript, take a look at our divorce papers."

I frown. "What?"

"The section that lists our joint property—as in who got what."

I shake my head. "Believe me, I'd remember if my manuscript were on that list."

"Just take a look. It's there. Not that it'll help much, but . . . " He raises his palms up.

Why can't he just tell me? "Okay," I say on a sigh. "I'll take a look."

"And Adda?"

"Yeah?"

"You probably won't believe this, but I hope you come out on top."

This is just too weird. I waver a moment, then lean down and press my lips to his forehead. "Good-bye, Richard."

EIGHTEEN

UEEN OF PLAGIARISM MAKES HER MOVE

As seen through the window of Starbucks.

I lower to a bar stool at my kitchen counter and unfold the newspaper. Four pictures. The first shows Richard and me leaning toward each other across the table—cozy. The second is an unflattering shot of my aggressive encroachment upon his space—that would be when he told me how much he owed Birgitta. The third, conveniently out of sequence, is a close-up of Richard's hand covering mine—I can guess where this is heading. And the fourth catches me leaning down and kissing his forehead—*um-hmm.*

Though I managed to evade the television cameras, I fell prey to a photojournalist who must have been tipped off by someone at the news station. And they've made it look like a lover's quarrel turned interlude.

I close my eyes in anticipation of a sinking feeling; however, it eludes me, and I realize I'm becoming numb to it all. Wish I'd felt this way last night when I flew in to La Guardia and was accosted by half a dozen blood-sucking reporters. I hid my eyes behind sunglasses and gritted my teeth against the temptation to spit and claw at their obnoxious probing. With the aid of two airport security guards, I finally made it into a cab. Call it what you will—denial or survival—I welcome the numbness. And I'll certainly need it tomorrow night when Birgitta hits prime time with her tale of woe and betrayal.

Opening my eyes, I quickly read through the accompanying article, and sure enough, the writer speculates on my involvement with my ex and what, exactly, the conniving Adda Sinclaire is up to.

When Nick sees—

I draw a sharp breath. When he sees it, he sees it, and that's the end of that. I mean, it's not as if it can make matters worse, can it? Bad is bad is bad.

"Right." I slap a hand to my thigh, push the paper aside, and look to the pile of phone messages Angel left me. A quick flip through them confirms that all but one—from Elizabeth Carp inviting me to hide out at her place—are headed for the round file. Well, that was easy. The mail produces a few more keepers, among them a letter from Jack and Jinx that had to have been sent prior to my departure, and a card from Sophia Farnsworth. I open the first, and my heart tugs at the grossly animated family picture Jack crayoned—Auntie Adda included—and the pink and green tea party scene Jinx watercolored. Boy, I miss them!

Lastly, I slide a finger beneath the flap of Snow White's envelope and remove the card within. *I believe in you*, she writes, *Love, Sophia (Psalm 31).*

I release my breath. "Well, at least there's one Farnsworth who doesn't think the worst of me." Not that I would ask her for anything—won't have her dragged into the middle of my mess. But I will write her back. Later.

I start to fold her note, but the Scripture referenced alongside her name pulls me in. Psalms, a recent favorite for all its carrying on about enemies and pleas for God to wreak vengeance on them through shame, breaking of teeth and arms, blinding, and even slaying.

Though I know Psalms was written during Old Testament times before Jesus arrived on the scene and taught about love and forgiveness, during my darkest moments I can't help but turn to this part of the Bible and draw comfort from it. What's that saying about misery loving company?

Curious as to why Sophia would refer me to the Old Testament, I retrieve my Bible and quickly locate Psalms. "Thirty-one," I murmur, drawing a finger down the page. And there it is. I read through the psalm of David, which begs the Lord for deliverance from enemies who slander and make him the contempt of his neighbors. Because of its mild take on revenge relative to other psalms, it's one I've disregarded during previous readings. And I almost discard it again—until I reach the last lines, "Be strong and take heart, all you who hope in the LORD." Struck by the comfort embedded in those words, I read it again. "Hope," I breathe, putting my finger on the word. "Hope in the Lord." But is it enough?

I return my gaze to Sophia's note, consider it, then fold and slip it in my shirt pocket. "Okay," I say, "I'll try."

And now it's time to pull out the divorce papers.

Though stung by memories, I determinedly search out the section that lists joint property, and there, pressed between the pages, find strands of bottle-dyed blonde hair—dark roots and all.

Eeew! Deciding it's time to let go—to grow up—I pinch the nasty reminder of my confrontation with Birgitta between thumb and forefinger and carry it to the wastebasket.

Good for you. Prim claps me on the back as I wipe my hands clean.

I return to the bar stool and begin reading through the joint property. Of course, Beijing is listed in Richard's column. Then there's the Corvette I bought and paid for, two motorcycles . . .

I clench my teeth.

. . . a motorized scooter, various pieces of furniture, a collection of sports paraphernalia . . .

I grind my teeth.

. . . a two-thousand-dollar bicycle he never rode . . .

I gnash my teeth.

. . . half a dozen fifteen-hundred-dollar suits—which met with the unfortunate fate of "accidental" laundering in HOT water the day before he came for them.

I grin. I know . . . I shouldn't.

Same thing with his leather riding pants and jacket.

I smile. Can't be helped . . .

Then there's the top-of-the-line laptop computer he had to have the moment it arrived in stores. Couldn't wait a couple of months for it to go down in price like they always do.

I drop the smile and grip the page tighter.

Ah, yes, the refrigerator, a stainless steel job with two compressors to keep food at its freshest. Birgitta probably still has it.

As the page begins to crumple between my fingers, I remind myself that *I* have Beijing, and as soon as it's feasible, I'll send for him. I continue through the list, item by infuriating item.

Underwear, socks, athletic supporter, all of which had a run-in with a new red sweater in the wash cycle. CDs, videos, DVDs . . .

I heave a sigh. "Okay, Richard, where is it? How did she get hold of my— " I blink, jerk my gaze up the list.

Laptop computer.

A chill pricking my flesh, I sit back and stare out the window above the kitchen sink. That has to be it. Richard and I argued over it. Though it was purchased for him, my *three-year-old* computer had required servicing. Thus, despite Noelle's insistence that I shelve the option book altogether, I had downloaded the manuscript onto the laptop for final editing. As Richard slammed around our apartment, selfish me—the sole breadwinner—had denied him access to his games of death and destruction.

Though remembrance leaves a bitter taste in my mind, I feel a momentary thrill at unearthing evidence of Birgitta's guilt. Momentary because Richard is right. Though I've found the source of the theft, that's it. Of little help to my cause and of even less significance than the affidavits Noelle has arranged to support my claim to *The Gifting*—hers and Joyce's. Hardly unbiased.

Numbness receding, the feeling in my emotions beginning to return, I suck a breath between my teeth. "That which does not kill me," I repeat a saying my mom could be heard murmuring often during my visit home, "makes me stronger—"

The phone lights up with an incoming call—the ringer having been turned off. Though it's undoubtedly a reporter, I flick my gaze to caller ID and startle at the name—Intrepid Publishing.

Nick? I reach to the handset and freeze. Can't be. He's not due back for another two days. Unless he returned early . . .

I grab the handset as the answering machine kicks on. "Hello?" I say over the outgoing message. Grimacing, I punch the machine's "off" button.

"Is that you, Adda?"

Kathryn Connell—a far cry from Nick. And it's too late to pretend I'm out.

"Kathryn. Hi."

"Long time, no speak."

"Yeah."

"How's it going?"

"The water's warm," I say. "Wish you were here."

"What?"

"Nothing. Just . . . fantasizing about a place I'd rather be."

"Oh."

I raise a hand, shake my head over unsightly nails. "I suppose you're calling about the pics of me and my ex."

"No, though you've got to admit that was a really bad idea."

"What? Trying to clear my name?" I laugh. "Considering how much support I've received from my publisher, it seemed the only course open to me."

A long, disapproving silence, then, "So did you get an admission out of him?"

I lower my hand. "Richard knows which side his bread is buttered on." I make a face. "Ugh. I can do better than that. How does this sound: 'He knows where his next meal is coming from'? Or maybe—"

"Adda—"

"I know. If I'm not careful, they'll start calling me the Queen of Cliché."

"Adda!"

With a half-groan, half-sigh, I say, "No, I didn't get an admission out of him, but regarding how Birgitta Roth got hold of my manuscript in the first place, he did point me in the right direction."

"Oh?"

"The laptop computer onto which I downloaded the story—he received it in our divorce settlement."

After a long moment, Kathryn says, "Interesting," then sighs. "Unfortunately, you're going to need more than that to beat this."

Hope in the Lord. . . . "I know," I say, biting back a retort.

"So how can I help you, Kathryn?"

"I just wanted you to know that we're doing everything we can to work this out between you and Birgitta."

Though I tell myself to calm down, to let it roll off my back, to go numb, words fill my mouth so full they have no place to go but out between my lips. "But of course you're doing everything you can. After all, Intrepid has a lot at stake, what with its lead author up on plagiarism charges — the same author who received a sizable advance for a book that may never see the light of day."

"Okay, Adda, calm down — "

"I was just telling myself the same thing, but," I shrug, "it sure feels as if I've been hung out to dry. Oops! Another cliché."

"Listen — "

"And I still haven't received the go-ahead — or should I say *permission* — from Mr. Nick Farnsworth to release a statement attesting to my innocence."

"I just got off the phone with him," Kathryn plunges in before I can go off again.

I still. "What?"

"Uh-huh. He asks that you hold off on your statement a bit longer."

That's all? But of course it is. What else would he have to say to me? "Then it follows he's also asked Birgitta Roth to hold off on her prime-time interview."

"He has, but she declined."

"Ah. So I'm expected to sit on my laurels while she's out

there inciting public opinion against me."

"Trust me, Adda, it's best that you wait."

"Best for who? Intrepid?"

"Look, Nick will be back Tuesday and— "

"Tuesday? I thought he was returning Saturday."

"Was, but something came up, and he had to delay his return."

"Oh." That secret fantasy of him appearing on my doorstep Saturday straight from the airport? Shot down. But that's all it was—a fantasy. Nick Farnsworth has more pressing matters to attend to than his attraction to a woman who's going down if she doesn't find a way to prove her innocence.

"He wants to meet with you," Kathryn continues, and my heart does a handspring a moment before she adds, "and Noelle Parker and Birgitta Roth on Wednesday at ten in his office."

Thud. I can hardly wait. "Okay, I'll put it on my calendar."

"Intrepid's attorney will also be present."

Getting uglier by the moment. "Thanks for the warning."

"Now don't get all worked up. We *are* going to find a way through this mess."

Of course *they* are—after they pull *The Feud*, demand the return of their advance, and drop a fat, juicy lawsuit in my lap. Fully aware of what I'm doing—way past the point of habit—I nip off the ragged edge of a thumbnail. "Sure," I mutter. "Of course you are."

"See you at ten on Wednesday."

"Uh-huh. You'll be there?"

"I will."

"Talk to you then." Don't know how long I sit there staring into nothing, battling the overwhelming urge to curl into a ball, but I eventually slide off the bar stool. Though I have every intention of going upstairs and unpacking, the phone lights again, and a moment later, the name of Farnsworth Publishing pops up.

Telling myself I'm a masochist, I wait for the machine to run through its outgoing message.

"Ms. Sinclaire," a New Yorkly accented voice rings its death-knell around my kitchen, "It's Joseph Blough, legal counsel to Farnsworth Publishing. I'd like you to call me back with the name and address of your attorney. I have papers to serve you."

Vacillating between the desire to indulge in a good old-fashioned pity party and an urge to give Joe Blow—what were his parents thinking?—a piece of my mind, I stare at the handset.

He clears his throat. "The number here is . . . "

Smoothing myself down, I turn away. Despite Nick's delay, there is some good in it, as it gives me six days to put on a little weight—*never* thought I'd aspire to that—get a haircut, buy a flattering outfit, and perhaps resort to artificial nails.

I halt at the base of the stairs to examine my nails. Yep. No way around it. I'll have to submit to a manicurist. With a sigh, I take the stairs two at a time and pass Angel's empty office. Poor thing's nerves were shot after dealing with the constant ring of the phone and the persistent reporters who came calling in my absence.

Thus, when she asked for the day off to get Doodle's name tattooed on her arm, how could I refuse?

Entering my bedroom, I cross to the suitcase that lies open on my bed. I hate unpacking! If Mom hadn't laundered most of my clothes, I would dump everything in a laundry bag and send it to the cleaners. Of course, one's clothes can never be too clean, can they?

I retrieve a bag from my closet and begin shoveling the clothes in, and that's when I find Jack's calling card—an orange plastic gun, half a dozen rubber darts strapped to the barrel with what looks like an entire roll of tape. And I can't help but smile.

Before I left Iowa, he had presented me with his prize toy gun. "In cathe that mean old Thtick Woman tryth to take another shot at you, Auntie Adda," he said.

I had started to laugh, but seeing hurt flicker in his eyes, swallowed hard and thanked him for trying to protect me. I'd then explained that the "shots" he'd overheard his mother and I talk about were nothing more than mean words. Though he remained adamant that I take the dart gun—just in case—I had put it back in his toy box when he wasn't looking. Guess he *was* looking.

"Oh well," I murmur. Fitting my hand around the molded grip, I lift the gun. As I gaze down its barrel, I'm struck by a thought that makes me smile.

● ● ●

She's in my sights—has no idea what's about to hit her. But rather than take the shot, I wait for the right moment. Timing has to be perfect. And a moment later, when she gives her best interpretation of a seductive smile, I squeeze the trigger.

My aim is perfect, nailing her right between the eyes.

"Wahoo!" I shout, bounding off the sofa. As I drop to my knees in front of her, the camera switches to the interviewer, and suddenly it's his nose from which the orange lick 'em dart protrudes.

"Shoot! Double shoot," I say when the camera returns to Birgitta, and she's leaning so near the interviewer the dart sits amid her hair.

"Oh, well." I put a fist around the orange shaft and pull. With a squishy sucking sound, the dart lets go of the television screen. I drag the other five free, all of which missed their mark by mere inches, and return to the sofa to reload.

I know—juvenile and not at all what Jesus would have me do—but the temptation was simply too much to resist.

As I insert a dart in the gun, Birgitta throws her head back and laughs.

About?

Though I've promised myself I'll only watch—won't listen to her big fat lies—curiosity burrows beneath my skin.

Uh. Uh, uh, Prim warns.

I grab the remote.

"Yes," Birgitta drawls, settling back in her chair, "every cloud does have its silver lining."

Talk about cliché!

"In fact, Heart Core, the publisher of *The Love Bounty*, informed me today that it's ordered another print run."

I feel my upper lip curl and teeth bare.

"You must be thrilled," the interviewer says.

Mute button! Prim fiercely reminds me.

Improper snorts. *Not on your life*.

Arching a pencil-thin eyebrow, Birgitta says, "Of course I'm thrilled. Who wouldn't be?"

"I can name one author," I mutter. "Ever heard of Adda Sinclaire?"

"Adda Sinclaire, perhaps," the interviewer suggests with a knowing smile that makes me gnash my teeth. No doubt whose side he's on.

"Yes, well . . ." Birgitta gives a one-shoulder shrug, "she has a lot to be unhappy about these days, doesn't she?" She sighs. "A lot to answer for."

"Which brings us back to the question of why she has yet to issue a statement—why she's refused all requests for interviews."

Mute, as in M-U-T-E!

Birgitta flips her hair back. "Considering the magnitude of what she's done by plagiarizing my work—"

Her work!

"—I'd say she's running scared. Think about it, Rob, what publisher is going to touch Adda Sinclaire after this? It's the end of her career, and she knows it."

Prim flicks my ear. *What about "mute" do you not understand?*

With a sharp crack, the dart gun's handle collapses. Heart pounding a hammer against my ribs, I toss Jack's offering aside.

"True," the interviewer says with an oxymoronic shake of his head, then frowns. "Ms. Roth, do you believe Ms. Sinclaire's plagiarism of *The Love Bounty* is an isolated incident?"

Birgitta hesitates before smiling what seems a forced smile. And is that a right-eye tic? I lean forward, narrow my gaze on her.

With a flutter of lids, she says, "I suppose it's possible I'm not the only author she's taken advantage of, but I prefer to think this is, indeed, an isolated incident. And I strongly believe that the sooner we in the romance writing industry put this ordeal behind us, the sooner we can hold our heads high again."

"What a crock," I mutter. Sounds more like she's worried. Of course, considering the weight of my defense thus far, what has she to worry about?

The interviewer, a long-faced rumple-headed man of thirty-something, taps his chin thoughtfully. "Then you believe this scandal has defamed the romance-writing industry?"

"Definitely, Rob. As you know, despite the fact that romance novels comprise over half of all popular paperback fiction, and generate well over a billion dollars in sales each year, it's been an uphill battle to gain the respect we're due. And now that we've finally made headway, something like this happens, and our books are once more being called 'trash.'"

"Hmm," Rob murmurs, and hands her a newspaper.

Damage control! Hit the mute button. That's right, that little button there. Better yet, the power button.

I slam the remote to the table.

You promised!

"I'm sure you've seen these pictures of Ms. Sinclaire with her ex-husband, Houston sportscaster Richard DeMarco, that were taken recently."

She sighs, shakes her head. "I have."

"Now you mentioned earlier that you and Mr. DeMarco became intimate following his divorce from Ms. Sinclaire."

"What?" I jump up.

"That's right," Birgitta says.

Some investigative reporter!

"What do you think Ms. Sinclaire hoped to achieve by meeting with him in Houston?"

"I have no idea, Rob, but she's obviously desperate."

I'm mad again. Real mad. Which, at the moment, is good. Real good. And I need to punch something bad. Real bad!

I grab a beaded pillow from the sofa and slam a fist into it. As she and Rob continue to shred my life and career for all the world to see, I take a bite of the pillow, then bury my face in it and scream.

I gasp another breath, but before I can let loose again, Rob says, "You've moved to Intrepid Books now, Ms. Roth."

"I have."

"There have been some rumors that its president, Nick

Farnsworth, is involved with Adda Sinclaire."

Oh, no . . .

"Think there's any truth to them?"

Birgitta scoffs. "In a word, Rob? No. Nick's too savvy to become inappropriately involved with one of his authors."

My anger breaks, and a moment later I sink to the sofa. "No, he isn't," I breathe. "Or, at least, he wasn't." *Ow . . .*

That mute button's starting to look pretty good about now, isn't it? Prim suggests.

"Yeah," I whisper, and reach to the table. I push the power button and watch as Birgitta's face darkens to a pinpoint of light. Staring at the black screen, I slowly lean back. "God, this hurts." I shift my gaze to the ceiling. "I could really use a little help down here."

And as is becoming an hourly habit, I pull out my Bible and read through Psalm 31. Over and over and over . . .

NINETEEN

ello Intrepid.

Or is it good-bye?

Amid the hustle and bustle of New Yorkers going about their busy lives, I halt and look up the building that houses one of the most prestigious publishers in the United States. Somewhere up there, Nick waits. And Birgitta and Noelle and Kathryn and Intrepid's attorney and whoever else they decide to throw at me.

Pushing my shoulders back in an attempt to ease the constriction in my chest, I tell myself that at least I look good, and a glance down my front confirms it. According to Elizabeth, my roommate these past three nights, the elegantly casual red jacket and skirt flatter my figure to perfection.

I almost smile. Bless her for standing beside me despite all appearances of wrongdoing. Though I hadn't wanted to impose by accepting her offer of a hideout, the journalists—not to mention an officer sent by Farnsworth Publishing to serve up a lawsuit—had converged on my home one too many times. But it turned out to be a good thing because I really needed the Christian support

Elizabeth offered. In fact, despite the executioner's ax hanging over me, I enjoyed our talks, which lasted into the wee hours each night and often included forays into Scripture.

Someone jostles me out of my reminiscence and, without apology, passes by. I glare at his retreating back. Good old New York.

Okay, going on ten. Time to brave the vultures. With a flash of Poppy Love-polished artificial nails, I adjust my jacket, skirt, and purse strap. Then, shoulders back, I step forward and pass through the glass doors I last passed through when Nick brought me here to sign copies of my books. Beginning to flush with remembrance of that night, I take a deep breath and make for the elevators.

"Ms. Sinclaire?"

I falter, and it's enough to confirm my identity to the man who suddenly appears before me.

"Ms. Adda Sinclaire?"

Why fight it? Knowing I'm about to be served, I meet his gaze through my sunglasses. "Yes?"

He reaches into a canvas bag and, sure enough, pulls out a legal-sized sheaf of papers. He hands them to me. And there it is, big and bold: Plaintiff—Heart Core Publishers; Defendant—Adda Sinclaire.

A chill goes through me at the culmination of the events of these past weeks. Clamping my teeth closed, I swallow hard to hold down my breakfast of toast and coffee.

"You've been served, Ms. Sinclaire," the man says.

Courtesy of Birgitta Roth. Who else would have let *The Love Bounty*'s publisher in on the meeting today?

"Have a good day," he says, and steps past me.

"Good day," I mutter, and my voice catches. Get a grip, I tell myself. If you can't handle this, you might as well turn around and walk your pathetic rear right out of here. Which, of course, will solve absolutely nothing.

"I can handle it," I mutter as my eyes tear. "I can." Remembering Snow White's note which I taped to my bathroom mirror, I close my eyes and whisper, "Be strong and take heart, all you who hope in the Lord." *Lord, my hope is in you. Please strengthen me.*

Grateful for the sunglasses, I draw myself up to my full height and resume my course to the elevators. Reaching them as two empty out, I step to the farthest one and, in hopes of making the ascent alone, jab the close-doors button. As they begin to slide together, I lean into a corner and lift the document that details the lawsuit.

A moment later, the doors jolt back open. With a groan, I look up as the intruder steps in. And lose my grip on the papers as Nick Farnsworth materializes before me. No fantasy, just wholesome, down-to-earth flesh with a generous sixteen-ounce serving of attraction. None of which I have any business appreciating considering he hasn't called me in over two weeks, likely believes the charges against me, and has surely seen the pics of me and Richard and drawn his own conclusions.

No business whatsoever.

"Adda," Nick says in that deep, dark voice that perfectly complements those chocolates of his.

And I could just melt. But I won't. "Mr. Farnsworth," I say, hating how choked I sound.

His brow darkens as the elevator begins its ascent, and I'm once more grateful for sunglasses—until I recall his ability to see through them.

He searches my face, lowers his gaze down me and up. "You've lost weight."

I shrug. "Well, you know the saying—one can never be too thin."

"You are."

Have he and Richard been talking? Are they in on this together? Or is it just "beat up Adda's self-esteem" week?

Nick considers me a moment longer, then bends and retrieves the papers. As he straightens, he scans the front page. "I expected as much," he murmurs.

I cock my head. "Did you, now? Well, there's more of that where this came from. Farnsworth Publishing is attempting to serve me as well."

He stiffens. "Peter and Damian at their best. Mind if I look this over?" He lifts the papers in question.

"As a matter of fact, I do." I pluck them from his hand.

A muscle jerks at his jaw as I roll the papers and shove them in my purse. Looking past him to the bubbled numbers counting up the floors, I say, "So everyone's present—Noelle, Kathryn,

Birgitta, Intrepid's attorney?"

"Listen, Adda—"

"I prefer Ms. Sinclaire, Mr. Farnsworth." Big smile. "Much less complicated, don't you agree?"

Nostrils flaring, he turns to the elevator control panel. A moment later, the elevator glides to a halt a dozen floors below Intrepid's offices.

I take a step toward him. "What do you think you're doing?"

He turns back. "Though I intended to catch you in the lobby before you came up, I was detained. We need to talk."

"Why? Hoping to avert a scene like that where I relieved Birgitta Roth of a hunk of hair? Well, don't worry. I won't do anything to scandalize Intrepid—excluding plagiarism, of course."

Despite my earlier attempt to control my anger, it's in the air and on the rise, and it's not just mine.

"That's not the reason I want to speak to you," Nick finally boils over.

"Oh?"

"I phoned you last night and got your answering machine."

I smile tightly. "That would be because I spent the night—the past three nights—with a dear friend." And he can take that however he likes. *And* the pictures of me with Richard. *And* his insecurity about Jake Grainger. I simply don't care. Really. Truly. Honestly.

Gauging by the overworked muscle in his jaw, he doesn't

take it well. "Ms. Sinclaire," he bites, "before we go in to the meeting, I'd like to discuss some new developments—"

"More accusations? More charges? More name-smearing?" I tell myself to stop, but I can't. "Or better yet, perhaps this whole debacle is just up and going away all by itself?"

"Adda!"

I startle at the force of his words but, goaded by my own anger, take a step toward him. "You're just like everyone else, Nick. Though you've gotten closer to me than anyone has in years, and feel something you probably haven't felt for a woman in a long time, you believe what they're saying about me, don't you?"

Emotion shifts across his face, and he inclines his head. "I did."

I stare at him as something fragile and hopeful cracks inside me. "Right," I breathe. Eyes stinging, nose tingling, I step to the elevator control panel. "Well, that about concludes our little chat, doesn't it? Time to feed me to the lions—though I warn you, I'll bite, kick, and claw all the way down their throats."

I punch Intrepid's floor number. Nothing. Again. Nothing. Harder. Nothing.

Nick steps alongside and grasps my hand. "Stop it, Adda."

I wrench my arm away before he can reduce me to a mass of quivering flesh. "Don't touch me." I meet his gaze through my lenses. "I can't stand it." And it's true, though not for the reason I'd like him to believe.

Face hardening, he takes a step back.

I return my gaze to the elevator panel and jab the button three more times. Nothing with a big, fat "N"! And if I don't get my emotions under control, I'm going to break down. I stamp my foot—courtesy of my favorite nephew—and jerk my head around. "I want out of here."

He reaches around me, flips a switch, and pushes the button. With a slight lurch, the elevator continues its ascent.

Waves of ache crashing over my heart, I settle back in my corner and look to the floor. He admitted it. Actually admitted it. Despite everything, he believed the lies about me—that I'm a thief, a user, a plagiarizer. He truly believed it—really did.

Hit by an echo of his words, I blink. *Did*? Was that what he said when I asked if he believed the lies? "I did"? Or was it, "I do?" Perhaps—

Get over it, I tell my pitiful self that so longs for him to believe in me. "Did" or "do," it comes down to the same thing. Nick Farnsworth, the man with whom I've fallen in love—oh no, have I really?—doesn't know me. And doesn't want to.

"Adda," he says as the elevator slows, "promise me that, regardless of what Birgitta and her attorney throw at you—"

I jerk my head around. "*Her* attorney? She brought *her* attorney?"

"She did."

I draw a shuddering breath. "I see."

He sighs. "Promise me you'll stick around long enough to hear out Intrepid's attorney."

I arch an eyebrow. "And what makes you think I'll keep my word? I mean, it's not as if the Queen of Plagiarism can be trusted, is it? Or have you forgotten Lake Tahoe and Jake Grainger? Oh, and what about those pictures of me with my ex? You did see them, didn't you? And judged me, I'm sure."

Something that looks a lot like regret flashes in his eyes, but my evolving instinct for survival dissuades me of it.

"Adda—"

PING! The elevator announces its arrival, and I look forward again as the doors ease open. "No promises," I say, "only an assurance that I won't take it too hard if you hang back a couple minutes, so no one knows you've been consorting with the enemy."

As I step forward, Nick curls a hand around my arm. "That won't be necessary," he says, and releases his hold as he steps past. "Follow me."

Momentarily blinded by his disregard for what others might think, hope trembles through me. But I know better. "Oh, right. Wouldn't want anyone to think I know the way to your office."

He halts, and I nearly slam into him. Feeling the regard of those milling about Intrepid's lobby, I step back and watch as Nick's shoulders go wider with a deep breath. Though I expect him to continue on, he turns.

"I deserve that," he says.

He does? I swallow. "Yes, you do."

Mouth grim, he motions for me to precede him. "They're waiting."

And so they are when I step ahead of him into his office. Avoiding looking at his desk and credenza for what it might do to me, I meet Noelle's gaze.

"Adda," she says, rising from the conference table where she sits opposite Birgitta and a suited, slicked-back, mustached man who has to be her attorney.

To Noelle's left sits Kathryn, and at the head of the table, a bald, fiftyish man sporting itty-bitty spectacles on a broad face. Intrepid's attorney? I lower my gaze to the thick folder before him. Has to be the attorney, meaning the folder contains my soon-to-be-void contract and whatever legal papers detail the action Intrepid intends to take against me.

Hope in the Lord . . . hope in the Lord . . .

Intrepid's attorney rises, and as he advances, I'm struck by the sheer size of him. The behemoth looks like he walked right out of a WWF arena!

"Ms. Sinclaire," Stone Cold says—yeah, I did it again, but at least it's not derogatory. He extends a hand and a warm smile that instantly puts me on guard.

What's he smiling about?

"Jeremy Littlefeather, counsel to Intrepid Books."

Not quite as amusing as the name of Heart Core's attorney—Joe Blough—but close. Knowing that if I continue to hide behind my sunglasses I'll appear shifty, I remove them. "Mr. Littlefeather," I say, sliding my hand into his great paw.

He gives me a firm shake, releases. "Join us, will you?"

As I follow him, I glance behind only to discover Nick is gone, and for a moment I'm stricken. But he's there, having positioned himself across the room in front of the windows. Hands shoved deep in his pockets, he stands with his back to us. That bad, huh?

"This all right, Ms. Sinclaire?" Stone Cold—er, Jeremy Littlefeather—asks, indicating the chair between him and Noelle.

"Fine," I murmur, settling my purse to the floor alongside the chair.

As I lower to the seat, withholding my gaze from Birgitta where she sits directly across from me, Noelle grips my shoulder and leans near. "Seen this morning's paper?"

Beginning to numb, I look around and whisper, "I don't read that trash."

"Well you should, Ms. Sinclaire," says the eavesdropping man beside Birgitta.

I meet his gaze. "I don't believe we've met."

He rises and shoves a hand across the table. "Bob Smith, Ms. Sinclaire. I represent Ms. Roth."

I glance at his moist palm, slide my gaze to his nails which extend past the fingertips. Someone ought to tell him about clippers.

"Bob Smith," I say, folding my hands atop the table. "Just . . . Bob Smith?" After all, once you've had Joe Blough and Stone Cold Littlefeather, it's a bit anticlimactic.

Frowning, Worm—aargh! I will beat this habit!—Bob Smith lowers to his chair. "Robert, if you prefer, Ms. Sinclaire."

I shake my head, smile tightly. "No, Bob is fine."

"And may I call you Adda?"

I try. I really try to summon a civil response, but the knowledge that this man wants to tear me apart overwhelms my good intentions. "Only if you intend to ask me out on a date, *Bob*." I slide my gaze to his left hand. "Oh, but you're married. Of course, I'm sure your client, Ms. Roth, wouldn't object." *Back off*, I tell myself, while beneath the table, Noelle grips my thigh.

I look around. "Yes, Noelle?"

She bends her head toward mine. "Stop it—now!"

"I agree with Noelle," Bob once more sticks his nose where it doesn't belong. "It's time to get down to business."

I chance a glance across the room and meet Nick's chocolates a moment before he returns his gaze to the pavement below. Though I expected censure, something else shone from his eyes—something too fleeting to name, though it jolted me.

"Today's paper, Ms. Sinclaire," Bob says, sliding it across the table.

I look at the headline:

FARNSWORTH PUBLISHING TALKS ABOUT ADDA SINCLAIRE

"Take a minute to read it," Bob invites.

Though I'd rather not, I steel myself and pick up the paper.

. . . interview with Damian Farnsworth, CEO of Farnsworth Publishing . . . Ms. Sinclaire was hard to work with . . . demanding . . . a prima donna. . . . had difficulty making deadlines . . . quality of work

was declining . . . until the charge of plagiarism is resolved to their satisfaction, has ordered all copies of The Gifting *pulled from the shelves . . . plans to seek damages that could run upward of a million dollars . . .*

Though nothing in the article comes as a surprise, seeing it in print causes my bile to rise; however, despite the appeal of retching across the table where Birgitta sits, I swallow hard to retain the contents of my stomach.

Lowering the paper, I look to where Birgitta watches me with her head at a slight angle, a satisfied smile stretching her mouth.

I clench my hands. "Psalm 31," I whisper in an attempt to once more draw strength from Snow White's Scripture. "Psalm 31."

"Some thirty-one what?" Bob asks.

For a moment, I'm mortified by my slip at having been caught speaking of the Bible—as if it's some dirty magazine—but then shame sweeps me. Other than my own reaction, I have *nothing* to be ashamed of.

I look to Bob. "Not 'some thirty-one.' *Psalm* 31, but I don't suppose you're familiar with Scripture."

"Scripture," he scoffs. "If that's what you're relying on to get you out of this mess, Ms. Sinclaire, you're going to be mighty disappointed."

The word "heathen" bounds forth, and I almost spit it at him; however, Scripture and name-calling don't exactly go together. *Steady on, Adda,* I tell myself and look to Birgitta. "Quite a work of fiction," I say, tossing the paper across the table. "You've done yourself proud."

Sneering, she pushes the paper aside. "So you still refuse to admit any wrongdoing?"

I nod. "Cry 'thief' all day long—sing it from the rooftops if you like—but you and I know the truth. And that truth doesn't change whether we're alone or among friends." I sweep my gaze from her, to Bob, to Kathryn, to Noelle, to Stone Cold who's watching me over the rims of his itty-bitty spectacles. I lean toward him. "I'm the sole author of *The Gifting*, Mr. Littlefeather, and no matter that this woman has disguised my hero and heroine by sticking them in the desert, dressing them in cowboy duds, and inflicting a twang upon them, they're mine. Anyone who's truly read me knows that."

Another glance at Nick finds him facing me across the distance, arms crossed over his chest.

"And eventually," I say, holding his gaze, "it will come out." Somehow . . .

"We have affidavits," Noelle says, reaching into her soft-sided briefcase.

Bob scoffs. "I've told you, those things won't hold up in court, Noelle. They're completely biased— "

"*Ms. Parker*," she says with an imperious lift of her chin. "The name is Ms. Parker, *Bob*."

I stare at Noelle. It seems I *am* more to her than just a bank account flashing before her eyes.

Bob forces a smile and nods. "All right, then, Ms. Parker, we can play it that way. So tell me, what else do you have to support your client's claim to *The Gifting*?"

Noelle plops the affidavits on the table, and atop them a copy of the joint property list I couriered over to her. "We've discovered how Ms. Roth obtained Ms. Sinclaire's manuscript." She taps the highlighted words. "Laptop computer, which my client's ex-husband was given in the divorce settlement, and which held on its hard drive the full, unpublished manuscript of *Wings of Love*—retitled *The Gifting* and released by Farnsworth Publishing this past January."

I look to Birgitta and notice that her right-eye tic has started up. Though I know the list isn't enough to hang her, I smile. Thus, when she glances my way, I'm rewarded with a tic at the corner of her mouth. Well, look at that—another one!

"As you know, *Bob*," Noelle continues, "Richard DeMarco lived with Ms. Roth previous to and following the divorce, during which time Ms. Roth had access to the laptop and its files."

He rolls his eyes. "If that and a couple of biased affidavits is all you have, Ms. Parker, you're really dragging bottom."

She slaps another paper atop the list. "Copy of a review of *The Love Bounty*, and I quote, 'Ms. Roth has finally found her voice between the pages of *The Love Bounty*, a beautifully sculpted tale that significantly narrows the gap between her writing and that of best-selling historical romance author, Adda Sinclaire. Watch out, Ms. Sinclaire, Birgitta Roth has your number!'" Noelle looks up. "Of course, what this reviewer meant to say was, 'Birgitta Roth has your *manuscript.*'"

I look to Nick, whose gaze is steadfast on the floor. Is he remembering the night he brought me here and himself admitted Birgitta had yet to repeat the success she enjoyed with *The Love Bounty*? I remember. And more. After all, how does one forget the beginning of the end of one's heart?

"Curious, isn't it," Noelle continues, "that Ms. Roth hasn't had another success like that one—not even close. Of course, *Wings of Love* was the only manuscript my client downloaded onto the laptop."

As I look to Bob, I catch Kathryn's eye, and she actually smiles at me. Why?

"Speculation, Ms. Parker." Tapping what looks to be a very expensive pen on his crossed knee, Bob shakes his head. "Won't hold water. Is that all you have?"

Noelle lifts her bottled water and takes a long drink, using the pause to compose a reply, I hazard. "There's more," she says, "but we're still verifying the data."

"Uh-huh." Bob sits forward, tacks his gaze to me. "Let me make this easy for you, Ms. Sinclaire. If you agree to certain terms, we can put this whole matter to bed today—make it go away. You'd like that, wouldn't you?"

I glance at Birgitta and frown. Is she holding her breath? And look at that tic go!

"Ms. Sinclaire?" Bob presses.

I draw a calming breath. "What terms are you suggesting, *Bob*?"

With a barely suppressed smile, he reaches into his briefcase and removes a document. "For the sake of the romance industry, Ms. Roth has generously agreed she will not pursue monetary restitution for the plagiarism of her work."

"Is that right?" Birgitta has *never* done anything for the sake of anyone other than herself. "Big of her."

"However, in exchange she requires a public apology."

I raise my eyebrows. "That's all?"

"Very generous of her," he repeats.

"Very," I say, and he startles when I reach to him.

"Uh," he mutters and fumbles the document into my hand. "Look it over. I think you'll find everything in order."

I lower it to the table, reach again. "May I have your pen?"

He blinks, and beside him Birgitta startles. "Certainly." Light dancing in his beady little eyes, he slaps the gold-tipped writing instrument into my palm.

Mmm, heavy . . . nice feel . . . superb workmanship . . . goes well with Poppy Love polish. . . .

"Adda?" Noelle squeaks.

Past her, I see Nick advance, urgency in his stride. Why? Wants an unobstructed view of my admission of guilt?

A hand touches my arm. "Ms. Sinclaire," Stone Cold says, and I realize I've forgotten about him.

I look at his paw on me, then into his magnified gaze. "Don't worry, Mr. Littlefeather," I pull my arm from beneath his hand, "I'm sure *Bob's* terms will in no way render negligible Intrepid's claim to monetary damages—nor Heart Core's nor Farnsworth Publishing's. You'll all get your whack at me."

Noelle grips my thigh again. "Adda, you're not going to—"

"What? Sign this nice man's document and put the whole matter to bed?" I slide Bob's pen into my breast pocket. "No." I pat my pocket. "But thank you for the pen, *Bob*. It's beautiful. Must have set you back quite a few bucks."

As his eyes widen, I sweep up the document and tear it in half, then toss the torn pages across the table and grin at Birgitta's stricken expression. "*The Gifting* is mine, as is *The Love Bounty*, and I make no apology for either—excepting the cowboy duds and that awful twang."

While beside me Noelle heaves a sigh of relief, out of the corner of my eye I see Nick has halted halfway between table and windows. "Anything else you'd like me to look at, *Bob*?"

Lips drawn thinner than Birgitta's eyebrows, Bob eyes my breast pocket and says, "You really ought to reconsider, Ms. Sinclaire. This will only get uglier."

"For your client." I settle back in my chair. "Sorry, *Bob*, but I'm not going to roll over and play dead."

His teeth snap. "Ms. Sinclaire, the longer this drags on, the more there is that's going to come out." He points a long-nailed finger at me. "Believe me, you don't want that."

And neither does Birgitta, as evidenced by her belief the plagiarism is an isolated incident—this from a woman who hates me, who stole my husband, then my book, and would steal from me again given the chance—

Realization broadsides me. And I gasp. "Oh, my word. That's it, isn't it?" I jerk my gaze to Birgitta. "Oh, my word." A laugh escapes me. "That's it!"

"Adda?"

I look to Noelle who sports a big question mark in the middle of her face, to Kathryn who appears to be holding her breath, to Nick who's once more shoved his hands in his pockets, to Bob whose calculating eyes are clouded by uncertainty, back to Birgitta who's busy adjusting her jacket and avoiding my gaze, and lastly to Stone Cold who arches an eyebrow above his spectacles and nods for me to continue.

Smiling so wide my face aches, I drop my head back and look to the ceiling. "Thank you, Lord," I whisper. Joy expanding my chest, I lower my chin and stare at Birgitta until she looks up. "That's why you don't want to pursue this further. You can't afford to."

All things smug and confident slipping from her despite her attempt to remain composed, she starts to rise. "As it's obvious Ms. Sinclaire cares nothing about public opinion or the dignity of the romance industry, it's time we leave."

I lunge to my feet, slap my hands to the table, and lean toward her. "Sit down, Birgitta," I say, amazed at how level my voice sounds despite the joy bounding through me.

She scoffs. "I have better things to do with my time than listen to more of your lies, Adda Sinclaire." She reaches for her purse.

"It's not an isolated incident, is it?"

Her hand freezes over her purse a long moment before she curls her fingers around the tortoise-shell handle. "No idea what you're talking about, but you really ought to seek professional help for whatever psychosis ails you."

"You're all that ails me, Birgitta, but I have the cure."

Her mouth puckers. "And what would that be? Another go at my hair?"

"Nothing so simple as that, but infinitely more painful."

She looks to Bob. "You heard her, Bob—she threatened me."

"No threat," I say, "just a little comparison shopping. Your books against mine, book for book, scene for scene."

Birgitta jerks.

"What are you saying, Ms. Sinclaire?" Bob leans forward.

"It's time to go, Bob," Birgitta says, voice wobbling.

"What I'm saying is that the reason your client is eager to put this to bed is for fear someone will take the matter a step further—will start comparing her other books with mine. Not that her plagiarism of the rest of my works will be as blatant. After all, whatever else she's stolen from me would have to be on a smaller scale as it would only be possible following publication of my books—a love scene here, a fight scene there . . . "

"As if I would even read your substandard little books!" Birgitta snarls.

Substandard . . . an insult one does not easily forget. Gotcha!

"Substandard," I muse. "Funny, but that's exactly what one

of my fans, who has read *all* my books, accused me of last year. You know her—goes by the name Brandy Reynolds. Initials big B, bigger R."

Though I didn't know a person's face could convulse, Birgitta's does. "You're reaching, Adda Sinclaire," she finally says. "How desperate can one get?"

"Not desperate enough to steal another author's words and call them my own. That's your gig, not mine."

Throat bobbing with a swallow that seems to resound around the room, she looks to Bob again. "I refuse to be harassed further. We're leaving."

Looking suddenly uncomfortable, he rises. "Yes, we should." With a parting glance at my jacket pocket, he snaps his briefcase closed.

I lift my hands from the table and straighten. "Give me a couple of weeks, Birgitta, then I'll have my attorney call yours, and they can do lunch."

"That won't be necessary," Stone Cold says.

I look around. "Excuse me?"

He opens his thick folder. "Ms. Roth, Mr. Smith, please sit down. I have some things you'll be interested in."

Bob makes a face. "Look, Jeremy, my client has taken about as much—"

"Sit down," Stone Cold says, "or read about it in the papers tomorrow. Your choice."

What is he talking about? I look to Noelle who, wide-eyed,

shrugs; to Kathryn who's staring at her clasped hands; to Nick who's returned to the windows to once more give me his back.

"Ms. Sinclaire," Stone Cold says.

As I turn to him, I see that Birgitta and Bob have resumed their seats. Stone Cold gestures for me to sit as well, and I slowly lower.

He sets out three stacks of binder-clipped papers. "Ten days ago," he says, "Intrepid contracted with three independent editors to compare ten books—six belonging to you, Ms. Sinclaire, four to Ms. Roth."

I stare. And stare. Is this for real? But how? Beginning to tremble, I peer at the nearest stack with its lengthy cover letter.

"All editors are in agreement," Stone Cold continues. "Though, as Ms. Sinclaire surmised, the incidences of plagiarism are less blatant than those found between *The Gifting* and *The Love Bounty*, they're there—love scenes, fight scenes, birthing scenes, etcetera."

My flesh pricks, heart convulses. Nick did this. For me. This was what he was trying to tell me in the elevator.

Realizing my hands are shaking, I lower them to my lap and look to Nick's broad-shouldered back. And the joy felt such a short time ago scatters. What have I done?

Noelle's hand is on my thigh again, and she leans in. "It's over, Adda," she whispers, tears in her voice. "Over."

It is, isn't it? All of it—including whatever brought Nick to my defense.

"And we have two affidavits," Stone Cold says, tossing them to the table. "One from Richard DeMarco—"

I snap my head around.

"—stating that he read *Wings of Love* prior to his separation and divorce from Ms. Sinclaire, that Ms. Roth discovered it on his laptop computer, and that he told Ms. Roth the publisher had declined the option book, and Ms. Sinclaire's new agent—Ms. Parker—advised her to shelve it altogether."

My throat tightens. Somehow Nick got what I couldn't.

I glance at Birgitta and watch as anger flushes her face. Poor Richard.

"The second affidavit is from the editor at Gentry Books who declined the book for publication. She attests to having read the synopsis and first three chapters of *Wings of Love* and concurs that it and *The Gifting* are the same."

I swallow hard. Nick again. Once more getting what I couldn't. For me, who'd refused to listen to his attempt to prepare me for this—to explain his long silence. And I suddenly feel sick.

"Do you understand what this all means, Ms. Roth?" Stone Cold asks.

Silence, and I'm not even tempted to look her way—to gloat or make smug with my triumph. I really am going to be sick . . .

Bob stands. "As Ms. Roth's counsel, I must advise her against making any statements at this time. You will, of course, send copies of all you have for my review, Jeremy."

"Certainly."

"Fine. Then Ms. Roth and I will be leaving."

Birgitta rises and stiffly follows Bob across Nick's office.

A great, hold-your-breath silence descends the moment the door closes behind them, and it's Noelle who pops it with a whoop and a "Hallelujah!" Then her arms are around me, squeezing me for all she's worth, and I'm too dead inside to even flinch. "It's over, Adda," she says again.

Over. "Yes," I say and look past her to Nick, who hasn't moved.

As Noelle releases me, Kathryn steps into the space between me and Stone Cold. "Told you we'd work it out," she says with a smile that's far from tight-lipped.

Stomach roiling, I nod. "Thank you." I look to Stone Cold. "And thank you, Mr. Littlefeather."

"Not me," he says and stands.

He's right, of course. I have Nick to thank, but the thought of doing so after my appalling behavior toward him makes me sicker than sick.

Stone Cold gathers the folder together and passes it to Noelle. "Whatever recourse your client decides to take against Ms. Roth, you'll need this."

Noelle positively sparkles. "Thank you, Mr. Littlefeather."

He inclines his head, looks to me. "A word of caution, Ms. Sinclaire. Self-serving though it was for Ms. Roth, it really would be best were this matter dealt with swiftly and put to rest—for you, the romance industry, and Intrepid."

And Nick, I realize. Nick who's suffered personal attacks not only against his character, but his judgment in signing me. Doubtless, his judgment in signing Birgitta will now come into question. "I understand," I say.

Stone Cold extends a hand. "Call me if I can answer any questions."

I stand and slide my hand into his. "A pleasure, Mr. Littlefeather."

"Same." He releases my hand and steps past me.

"Thank you, Jeremy," Nick says.

Stone Cold nods. "Any time."

As Kathryn follows Stone Cold toward the door, she looks to Nick. "If you've got an hour or so this afternoon, I'd like to go over the marketing campaign for the new line."

"I'll let you know," Nick says, and looks to me as I fall behind Noelle to become the caboose of the train leaving his office.

"Thank you for everything, Nick," Noelle says.

He inclines his head, returns his gaze to mine.

"Thank you" sticking in my own throat, as it seems so shallow under the circumstances, I look away. In the gathering silence, I continue toward the door, aching at the realization he's going to let me walk away. Just like that.

"How about lunch?" Noelle asks over her shoulder as she precedes me into the corridor. "My treat."

No. I am *not* going to walk away! I halt in the doorway. "Another day," I say, "but thank you, Noelle. For everything."

"Sure." She looks to Kathryn's and Stone Cold's retreating backs, then past me to Nick's office and raises her eyebrows.

I bite my lip, nod.

"All right, then," she says. "Call me."

"I will." As she prances down the corridor, I turn back into Nick's office, close the door, and lean against it.

He and I stare at each other across the empty space that not even the unspoken words between us can fill.

Although I know an apology is the best place to begin, followed by heaps of gratitude, for lack of the right words I hear myself ask, "You met with Richard?"

"I did." His hands shove deeper in his pockets. "And your Gentry Books editor."

I moisten my lips. "How did you convince them to cooperate?"

He smiles tightly. "When presented with the independent editors' reports, they had no choice but to attest to the truth or be named co-conspirators when the story came out."

I nod. "Of course."

He rocks back on his heels, raises his eyebrows as though to ask, "Any more questions?"

Slow, deep breath. "Look, Nick, I'm sorry. I didn't know. I thought—"

"You thought right." His shoulders rise with a deep breath of his own. "From the moment the rumors took hold, I doubted you. Then, when Kathryn revealed she'd had to grant you an extension on your deadline at Farnsworth Publishing, and that the manuscript you submitted in no way resembled the proposal she approved, I began to believe the charge of plagiarism."

Ouch.

Of course, it's no different from what he admitted in the elevator. And in the end, he did rally to my defense. Grasping that thread of hope, I look to the vacated conference table. "Yet you did this for me." With a tremulous smile, I return my gaze to him. "I have you to thank—"

"No." He presses his shoulders back, causing his jacket to strain the breadth of him. "You have Sophia to thank. She's the one who believed in you."

The thread of hope tugs taut, and I shake my head. "I don't understand."

"She called me in Sydney and demanded I do something to help you. So I humored her, though only to prove she was as wrong about you as I'd been."

Snap!

I look down. "Oh." That hurts.

"Then I received the independent editors' preliminary findings," he continues, "and discovered I'd wronged you—again."

Findings that he'd set in motion to prove I was more of a thief. *Yeow.*

He sighs. "Thus, you're the one owed an apology. And I *am* sorry, Adda."

As the space between us yawns wider, I look up.

He shoves a hand back through his hair. "Psalm 31, hmm?"

I blink. "Yeah."

"Sophia?"

How does he know his daughter quoted the Scripture to me? Surely she wouldn't have told him. Would she? I frown. "Yeah?"

He smiles wryly. "She gets a lot of mileage out of that particular one—wrote it on my bathroom mirror with soap a few years back when I had a particularly bad run-in with her mother."

As the specter of his ex-wife rises between us, I realize she's been there throughout, casting suspicion on everything I do and everything I am. And apparently she's not going away. "It's a good Scripture," I say, dumbly. "Helped me a lot these past days."

He draws a deep breath. "I really am sorry, Adda. It's hard for me to trust women."

"Yeah. I noticed." I will not cry in front of him. Will not! Unless I don't get out of here soon . . . I push off the door. "I really should be going."

He stares at me. "I prefer that you stay."

"Stay?" A brittle laugh pops from my mouth. "Whatever for?"

"There's something I should have explained months ago. Will you hear me out?"

Needing desperately to shore up my emotions, I say, "I appreciate all you did for me, Nick, even if it was for the wrong reason, but— "

He strides from the windows and, as I stare wide-eyed, halts before me. "Ten minutes, Adda. It shouldn't take more than that."

Throat so tight it feels as though I'm breathing through a coffee stirrer, I shrug. "All right."

He gestures to the chair before his desk. "Have a seat?"

Though I know it would be best to remain standing, I nod, and he steps aside. A few moments later, we're both on edge—as in the edge of the chair to which I lower myself and the front edge of his desk to which he settles back against.

He considers me, then says, "What I need to tell you—"

His phone buzzes. "Mr. Farnsworth?"

"Yes?" he clips, holding my gaze.

"Wilson Howell calling, sir."

Howell, as in CEO of Intrepid—Nick's boss, who takes precedence over me any day. I start to rise.

"Tell him I'll call back," Nick surprises me.

As he obviously surprises the woman. "Uh . . . yes, sir."

I lower back to the chair and clasp my hands in my lap. "So what do you need to tell me about?"

"Gwyneth."

I frown, but the hoity-toity name and the transformation of his eyes from chocolate to black licorice clue me in. "I assume that's your ex."

"That's one way to describe her." He crosses his arms over his chest. "Our marriage was a mistake. Not that I wouldn't do it again to gain Sophia."

Under different circumstances, I might melt. "Go on."

"Gwyneth came from a prominent family, was beautiful, sophisticated, and demanding. But even as I told myself it was a mistake to pursue a serious relationship with her, I allowed myself to be pulled along. We married a year after we met, and two years later, when everything was crumbling around us, she informed me she was pregnant. It was then my suspicions came to a head."

He lowers his gaze to the floor, and that muscle in his jaw looks as though it might jump right off his face. "She was restless—always on the hunt for the latest clothes, jewelry, cars, furniture and, as it turns out—" his gaze locks with mine, "—men."

"Oh." I blink. "Then she . . . ?"

"She did."

Just as Richard did. Just as Richard hurt me. Just as Richard's betrayal made me wary of all things male. Gwyneth Farnsworth could not have betrayed her husband in a worse possible way—unless she'd—

"Oh," I breathe.

"Sophia is mine," Nick says.

I gulp guiltily. "Well of course she is. I mean, there's no denying she has the look of her grandfather."

With a grim turn of his mouth, he says, "And no denying my brother, Peter, also has his looks."

I stare at him, and my stomach rolls. Then Peter and Gwyneth . . . oh. Wow. This, then, the difference between my family woes and his. BIG difference. HUGE difference. DON'T TOUCH THIS WITH A TEN-FOOT POLE difference. And suddenly Nick's distrust of women makes sense. Even if, in my case, it's unjustified. Even if it hurts.

"Though I had every intention of ordering a paternity test when Sophia was born," he continues, "once I held her, she was mine."

Even though she might not be . . .

I swallow. "I'm sorry, Nick. It . . . explains a lot."

"It's meant to." He lowers his arms, curls his fingers around the desk edge as though in need of something to choke the breath out of. "Thus, since my divorce, I've made a point of dating what Sophia calls 'plastic' women." He sweeps his gaze over me. "Then came you."

My heart loops the loop.

"Though I told myself I wasn't interested, every time we met, I wanted to see you smile, hear you laugh, know the woman beneath the author—and discover how it was possible for Adda Sinclaire to understand men so well on paper and yet not apply that knowledge to her life."

I grimace.

"Of course, when I realized how deeply you were affecting me, I grabbed every opportunity to make you into Gwyneth."

"As in Jake Grainger."

He nods. "As in Grainger."

I take a deep breath. "Then along comes the plagiarism debacle."

He closes his eyes briefly as though pained. "It was exactly what I needed to shake you off. I was . . . almost relieved." He shoves his hands in his pockets, the familiarity of which makes me feel a part of him. "Then I got angry. Although I'd gained Peter and Damian's lead author and best editor and was ready to launch a new line that would put Intrepid in the forefront of women's fiction, the scandal gave my brothers the last laugh.

"As the rumors and speculation over our involvement resurfaced and became grossly exaggerated, I felt like a fool for once more falling prey to a deceitful woman—something I'd vowed would never happen again."

I stare at Nick, aching for his ache, pained by his pain, wanting to go to him. But he has more to tell, and all I can do is wait.

"When the editors' preliminary reports finally came in, I didn't open them, Adda—not until the following day." His shoulders go wider as though to bear a great burden. "I didn't want to see what was in them—didn't want to prove to Sophia she was wrong about you."

"And when you opened them?"

"I was relieved. And ashamed."

My nose tingles as he stares at me with an intensity that almost hurts.

"But for all that, I thought I could make things right with you—until I caught up with you in the elevator and saw how much pain I'd caused." He shakes his head. "Not that I didn't know you were hurting, but I believed an apology for my silence would suffice, only to realize it would take more—that I'd have to explain Gwyneth."

This, then, was what he'd brooded over throughout the meeting?

He straightens from the desk and takes a long stride to where I sit.

Looking up, I see his struggle, feel it, almost breathe it.

Finally, he says, "Though my failed marriage in no way excuses my behavior toward you, Adda, I've told you that you might better understand me. And, given that, perhaps allow me a chance to make up for the hurt I've caused."

I stare at him, heartbeats tripping one over the other, which feels infinitely better than the terrible ache felt as I followed Noelle from his office. "Then you . . . weren't going to let me walk away?"

A corner of his mouth tilts slightly. "I knew you'd be back."

I blink at what sounds a lot like arrogance, even if it doesn't look it. "And just how did you know that?" I ask with a snip of irritation.

He glances over his shoulder toward the conference table. "Your purse."

I snap my head around, and there, just visible between the legs of the chairs, is my shoulder bag. Warmth suffusing me, I mutter, "Oh." I meet his gaze, gather a deep breath. "And if I didn't come back for it?"

His eyebrows slide up his brow. "What better excuse to show

up on your doorstep again?"

Where a pathetic, blubbering idiot would have opened the door to him. Imagining myself in an oversized T-shirt, fake-fur slippers, nibbled false nails, and swollen eyes, I bite my lip and look down.

"I don't require an answer now, Adda. All I ask is that you think about it."

Might this be a dream? And if it's not—if he really wants to make up for the hurt—dare I risk the last of my heart? What happened before could happen again. After all, it's taken him—what?—twenty years to look seriously at a woman? It might not work out.

But it might, Improper says—or is it Prim? *If you don't try, you'll never know, will you*?

But—

Nothing ventured, nothing gained, the voices meld.

With bated emotion, I look up at Nick and imagine walking away from him. Could it possibly hurt any less than giving him another chance? And isn't one of life's greatest tragedies waking up one morning and asking one's self "what if?"

I grip the chair arms, press to standing. "I've thought about it."

Nick's face tenses, and I realize he expects me to decide against him.

"This . . . second chance . . . " I watch his face so near mine. "Perhaps you'd care to define it?"

His lids flicker. "All right. The night I returned to the loft and heard your voice . . . looked up and saw you there on the stairs . . . " He shakes his head. "Despite the shock, it felt right, Adda."

Ooh. Nice.

"Go on."

"And when I drove you home and watched you walk away, I knew that when I returned to the loft it would feel more empty for you having been there and gone."

Real nice. Great, in fact. "Go on."

Some of the tension drains off him, and his mouth begins to curve. "What I'm trying to say, Adda, is that I want to be with you—that at the end of the day, I want you in my arms."

Goin' to goo.

"And?"

A bit of his teeth show, and a moment later, his smile comes through, left cleft dimple and all. "Not enough?"

I sober, shake my head. "Not for me."

"Hmm." He lifts a hand, pushes a tendril of hair off my brow. "Then I suppose a confession is in order."

Dare I hope?

"What might that be?"

He draws the backs of his fingers down my cheek. "Something I've only ever touched the fringes of."

"Keep going."

His dark chocolates melt into me. "Fight it though I've tried, Adda Sinclaire, I'm in love with you."

Emotion rolls through me. The "L" word. Nick Farnsworth just said the "L" word to me. Joy careening through me, I slide my hands up over his shoulders. "What a coincidence." I smile. "You see, I'm in love with you, Nick Farnsworth."

His taut muscles yield beneath my hands and warm breath stirs the hair at my brow.

Staring at him through tears, I push my fingers into the hair at the back of his head. "So what now?"

He angles his head. "I believe this is where the boy kisses the girl."

Be still my beating heart!

However, as his lips brush mine, I pull back. "What about the media? They bite, you know."

He arches an eyebrow. "Do you care?"

I shake my head. "Do you?"

"Not anymore."

His mouth lowers, and again I draw back. "The three nights I spent with a friend, that was— "

He shakes his head. "I know, Adda."

He does? I search his face. Of course he does. Stepping up to my toes, I say, "Then the boy should probably kiss the girl, hmm?"

A moment later, Nick claims my mouth, my heart, and my future.

EPILOGUE

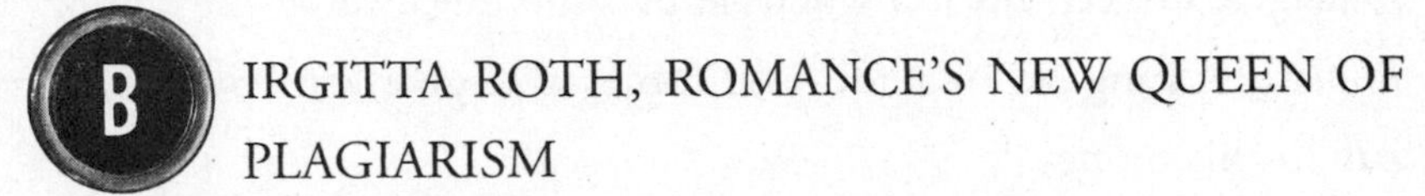

BIRGITTA ROTH, ROMANCE'S NEW QUEEN OF PLAGIARISM

FARNSWORTH PUBLISHING ISSUES APOLOGY, WITHDRAWS LAWSUIT

HEART CORE FILES FOR BANKRUPTCY

ADDA SINCLAIRE'S *THE GIFTING* GOES TO THIRD PRINTING TO LAND ON BEST-SELLER LISTS

INTREPID LAUNCHES NEW LINE WITH ADDA SINCLAIRE'S *THE FEUD*

All this without even trying.

I sigh, push aside the collection of headlines Joyce laminated into an enormous birthday card for me, and take a sip of hot tea. Though it's been months since Birgitta released a statement admitting she plagiarized my work during a "time of great stress," I've added no fuel to the fire. I have gracefully accepted her apology without exposing the true depth of her theft. Not that romance readers haven't discovered it for themselves. Even after all this time, online chats buzz with private analyses of other instances of plagiarism. But most of it slips right past the media, which has moved on to bigger and better scandals. In fact, the only mention of Birgitta in today's paper is by a gossip columnist who wrote that Ms. Roth is considering an offer to host a late-night television tabloid show. There's just no accounting for taste. But then, there's no accounting for tabloid television, is there?

Hmm. Maybe Birgitta and Richard—who, by the way, managed to keep his job when he became engaged to the station manager's daughter—could join forces and give Jerry Springer a run for his money.

I smile, and I'm still smiling when the doorbell rings. I look to Beijing, who lifts his head from his pillow and quirks his clamshell ears.

"Stay put," I say, "I'll get it." He's not getting any younger, after all.

A few moments later, I open the door to Nick—a half hour sooner than expected. Meaning I'll have to make do with the slightly worn Scheherazade Nights polish applied two days ago. Whatever . . .

"You're early," I say, stepping forward and turning my face up.

Nick gives me one of his deliciously dimpled smiles. "I know." He lowers his head. As the kiss deepens, I sigh in remembrance of all we've been through to get where we are, beginning with cheating partners and culminating in Birgitta's thievery.

Not that I have anything against the woman. After all, I

have a lot to thank her for, such as *The Feud*'s appearance on the *New York Times* Best Sellers list for the past eight weeks and counting—both versions. Of course, the books would likely have made it there on their own, but the scandal certainly gave them that extra boost.

Thank you, Birgitta Roth.

Then there's my backlist books, nearly all of which have reappeared on one best-seller list or another—meaning print runs are up and royalties are rolling in.

Thank you, Birgitta Roth.

And of course there's the reconciliation with my sister and the shocking but welcome discovery that my mother does possess motherly instinct.

Thank you, Birgitta Roth.

As for Snow White, she has become a dear friend and confidante in my journey toward deeper faith.

Thank you, Birgitta Roth.

And mustn't forget Josh Holman—as if I could! Just last month, the youth who gave me his New Testament reappeared on my doorstep. His joy at learning I had become a Christian nearly burst from him. Though it turns out I'm not the first nonbeliever he led to Christ, doubtless I won't be the last. Before he left, I tried to return his New Testament; however, he told me it would mean more to him if I passed it on. And I will—I'm thinking Angel, who has not only toned down her Gothic getup but has started asking questions about my fledgling faith.

Thank you, Birgitta Roth—er, actually, that wasn't Birgitta at all, was it?

Then there's Nick. Nick. Nick.

Thank you, Birgitta Roth.

Oh! And my nails, which are looking better every day in anticipation of the engagement ring I expect will soon brighten my left hand—perhaps this very evening.

Thank you, Birgitta Roth.

Last, but never least, there's Jesus. Although it's true I have much to learn—a lifetime's worth—I know I'm on the right path.

Thank you, Birgitta Roth—kind of.

No, I have nothing at all against the woman. In fact, I've practically forgiven her. The next hurdle? To pray for her as Christians are called to do—enemies and all that. But I'll get there. After all, I can do everything through him who strengthens me. Some things just take longer than others.

Thank you, God.

READER'S GUIDE—BONUS SCENE

Dear Reader,

Thank you for taking the time to get to know Adda. As you prepare to move on to the next chapter–er . . . paragraph?–of *your* life, it is my hope that the characters between these pages stay with you in some measure (why should I be the only one to suffer, hmm?).

Seriously, though, what I hope you take away with you when you set this book on the shelf (hint: "keeper"), is a healthy dose of chuckles and a satisfied sense of curiosity over the life of a romance writer. But that's not all. It is my greatest hope you found something in Adda's spiritual journey that will impact your relationship with those who are still searching for something beyond themselves. Heavy . . .

So now that our visit is over, our bags are packed, and we're heading for the door, we come to a time of reflection . . . deep introspection . . . soul searching —

Eeerrrrkkkkk (cue the sound of a needle being dragged across a record).

Introspection? Soul searching? As my editor, Lissa Halls Johnson, would say, that's not very Adda-like. So what *would* Adda do?

Hmm . . . hmm . . . um hmm . . .

Light bulb, please!

Rather than fill the pages of this Reader's Guide with a series of discussion questions—dull, very dull—let's plug them into a "bonus" scene featuring Adda herself. Like the idea? Me, too (note to fence sitters: Stay with me. I know what I'm doing. I think. . . .).

Ahem. The following will serve as your Reader's Guide—granted, a rather different guide, but different is good. Enjoy!

Tamara Leigh

● ● ●

"Is it working?" I tap the mic clipped to my lapel.

Janine Calhoun, host of *Christian Entertainment Review*, jerks her chin and gives a quick nod in the direction of the cameraman.

"Oh . . ." I make a face. "Then we're . . . ?"

Another jerk of the head, followed by a bright smile for the camera. "Thank you for joining us at *Christian Entertainment Review*. Today our guest is best-selling romance author, Adda Sinclaire, of 'Queen of Plagiarism' fame."

I nearly choke; however, all too aware that my face is being broadcast across the land, I feign the necessity to clear my throat. Queen of Plagiarism! Not anymore! In fact, *never* was!

Seemingly oblivious to my reaction, Janine smiles brighter.

"Did I say 'romance'?" She wrinkles her cutesy nose. "I did." Wink. "I most certainly did. *Main . . . stream ro . . . mance.*"

I cringe. Though I've become practically numb to "romance" being made to sound like an obscenity, she's somehow managed to take it to the next level. Of course, this *is* a Christian program and romance novels aren't exactly esteemed in such circles. Actually, they aren't esteemed in most circles, are they? Not that it stops millions and millions of readers from buying in excess of a billion romance novels each year—

"When we were in the green room earlier," Janine says, leaning forward to pat my fashionably jean-clad knee, "you shared with me your journey toward salvation."

Now we're on track. Relieved, I smile and say, "I did, Janine."

"And therein lies quite the tale." She settles back in her chair and launches into a retelling of my encounters with Josh. After I answer the questions she lobs my way, she turns to the camera and addresses her viewers.

The young man who selflessly gave his copy of the New Testament to Adda took the first step in leading her to Christ. Has there been anyone who, despite short acquaintance, had a positive, lasting impact on your life? Initially, how did you receive this person? How much time passed before you realized the importance of that encounter?

After allowing the questions to sink in, she returns her attention to me. "Now, Adda, you mentioned a habit you had previous to accepting Christ into your life—that of giving others so-called 'pet names.'"

Ooh. I didn't realize she was going to work that in. For fear of succumbing to rigor mortis, I force a nod. "Yes. It was a bad habit."

"Especially with regards to derogatory 'pet names.'"

This is what I get for running on at the mouth. "Well, I wouldn't say 'especially,' but I admit the 'pet names' weren't all endearing." I give a short laugh that comes out all jittery.

Janine looks to her clipboard, flips a page. "Let's see . . . Ah! 'Stick Woman' was a favorite, you said."

I nearly choke again. How did this cute little woman disarm me so completely that I spilled my guts—guts which are now splattered all over television? Well, maybe not "all over," as this is a *Christian* channel. Of course, there are lots of them—er, *us*–aren't there?

"Adda?"

"Um . . ." I nod. "Yes, that's one I used often." A favorite. Definitely a favorite. In fact, even now, late at night when I'm all alone, I sometimes catch myself—

"And would you like to tell the audience to whom 'Stick Woman' referred, Adda?"

Surely she didn't just ask what I think she did. I narrow my gaze on her. She did. Why did I agree to this interview? What was I thinking? Elizabeth said it would be fun, a way to reach out to others—

"Of course . . . " Janine wrinkles her nose again. " . . . anyone who's followed your story can probably guess who 'Stick Woman' is." Wink wink.

Oh, Elizabeth, why did I let you talk me into this? I press my shoulders back. "It was a fellow author." And can we *puh-lease* leave it at that?

Janine arches an eyebrow. "She-who-shall-not-be-named, hmm?"

Tight smile. "I think you'll agree that's best."

"I most certainly do."

Then why did you bring it up?

She gives her hair a toss, reaches forward, and pats my knee again. Does she have to do that?

Once more addressing her viewers, she says:

Do you give others derogatory "pet names"—strangers, acquaintances, coworkers, friends, family members? How does it make you feel? Justified? Superior? How do you think the recipient might feel if they knew what they had been labeled?

Realizing my nails are digging into my palms, I open my hands and spread them on my knees—only to wince. Ugh. Could have used another coat of nail polish. Why, oh why didn't I drag myself away from the computer a half hour earlier? One more layer of "Double-O-Red" would have done wonders–

"Speaking of 'Stick Woman'–" Janine smiles knowingly "–and the scandal that surrounded you during those weeks leading up to the exposure of the rightful heir to the title of 'Queen of Plagiarism,' what kept you from losing all hope?"

This one's easy. "That would be the support I received from family and friends, as well as Scripture."

"Scripture?" She's so thrilled, her hands tense as if it's all she can do to keep from clapping.

I nod. "Psalm thirty-one, verse twenty-four. 'Be strong and take heart all you who hope in the LORD.'" Ha! Memorized that one!

"Beautiful," Janine says on a sigh. "One of my favorites." With a look of divine contentment, she eyes the camera.

When you feel you're hanging by a thread of hope, what do you reach for? Family? Friends? God's Word? Is there any specific quote or Scripture that strengthens you?

Janine looks back at me. "So tell me, Adda, when are you going to make the leap?"

"Hmm?"

"The leap." She opens her lids wider as if to allow me to peer into her mind. "You know—answer a higher calling?"

"Er . . ."

With a playful roll of her eyes she says, "As in write something Christians are comfortable reading." *Pat, pat.*

I narrow my gaze on her hand as she draws it from my knee. I'll just bet she owns one of those trendy dogs that tuck under one's arm.

Hoping I'm not showing too much teeth, I smile. "Well, actually, according to the fan mail I receive, quite a few of my readers are Christian."

She snorts, wrinkles her nose. "As in closet readers, hmm?"

Some things never change. "I wouldn't know, but what I am

certain of is that readers of romance place a high value on tales of love, fidelity, and the triumph of good over evil."

Janine's eyebrows bounce. "Touché," she says with surprised admiration. Then, smiling big, she once more looks into the camera.

What are your feelings about mainstream romance novels? What do you like about them? What do you dislike? How do they differ from Christian romance novels?

Following a long pause, Janine refers to her clipboard again. "Perhaps that boyfriend of yours—Nick Farnsworth of Intrepid Publishing—might be convinced to start a Christian imprint."

Gulp. I didn't say a word! Not a word! For fear Nick will think I leaked what he asked me to keep in confidence regarding Intrepid's research into the viability of a Christian division, I nearly groan. Surely he'll believe me. He *has* to.

"Speaking of which," Janine continues, unaware of my sudden compulsion to chew a fingernail, "I understand Mr. Farnsworth is also a Christian."

Jabbing my nails into my palms, I manage a smile. "He is."

"Tell me, did he figure into your decision to accept Christ?"

Did he? "I haven't really given it much thought, but . . ." Remembering the ride to Lake Tahoe when I learned Nick was a Christian, I start to smile. "I guess I'd have to say he did figure into my decision. In fact, not only was I moved by Nick's beliefs, but his daughter was instrumental in pointing the way."

"Then you have a good relationship with his daughter?"

"Very much so."

Janine nods. "Looks like the place to give our viewers more food for thought."

How do your relationships with others influence your personal beliefs in a higher being? Which Christian qualities appeal to you? Which qualities are off-putting?

"Let's return to Nick Farnsworth," Janine says.

Why do I have the sinking feeling we shouldn't?

"I understand he's divorced." She puts her head to the side. "As are you."

Is that a judgmental gleam in her eye? I nod warily. "That's right."

"Divorce." She shudders. "Messy."

Is she speaking from personal experience or just trying to make me feel bad? "Yes, it is."

"The two of you are pretty serious."

"We are."

"And yet . . . " She looks to my left hand. " . . . no engagement ring."

Was that really necessary? Pretending an engagement ring is the farthest thing from my mind—which it most certainly is not—I shrug. "Based on the failure of our past marriages, we're taking our relationship one step at a time." As in *trudging*.

She nods. "Wise. As everyone knows, the baggage that comes with divorce can be preeettty heavy."

Even as I offer the obligatory nod, I find myself frowning.

Baggage—it's what's holding Nick back, isn't it? Surely it's not me. Or maybe it is. Maybe he isn't as serious as I am. Maybe—

"I'm pleased you're still with us, viewers," Janine says. "I have another one for you."

What issues do you think Adda and Nick must confront and resolve before they commit to each other? Before they "tie the knot"?

This time the groan escapes. Catching my breath, I glance at Janine. Though she continues to face the camera, the tightening of her mouth reveals my slip didn't go unnoticed. Hoping the camera was on her when the sound escaped, I sit straighter, cross my legs, and force a smile that sharply contrasts with the anxiety zip-zinging through me. First, talk of Intrepid's venture into the Christian market, now of Nick and Adda's venture into marriage. How long before Nick gets wind of this?

"Your personal assistant told me you've been witnessing to her," Janine says.

Oh . . . dear . . . God.

Feeling as if my smile is glued to my teeth, I meet her gaze. "Oh?" And just when did she and Angel talk? I thought it was Janine's assistant who set up the interview.

"I called her this afternoon before your arrival at the station and—" Janine makes elegant quotation marks in the air "—picked her brain."

Forgot to mention that, hmm, Angel? Of course, maybe I'd already left for the interview.

Tugging at the waistband of my sagging composure, I sweep

my palms up. "I wouldn't exactly call it 'witnessing.'"

"Oh?"

"Well, as a new Christian, I'm hardly qualified."

She cocks her head, considers me a seemingly thoughtful moment, then says, "I understand Angel is a Gothic."

Great. "Uh . . . she definitely likes the color 'black.'"

"And body piercings."

Wonderful. "Yeah."

"So how has she responded to the good news of Christ?"

Smile, Adda. Keep smiling. "She's . . . interested." But not interested enough to accept Josh's New Testament that I offered recently. Not that I was offended. Well, maybe I was offended. A little.

"Glad to hear it," Janine says, then once more leaves me for the camera.

Adda doesn't feel that, as a new Christian, she's qualified to witness to others. How mature in one's beliefs should a person be before attempting to influence the beliefs of others?

Janine folds her hands atop her clipboard, "That's all we have time for today, beloved viewers. Join us again tomorrow when we feature Christian pop sensation, Brandon Bernardo." There goes that nose of hers again. "I promise you, *this* one, you won't want to miss."

Meaning they should have passed on Adda Sinclaire? Hmm.

Janine gives a little wave, brightens her smile, then turns to me and . . . pats my knee.

For the benefit of the camera that continues to film as the credits roll, she animatedly thanks me for joining her. I thank her back, nod, nod some more, glance at my watch.

Three hours until Nick and I meet for dinner. Three hours during which he's sure to hear about the interview. I am so toast.

ABOUT THE AUTHOR

Since 1994, TAMARA LEIGH has been writing nationally best-selling, award-winning historical romances, including *Warrior Bride, Unforgotten, Misbegotten Saxon Bride, Pagan Bride,* and *Virgin Bride*. Her most recent release, *Blackheart*, made the USA Today Best-seller List. *Stealing Adda* is her first book with NavPress.

At age nine, Mara knows many things (how to do laundry, for instance), but there are lots of things she doesn't know – like her mother, or her father, or even God.

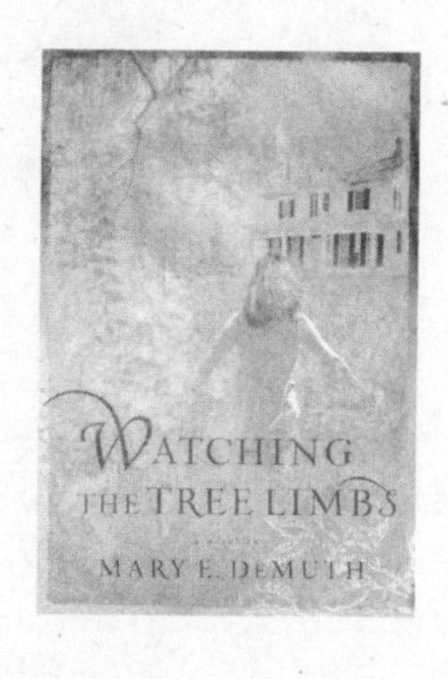

Watching the Tree Limbs

Nine-year-old Mara loves playing Nancy Drew with her best friend, Camilla. With an attic chock-full of treasures and a whole summer ahead of them, they're set to find the home of the mysterious and controversial radio disc jockey Denim. But then there are the mysteries that Mara's afraid to share: Who is her mother? Her father? And how can she stop the biggest criminal of all: General?

Mary E. DeMuth **1-57683-926-5**

Visit your local Christian bookstore,
call NavPress at 1-800-366-7788, or log on to www.navpress.com
to purchase.

To locate a Christian bookstore near you, call 1-800-991-7747.

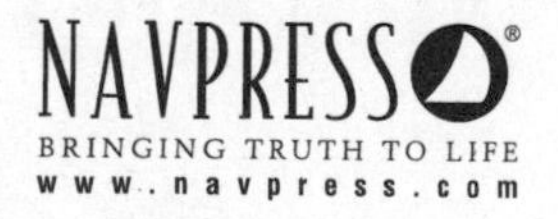